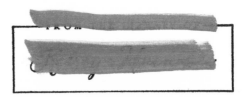

EMBER

OF

NIGHT

MOLLY E. LEE

Entangled Publishing, LLC
10940 S Parker Road
Suite 327
Parker, CO 80134
rights@entangledpublishing.com

Entangled Teen is an imprint of Entangled Publishing, LLC.

Visit our website at www.entangledpublishing.com.

Edited by Liz Pelletier
Cover design and illustrations by
Elizabeth Turner Stokes
Interior design by Toni Kerr

ISBN 978-1-64937-031-0
Ebook ISBN 978-1-64937-044-0

Manufactured in the United States of America

First Edition May 2021

10 9 8 7 6 5 4 3 2 1

ALSO BY MOLLY E. LEE

Ask Me Anything

THE GRAD NIGHT SERIES

Love in the Friend Zone
Love Between Enemies
Love Beyond Opposites

To Molls—the coolest half of #MollySquared. Thank you for reading every line, every draft, no matter how many times you've read them before. Your insight, support, and friendship are everything. I love you. That's all.

Author's Note: This book depicts issues of emotional and physical abuse, violence and gore, suicidal thoughts, and some sexual content. I have taken every effort to ensure these issues are handled sensitively, but if these elements could be considered triggering to you, please take note.

If you are suffering from abuse, please know that you have done nothing to cause this, and there are places ready and willing to offer help and guidance.

For ChildHelp National Child Abuse Hotline, call 1-800-422-4453 or visit childhelp.org.

For the Domestic Violence and Intimate Partner Violence Hotline, call 1-800-799-7233 or visit ncadv.org/get-help.

If you or someone you know is contemplating suicide, please know you are not alone. Visit bethe1to.com and help save a life.

PROLOGUE

DRAVEN

Even from our position on the roof, the alleyway reeks of cured meats and rain-soaked garbage, the stench curling upward like it's as desperate to leave this place as I am.

A metallic groan splits the silence coming from below us, and my gaze sharpens as a fainter scent penetrates the rotten odor, almost hidden beneath it—something *different*.

The door swings open, and a thick streak of yellow light darts across the cracked pavement. A girl shoulders a bag of garbage into the alley, striding quickly toward the dumpster still in the shadows.

"She doesn't look like much," Cassiel says from my left, his obsidian wings tucked in tightly behind him. His eyes are as sharp as mine, piercing through the night without difficulty. The girl wrestles the garbage over the lip of the dumpster like the bag's filled with bricks. "Certainly not enough to tear a hole through the world."

I cut a glance at Cassiel. "That's exactly what the lion says to the honey badger right before getting his ass handed to him."

Cassiel arches a brow but then returns his attention to the girl.

She wipes some of the misty rain from her forehead, lingering by the dumpster like it's the only quiet break she's had all day. Then her gaze snaps down the alley.

Her spine straightens, and my heightened senses prickle as she effortlessly shifts into a defensive stance.

"Two of them," Cassiel says, his voice low and cold.

"Humans," I say, scenting them on the air.

A woman cries out, and the girl rushes toward the sound.

It's like her instincts push her *toward* the danger instead of away from it.

Cassiel and I move silently along the deli's roof, keeping her in our sights.

"Todd, stop!" the woman cries out. "This isn't funny anymore. Stop," she pleads again as she struggles against a much larger man's hold.

"Hey!" The girl skids to a stop before the struggling pair, and the man jerks his head in her direction.

"This is none of your concern, kid," he spits at her, never taking his hands off the trembling woman. "Get lost and keep your mouth shut."

"Didn't anyone ever tell you? You're supposed to be nice to your friends," the girl says, eyeing the woman who'd spoken the man's name with familiarity. The girl hasn't missed that detail. "If you're looking for a fight, you'd be better off picking on someone who isn't worth a damn to you." She raises her brows at him.

I flash a questioning look to Cassiel, who appears as shocked at the words as I am.

"The hell you say?" The man shifts a bit, focusing more intently on the girl instead of the young woman.

The girl smiles—a whisper at one corner of her lips, nearly imperceptible. She nods toward the woman. "Save yourself the grief. It's easy picking a target you already know," she says. "Why don't you give yourself a challenge?"

The man releases the young woman's shirt, turning to fully face the girl. "You think you're a challenge?"

The girl tips her chin and shrugs. "Why don't you come find out?"

Slowly, she lifts her hands from her pockets, raising them horizontally. I internally cringe at the vulnerable position it puts her in, my instincts thrashing to intervene.

Which is as impossible as it is ridiculous.

The girl is as much my prey as this worthless scrap of a human.

A vein pops in the man's neck, his fists curling at his sides. She shifts her feet, a subtle move the man doesn't notice.

He *should've.*

He should've realized that a regular person who'd distracted him enough to save his victim would have bolted by now. Would've run back inside the deli and called the police.

A regular person might've done that *first*, before ever thinking to rush for help.

But not this girl.

I tilt my head. She doesn't flinch, not even when he raises that meaty fist and swings. She moves quickly enough to miss it, ducking out of the second attempt, too. But the third swing connects with her face before she can dodge again.

Even I flinch from the resounding *crack*.

Cassiel hisses, his dark wings unfurling partially behind him as if he might fly down there and stand between them.

The impact of the hit shakes the girl's body, twisting it to one side, but she doesn't lose her footing. Blood glistens at the corner of her lip, and she spits a mouthful of it at his shoes.

And laughs.

The girl *laughs*.

"My drunk father hits harder than that," she snaps.

Another shock rolls through me. The words that come out of her mouth…

She widens her gaze at the young woman, who remains pressed against the alley wall. "Now would be the time to run," she says, almost exasperated as the man approaches her, his victim forgotten behind him.

The young woman blinks tears out of her eyes and bolts toward the main street at the cusp of the alley.

He leaps at the girl, but she dances out of the way. She swipes her leg, trying to knock him off-balance, and almost does, but he catches the move, slamming her back against the dumpster. The light from the open door casts them in an eerie glow.

She laughs again as he hauls her harder against it.

"You like pain, girl? Is that it?"

No, no, that isn't it. I can see it in the cold, shattered bits of her blazing green eyes.

"You call this pain?" She scoffs at the man who has every advantage over her.

She's used to this kind of assault.

My stomach twists, sharp wires tangling and threatening to choke me. I shove them down, remembering why I'm here in the first place.

"We should stop this," Cassiel whispers.

He isn't wrong. The girl is *mine*. I don't need this human spilling one more drop of her blood.

The tip of my black boot touches the lip of the rooftop as I prepare to jump down—

"Harley?" Another man's voice sounds from the doorway, quickly followed by a looming shadow. "What the hell?" he growls as he sprints through the door, a frying pan raised over his head. "Let her go! I'll call the cops!"

The man ducks, barely missing a crack to the head, then hauls ass down the alleyway.

The girl—*Harley*—glares at the man. "I'm fine, Nathan," she says.

Nathan shakes his head, his mouth half open as he gapes at her. He reaches a hand toward her split lip, then seems to think better of it and drops it. "How many times have I told you, Harley? I'll take out the garbage on night shifts."

"You own this place," she says. "You aren't supposed to get your hands dirty." She glances down at her fingers like an invisible layer of grime always cakes her skin. "I'm seriously fine. You stopped him the second he came at me."

Liar.

The man sighs, the lengthy one of someone who's had this conversation more than once. "Come on," he says, motioning toward the open door. "Let's get you cleaned up. I know you have a concert to get to."

Harley flashes him a *what's the point* look but follows behind him. She lingers in the doorway, glancing over her shoulder as if she senses something else out here. Some other danger she can't see.

Or perhaps she's always looking for danger.

The door shuts behind her, the light winking out.

"Honey badger indeed," Cassiel says after a few silent moments.

I turn toward him, something gnawing at my insides.

"How long until you know for sure?" he asks.

"My source informed me something ancient and powerful is on the brink of surfacing here. And that someone else has taken extreme precautions to cloak it."

"The Key," Cassiel says, and I nod.

"She'll come of age in eight days." If this girl is the Key, then her eighteenth birthday will unleash what's in her blood.

"And if she shows powers?" Cassiel asks, his silver eyes glowing in the darkness.

The image of her fearlessly facing down that vile human flashes behind my eyes.

"Then I hope she enjoys these last few days on earth." My voice is as cold as ice.

Cassiel tilts his head. "I can help you, Draven," he says. "If you don't want to do it yourself."

Something clenches the center of my chest—my Angel of Death friend offering to break his own moral code and take a soul that isn't on his list is a testament to our unorthodox friendship. Especially since he views himself as the be-all, end-all of baddies when in reality, I'm so much worse than he is.

"I won't ask that of you," I say.

"Do you think she's the Key?" he asks.

I inhale through my nose, the faint smell of a crackling fire igniting an internal flame in my blood. "Could be."

"And if she is?"

I glance down the dark alleyway, my eyes seeing her selflessness, her strength, before I look at my friend again.

"Then I'll kill her myself."

CHAPTER ONE

"Are you sure you don't want to bail after..." Kai—my best friend and total worrier—motions to my split lip and bruised cheek as we hustle down the crowded sidewalk toward Bottom Lounge.

"It's nothing," I say, shaking off his concerned stare. "You've been planning this for months, Kai," I continue, allowing real excitement to chase away the grittiness from earlier.

Adrenaline still thrums in my blood, but the buzzed sensation isn't anything new to me. At least the woman got away. Rather me than her.

"Besides," I say, forcing myself out of my head, "Nathan is watching Ray." My boss is my absolute second-favorite person on this planet, right behind my baby sister. With her safely taken care of tonight, it's my one chance to pretend to be someone else... *anyone* else. "My dad thinks I'm working a double shift," I add. "I'm ready to have fun." I loop my arm through his.

Kai looks like he wants to argue, those green eyes searching my face and lingering on what will be a hell of a bruise tomorrow. But we've been friends for almost a decade, so he knows not to push me on this.

"Be honest," he says as we round a corner and the small bar comes into view. The brick building's black lettering is illuminated by a single backlight, and a few concertgoers hurry through the doors. "How excited are you?"

I grin up at him, one of the few unhindered smiles I've mustered lately. I've had a countdown for this concert since he snagged the tickets—a rare escape. Any nights away from Ray are a struggle, because the distance feels like a physical strain on my heart. But I know Nathan will keep her safe, and in the end, that's all that matters.

Tonight—and *only* tonight—I get to act like a normal girl headed to a concert with her best friend.

Not the real me—a girl who has worked tirelessly to survive her home life and graduate high school, raise her baby sister, and eventually, help her escape. At least I get a gold star for multitasking, right?

But tonight? Tonight, I want to be someone else entirely.

"Beyond pumped," I finally answer Kai, dropping his arm as we show the bouncer our tickets and head through the doors.

Instantly we're hit with the opening act's music—loud bass filtering through the small space. Dim lighting illuminates the stage and half the dance floor, while the rest of the place is covered in a faint darkness that sets the electric mood—which is exactly what I'm looking for tonight.

"Dance floor or bar?" Kai asks, his voice barely heard above the music and chatter.

I bite my lip, torn between my craving for a strawberry lemonade and my need to move. My muscles itch to sway, to lose myself to the music and simply *be* for a few blissful hours.

"Dance floor," I answer, tugging him through the crowd of people covering the floor.

The opening act finishes up, and after a small break, my favorite artist takes the stage. Bishop Briggs isn't just a phenomenal singer—she writes songs I can relate to. Pain, secrets, having a dark side—they're fire.

"Happy early birthday, Harley," Kai says after I've stopped cheering at the sight of her.

"You're seriously the best," I say as we dance in the small space we've claimed—well, *I* dance, while Kai sort of shuffles side to side a foot away. He's not big on dancing, but he's not about to rob me of my fun tonight. Something I'm forever grateful *and* guilty for. I'll never be able to repay him, even when he says I don't need to. All the money I earn from the deli, I save to keep Ray and myself fed, clothed, and, hopefully soon, free.

Once I have enough saved for an apartment—

Stop.

I squeeze my eyes shut, focusing on the music. I'm not going down that road now. Not tonight, the one night of the year I've allowed myself to be the version of Harley I wish I could be—fun, baggage-free, maybe even a little wild.

I laugh at myself then, and Kai tilts his head, but I wave him off. Even if I can explain it, he won't be able to understand. And why would he? Kai has the perfect life—loving family, wealthy, smart as hell. He'll never need to pretend to be anyone else.

The band transitions to a slower, sultry song, and I adjust my pace, escaping in the notes that tumble over one another like honey dripping from a bottle. Sweat beads on the back of my neck, and I lift up my long red hair, gathering it in a knot atop my head.

"You need a drink?" Kai asks, hunching down a bit awkwardly for me to hear him over the music.

"Please." I nod without stopping my moves.

He flashes me a thumbs-up, then slips through the crowd at a slow pace, heading toward the bar.

A sudden rough shove and a quick "sorry!" have me tumbling backward—another overzealous dancer knocking into my space.

Warm, strong hands steady my shoulders from behind, but I quickly right myself and shake them off.

I whirl around, ready to apologize for the domino effect, but the words die in my throat.

I look up and *up* to lock gazes with a pair of amber eyes that stare at me with such intensity, the hairs on the back of my neck stand on end. His skin is a rich golden brown, his hair a mess of black curls atop his head. A black T-shirt is molded to tons of corded muscle.

I suck in a sharp breath—not from how hot he is, though *yeah*—but because of his eyes. There is something there, a churning intensity I can't put my finger on. It stirs up my insides, anticipation and curiosity and just a hint of fear.

"You're welcome," he says before I can get a word out.

"Excuse me?" I barely hold back my laugh. "I didn't need your help. I totally meant to do that."

A smirk shapes his full lips, equal parts mischief and danger. He raises his hands in defense. "I guess next time, I'll let you fall."

"You could," I say, a smile teasing the corners of my mouth. "But I'll take you down with me."

"Well, that would be one way to get me horizontal," he says, deadpan, his eyes practically gold in the flickering lights bouncing off the stage. The music swells to a new song, the concert still going full swing despite everything in my world narrowing to him.

My next words leave my mouth before my brain can catch up, can remind me I've never flirted a day in my life before now. But tonight, I'm not the real Harley. Tonight, I'm just a normal girl teasing a hot guy at a concert. "There are other ways?"

"Many." He draws the word out, arching a brow at me. "Should we dance and find out if that's one?"

A laugh rips from my lips. "You think you can dance my pants off—literally?" I ask, rolling my eyes. "I can tell you right now, it'll take more effort than that."

I didn't think his brow could go any higher. It can and does. "Do you answer everything with a challenge?"

"Is there any other way?" I ask, my heart racing from the back-and-forth. I can't deny the electricity buzzing in my blood from the verbal battle, or the fact that I should have reminded myself a half a dozen times by now that this isn't my life—this isn't who I really am, carefree and interesting—and just walk away.

But here I stand, unable to resist finding out what he'll say next.

"I think you truly believe that," he says, then shakes his head.

My lips part, a tiny gasp escaping. He's pinned me—my default setting is defensive, but I have my reasons.

He stretches his muscled arms out in an offer, flashing me a questioning glance with just a hint of dare behind it.

And I'm almost as shocked as he looks when I step into his space and start to move.

Maybe it's because he's a stranger. Maybe it's those eyes. Or maybe it's because I want so desperately to be a different Harley tonight. One not weighed down by an anvil of rejection and held back by a chain of unworthiness.

Either way, I purse my lips. And *move*. "Can you keep up?"

"Another challenge?" His lips slowly stretch into a half grin now, like he tried to stop them but didn't have complete control.

When he doesn't start to move with me, I decide maybe I've gone too far. This flirting thing doesn't come naturally. Why do they make it look so easy on TV? I'm about to turn and walk away, but then his hands fall lightly to my hips.

And his touch is *searing*.

Then we're moving together.

Instantly, like a magnet, he falls into my rhythm, that half grin lighting up the sharp angles of his face.

I force myself out of my own head and dive into the music, the dance, the way this stranger laughs when I tease him to match a more complicated move. Daring him to keep up. An answering laugh echoing in my chest when he does. It's like dancing in a mirror, every move almost anticipated and perfectly matched with mine. Like this music itself was created just for us to dance to.

"You like this song?" I ask when the band shifts to a new tune.

"It's…enjoyable," he says, the words low and rough.

"From the way you're smiling, I'd say you're *more* than enjoying it."

"It's not the song," he says, his breath warm from where he leans down to speak into my ear.

The fingers on my hips flex, and I whirl out at his gentle nudge. Another laugh escapes my lips as he beckons me back in with a flick of his finger, and I can't help it—I love the way he dances. Love the way he dives in headfirst, matching my moves and upping the game with some of his own.

"What is it, then?" I ask once I've caught my breath.

"It's you. You're a bit reckless when you dance." My heart stutters at his words, at the way he's watching my every move. "You consume the space."

I raise a brow, a bubbly sensation filling my lungs. "Do lines like that *ever* work?"

"Depends on the girl," he says, shrugging.

"Not this one."

"Definitely not." His gaze holds mine, the music a throbbing pulse under my skin. "Give me time," he finally says. "I've been told I'm an acquired taste."

A warm ripple races down my spine as I'm suddenly thinking about what he tastes like. From the smell of him—all citrus and cedar and amber—I'm guessing pretty damn great.

"I don't have time," I say, the truth in that statement catching up with me. I have tonight—this one night of freedom I'm allowing myself. The rest?

Take care of Ray at all costs.

That thought suddenly evaporates all the wildness coursing in my veins, leaving me slightly cold inside.

He leans down, his full lips at the shell of my ear. "That's the first true thing you've said all night."

"And it's the last," I say, stepping away as the band shifts to another tune. "Thanks for the dance." I back up another foot, both relieved and disappointed when he doesn't protest.

"Harley!" I hear Kai call from behind me. I glance over my shoulder and spot him at the edge of the dance floor, two drinks in his hands as he motions me over. I turn back around, my hand prepped for a wave goodbye, but the boy is gone.

I scan the area around me, almost desperate to lock on to those golden eyes.

Nothing but dancers laughing and cheering.

I ignore the hollow disappointment that sucks at the bottom of my stomach.

I already stopped the dance—of course he left after my obvious shutdown.

I start toward Kai, forcing myself to smile.

Forcing myself to forget the heat I feel lingering from the dance.

Tonight isn't over, but I can't help but feel like I've lost something.

I continue to give the place furtive glances, but even after an hour, the dark stranger never shows up again.

Probably for the best.

Because I've never allowed myself to *want* anything before, and I sure as hell can't afford to start now.

CHAPTER TWO

My baby sister holds the colored pencil to paper like a conductor creating a symphony as swirls of black crash with sharp angles of indigo.

I fold myself into the booth in Miller's Deli and watch Ray across from me. She hates it when I do, but I'm stopped dead by the absolute peaceful concentration that shapes her beautiful face. The blond braid down the back of her head leaves nothing hidden from her crystal-blue eyes—peace, hope, joy.

She may only be my half sister, but she's the Disney princess to my villain, and has been since her mom gave her up to my father and me when Ray was a baby. Really, she gave her up just to me, since he's been a worthless parent every day of his life.

"Stalking is a crime, you know?" Ray says without looking up from her paper, and I shake my head. She's only seven, but she's always been hyperaware of her surroundings. Me constantly having her run and hide from the big bad at home will do that to a girl.

I absentmindedly touch my sore lip, still tender from the fight two nights ago but almost completely healed now.

My thoughts race as I think about the rest of the night—more specifically, the stranger at the concert. The dance. The way warm shivers continue to burst along my skin whenever I think of how he barely touched me and yet it felt electrifying. In truth, he'd only put a whisper of touches on the jeans over my hips, but I still can't get him out of my head—his scent, those eyes...they haunt me.

"I brought you lunch," I say, shifting the paper-wrapped pastrami sandwich in my hand.

Ray finishes the last swoop of black over her most recent anime original character and sets down her pen.

"Working on Marid again?" I ask, nodding toward the paper. He's her latest obsession; her sketchbook is filled with him.

"Can't get him out of my head," she says, something wary in her eyes as she studies her work—the mass of black hair, the vivid indigo eyes, the slick midnight suit covering sharp shoulders and a trim frame. Ray shifts in the little plastic seat and looks up at me.

"Thanks." She unwraps the sandwich and sinks her teeth into it like she's not eaten all day.

She hasn't.

Neither of us has. I cringe against the truth.

Summer vacation—while awesome because of the whole *lack*-of-school thing—sucks because it means Ray goes without two guaranteed meals a day.

Luckily, my boss—Nathan Miller, owner of Miller's Deli— happens to be the nicest man we've ever met and doesn't charge for any of the food we eat. I always make her a sandwich the minute we get there.

Also lucky for me, he's let me work five days a week every summer for the past five summers now. He took pity on me when I showed up the summer of my thirteenth birthday begging for a job. I still remember the skepticism on his face, the way he laughed and rolled his eyes but handed me a mop and a bucket and told me to get to work. He joked that I wouldn't show up for the second shift.

I've shown up every summer since, as well as after classes during the school year when I could.

And now that I've graduated? I'll work here as long as he lets me. In fact, I'm going to need this job more than ever in seven days. The minute I turn eighteen, I'm going to rent Ray and me an apartment and finally, finally be free.

"Marid looks badass," I say. The character has a fondness for suits and a penchant for thievery and violence.

I reach across the table and run my fingers over the art kit open next to her pile of papers. The little leather satchel unrolls to reveal rows and compartments filled with the best art supplies I can afford. Erasers, graphite pencils, charcoal, colored pencils, dip pen nibs and holders, a half-empty bottle of black liquid, and brushes for inking—Ray cleans the bristles religiously to ensure they last. It took me half a summer to save up for that kit, but the look on her face? The magical pieces she creates? Worth it.

"Have you heard anything about the art summer program?" she asks.

I grit my jaw. I just graduated a few weeks ago, but Trenton's summer office seems hell-bent on ignoring me. Ironic since when I was a student they constantly pushed agendas on me like *"pursue a career in physical therapy, they always need people"* or *"you'll never survive college if you don't study for this final." Please*, college isn't even on my radar. Not necessary when I already have a degree in go-fuck-yourself and survival 101.

Can't really complain, though—I'd trade more classes and a cupboard of a dorm room to hang with my sister any day.

"I emailed them again yesterday," I say. "The program doesn't start for a couple of days. I'm sure you're accepted. I'll check tomorrow after I meet with Coach Hale."

She flashes me a look of doubt no seven-year-old should even know how to make.

I press my lips together, both hating and admiring the maturity in her eyes. It isn't fair. She shouldn't be stuck in a deli for eight hours at a time because it's not safe to go home without me.

After he hired me years ago, I carted in my two-year-old baby sister and begged him to let her stay with me. We all took turns watching her back then, and she became the little mascot of Miller's. Some customers grew so attached to her that they came with little gifts of clothes or toys.

"Hey," I finally say, and she looks up at me. "They'll know a true artist when they see one." I nod to my left, eyeing her most recent work. "Once they see yours? I'll get that call. I have no doubt."

She smiles, returning to her food with a nod.

"See you in a bit," I say, standing up again, glancing around the tiny seating area to ensure we're not taking up the last available spot. When the deli gets too busy, Ray doesn't mind working in the tiny storage closet in the back of the restaurant. In fact, some days, she prefers it.

The artist in the storage closet. The fact that she doesn't mind being shut away during the occasional rush makes my heart squeeze. She always says she can find inspiration anywhere, and not for the first time, I wish I were more like her.

Ray sees the world in sweeping colors of hope and possibility.

I see it in jagged pieces of black and gray, but hey, maybe we're just watching different channels.

"Don't forget your net," Nathan says as I make my way through the door marked EMPLOYEES ONLY and toward the deli counter.

"Got it!" I call, fishing the hairnet from my back pocket. I wrap my hair in a bun and secure it with a tie, then put the net over it. A white paper hat covers the black webbing, completing my super-lit look. Not that looks matter—only the paycheck.

"Harley?" Nathan has *that* tone to his voice—the one full of concern. The one that makes acid swirl in my stomach. He adores Ray; I've known that since the moment he laid eyes on her. Everyone does. But I sometimes wonder if she's the only reason he continues to tolerate me.

My cheeks burn despite my mental effort to cool them, and I try to casually cross my arms at my stomach, as if bracing for a blow. "Yeah?" I ask, stopping just shy of the deli counter.

Nathan drops the box of spices he's sorting and makes his way over to me. He's young for a business owner, a little over thirty, but sometimes he acts like he's a hundred when his gaze hones in on mine—or on my arms, where my rolled-up long-sleeve shirt has exposed a new bandage.

"I've got some antibiotics in the first aid kit for cuts...or burns," Nathan says, jerking a thumb toward his office past the kitchen. "After your shift is up, come get some. Understand?"

I stiffen. I only ever wear long sleeves for this reason—so no one asks questions—and I'm forever grateful when Nathan doesn't now. I've established over the years that I'm a klutz—I know totes cliché, but I had to come up with some sort of cover. And either it's what he wants to believe or I've just gotten that good at lying. I'll never know. Either way, we both drop the topic and thankfully move on.

"Oh," he says as I turn to head to my station. "Hired a new guy today. His shift is in a half hour." He flashes me a pleading look. "Don't scare him off, 'kay?"

I stare at him, the threat of a smile on my lips. "The last guy was a creep! He never took no for an answer and constantly begged me to watch sea-turtle videos with him."

Nathan raises his hand toward me, nodding. "I get it. But the one before that wasn't a bad guy."

"Debatable." The one before that told me I'd sell more add-ons like sodas, chips, and sides if I *smiled more.*

Nathan rubs his palms over his face. "Fine," he says. "If you could determine quickly if this one is a jerk or not, that'd be great. I need the help, and I hate going through the hiring process."

I soften at his acceptance of my opinion, at the value he places on mine above all other employees'.

"I'll do my best." And I mean it. I don't want to cause Nathan any problems—I just can't stand to work with misogynist assholes who *live* to tell me what to do.

I have to deal with that enough at home.

"You always do," he says, then returns to his work.

I swallow hard as I hurry behind the deli counter.

For the next thirty minutes, I lose myself in the steady stream of regular customers—the process of *bread-spread-meat-side* a soothing kind of hypnosis. Here, making the city's most popular sandwiches, I don't have to *think.*

Don't have to contemplate the next hour, the next night.

Don't have to worry if tonight will be the night I won't survive.

Don't have to feel the guilt of sometimes *wanting* it to be the night I don't wake up.

But no matter how bad things are, I'd never leave Ray to face this life alone. Plus, I could have it a thousand times worse. I could be jobless or an only child or God forbid, be totally obsessed with brussels sprouts and kale. I remind myself of those facts and add a little mental kick in the ass for good measure. Pity parties are so ten years ago.

"Can you hand me a pair of gloves?" A masculine voice behind me jolts me out of my thoughts, and a warm shiver skates down my spine.

I know that voice...

I whirl, and the air freezes in my lungs.

A pair of amber eyes—the same amber eyes I haven't been able to stop thinking about—stare down at me. His gaze is narrowed, almost like he's sizing up an opponent, and his lips? They're quirked up in the barest hint of a smirk. He's wearing another black T-shirt, but this time he's paired it with ripped jeans, and I can't help but like that he doesn't go out of his way to look perfectly put together.

"What the hell are you doing here?" The words burst from my mouth before I can filter them as heat flares beneath my skin. I mean, sure, I might've possibly fantasized about him wandering in by accident as a customer, but I didn't expect him to be on *this* side of the deli counter.

Shit. This guy is going to see the real me now, every scar and bruise clearly visible under the bright fluorescent lights of the deli—and not just the physical wounds. I am broken inside in ways that can never be fixed, and he'll see it all. With a *hairnet* on, of all things. I know it's silly that that's my first thought, but as my hand goes up to fiddle with the netting, ensuring it's tucked under my hat as much as possible, there you have it. Oh vanity, where have you been hiding my whole life? And can you please skitter back under that rock again?

"Glad I made such an awesome first impression." His tone drips sarcasm.

I blink a few times, the shock of seeing him in my deli having completely stolen my words.

"Want to hand me a pair?" he asks when it's clear I don't know what to say. He glances behind me and down, at the cubby beneath the register I block.

"Gloves," I grumble, realization donning on me. "Right." I move out of the way but don't turn my back on him. I hurry along the prep station to help the next customer. The boy grabs the gloves, then is back at my side in two seconds flat.

I flash him a *what the fuck* look. "What *are* you doing here?"

"I'm here to watch you," he says, arms folded neatly behind his back.

I arch a brow at him, trying to look unfazed even though his words cause ice to slither along my veins. "Did you know—"

"Who you were when Nathan hired me?" He cuts me off, and I glare up at him. "Yes. Our brief dance was so memorable that I tracked you across the city and begged your boss to hire me just so I could slap mayo on bread all day to be near you." He rolls his eyes. "Trust me, I got your message loud and clear that night that you weren't interested."

I swallow hard, my gaze darting anywhere but at his. "Not what I meant," I say, hating that I sound breathless, and I can't tell if it's because I want to run from him or get closer so I can catch a smell of that damn invigorating scent of his. Citrus and cedar and amber must be the kryptonite cologne I never knew existed.

"So you're the new guy," I start again, as if I'm trying to get my brain and my heart to sync up. To shake the shock and wake the fuck up. Our dance keeps flashing behind my eyes, as does the way I've replayed it more than a dozen times in the past two days. Escaping into it like the little slice of fantasy it is.

Mortification threatens to shrivel me on the spot—I'd been so open at the concert, so wild and teasing and...*not* me.

"Yes," he says. Nothing else. As if that says it all, in fact. And I suppose it does.

I nod, then take a ham sandwich order from the next customer.

I grab a fresh hoagie and slice my knife through the middle of it. I made too much out of a simple dance, that's all. I dip my knife into the mayonnaise and lather it on the bread. It was just a chance encounter, nothing more. I reach into the ham container and grab a little too much, shoving it into the bread anyway. Normal people go to clubs and dance with strangers all the time—they don't turn the experience into some sort of fantasy reel of what life could be like. I randomly toss in lettuce and cheese and slide down the line. I need to move on. I'm going to be working with this guy now. Nothing to see here. I wrap the sandwich quickly, grab the customer's sides, and ring him up—all with the new guy's gaze burning on the back of my neck.

I don't turn around, though, until he hums a familiar tune—a Bishop Briggs song I know by heart—and I cringe. It's the song we danced to. There is laughter in his eyes as I stare up at him. "I should thank you," he says. "I didn't know the singer very well, but your…*enthusiasm* that night urged me to download every song she has."

I clear my throat. "You're welcome," I say, forcing myself to focus more intently on the incoming customers than necessary.

For the next few hours, he goes so silent, I want to scream.

Normally, I relish silence. But come *on*—he just teased me with his humming, and he'd practically held a verbal battle with me about how to get him horizontal at the concert. All while meeting me move for move on the dance floor. How could he not say something now? Put me out of my misery and at least get us to the point where we laugh about it and then never mention it again. That's a thing, right?

But no, he seems content with his silent, efficient, and *just this side of broody* mood. And sure, I haven't really given him an opening, but I've been too busy trying to un-mortify the situation. He probably expects me to be that girl from the concert, someone maybe even interesting to work with, but it has to be more than clear that I'm not her anymore. And I hate that. Hate that I put myself in a situation where someone can clearly see everything I'm not but wish I were.

I have no idea what he's thinking, and I'm almost more mad that I *want* to know.

"I've got that," he says as I go to gather the garbage from the numerous bins throughout the shop. He moves so quickly, he makes it to the bag at the first can before I do.

"I'm fine," I say, reaching for it, but he's already hauling the bag out and twisting it closed. His boots are near silent against the tiled floor as he hustles to the next. I glare at his back, then shake my head and put a clean bag in the bin.

I follow him to each can, the silence deafening between us except for the swish of the plastic bags as I refill the cans. Once he gathers all five bags, I reach for the two in his right hand, but he jerks away.

I clench my jaw, heading toward the door to *at least* hold it open for him, but he beats me again, using his long legs to eat up the space. A cocky grin shapes his full lips as he disappears through the door, dumpster-bound.

Fire bubbles in my chest at his arrogance, at his *immediate* assumption that I can't possibly manage to lift all the bags on my own. I fold my arms over my chest, waiting at the prep station.

"What's next?" he asks when he returns from washing his hands, his eyes flickering under the lights as he stares down at me, waiting, expectant.

"Two things," I say, hating that my voice cracks. He's easily the most gorgeous person I've ever seen in my life, but I know better than anyone that looks can be deceiving as fuck. And sure, we shared *one* dance together, but he could be a monster—an attractive, intriguing monster, but still. "I can handle myself," I say, pointing toward where he hauled all the garbage. "Like, *literally* anything that comes through any of these doors, I can handle." I point toward the front of the shop to include the entrance, too.

"Well, you do love a challenge." He has the nerve to raise a brow at me, his lips shaping this crooked, mischievous grin that makes my blood boil.

"That doesn't mean it's not the truth." I scrunch my nose. *I'm more than capable of taking care of myself*, I think, but then hate it when I reach down to tug the sleeves of my shirt down to make sure the bandages beneath are hidden.

"It means you seem like the type of girl who would insist she's fine even when she's literally drowning."

My heart stutters.

He takes a step closer, the smell of citrus rolling off him. I shake away my reaction to it and narrow my gaze.

"And you seem like the type of guy who would insist someone is drowning when in reality, they're happy keeping their head above water," I say.

He sighs and shakes his head. "What's the second thing?"

Shit, what was *the second thing?*

I hurry to come up with something to say, motioning to the prep station. "This all needs to be wiped down." Then nod. "My shift is over."

He bows slightly, and I spin on my heels, shirking the paper hat and hairnet as I head to the back to grab my things. Ray will be packing up by now, and I want to clear this place as quickly as possible.

"Your name?" he asks, having followed me—silently.

Can't he tell already that the girl he met at the club is gone? As gone as I want to be right now.

"You didn't tell me the other night." He stands there patiently, like he doesn't mind waiting all damn night to hear my answer.

"You didn't ask," I fire back.

"Harley?" Ray calls from behind me, and I glance over my shoulder, keeping the new guy in my peripheral vision. Her leather satchel is rolled up and tucked against her chest, her eyes darting between me and him. "You ready? Or did you get a double shift?"

"Yeah, I'm ready," I say, returning my focus to him.

"You work sixteen-hour shifts?" he asks, his brow furrowed.

"Sometimes," I say, and I've never been more glad tonight

isn't one of them.

"Who are you?" Ray asks, stepping to my side.

"Draven," he answers, and the sound of his name makes my stomach flip. Seriously? What the hell is wrong with my body today?

Draven drops to a crouch to meet Ray at eye level, and my jaw just about comes unhinged. "What's your name?"

"Ray," she answers, a soft smile on her lips, but her eyes are still sharp. Good girl. I taught her never to be mesmerized by a pretty face—regardless of gender.

Draven glances up at me, then back to Ray. "Sisters."

She nods.

I purse my lips. Not many people make that leap—Ray is all blond hair, blue eyes, and has the optimism of a unicorn. I'm all red hair, green eyes, with a signature vibe of damaged, dirty, and back-the-hell-away. It doesn't bother me, though, I'll be the scary ogre that guards the unicorn any damn day of the week.

"You like to sing with your eyes closed," he says, and she tilts her head. He nods to her art kit. "Painting. Pablo told—" He clears his throat. "Pablo Picasso said that once about creating art."

Ray's eyes widen as she files away that gem.

"What's your style?" he asks.

"Manga," she says.

"I've always wanted to read that," he says. "But I've never known where to begin."

Her eyes light up—he's just won her over for life.

"You should start with Death Note," she says. "Or Fullmetal Alchemist. You seriously can't go wrong with those two."

"I'll be sure to pick them up." He stands, and I step in front of Ray.

"Yeah, we need to go," I say before I can stop myself. The more he chats with Ray, the more I'm tempted to linger, and I don't have the luxury of hanging around. I need a serious redo on today, the mortification of this guy seeing a wilder side of me still clings to my skin.

Something like confusion flickers in his eyes, and I rake my palms over my face. It's been a long day, and it's about to be an even longer night. I shake my head, ushering Ray to the exit with my hand on her back.

"Bye, Draven!" she calls over her shoulder.

"Bye, Ray," he calls back.

I promise myself I'm not going to give in to the urge to see if he's watching me walk away. I will not allow him the satisfaction of knowing how much it matters if he is. I will not turn around to spy the smirk he's probably wearing right now. An army could not make me look back.

I totally look back.

And then wish I hadn't.

CHAPTER THREE

"He was cute," Ray says as we make the walk toward the El. The heady Chicago air is comforting like a warm blanket.

I scoff. She hadn't seen that obnoxious smirk on his face when he caught me giving him one last look before we left. He's going to be insufferable to work with tomorrow.

"Come on, admit it."

"He's okay."

More like gorgeous.

"Not every guy is bad," she continues after the train has barreled us toward our stop.

"I know that," I say. "Kai is my best friend, remember?" I challenge. "And he's a guy." One of the good ones, thank God. He's always been a rock to lean on when shit gets real and when it comes to my life? That shit is more constant than the sun rising in the east.

"Yeah, and *he's* cute, too."

I glance down at her while we hop off the El and start our walk home. "What is it with you and cute boys all of a sudden?"

Oh fuck. Have we reached this point? Is she in the getting-crushes phase?

"I'm just making an artistic observation, Harley. Don't freak out."

"I'm not freaking out," I tease but tuck her under my arm.

The closer we make it to home, the more tension grows between us. Like a rubber band pulled from either end.

Our trailer comes into view as we navigate the small pathways between homes, and I stop by the wooden steps outside our front door. "You ready to play our traditional game of hide-and-seek?"

Ray grimaces. "I'm getting too old for that game."

I swallow around the rock in my throat. She'll *never* be too old for this game.

One more week—we can make it. Maybe he won't even notice I've taken Ray with me.

Acid churns in my gut. I know that's not true. He'll notice, and he'll come after us and ruin my chance at ever legally obtaining guardianship over Ray. I have to play this smart, or I'll lose her forever.

"Please, Ray. For me?"

She hugs me close. "Maybe tonight will be different."

It won't. No matter how many times she says that, it won't.

Not for me.

And honestly, the closer we get to my birthday, the more frequent the beatings. It's almost like Dad knows he's about to lose his hold over me and wants to get a lifetime of punishment in these last few days. Jokes on him, I'm going to outlive his ass just so I can stand over his grave flashing two middle fingers. Maybe I'll bring donuts, too.

"Go," I say.

She nods and hurries around the back of the trailer where our shared room is. I rigged the window to easily open from the outside and stacked a couple of milk crates outside it so she could climb in and out without making too much noise.

Dad has never hurt her, never even come close. But I can't stand the thought of her seeing what he constantly does to me. It's bad enough she has to hear it—no one needs that image planted in their brain, either. Except maybe, Tarantino—he'd probably take that inspiration straight to the bank. Maybe I could grab a percentage of the sales.

I count to twenty, forcing myself to the present.

I unlock the door, the smell of vodka and stale sweat souring the air. I sigh, wondering why he couldn't pick a liquor with a better smell—something citrus or mint flavored at the very least.

It doesn't matter how many hours I spend cleaning the trailer, it's always the same. I can usually smell it on my clothes even in the fresh air.

I lit a candle last night, trying to find my Zen while also freshening the trailer.

I thought Dad was out with his buddies, drinking himself into a stupor.

Fuck me, had I been wrong.

He found the vanilla spice candle Nathan gave me for my birthday last year and immediately reminded me exactly what fire could do.

I can still feel the sizzle on my skin as he held my forearm over the flame. Can still smell the burning flesh. But, bonus, he didn't even think to go for my hair. That would've been a bitch to try and hide. Some girls can rock the hell out of a beanie or cute hat—me? Not so much.

I shake my head, forcing the images out of my mind.

"You're late." Dad's voice drifts from the kitchen, a sharp edge in it like he's been waiting for a fight—yay, me, I get his default setting tonight. I'd kill for an *upgrade needed* night—the ones that take hours to run. "Work was long as hell today, with that tight-ass supervisor bitching at me nonstop about how my line's quota is slipping. I should've had a warm meal waiting on me when I got here."

I force my face into a smile. "We came straight home from work."

"You better not be late with rent this month." The fridge door slams shut; then the familiar *pop* of a freshly opened can fills the silence. "That's the only reason I even let you work, you hear me?"

Yeah, that's why he *lets* me work. He charges me double our trailer rent for my "share" of expenses and thinks I don't know that he pockets the rest of the money. Of course, he doesn't know I actually make double what I've told him I'm paid, so I guess it could be worse.

"Where is Ray?" he asks as he walks out of the shadows of

the kitchen. The exposed bulb that lights up our meager living room illuminates his face. He has the same blond hair and blue eyes as Ray, but there's nothing but contempt on his face when he looks at me.

"She's going to bed. Art program tomorrow," I lie... Well, I hope it isn't a lie. She needs the extra meal that comes with it, not to mention the class that will fuel her passions.

Dad glares at me. "I didn't tell her she could do that." He cracks his neck and turns toward the lone hallway that leads to our room. "She should know better than to do something without asking." He stomps toward our bedroom door, and I freeze as I imagine what he'll do—what he's done to me too many times to count.

Threats. Always just threats. I know he'll never touch her. He just wants me to *believe* he will. To live in a constant state of fear of the possibility. But that doesn't stop the terror from shaking my body.

"No," I say.

He pauses and slowly turns to face me, his smile showing he wanted me to say exactly that. "What the hell you say, girl?"

"It was me," I say, watching his every step toward me. The fists curling at his sides, the malicious glint in his eyes. "I signed her up."

He looms over me. "You should know your place," he snaps.

"I—"

He moves so fast, I don't register the backhand. Stars burst behind my eyes.

I clutch my cheek, shifting my stance and using my core to help me stay on my feet. He's so much worse when I'm on the ground.

"You never listen," he says. "You never learn. You keep disobeying me, keep trying to be more than you are. And you know what you are, Harley?" He slams his fist toward my face.

I fling up my right arm, blocking it, my muscles barking in protest.

"Worthless," he spits. "Weak."

I dig my fingers into his flesh with my other hand, baring my teeth. His eyes flare wide at my pathetic attempt to stop him.

Then he *laughs*.

It turns my blood to ice.

"You want to play?" He seethes. "Fine." He shakes me off.

I can't blink before my hip hits the floor, my teeth singing from the impact. The tip of his foot sinks into my stomach, knocking the breath from my lungs.

And I curl around myself. I tighten my stomach muscles so the next kick does the least amount of damage. It hurts, but I'll survive. I've survived much worse.

Hit.

Smack.

Bursts of pain. My cries escape through gritted teeth. But inwardly, I *feed* off the pain. Relish it.

I used to lie awake at night and wonder what was so wrong with me, so worthless that even my own father could look at my bruised and bloodied body on the floor and feel nothing. Not an ounce of love or kindness. He'd treat a dog better than he ever treated me. But then when I was fourteen, a group of boys cornered me in an alley—and it was the most freeing moment of my life.

I fought and screamed and just barely escaped, but those boys had given me something they hadn't intended that night—a purpose. Later, as I hunkered in the shadow of a bush near our trailer, the adrenaline still sucking the strength from my body, I heard Ray's tinkling laughter in our room, and I just knew. I finally *knew* why I didn't get to have a life free of pain and suffering. Why I was never meant to be loved.

Dad wasn't the only monster out there. The world was apparently full of them.

With every hard swing of my dad's boot into my hip, into my thigh, with every vile word he spits at me, all he does is light a fire in my soul.

I may be bleeding, aching, burning.

But no one as pure as Ray can survive in this world. It's harsh and cruel and it will slowly kill every ounce of hope inside her if I don't protect her.

That night, I realized my father wanted to turn me into a monster just like him.

And I would let him. I would let him teach me to take pain. I would let him make me relish the fight. I would let him kill even the tiniest sliver of trust I might harbor.

Because Ray was an angel sent from heaven for *me* to protect.

I'll become *her* monster, and the evil of this world will have to go through me first.

CHAPTER FOUR

My spine cracks against the mat that stretches across half of Trenton High's gym floor, and the air *whooshes* out of my lungs.

In an instant, Coach Hale is on top of me, her slight frame somehow pinning me to the ground. Her delicate hands wrap around my throat and squeeze until I can't drag a breath into my aching lungs.

"You know what to do," she says.

Panic overtakes me, and I flail beneath her. Smack and scratch at her fingers clutching my throat.

"Focus!" she snaps as I struggle. She grips my hips with her knees, rendering my legs useless. "You begged me to teach you how to fight. Then *fight*. Channel your anger," she orders. "Use it!"

Monkey grip.
Elbow clutch.
Pivot.
Push.

The answers play like a movie in my head, the result of three sessions a week with Coach Hale for more than a year now.

Quickly, I grip one of her wrists, ensuring I don't leave my thumb vulnerable, and hold the back of her elbow with the other so she can't break it. Pivoting left, I use the strength in my hips to throw her off-balance. I roll, gathering all the force I have left in my body to propel her off until *I'm* the one pinning her to the mat.

"Good," she says, sweat sliding down her smooth, dark skin.

I hurry off her, extending my hand to help her stand. She takes it, hauling herself to her feet. She's an inch or so taller than

I am but a shit ton stronger. It doesn't matter how many times we practice or how much cardio and strength training I do in the alley behind Miller's, I can never truly match her. Some inner flaw in my muscles—weakness, just like my dad always says. I hate that he's right.

"You're getting faster," she says as we walk off the mat to where our water bottles sit near the wall of the gym.

I take a fast drink, then shake my head. "Not fast enough. I should've seen that palm strike coming."

Coach Hale wipes her face with a towel. "I haven't been holding back," she says, and I eye her. "Not really. It would be hard for anyone with years of training to see that move coming, let alone—"

"A recent high school grad who can barely walk without tripping into a wall?"

She gives me a chiding look. "You've improved so much since we first started."

I nod, unable to deny that. But my body still feels…weak. I have no other way to describe it, like something went wrong when I was made. I can never quite gain enough energy or strength to stop my father. I can take hits, sure; that's the easy part. Actually holding my own against him? Impossible. I guess there'd be no challenge if it was easy.

I fiddle with the small cord bracelet wrapped around my left wrist. A thin, circular black gemstone hugs the center of the cord, the lone piece of my mother I have left. I remember her wrapping it around my wrist when I was four—the cord cinched as tight as it could go back then. Over the years, though, the cord stretched with my body, but never too tight. She told me it was a wishing bracelet and that the minute the cord snapped, the wish would come true. It had to snap on its own, she said, and I knew as I grew, my body should have broken it. But I couldn't even get that right.

Still, I never take it off. Not when it's the last memory I have of her before she disappeared. When I was younger, I clung to the token as a beacon of hope—a fantasy that she'd return for me. The bracelet her promise.

That hope died after the age of seven.

And now…now I wear it both as a reminder that silly dreams are useless and that I once had a mother. One who left, but a real one out there all the same. Some other piece of me that isn't made entirely of my father. And since there is no proof otherwise, the bracelet also serves as a comical what-if game I like to play—I mean, for all I know, she could've been a contestant on *The Great British Bake Off.*

"It's not enough," I finally respond to Coach Hale's praise, letting go of the spiral my mind just slid down.

"You came to me last year because you wanted to know how to defend yourself in the event that something happens after one of your night shifts." She eyes me. "You've proven yourself over and over again. Why is it never enough?"

I rub my palms together. How can I explain without telling her the truth? I can't be honest with her, obviously. I can't risk her telling the authorities about my abusive father and run the chance that I'll be separated from Ray.

"I guess I just never feel like I'm doing enough," I admit. At least it's a portion of the truth.

Coach Hale furrows her brow, then rolls her eyes. "You're the hardest-working kid I've ever known." She nudges her shoulder against mine. "You should be planning your wild eighteenth birthday party, not adding on more grueling lessons with me."

"I enjoy your grueling lessons," I say, laughter in my voice.

"That's what worries me," she teases. "Come on, what are you doing to celebrate?"

Every year on my birthday, Kai, Ray, and I gorge ourselves on Nathan's famous chocolate chip cookies. Nathan always makes sure to sneak Ray a few extra, and it's a day I look forward to each year.

But…this year…

My life will change.

"Not really a party person," I say when Coach Hale raises

her brows at me. It isn't like I have a long list of friends secretly planning me the bash of a lifetime. And I'm cool with that. I learned a long time ago that people have an innate sense for sniffing out the damaged, the dirty.

"You should live a little, Harley," Coach Hale says. "High school is over. You're about to be old enough to vote. You should enjoy life while you can."

My eyes widen.

"Life is short," she hurries to add. "And turning eighteen equals college, paying your own bills, and more."

I don't have the energy to explain I've been an adult for much longer than she can guess.

"I owe you big for keeping up our lessons in the summer," I say, forcing myself to the present. "I'd be beyond bored without them."

Most of the defensive techniques she's taught me are the sole reason I'm better at hiding my wounds. With the blocks she's drilled into me, I've been able to spare my face more than I ever have before. Face injuries are incredibly hard to explain away—though, in my defense, I do actually have an issue with walking—at any given moment, my legs will get tangled and I'll trip right into a door or fall down the stairs. What can I say, I've never been comfortable in my own skin.

Coach Hale nods, her shiny black hair secured in two braids that make her look like she has a vertical crown down the center of her head. "You're a good student," she says. "Same time Friday?"

"I'll be here."

She flashes me a smile then we gather our things, and I head out of the gym while she walks to her office inside the girls' locker room. I make a quick stop by the admissions office, mustering up my polite face.

"Hello, Miss Ward." Mrs. Campbell greets me from behind her desk. There's a smile in her cheeks, but it never reaches her eyes. I'm sure all she wants is to be out of this place for the summer as much as I do. "What can I do for you?"

"Hi, Mrs. Campbell," I say. "I'm sorry to bother you, but I'm wondering if Ray's application for the arts program has been process—"

"Oh!" Mrs. Campbell cuts me off, sifting through a stack of folders on her desk. "Yes," she says, passing a thick folder to me. "I've tried contacting your father for more than a week now to let him know she was accepted, but I understand how busy single parenting can be."

I swallow hard, tucking the folder under my arm. "You should have…" I stop myself, softening my tone. "I mean, I thought the school had my number as the primary contact."

Mrs. Campbell arches a brow. "We're required to contact the parent first, Harley."

I force my face to stay even, to stay calm. They don't know my father like I do. He never shows anyone anything but a perfect, pretty face outside our home. "Okay," I say. "I get that, but he's super tech-deficient." If you can call being too drunk to work your cell tech-deficient. "So if you ever can't get ahold of him, I'm almost always by my phone." A phone I saved up for and secured thanks to Nathan adding me to a family plan, with the condition he takes the bill from one of my checks each month. Another kindness he's offered me on Ray's behalf so I can stay on top of things for her.

Mrs. Campbell opens something on her computer screen and takes a few moments typing away. "I've made a note," she says. "But I can't guarantee we'll be able to do that."

I nod. "Thanks for making the note."

She smiles again, this time the motion actually crinkling the corners of her eyes. "I look forward to seeing Ray soon!"

My heart swells as I grip the folder in my arms. "I can't wait to tell her," I say and hurry out of the office as if she might change her mind any second.

I knew Ray would get accepted. She's wicked talented, and now this means she'll be at school for four hours, five days a week, with a lunch served every single day. Tears threaten to sting my eyes as relief pools in my stomach.

"Harley!" Ray shouts as she runs toward me when she spies me exiting the front of the building. She gives me a quick hug, and I hold her close while flashing Kai a smile as he follows behind at a much slower pace.

"Thanks again," I say, grinning at my best friend. Kai had offered to watch Ray when I first started working out with Coach Hale, and I swallowed my pride and accepted.

"No problem," he says, tucking his hands into his maroon blazer pockets. His warm brown hair is perfectly styled in an ultracasual way, his light-green eyes saying what they always do at times like these—*there's no need for thanks.*

But I will always thank him. Always *be* thankful for him. Thankful for him crashing into my life at seven years old and never judging my lifestyle, which is so different from his. His family can afford to live in a mansion and travel the world on a whim. Ray and I share a tiny room in a trailer that's one strong gust from destruction. But you can't have the *haves* without the *have nots*, and I'm not complaining. Once I'm eighteen, I'll make sure I do everything I can to put Ray in the *have* column.

"Did you eat?" I ask, glancing down at Ray.

She grimaces slightly, but only enough that I notice.

"I took her to Donavan's," Kai says as we settle in a walk toward the El.

I flinch internally. Donavan's is Kai's favorite restaurant in the city that serves pretty decent Italian food, but Ray doesn't really like it. Not that she'll ever admit that to Kai, who I'm sure paid for the meal, but I could've sworn I brought it up to him before.

"I'll pay you back," I say, but Kai rolls his eyes.

"Do you want to have this argument again?"

"Always," I say. "It's already bad enough that you don't take money for watching her—"

"I'm not a baby," Ray cuts me off. "I can take care of myself."

"I know you can," I say honestly. "Kai hanging out with you when I can't is for *me*, remember? I can't focus if I know you're at home alone."

Ray nods.

"Besides." Kai winks at her. "You know I'd do anything for Harley."

I roll my eyes at him. He's such a goof, but I love him.

The El ride is quick and painless—although Kai and Ray spend the entire trip arguing over the merits of manga—and we're all soon heading into Miller's through the employee entrance.

"You should at least give it a chance before you knock it," Ray says, a slight annoyance in her tone.

Kai sighs, rubbing the back of his neck as we walk toward the front so Ray can set up at her regular booth. "Just because you love manga doesn't mean the entire world has to."

I cringe at his response. I know normal siblings fight and Kai isn't her brother, but he's as close as she has to one, but Christ these two's debates can sometimes be a recipe for a migraine … for *me*.

Once Ray drops her supplies down on her table, I grab the folder the school gave me from my bag, happy as hell to distract her.

"What's this?" she asks, and I can barely contain my smile as she flips open the folder.

Her blue eyes light up, her eyebrows climbing. "I got in?"

I bite my lip, nodding as she bounces on her toes.

"I got in?" she cries, tears rolling down her cheeks.

I drop to her level, opening my arms as she nearly tackles me in a hug.

"Thank you! Thank you! Thank you!" she squeals, and I flinch from the high-pitched tone drawing looks from customers but laugh as I squeeze her tight.

"What's all the screaming about?" Nathan asks as he comes to stand just outside the open doorway. He nods to Kai, who high-fives Ray in celebration.

Ray disconnects herself from me and hurries over, handing Nathan the piece of paper from the file she left on the table.

"Dear Miss. Ward, we're pleased to invite you to attend our

limited and select advanced arts program…" Nathan's voice trails off as he grins down at Ray. "I told you!" he says as he scoops her up into a hug.

I swallow back a lump in my throat at the way Ray effortlessly throws her arms around his neck.

"I'm so proud of you." He sets her back on her feet. "Tell you what," he says, glancing at me with a question in his eyes. "If it's okay with your sister, I'll take you down the street for a celebratory sundae while she works."

Ray whirls around, her eyes wide. I nod, hating how tight my chest feels. She whips back to Nathan. "Can I get extra sprinkles?"

Nathan grins. "Only if you promise I can hang the first piece you create in the program on our front wall."

A blush rises on her cheeks, but she juts out her hand. Nathan shakes it.

"Deal," she says with much more distinction than any seven-year-old should be capable of.

"Let's go," he says, holding on to that hand and tugging her toward the employee entrance in the back. He meets my gaze over his shoulder, and I mouth *thank you* as they round the corner.

Kai shifts off the wall he's leaning on, his smile perfect and infectious as always. That's Kai—clean-cut, pristine, polished. It's a marvel I've never rubbed off on him, honestly.

"Guess that means you won't need me to watch her anymore," he says as he follows me through the kitchen and to the deli counter.

"She'll get to spend the week doing what she loves *and* be safe," I say, sliding my hairnet and paper hat into place. The truth of those words sinks into my already tight chest, and the smile I wear *hurts* my cheeks. "Do you know what that means?"

Kai steps a bit closer, his eyes on my lips. "You don't do that enough," he says, glancing down at me. He's a head taller than I am and where he used to be gangly, he's now all lean muscle. I don't mind how close he stands because I feel safe around him. Comfortable. Something I'm always worried will snap any second because I'm not used to comfort. Awkward, anxious, and downright defensive are more my jams.

"Do what?" I ask, hurrying through my prep tasks.

"Smile," he says, and I stiffen.

"Smiling is only good for a handful of things," I say, a tease in my tone. "And one of them happens to be scoring extra-special sauce at the Fry Shop."

Kai laughs, shaking his head before he steps into my path.

"Kai," I grumble as his fingers lightly trace over the bandages on my arms just barely visible at the ends of my sleeves.

"Cuts or burns?" he asks, not needing to know the source behind them. He's simply worried over how long it'll take me to heal. He's been in my life long enough to know who put the wounds there.

But I swore him to secrecy a long time ago for fear of being taken from Ray. And I'd guess he didn't want to lose me, too, if I were taken away, so he's always kept his mouth shut.

"Burn," I whisper, shaking out of his touch.

He hisses as he tracks my movements along the prep station. Thankfully, we're in that sweet lull between customers, but our four o'clock rush will happen any second now.

"I hate him."

Well, that makes two of us.

"I've had worse." I shrug. My skin grows too tight, and I try to breathe around the shame coating me like a layer of oil. I can't stand the pity clinging to Kai's eyes, and I sure as hell don't want that oil to stain *him*.

"I know you have," he says. "Doesn't mean I have to like it."

I finish my tasks, then turn to him. His eyes are on the bracelet I never take off before he flashes me a pained smile.

"Harley—"

"Where do you want me?" Draven's voice cuts Kai off, and he whirls at the sound.

Can't blame him, because that's the second time Draven has entered the space without making a damn sound. I'm beginning to think he's a ghost.

"Register," I say, then straighten my spine as I realize Draven isn't even looking at me. No, those gorgeous eyes are locked on Kai, a lethally amused sort of look. "Right," I say quickly. "This is my best friend—"

"Kai," Draven says, and it's my turn to look shocked. I turn to Kai, who steps in front of me, blocking me from Draven's view. "It's been a long time."

"Not long enough," Kai says, his jaw clenched.

CHAPTER FIVE

"Wait," I say. "You two *know* each other?" I furrow my brow, stepping around Kai to stand between them. There is so much chest puffing, I almost don't fit.

Draven doesn't flinch from Kai's death glare. He stands his ground, smirking at Kai two seconds past awkward. Then he dismisses him as easily as if he never spoke and gives me his attention.

"Register," he says in a reserved tone. He gives me the slight bow thing he's done several times now, then spins on his heel to take up vigil behind the cash register.

I blink a few times, wondering how the hell Draven manages to make my stomach drop, my muscles tighten, and my mind spin all at the same time with the simple *dipping* of his head. Jesus, this guy is a mystery with a capital *M*.

"Kai," I say, grabbing his elbow and guiding him through the back until we're out of Draven's earshot. "How do you know Draven? He just started here, and I've known you since we were seven."

Something like pain crinkles around Kai's eyes, and I tilt my head.

"Why didn't you tell me Nathan hired a new guy?" he asks instead of answering me.

"Why would I tell you? Nathan hires new people every summer."

Kai rakes his palms over his face. "You have to stay away from him, Harley."

I arch a brow at him. He knows better than to tell me what

to do. It's an instant trigger of mine—men explaining what I should or shouldn't do, what I should be wearing, how I should be speaking, what I should be listening to, behaving like, all of that crap.

He huffs, realization clicking in his eyes. "I didn't mean to…" He stumbles over his words, his eyes shifting over my head like he can see Draven around the corner. "He's not a good guy," he says.

"How do you know him, Kai?" I ask again, folding my arms over my chest. A prick of pain stings at his declaration about Draven. Why? Is it because he preceded it with a command? Or is it because Draven has popped into my thoughts constantly since the night of the concert and I don't want Kai's words to be true?

Kai visibly swallows, and I take a step back.

He's never lied to me before, but I can see it in the tense set of his shoulders, the flexed line of his jaw, the regret and anger churning in his eyes.

He's about to lie to me.

Hurt snakes down my chest, settling heavily in the bottom of my stomach.

"I don't really know him. Just trust me—he's bad news," Kai says, glancing down at the watch that's worth more than my life savings. "I have to run. I'm due at the airport in an hour."

My shoulders drop. I forgot he has another family trip this week. I hate it when he travels, how much I miss my friend when he's gone. How much it reminds me how alone I am. Yes, I have Ray and she's my entire world, but with Kai? I can just be myself, not the big sister/parent.

"Oookay." I shake my head as I drag out the word. I take another step away from him, resisting the urge to beg him to stay. "Forget I asked." I wave him off, turning to walk to my station, but Kai stops me with a gentle touch on my shoulder.

"I'll be back soon," he says, his smile soft, melting the tension between us. "We'll talk about it then, all right?"

I nod, and he pulls me into a hug. His cheek presses against my hair, his lips at my ear. "Be careful, promise?"

"As much as I can," I answer with our custom response. Every time he leaves, he makes me promise to be careful. I never *fully* agree because it isn't something I can control. It's not like I go out looking for danger; it just somehow always finds me. I'm super lucky like that—like I won a reverse lottery where the prize is pain instead of money. But hey, at least I'm a winner at something, right?

Not that I can be mad. Like with the man in the alley behind the deli a couple of days ago—that woman didn't deserve to be attacked. And me? Well, I'm used to it. If someone needs to take a hit, might as well be me.

I release Kai, his crisp, soapy scent lingering on my clothes for a second. One breath and it's absorbed by my much earthier one I can never get rid of—no matter how many showers I take or how many loads of laundry I do.

I make it to my station behind the glass partition just as a few customers stroll through the doors.

I lose myself in the controlled tasks of building sandwiches and greeting customers. Force myself not to contemplate how Kai knows Draven or how or *when* the two would've even crossed paths. Try to ignore the sinking feeling in my gut that the answer is something worth my best friend lying to me about.

"How long have you known Kai?" Draven asks a few hours later as we wipe down tables after closing.

"We met when we were kids," I say. "I snuck out to the park, and he was wearing a Thor shirt, my favorite, and—" I cut myself off, internally cringing at the memory rolling off my tongue. Meeting Kai is one of the few good ones I have. Though when I returned home from the park that day? *Not* so much.

Draven's brow furrows. "And he's your…boyfriend?" he asks.

I sputter, choking back a laugh at the way the word comes out of Draven's mouth. Almost like it's a foreign term to him.

"He's my oldest *friend*," I say. Draven and I worked in a peaceful sort of silence all night and now this?

"True friendship is often the basis for deeper love," he says as he continues to clean the tabletops. He doesn't say it like an accusation or a question, more like stating a fact. And the more time I spend with him, the more I realize when Draven isn't throwing snark left and right, he's making unusually annoying and profound statements that make me *think*.

Do I love Kai? Sure, yes. In a friendly way. Not in any romantic sort of way. It's never been like that between us.

"Maybe that's true for some people," I answer, finishing my last table.

Draven tilts his head, those eyes of his silently urging me to continue.

"Love is a fairy tale," I huff. "Sure, some people fall in love and live happily ever after, but others? Those people have to claw and dig and *bleed* for a shred of happiness, and even then…" I struggle for the right way to explain it.

"Even then," Draven says, taking a step toward me, the heat from his body washing over mine. "The happiness they cling to is mere drops where others have bucketfuls."

My lips part as I gaze up at him. "Exactly."

I try to tear my eyes away from his, but I *can't*. My brain tells me to stop staring into those golden depths, but my body won't listen. I just stand there, letting Draven hold my gaze as intently as if he was trying to read my mind. It doesn't matter that the boy is gorgeous and likes to challenge me — which I secretly relish — but when he speaks…

There's something about the way he shapes his words that has me wishing he'll say something else, something *more*.

A slight upturn of his full lips has me blinking out of his stare, and he finishes cleaning his last table. He moves around me, flipping chairs upside down and setting them on the tabletops with ease. Ray moved to the storage closet hours ago when the rush hit, so she isn't in her usual booth, which kind of sucks because this moment could really use a tension breaker like only Ray can deliver.

I force myself to tear my eyes off Draven, off the way his arm muscles ripple with each chair he lifts like they weigh nothing. Jealousy bites my chest at his strength, at the effortless way he moves around the room in silence, lifting and shifting furniture without a hint of strain on his face.

Not his fault you're so weak.

I swallow the unmerited jealousy. I grow stronger with each lesson with Coach Hale, but I feel like I should be further along by now. Feel like I should have more balance and core strength and all the things that will give me an advantage for surviving what awaits me.

Instead, my muscles tremble even now…an endless sort of tired I can never shake. Maybe it's fear constantly eating away at any semblance of solidity I can manage. Or more likely, it's the fact that I live on sandwiches. At least they're tasty. Gotta find that silver lining, amirite?

Draven lingers as we finish closing tasks, and I find myself staring at him while I shuck my hairnet and paper hat.

"What's troubling you?" he asks, turning as if he knows I've been staring at him this whole time.

Great.

"How do you know Kai?" I ask, wondering if I'll have more luck with him—a stranger—than I did with my own best friend.

Draven's amber eyes go distant for a moment before he slides his hands into the pockets of his jeans. "We worked together once."

I raise my brows. "He's never had a job in his life."

Draven challenges my words with a simple look.

Heat flares on my skin at the idea that *I* could be wrong. That I might not know my friend as well as I think I do. There's an explanation. Kai has been around forever—sure, his family goes on long summer trips that I dread—but he would've told me about a summer job. Right?

"You going to tell me to stay away from him?" I half joke as I repeat Kai's words from earlier.

"As if anyone has the grounds to make a demand like that?" Draven scoffs. "You decide what company you keep."

A warm shiver races across my skin at his words, at the effortless way he illuminates my independence as a human being. He doesn't act like he knows better, doesn't force advice, or make commands because he believes *he* knows better.

"Even if the choice in company is riddled with entitlement and disdain for anything that doesn't fit into a nice, pretty box. Usually one with a golden label," he adds, instantly killing the warmth in my blood.

"What the hell is that supposed to mean?" I snap. "So Kai has money. He doesn't act entitled toward people who don't." I'm living proof of that. He's never once shown any judgment toward Ray or me, and we'll never afford luxuries like cars or overseas trips.

Draven slowly arches a brow at me. "No, he doesn't *act* that way at all, does he?"

I glare at him. "You work with him once and you think you know him?"

Draven shrugs. "First impressions should be trusted," he says. "People usually tell you more of who they are in those initial few moments of meeting them than they do in an entire lifetime afterward."

I choke on a laugh. "So according to you, all you want is to get horizontal with me?"

Draven's eyes flare.

"That was my first impression of *you*—when you told me how to get you *horizontal*."

A smile turns up the corners of his lips. "I rest my case."

Heat rushes to my cheeks, but I shove down the butterflies trying to climb up my throat.

"Bullshit," I insist. Now that we've worked together, I know there is *no way* his first impression is one hundred percent dead-on like he implies—sly grins, slick innuendos, and sharp challenges, sure, but there is a whole other layer to him he tries to bury. The same one that I catch when he slips in a deep, thoughtful comment between his snarkier ones. "People hide behind masks,"

I continue. "Slap a filter on their thoughts and only show their true colors when angered." That's the only way my father ever got away with anything—hiding behind a charming mask to fool the world. Only those who provoke him—namely, *me*—ever see the monster he really is.

I take a step back, ready to lock up the shop and leave. Draven may be mysterious and gorgeous and smell infuriatingly good, but Kai is my best friend. I spin around, nearly stumbling over the freshly emptied trash can. Draven darts his arm out like he'll catch me, but at the last second thinks better of it and draws his hand back.

Good, I think as I right myself and straighten the trash can. He's learning quicker than the other employees Nathan has hired—I don't like being touched, and I certainly don't like help I didn't ask for. Especially from some jerk who just insulted my best friend.

Ray's giggles echo through the back of the deli, bursting the tense bubble between Draven and myself. He dips his head in my direction, then slowly walks toward the back exit. He's stopped by Ray and Nathan coming his way, so he leans against the wall.

I force the confused and angry look off my face, conjuring up a smile as Ray skips over to me. "So what sundae did you get earlier with Nathan?" I ask.

"We got deep dish," she says, grinning up at me, "*and* sundaes."

"Deep dish, huh?" I ask, glancing at Nathan, who stands behind her. "I'm jealous."

"Nathan let me take the leftovers," Ray hurries to say. "They're with my art gear. You can eat it on the way home."

I flash Nathan a look, but he just shrugs. "I'm so full, I'm miserable."

"Thank you."

He points at Ray. "She deserved a little celebration. It's not every day you're accepted to a prestigious art program."

"That's an incredible accomplishment," Draven says as he shifts to kneel at Ray's level. "Can I expect you to create some fantastic manga for me?"

She blushes but nods. "You know it."

Draven makes the universal *yes* motion with his fist, and she giggles again.

I try not to sputter at how quickly he shifts gears. One second, he's insulting Kai and my choice of him as my friend and the next he's making my baby sister giggle? It's hard to ignore the easy way he interacts with her, the genuine respect in his gaze, or the way my skin tingles at the sight.

I also try and fail miserably not to hate how he disappears while Ray and I gather her things. What did I want? To continue arguing with him?

Yes, yes, that's exactly what I want.

Because arguing with him feels more like playing chess—a slow sort of battle where I never know what he'll do or say next. And focusing on that is infinitely easier than focusing on the shift in my life I know is coming.

Six days and counting.

I try not to let the hope of freedom fill my shattered soul.

Because hope is a dangerous thing for me, and I've had enough danger to last me a lifetime.

CHAPTER
SIX

"Are you training with Coach Hale today?" Ray asks as we linger outside Trenton High's building.

"Tomorrow," I say, my muscles still sore from our last lesson. The other night, I tested out one of the evasive techniques she'd drilled into me, and my father only hit harder because of it. The bruise on my lower back throbs at the memory of his boot sinking into my flesh.

"What will you do?" Ray asks as she clutches her art kit to her chest. Worry colors her blue eyes, as does the purple beneath them from fatigue. I tuck her into a side hug.

"Don't worry," I say. "I'm not going home. I'll be right here when you're done at the end of the day."

Her tight shoulders loosen at that.

"Did you have another nightmare?" I ask, examining the exhaustion on her face a little closer. I hadn't heard her — normally she's pretty vocal with her night terrors — but there are times her dreams take her so far under, she can barely move, let alone cry out.

"It was a long one," she says, shrugging. "But it was just a dream."

I purse my lips, my hand lingering on her shoulder as if I can siphon off the exhaustion and replace it with what little strength I have. Ray has had vivid nightmares since forever, but they seem to be getting worse as she gets older.

"I'm fine now," she says. "I promise." She smiles up at me to prove just how *not* tired she is.

The weight in my chest lifts at the sight, and I make a mental note to listen better tonight. If I hear her struggling, I'll wake her up.

"Okay then, artist," I say, pushing her toward the school's double doors. "Go enjoy this. You've worked so hard to be here, Ray—you deserve every bit of this. Don't waste one second worrying, okay?"

She nods and sucks in a long breath. "Thanks for making it happen."

"I didn't. This is all you. Your talent." I smile down at her. "The talent I didn't get a drop of. Your mom must've been cooler than mine."

"Not cool enough to stick around, either," she says. "They have that in common, anyway." Ray rolls her eyes but squares her shoulders and walks toward the doors.

"I'll be right here when you get out," I say again, pointing to exactly where I stand. "If I'm not, don't leave. I *will* be here."

She gives me a nod over her shoulder before disappearing into the school. Some inner anxiety soothes as the doors seal shut behind her. A building full of art teachers and advisers and summer staff serving meals during the program ensures her safety. And since I don't have a shift at Nathan's today, I need to find a way to pass the next four hours. A rarity I won't waste.

Twenty minutes and one train ride later, I stand outside Myopic Books and set an alarm on my cell. No way in hell I'll be late and make Ray worry, but it's easy for me to lose myself in my favorite used bookstore in the city. I like to err on the side of caution when it comes to time constraints.

My phone buzzes in my hand, and I furrow my brow at the unknown number.

2125551247: I'm in need of manga. Since I'm new here, can you direct me to a good place to buy some?

The air in my lungs tightens as I realize who the unknown texter has to be.

ME: How did you get this number?

2125551247: It's on the schedule at Miller's.

Right. All employee numbers are listed in case we need to switch shifts. I resist the urge to face-palm myself and instead stare suspiciously at my phone. What are the odds I stand outside my favorite bookstore and Draven texts asking about one?

Ray told him what manga to start reading to get him into the genre. And we both have the day off. Coincidences all around.

ME: Myopic Books is the best in the city. I'm actually here now.

I cringe as I hit Send. Why did I tell him that? I shake my head at myself and save his number in my phone.

DRAVEN: Maybe I'll see you there.

A thrill rushes through the center of me, and I roll my eyes. Maybe it's adrenaline at the idea of running into him and retuning to our argument from last night about first impressions and trusting people and his general disregard for my best friend.

Maybe it's because the idea of him distracting me is an easy out for the day.

Maybe I'm really just a sucker for those damn golden eyes of his.

Either way, survey says I have some serious priority issues.

I pocket my cell and step underneath the hunter-green awning, the tightness in my chest loosening with each step I take into the store. If I had to describe myself in one image, it would be a cup of coffee holding an old book. I inhale the glorious smells of pages crinkled with time and rich coffee as some inner piece of me clicks into place.

I head up the creaky wooden stairs that lead to the third level. I scan the spines and relish the quiet. After losing myself in the cookbook section for thirty minutes, my mouth watering at all the possibilities awaiting Ray and me when I secure my own place, I head back to the main level.

"Harley," the manager, John, calls from behind a glass case hidden among piles and piles of colorful and fraying book spines. "It's been a month, young lady."

I make my way over to him, an apologetic grin on my face. "I've been busy," I say, scanning the new wrinkles grooved into his forehead. He seems to get more ancient every time I see him, his salt-and-pepper eyebrows wild, his hair much the same.

John waves me off. "I know," he says, shuffling behind the counter to dig through a box tucked in the corner. "With work and graduating high school, I can't imagine." He sets a stack of thin black books on the counter, and my smile deepens. "These came in a few weeks ago," he says, setting his hand atop the stack of mangas. "I wasn't sure if Ray had these or—"

"She doesn't," I cut him off, my eyes looking over the titles like he's laid out a bag full of cash. These are like gold to Ray, and we can't afford them fresh off the shelves as often as I wish. "How much?"

John settles back into his plush chair behind the glass case holding rare first editions, and he lays his hands over his belly. "Twenty."

I tilt my head. "That's grossly underpriced."

He shrugs. "I know if I say twenty, you'll still spend double that on books for yourself, too. It's good business."

It's damn near charity, but I don't say as much. Whenever I have any extra money, I always dump it here. Either on books or treats from the café or both.

"All right," I say. "Keep them here for me, please?" I motion to the rest of the store. "I haven't hit the basement level yet, and I have several hours to kill."

"Wonderful," John says, nodding toward the stack. "I'll keep them safe."

"Thank you." I navigate down the main path between giant shelves stacked to the brim with used books. A few more twists and turns, and I find the stairs leading to the basement level of the store.

The wooden steps groan under my boots, my stomach growling right alongside the sound. I haven't eaten since work yesterday. I gave what little breakfast we had in the house to Ray this morning.

It's always harder on days I don't work at Miller's—I've become so dependent on Nathan's generosity. And I'm reluctant to dip into my savings too many times, knowing I need it to prove financial stability to the family courts to gain guardianship. I blow out a breath, eager to snag a comfy spot downstairs and use my phone to set an appointment at the apartment complex I've eyed for months now.

I ignore the gnawing hunger and the slight tremble in my thigh muscles as I continue my trek down the ancient stairs, finally landing on an expanse of concrete with peeling green paint strewn across the surface. Rows upon rows of wooden bookshelves scatter about the open-floor-plan space, creating a near-chaotic maze.

Grabbing a few hardbacks from my favorite section, I settle into one of the ancient red-leather wingback chairs circled around a low-sitting wooden table tucked into the farthest corner of the basement. I set my meager stack on the table, then select the first book that catches my eye. The cover is all blue and gold swirls, like someone melted and mixed gemstones to create a hypnotic design.

I only make it ten pages into the introduction when footsteps sound from the stairs beyond the row of stacks. The sound all but disappears once the person hits the concrete floor, the steps too light, too quiet to be anything other than on purpose. The hair on the back of my neck stands at attention, but I keep my eyes on the pages, the words blurring in a mess of black and beige as I truly focus on the room around me.

On whoever is heading my way like a goddamn thief.

CHAPTER SEVEN

"*Projection of the Astral Body*," a familiar voice says, and I snap my eyes up. "Light reading?"

I lay the open book against my chest, gazing at Draven. No wonder his footsteps disappeared—he's as quiet as a ninja. "This isn't the manga section."

He shifts the two books he holds under his arm and sinks into the chair directly to my right. His eyes are on mine, no trace of aggravation from our heated discussion yesterday.

I eye the other free chairs, wondering why he chose to sit so close.

"You're in my seat," he says.

My mouth drops open. "I was here first."

"Not what I meant." He smooths his hands over the leather armrests, scanning the area around us before pointing at me. "Wherever I go, that's the seat I choose."

I raise my eyebrows, my chest tightening as I lift my chin, just a hint of a challenge. "Why?"

"You know why."

I swallow hard. Can he read me so well? Sure, we've worked the last couple of shifts together, but sixty percent has been spent in silence and the other forty, we've argued.

Draven motions to the room—the shelves, the pathways curving this way and that between them, the stairs beyond sight. "I like to be able to see everything, back against the wall," he clarifies, though I didn't really need him to.

I just wanted to hear him say it. I find myself looking forward to the sound of his voice, if only because he so rarely speaks when we work together. And when he does, it's either intriguing or infuriating. A combination I apparently can't resist.

Plus, there is something about his deep tenor, the slow, almost calculated way he chooses his words. Like he'll never be caught dead saying something he doesn't mean. Or perhaps, he's been in a situation where rushed words had consequences.

That I can totally understand.

I hedge. "I like to have the best vantage point." I can see anyone coming my way.

"Why?" he asks, his voice almost a whisper between us.

I chew on my lip for a minute, wondering how many truths I should lay bare to the boy who's gone from stranger to infuriating coworker. "The instinct to have a layout of my surroundings is kind of ingrained in me." I shrug. "I almost don't notice it anymore." I arch a brow. "Until random people point it out."

Draven coughs a laugh. "I didn't mean to pry."

"Sure you did," I tease, and all of a sudden, things between us feel like that night at the concert. Easy and yet complex at the same time.

He blows out a breath. "It's not every day I meet someone who…" His voice trails off, and I note the weight in his eyes. A weight I recognize—anxiety. The result of constantly frayed nerves, of holding your guard even in sleep. Maybe that's what drew us to each other that night—like recognizes like. I hate that urge gathering in my chest—the need to reach out and comfort him, to tell him I understand. That he can talk to me.

Right, and if he did that to you?

I'd snap his olive branch in two. I hate pity almost as much as I hate the reason behind it—so I keep my hands firmly on the book I hold.

"Besides," Draven says, never finishing his previous sentence. "I'm not exactly 'random people,' am I?"

I narrow my gaze. "No," I say. "I guess you're not."

He smiles a crooked grin that makes a bit of gold shimmer in his eyes. God, I hate how my heart kicks up in speed, that I can't *stop* looking at him. At his smooth skin, the unkempt hair atop his head that falls just so to give him a bit of a reckless edge. The way his jaw ticks sometimes like he's holding some internal battle-to-the-death cage match.

"So," I say, glancing around at the shelves. "Did you really text me for a recommendation, or did you seek me out to apologize for last night?"

He furrows his brow, like he's totally forgotten about the shade he threw Kai's way.

"For you saying those things about Kai," I remind him.

How could he forget the words that left me fifty shades of salty? I haven't been able to stop replaying the convo in my head, trying and failing to fix it. And it irritates me twice as much as the argument itself that I *can't* stop thinking about it.

"Ahh, that." He shakes his head. "No, I did not come here to apologize to you."

My eyes widen, and I fold my arms over my chest.

"That makes you angry?" He smirks. "That I have an opinion different from yours?"

"Oh, you can think pancakes are the devil or tell me that music will never be as good again as it was in the fifties, and I won't care either way. But when that opinion is speaking negatively about my friend, then hell yes, it does."

Draven never drops his gaze from mine. "My intention is not to anger you."

Not an apology, but answer enough that I'm not going to get one. I have to give him credit—at least he stands his ground. I like that, even if in this situation it's frustrating as hell. Most people fold under direct pressure. I wonder what Kai did in the short time they worked together to give off the asshole vibe...and vice versa?

Mystery indeed.

"Fine," I relent. "But you really should give Kai another chance. He's not entitled like you think."

"It's admirable," Draven says, "how you stick up for your friend."

"Wouldn't you do the same for yours?"

A slow, sharp grin. "Yes," he says. "I most certainly have and will likely be called to do so again and again." He leans forward a bit, rests his forearms on his knees. "He's always getting himself into trouble. He'll be the death of me one day." Draven laughs softly, the sound grazing over my skin like warm silk.

I swallow hard, and he leans back in his seat again before saying, "You don't trust many people." Not a question.

"Not something I hand out easily."

"Smart," he agrees, then tilts his head. "Trust is both a gift and a curse. Heady in the right hands and a weapon in others.'"

I glance at him, a laugh on the edge of my lips. "How old are you?"

"I'm the same age as you," he says, glancing at the cover of the book on the table. "Aren't you turning eighteen in a few days?"

Damn Nathan and his birthday board. "Yes."

"What will you do until then?"

"What do you mean?" I set my book on the table and reach for the phone vibrating in my pocket.

KAI: Back early. Want to meet up? I miss you.

ME: Definitely. @ Myopic.

KAI: Be there in fifteen.

Excitement curls around me, despite the way we left things. I know Kai. He'll tell me all about his job with Draven, and then we'll laugh at how insignificant this whole thing is...hopefully tacos will be involved. Besides, maybe this is a good chance for them to talk, to get over whatever bullshit there is from their past, especially if I'm the common denominator between them.

"Last days of freedom?" Draven asks, and I blink up from my phone. "Isn't that usually how people feel before they enter adulthood?"

I laugh again. "Adulthood?" I arch a brow at him. "Again, how old are you?"

"Apparently over a hundred." His strong jaw flexes.

I grin, a flare of delight storming my blood at the notion that

I'm getting under *his* skin. *Welcome to the club, Mr. Mystery*. "I can't help it. You talk like you've either lived a long life or your favorite books are by Aristotle and Confucius."

"I'm more of a Nietzsche fan." He shrugged, then did a double take. "Wait, are you saying I'm thought-provoking?"

"Or ancient," I fire back, scrolling through the websites I have up on my phone. The apartment complex's site is the first page, and I click on the *Contact Me* link.

"The ability to speak properly doesn't make one ancient."

"Okay, Yoda," I say, widening my eyes at him before returning to my phone.

He huffs. "What are you doing now?"

"Not that it's any of your business, oh wise and ancient one, but I'm making an appointment to look at an apartment. You know, *adult stuff*."

"When do you plan on moving?"

"My birthday," I answer, typing in my contact info. This is the second message I've sent them, and from our previous discussions, I know there is a one-bedroom apartment coming up for rent this week. All I have to do is show up, look at it, and then sign the papers. Along with a check for a good deal of my savings. But it'll be worth it. Step one in proving I'm the best guardian for Ray.

"So soon," he says.

I pocket my phone. "Not soon enough. I wish I had an earlier birthday."

"Why?"

"I would've already moved out."

Something dark flickers beneath his gaze as he slips into that internal-stare thing he loves to do. I respect the retreat, knowing the introvert in me needs the same reprieve sometimes.

"I had my own place back in New York," he says after some time. "I can go with you if you want."

"Because a little girl like me can't handle signing a lease on her own?" I challenge.

"No." He sighs. "Because moving out on your own can be a

lonely process when you don't have family to help you."

I swallow the knot in my throat. Of course, he could tell I had no home life to speak of, beyond Ray. I was practically sprinting away from it.

And fuck me, but my knee-jerk reaction is to say *yes!*. This guy is nothing if not distracting…infuriatingly distracting. When I'm constantly analyzing the next second, next day, next attack, distraction is as an addictive escape for me as reading one of these books from Myopic. "Or you could do it alone like you do everything else," he says after I don't respond. "Easier to push people away than accept help and burn for it afterward."

"You don't know me," I insist.

He leans his elbows on his knees again, his eyes slicing into mine like he can see through me. "Don't I, Harley?"

My skin buzzes at the challenge in his gaze. At the unflinching hunger there, as if he enjoys the battle of words as much as I do. As if he, too, relishes the sting that comes with a good brawl.

I know it's wrong. Know I *shouldn't* enjoy it. But I do. And the idea that he might, too? That maybe there's someone out there as broken as I am, who can't get a thrill unless there is a bit of danger involved. It makes me feel less alone in a world that has done nothing but make me feel just that.

He blinks a few times when I don't shy away from his stare. "Honey badger," he mutters, then shifts in his seat, eyes falling to the book on the table. "So," he says, his tone much lighter. "Have you tried it?"

"Astral p-projection?" I sputter, my mind whiplashing between the topics.

He nods.

"Maybe." I laugh.

His brows raise. "Very *Doctor Strange* of you," he says, and I warm a bit at his Marvel reference. Comic book movies are my fav. I'd give anything to get into a freak accident and then suddenly have the power to destroy my enemies.

"Did it work?" Draven asks.

"Of course not." I rake my fingers through my hair.

"You can't settle enough to focus?" he asks as casually as if we're discussing a math test, not astral freaking projection.

"How do you know?"

He shrugs. "I know a lot of things about you."

My heart starts beating a little bit harder at the odd comment. "Is that right? One dance and a few days working together suddenly makes you an expert?"

"Not hard when you know where to look for the information."

"This sounds dangerously close to stalking."

Draven leans forward, so close that I can feel the heat from his body buzz against mine. But his knee doesn't brush mine, nor his elbow. Close yet not touching, but the sensation warms the air between us. He lifts a finger, slowly tracing several inches in front of my face. "It's all right there," he says.

My breath catches.

"Everything you need to know about anyone can be found in their eyes. In the moments when they think no one is looking."

I swallow hard. "And what have mine told you?"

"You love your sister more than your own life," he says, leaning back in his chair again. I nearly whimper at the loss of heat. "You have poor taste in friends, you're hyperaware of your surroundings, and you walk through life wound tight, like at any moment one of the fractured pieces of your soul will snap off and shatter..." His voice trails off, and I'm not sure I'm breathing.

He may as well have flayed me open right here and let me bleed out on the table.

"You don't waste time trying to fit yourself into the public norm of standards," he hurries on. "And your mind," he adds, pressing his lips together for a moment, "races. Constantly. Scenarios, future and past, play on a loop you're desperate to break." He pauses, as though he's uncertain he should share this next part, but then says, "And you have terrible, awful thoughts that rack you with guilt, that you pray no one will ever know about."

I hug my arms across my chest, wondering what else I've let slip through my mask.

"How?" My fingers dig into my arms for support. "How do you know all that?"

It can't be from my eyes. No one, not Nathan or even *Kai*, has seen through to the heart of me so easily, and they've known me much, much longer.

"You know, it doesn't feel good to be the only person under a microscope." I try to joke, to hide how much of my blood is gushing out onto the floor right now.

"I could offer to let you see behind my walls, Harley, but we both know you'd run away screaming first."

"Because you think I wouldn't understand you?"

He shakes his head. "Because I think the only emotion you're comfortable feeling is anger."

My eyes widen. Is he really challenging me to get to know him better, to risk feeling something more for him? And screw him for knowing me well enough to know that's the one thing I'd never risk. "Maybe you just bring it out in me." I arch a brow, trying to lighten the situation that is twisting me up in knots.

Draven shrugs and scoops up one of the books he set on the table, flipping it open. "Perhaps I'm wrong," he says as he focuses on the pages.

I stare at him, practically ogling, before my eyes fall to the cover of the book. "You got *Death Note,*" I say, pointing to the manga he holds.

"Well, of course," he says, flipping another page.

"Why?"

"Ray told me to read this one first."

I blink. "You listened."

He parts his lips but suddenly goes ramrod straight in his chair. His amber eyes harden, darting to where the basement stairs rest beyond a giant shelf of books.

I crane my head, listening, but hear nothing.

"Draven," I say. "What—"

"You invited him, too," Draven cuts me off, his voice a cool whisper between us.

CHAPTER EIGHT

"Harley?" Kai's voice echoes throughout the basement of the store. His sudden appearance makes me jolt in my chair. I didn't hear or see him come around the stacks—I'm *that* worried about why Draven suddenly looks like he wants to crush something.

"Kai," I say as I hop up from the chair. "You're back." I throw my arms around him, inhaling his crisp, clean scent.

"I was only gone a night," he says, a laugh in his tone as he squeezes me back. "And you didn't listen to me," he says, releasing me. Kai glares at Draven but then turns back to me. "I need to talk to you. Alone."

"Be right back," I say to Draven, who doesn't move from his seat. I tug on Kai's arm until we're on the opposite side of the basement and out of Draven's earshot.

Kai tucks his hands inside his khaki pockets. "Look, I'm sorry," he says. "I know Draven from one of my summer gigs a few years back."

"He told me you worked together," I say.

"What else did he tell you?"

I bite my lip, not wanting to rehash Draven's opinions of Kai. "Not much."

"Well, we did. You remember," he urges. "When my parents took me to New York City?"

I nod, vaguely remembering.

"Anyway," he continues, "we didn't get along." He sighs. "He's selfish and…he's just a prick, Harley."

I arch a brow at him. Draven may be a lot of things—cocky

and mysterious with a side of *bite me*—but nothing about him screamed *prick* to me. And I prided myself on my prick-radar. Thanks, Dad. "What job did you get again?"

Kai opens and shuts his mouth a few times. "It was a messenger service."

"Oh," I say. "Like one of those bike messenger things?"

Kai nods, rocking on his heels. "I saw him, and all those memories came rushing back. It was an awful summer." Something hard cracks in his eyes. "And I don't want him…"

"Don't want him what?" I ask when he doesn't continue.

"He's just bad fucking news," Kai says, and I purse my lips at the sharpness in his tone.

Draven may like to challenge me at every turn and leave me breathless the next, but at least he owns who he is.

And maybe it's because I feel that connection between us—the one that screams he not only knows what it's like to be damaged but has thrived on fighting against it his whole life, too—that draws me to him. Maybe that's why every cell in my body roars to fight Kai on this matter, to fight for Draven—

"But I was wrong," Kai continues before I can respond. "I shouldn't have told you to stay away from him. Shouldn't have acted like I have some claim on you."

Heat flushes my cheeks at the way his eyes sweep over me. "You're my best friend," I say. "I know you want to protect me."

Kai visibly swallows, his eyes falling to my bracelet. He reaches for my hand and runs his thumb over the black cord, the smooth stone in its center. "Right," he says, his voice soft, defeated.

I tug my wrist back, the touch too gentle, too…something.

When did things get so complicated between us?

Oh, probably right around the time Draven walked onto that dance floor and stole my breath.

No, even before that.

"Are we good?" he asks, and I nod.

"We're good," I say. "But I think you're wrong about Draven."

He parts his lips, then shuts them. "You hungry?" he asks

instead of arguing. "Let me buy you lunch as an apology."

I grin. "Let me say bye to Draven," I say, motioning behind me. "Then I'll buy my books and meet you outside."

He looks reluctant to let me out of his sight but finally relents and heads up the stairs.

I hurry around the stacks, navigating my way back to the secluded corner...

Only to halt my steps.

The chairs are empty.

CHAPTER NINE

A quick glance around the room tells me Draven isn't hiding in the stacks somewhere. My shoulders drop, and I sigh as I tuck the astral projection book under my arm and put the rest of the stack back in their places. John gives me another massive discount on the books, but I know better than to argue with him. Once armed with my bag, I meet Kai outside.

"Did you see Draven leave?" I ask him as we walk down the street lined with shops and bars and restaurants.

"No," he says, his voice slightly cold. "Why?"

I shrug, swaying the bag back and forth as we walk. "He left without saying goodbye."

Kai stops outside the best burger shop in the city. "Harley," he says, holding the door open for me. "Draven is the kind of guy to do that. *Often*."

"Do what?" I ask as I walk into the restaurant.

"Disappear."

A heavy weight sinks in my stomach.

I can't figure out why I care so much, since I don't know Draven, not really. Nothing beyond that connection I assume we share—though I have no real proof of that, either.

But he knows you. *He sliced you open in that bookstore…*

My heart echoes the words he spoke when describing me. He sees me, in a way that leaves me feeling exposed. Naked. And it's *that* realization that makes the idea of him disappearing feel like a physical blow.

He *sees* me. When no one else has even bothered to look.

Of course he left without a backward glance. And that really sums everything up, doesn't it?

"So," I say once we settle at a table in the restaurant and order our food. "Tell me all about this job in New York."

Kai chokes on the sip of water he's just taken, setting down the red cup with an audible *smack*.

"You all right?" I ask as he clears his throat.

"Yep," he says tightly. "Wrong pipe."

"I remember that summer," I say, fiddling with the straw in my cup. "You mainly talked about the sights you saw, the plays, the food. Not a job."

Kai rests his hands on the table, his fingernails so clean that they look polished. I glance down at mine. My dollar-store black polish is chipped on almost every nail. I quickly fold them in my lap beneath the table.

"Those things are part of the gig, really," he says, shrugging. "Being a bike messenger took me all over the city."

"Just funny that you left it out," I say, and he grins.

"Well, I didn't want to get another lecture about how I took a summer job there but not here."

I side-eye him but laugh. "Come on," I chide. "I've only asked you once to apply to Miller's."

"Okay, sure," he fires back. "If more than a dozen times counts as 'once.'"

Something wilts in my chest, but I cover it with another laugh. "Can you blame me? Who wouldn't want to work with their best friend?"

Kai's laughter fades, his grassy green eyes scanning every inch of my face. "You know I would if we didn't travel so much."

I nod quickly, taking a fast sip of my drink as our waitress sets our baskets of food on the table. Kai thanks her, then focuses on me again, not even going for his food.

I resist the urge to shovel the burger into my mouth, my stomach practically screaming at the sight of the meal. Instead, I delicately pluck a hot fry from the basket and munch on it. Points to me for not moaning.

"But it was fun?" I ask after a few more fries and a good chunk of my burger.

"Sure," he says, picking at his food. "Most of the time. Other times…" His voice trails off, and I inwardly cringe. He's probably referring to those times with Draven, and I seriously don't want to hear him talk shit. Then I'd have to argue with him just like I had Draven—wait. Am I actually considering defending Draven on the same level as Kai? What the hell is this guy doing to my common sense?

"Other times," I prompt despite myself. Kai normally tells me everything. I can't help but be curious about the one story he's left out.

He takes another bite of his burger before plopping it back in the basket. "Other times I'd get an order that took me to a sketchier part of the city. Those times, I saw things. Things I wish I hadn't."

I furrow my brow. "Like muggings?"

He nods. "Assaults, drug deals, all kinds of stuff."

"What were you delivering that took you to places where that's normal?"

"Messages," he says flatly.

"Well," I say, swallowing hard. "I'm glad you didn't decide to move there and keep the job." The idea of something happening to him literally makes my stomach sour. Then it fills with acid. If anyone hurt him…I'd hunt the person down and use everything I've ever learned to return the hurt times ten.

Or I'd try, since I've only proven I can *take* a hit, not deliver one, so far.

"It's nothing new, Harley," he says. "The shit going on in today's world? It isn't isolated to certain cities. It's everywhere. A constant stream of darkness shitting on anything that has a scrap of light in it."

I raise my brows but don't respond. Kai is a news fanatic, constantly staying up-to-date on current events and politics, whereas I feel lucky enough to survive the day without getting my teeth knocked out.

Feeding my baby sister or myself? *Those* are light days. That darkness he speaks of? I fucking live it every single day. Not that he can ever fully understand that. And how can I expect him to? He may have witnessed some things during his travels, and he may read every horrible story reported in the news, but he doesn't *know* what it feels like to truly fear for your life.

To go to bed and wonder if the hit you took earlier will keep you from rising in the morning. Because the one person who's supposed to love you, care for you, doesn't. Because your father sees you as a weed that just won't die—no matter how hard he tries.

"Hell, there were three mass shootings last week," Kai continues, drawing me back to the table. "Didn't you read about them?"

I shake my head. I've told him a hundred times, I can't read about that stuff. I have enough to deal with on my own. The world could burn for all I care. But I can tell that's not what he wants to hear.

"Our country needs a better health care system," I say, sighing. "With a focus on mental health."

We've had this conversation a hundred times, too, but whenever he brings up the horrid state of the world, I can't help but respond with this.

"You honestly think that's all it will take to fix things?" Kai challenges, and I tuck my chin, questioning my thought process.

He went to private school and is world-traveled. I have to hand it to private education—they've certainly molded him into a model citizen with a passion for change. A change for *good* in the world.

Wholesome, pure Kai. I have no doubt he'll fix the world someday, for the better. He'll find a cure for a deadly virus or become a politician with real compassion in his plans.

I lift my shoulders. "Mental health needs to be an early focus. Like, elementary school age. It should be a required education class—as common and frequent as physical exercise."

Kai sighs. "The shootings, the kidnappings, the serial killers. You think all of that will magically disappear with mental health awareness?" He doesn't say it with disdain—he *doesn't*.

That's Draven's voice sneaking into my head. Kai likes to challenge me and push me as any best friend does. He wants me to be better, so much so that sometimes I wonder if he truly is disgusted by the dirt I never scrub off. But then I know better— know him better. Kai listens when I speak, encourages me when I feel worthless, and pushes me on the things that matter. What more can I really ask for in a friend?

"I think there are people in the world who are made wrong," I answer, my voice heavy, thick, and for a second I don't know if I mean my dad or myself. "Maybe," I force myself to continue, "if mental health is given as much focus as physical health...maybe those people could find a better way. Maybe the world wouldn't need to give up on them." I know I, for one, would've relished chatting with a professional—even if I would've kept the truth to myself—ten times more than climbing a damn rope or running laps in the gym.

"Maybe," he says, his gaze fixed on something over my shoulder. "That could help some people, but definitely not all. Some evil..." The line of his jaw sharpens. "Some evil can't be countered no matter how much good you throw at it."

A chill skates over my skin, the sinking feeling in my stomach threatening to suck me down with it. I can't argue with his logic. Can't bring myself to muster words of hope and encouragement—I save those near-evaporating dregs for Ray.

Besides, I never have the heart to tell him he's living a fairy tale, seeing the world through a privileged lens I'll never know. That's his first setback right there. Not that I want him to understand like I do, of course.

"Everything going on recently?" he continues. "Not just the shootings or the kidnappings all over the news, but the wildfires? The spread of viruses we don't have the support to combat?" He sighs. "It's just the beginning, Harley."

I push away my empty basket, looking around for the sign to the restroom. "The beginning of what?"

"The end," Kai whispers so quietly, I'm certain I've heard him wrong. But then he shakes off the mood and says, "Let's talk about something good." A smile turns up his lips. "Have you decided what you want for your birthday?"

My shoulders sag with relief at the change in topic. "You already took me to the concert. You know I don't want anything else."

"What if I *want* to buy you something else?" he asks, "Remember that time I snagged you those limited-edition Vans? You wore those until there were holes in the bottom."

"You got those for me?" I furrow my brow. I remember the shoes—they were red and white and probably the nicest pair I'd ever owned. My eleventh birthday... That was before I'd met Nathan, so there wasn't any celebrating. But Kai... "Oh, wait, that's right. You did." I blink a few times, wondering how I could've forgotten something like that.

He glances over the table at the bracelet I currently fiddle with. "Maybe a new bracelet?" He raises his brows. "That one looks ready to fall off any second."

I quickly shake my head. "I love this bracelet," I say. "And you know it'll never fall off." I've told him the story of the wish, and he's familiar with my luck. It's never going to happen, and I made peace with that a long time ago.

"You could force it, you know," he says, his tone teasing. "Break it on purpose and make your own wish come true."

"I don't need a bracelet to do that," I say. "I'm making that happen all on my own."

"Oh yeah?"

I nod eagerly. "I have an appointment at that apartment complex I told you about. The day of my birthday. I'm planning on signing the lease that day."

Kai's eyes widen. "You were serious about that?"

"Dead," I answer as he hands his card to the approaching

waitress. I learned a long time ago not to argue with him over buying my meals when we ate out together. "Why wouldn't I be?"

"I think you need more time," he says, his gaze still wary. "With the family courts—"

"I don't need permission to move out once I'm eighteen," I cut him off.

"But to take Ray," he says. "You need a hell of a lot more than an apartment."

I swallow the sudden rock in my throat. "I know that, and I'm working on it. But she could stay with me. I doubt he'll even notice she's gone at first." We've stayed at Nathan's a few times without Dad even batting an eye. Sometimes he's so drunk, he can't muster the strength to get out of bed, let alone realize we aren't there. I relish those days—usually around payday.

"I'd tread carefully with that, Harley," Kai warns. "He could use anything against you in court, once you take him there. And bringing Ray to your apartment without his knowledge or permission? He could say you kidnapped her—"

"As opposed to not feeding her if I'm not there? Being too drunk to even notice she's *not* there?"

Kai raises his hands in defense, and I take a steady breath.

"Harley." He says my name like he's soothing a wild animal. "I'm on your side. Always. You know that. I'm just trying to help you see it from his perspective."

I scrunch my nose at the mere notion of thinking like my father, but I can't deny Kai has a point. I sigh, my shoulders sinking. "You're right. I have to be careful. More careful than usual." This won't be a random and much-needed escape to Nathan's for a few nights. This would be a direct threat to my father's image as the perfect parent.

"I'll be smarter," I say, determination coloring my tone.

Kai smiles at me. "I have no doubt." He reaches across the table, his hand turned palm-up, and I lay mine in his, the touch not unfamiliar, but something about the look in his eyes...it's shifted lately. Something deeper I don't want to acknowledge.

I quickly withdraw my hand, glancing at the time on my phone. "I have to pick up Ray from art."

Kai stares at his empty palm for a few seconds before looking up at me as I stand from the table. "Okay," he says, his tone a bit clipped. "I'll see you soon?"

I nod. "Thank you for lunch," I say, hurrying to give him a fast hug before bolting out of the restaurant and toward the El.

Once safely on the train, I succumb to the gentle whir of the machinery whizzing through the city. I don't have time to worry about the look in Kai's eyes or the state of the world he brought up.

I can't worry about any of that right now. I have five days to figure out how to take Ray with me when I leave—or as big as my plans are, I know I won't go anywhere.

CHAPTER TEN

I carefully slide on my hairnet and hat as I head to my place behind the counter. Last night was rougher than usual, Dad deciding to use his favorite rock paperweight on my temple, and I have a bitch of a headache from it today.

Luckily, I'm a notoriously fast healer, probably all the practice my body gets. My bruises turn from scary-purple to healing-green within hours, and this one has already started to fade to the point I hope no one comments. But I'm definitely going to need to dredge up some Tylenol on my first break today.

I grab a rag and immediately start wiping off the already clean counter.

"No way!" Ray's voice reaches near-glass-breaking levels. And the joy in it? It's enough to wobble my knees.

"How did you do this?" she squeals, and I hurry to the storage closet.

I stop dead in the open doorway.

Draven stands a few feet away from Ray's art table, looking down at her with an easy smile.

Ray is gazing up at him, a frame in her hand, the paper inside like puzzle pieces—

I cover my mouth so I won't gasp.

"I saw you when you got here earlier," he says, shrugging. "When you tossed the pieces into the kitchen garbage."

"I tried all day, but I couldn't get it to go back the way I wanted it," she says, her eyes on the paper inside the frame. On the picture our dad ripped to pieces—her favorite drawing of Marid. I thought I could literally hear her soul rip with it, and after I got her out of there, I'd charged him like a bull.

I rub a gentle hand across my temple. Not my best move, for sure, but at least Dad stopped shredding up the art on her walls, so not a bad sacrifice, either.

"I thought I'd take a crack at it." He leans a little closer to her, lowering his voice. "I nicked the frame from Nathan's office—our secret?"

She clutches the frame to her chest. "How'd you get it together so fast?"

Draven waves her off. "Don't worry about it," he says. He steps toward the door, but his eyes remain on her. "Just because something is damaged doesn't mean it isn't beautiful. *All* things have value. Don't let anyone tell you differently."

Ray nods, understanding flickering in her eyes.

"I have to get back to work," he says, then points to her table and the blank sheets of paper that have sat there all afternoon. She hasn't sketched a thing since school—electing to use her time to read a chapter book instead. "You should, too."

Ray glances at the blank sheets, to the reassembled piece in her hands, to Draven. "I will." There is such determination in her eyes. "Thank you."

Draven nods, then turns, stopping when his eyes find mine. I move out of his way, allowing him to pass by without a word.

Because how can I possibly express the enormity of what he's just done?

Fuck, he might as well have just reassembled my broken heart.

Warmth pools in my chest, soothing my frayed nerves. She hasn't wanted to draw since she saw my bruise when I picked her up from school. Thankfully, I'd sent Ray to Nathan's when I realized just how drunk Dad truly was last night. She didn't have to witness what he'd done to me. And also lucky for me, Nathan gave her a ride to school, as it took me hours to wake up this morning, still on the carpet in the living room where my dad had left me.

Customers pour into the deli, and I have to hustle on order after order, my mind reeling with words, actions, *anything* to show

Draven what he's done. What he's given Ray.

Hope.

He's restored that with a simple, selfless action.

"Staring is considered an invitation for a fight to the death in some cultures," Draven says a few hours later, a grin on his lips and a challenge in his eyes. He fingers through the bills in the cash register as we close down for the night. "Don't mistake me," he continues when I say nothing. "I love a good fight to the death as much as the next person." He cocks a brow at me. "But I'd hate to kill you before your birthday."

That quickly, the bliss at what he's done for Ray evaporates in a flame of cocky smoke.

"Please," I say, flustered. "I can absolutely take you in a fight." I shake my head. "That's not why I'm… I *wasn't* staring at you." Okay, I was. But only because I'm trying to figure out how to thank him properly.

Draven writes down the figures, bagging the larger bills and slipping them into the safe below before he shuts the register. "Come now, Harley," he says, and chills race over my skin at the way he says my name.

"You think I want to battle you to the death?" I glare at him, my hands curling into fists at my sides.

"I think you live for bursts of danger that remind you why you're alive."

Jesus. This guy is like a Ouija board. "Not. True."

"You're a horrible liar."

"I am *not*."

"That isn't an insult," he says, leaning against the counter. "Me, on the other hand? I'm a fantastic liar. I'm sure your"—he makes air quotes—"'best friend' has told you all about that."

I furrow my brow, shifting on my feet. "Wait, what?"

He shrugs. "I assume the stoic and perfect *Kai* has told you what an awful person I am. That I lie and cheat and steal. Kick puppies."

"Do you?" I counter, my mind whirling from the whiplash.

How can someone be so gentle and selfless toward my baby sister and then so...infuriating toward me? Do I simply attract that kind of mood?

"If it benefits me," he answers.

My lips part as I scramble for something solid to hold on to. I meet his unfathomable gaze, searching those eyes for the truth.

There—just past the confident front, just shy of the flecks of gold—is *fear*.

But why is he scared? Why would him catching me staring at him—

Oh.

Because I'm staring at him like he's amazing, like what he did for Ray is amazing. Like he's a good guy, someone *worth* something.

In the rare times someone looks at me like that—Kai or Nathan usually—I hate it. Absolutely *hate* the hope in their eyes as they see through the darkness of my life and envision me as a person worth much more than I actually am. It only reminds me not of what I am but what everyone *wishes* I were.

Realization clicks into place, and I nod, my previous flustered state slipping.

"Now, *that's* a new look. What's happening in there?" he asks as he slowly traces the air before my face.

I take a step toward him, sighing. I don't know how to respond to compliments and praise and affection. Normally, I combat that with my default prickliness, and it seems like Draven uses his overconfidence and choice words to do the same.

Maybe we're the same kind of damaged after all.

I cringe against how...*comforting* that notion feels as it settles into my blood.

But I can't *not* say anything.

"Why did you do that for Ray?" I ask, stopping only an arm's length away from him.

He raises a brow. "I was bored."

I shake my head, remaining silent.

"She's been mopey all afternoon, not a good vibe for the deli."

I purse my lips, never breaking his gaze.

"All right," he relents. He casually slides his hands into his pockets, the graceful move looking almost practiced, as if it's a type of defense mechanism. And it works, because the motion shows all the considerable muscles rippling beneath his golden skin and distracts me entirely. "It was in my power to do, and she needed it done."

That's closer to the truth, but not quite.

"Draven," I say, giving him a rare *true* smile I usually reserve for Ray and Ray alone. Something in his gaze flickers as he tracks the grin. "She'll never forget it," I say, emotion clogging my airways.

"It's not anything of consequence." His voice is a whisper between us.

"It is," I assure him. "That's pure, selfless kindness." Nothing like what Kai said about Draven being selfish. And maybe Kai knew a different Draven. Maybe the Draven Kai knew had only been the one Draven masked over the walls he'd built.

Walls I suspect mirror the ones I've spent my life constructing brick by brick, too.

"I'm not that person," he says, a near growl in his tone. "Don't delude yourself into thinking I'm some sort of hero."

"Then what are you?"

"The villain."

"Villains are usually misunderstood." I shrug, knowing how many times I felt like the villain—the person ready to do whatever is necessary to protect what they love, regardless of what they destroy in the process. "But I don't believe you're one of them."

"Then you're not as smart as you look."

I glare at him but ignore the sting. I know what he's doing— pushing me away. Which means I'm getting closer. Closer than likely anyone has in a while.

"I just wanted to thank you."

"Gratitude can function as one of life's *finest* sedatives." The bite in his tone doesn't reach his eyes.

I hiss, my muscles recoiling at all the shields he keeps throwing in place between us. I understand it, sure, but it's frustrating as hell.

"I won't ever forget it, either," I say, ignoring his attempt to rile me, to make me forget what I wanted to do. I reach for his hand—to squeeze it in a silent show of support, of understanding, of the need to touch him, or I don't know—

Draven steps away before I can make contact, the motion so fast and jarring, I jump backward, my feet instinctively shifting into a fighting stance.

He tracks the movements, something like pain flickering in his eyes, and he shoves off the counter.

"Draven," I say as he walks by, and I reach for him a second time.

"Don't," he snaps, drawing his arm just out of reach.

I flinch at the command in his tone and wrap my arms around myself. Draven looks me up and down, his face a mask of steel before turning on me and disappearing through the employee entrance in the back.

I stand there, gaping at the spot where he left for longer than I want to admit.

Because his reaction to my attempt at an innocent touch confirms everything I ever thought—Draven *is* broken like me. Has experience with the darkness like me. It explains the need for the walls, for the emotional distance, for the brief moments of connection where he lets down his guard and I slip past. Because he sees himself in me, someone who will understand, who won't judge.

And I should've *known* better than to try and breach those walls without an invitation.

I can only hope it doesn't make him retreat further.

Because now I know what I'm going to do next… What I *have* to do.

Fear pounds in my ears as I grit my teeth. I'm going to take Draven up on his offer in Myopic and look behind his walls at the monster he keeps hidden.

CHAPTER ELEVEN

"Can you pass me a clean dishrag?" I ask over my shoulder as I crouch before the prep station. We closed the deli a half hour ago—after Draven came back from storming off—and I'm almost done with my cleaning duties.

Draven's boots move in my peripheral vision, but he still doesn't make a sound as he grabs a clean cloth and heads toward me. I glance up at him from my kneeled position, hating the distance in his eyes.

We haven't spoken since I reached for him earlier—since he told me not to touch him and took a much longer break than usual. I'm missing our easy banter. This new cold shoulder? It's much worse than the glittering verbal challenges and debates we've had before.

A muscle in his jaw ticks as I outstretch my hand, waiting for him to give me the rag. He drops it without a second glance, the cloth missing my hand and landing on my boot.

Okay, then.

I scoop it up and clean the globs of dried mustard off the bottom of the prep station with a bit more force than necessary.

"You about done?" Kai's voice calls from behind me, a lightness to his tone that sets my shoulders at ease as I push off the floor.

"Almost," I say, tossing the rag in the dirty laundry bin in the back, then wash my hands at the industrial sink. "You ready for tonight?" I ask, a smile coming to my lips.

It's pier night—a long-standing tradition of ours—and after all the confusing tension between Draven and me, I'm more than in need of it.

"Haven't eaten all day," he says, patting his hard stomach as I dry off my hands. "I'm ready to hop at least three shops. Any idea where you want to start?"

I tilt my head, my eyes instantly darting to where I can see Ray finishing up one of her pieces in the storage closet. I invited her to come with us like she normally does, but Nathan asked if he could watch her tonight for a Netflix and pizza marathon.

"It's a Brown Sugar Bakery kind of day," I admit.

"That bad?" Kai asks, his gaze cutting to where Draven silently cleans behind us.

"No," I say a little too quickly. I can't possibly explain the feelings I don't even understand myself.

I mean, why does Draven's silence really bother me? We barely know each other, despite that aggravating connection I can't stop from tugging tight in my chest. And sure, I enjoy his banter, his quick but deep wit, and how it offers the perfect distraction for my constantly chaotic mind, but in reality, we owe each other nothing.

Hell, I doubt he even considers me a friend. And it stings for some reason. Hence the need for sugar. "Just craving the sugar high," I finally finish, Kai returning his gaze to me, a soft smile on his lips.

"Then sugar it is," he says, motioning toward the employee exit in the rear. "I'll wait for you."

I nod, watching him walk toward the back of the kitchen. I can practically *feel* Draven hovering near the register not far away. Something heavy settles inside me as he refuses to look this way. Since he came back from his break, I tried about a dozen times to get him to talk to me, about anything, but he dodged every question.

With a considerable effort, I manage to make my feet move in the opposite direction and hurry to double-check with Nathan that everything is all good for tonight.

"Gonna introduce Ray to *Little Witch Academia*," Nathan says as he straightens the clutter on his desk in his office. "It's trending on Netflix right now."

I grin, recognizing the name of the anime show. "You know she may never want to leave if you keep queuing up anime, right?" I tease.

Something serious flashes in his eyes as he rounds his desk. The look is gone in a blink, and he gives me a half smile. "I wouldn't argue with that," he says. "She could help me keep the place clean for once," he jokes, but the words are forced, and that weight is back in my chest.

This isn't the first time he's joked about keeping Ray forever. He may not know about the abuse I suffer on a near-daily basis, but he has to at least suspect our home life isn't the best. I mean, who else demands her baby sister come with her to every shift? I'm certain if Ray showed up with even a *shade* of an unexplainable bruise on her body, Nathan would flip.

I shudder at the thought.

"Thanks again," I say quickly, needing to escape the suddenly small confines of his office. "I'll pick her up by midnight," I say. "As long as that's all right with you," I add as I head for the door.

"Midnight is late," he says, eyeing me. "Either get to me by then and crash in the spare bedroom again or just come get her in the morning. I have a new waffle maker I'm dying to try out."

I press my lips together. Ray and I have stayed at Nathan's sporadically over the years—times when he thought we just needed to change up our routine. But I don't like to take advantage of his kindness more than I already do.

"It's shaped like a Death Star. You can't resist the dark side," he teases in a super-bad imitation of Darth Vader, and I laugh. I need to loosen up. Ray will be safe with him, and she'll be fed. Win-win.

"Thank you," I say, turning out of the doorway.

"Hey, kid," Nathan says, poking his head out of his office.

I raise my brows.

"You still have that birthday gift from last year?"

I snort. "Which one?" He gave me several, but I know which he meant.

He eyes me.

"Yes," I say, patting the bag strung over my shoulder, right where I keep the bottle of pepper spray.

"Good," he says. "Don't hesitate to use it." His eyes drift behind me. "Even on friends if they choose not to listen."

I glance over my shoulder, following his gaze to where Kai leans against the industrial sink across from the storage room. Draven leans on the opposite wall next to the doorway, arms folded over his chest as he stares down Kai. The two look like battering rams waiting for the other to blink the wrong way. I roll my eyes, hurry to kiss Ray one more time, then step in front of Kai.

"Ready?" I ask him.

His eyes flicker up to Draven behind me; then he wraps an arm around my shoulder and leads me toward the employee exit. "Absolutely."

I hate how overwhelming the need is to say goodbye to Draven, to say I'm sorry for earlier, but I somehow squash the urge and put one foot in front of the other until Kai and I exit Miller's.

After a quick train ride, Kai takes my hand and leads me down the crowded pedestrian path of Navy Pier. Evening transitions to night, the sky a deep purple and the moonlight glittering on the water hugging the pier.

The light breeze off the water is a soothing combatant to the sticky summer heat. The tension in my muscles loosens the more we walk, and I once again find myself grateful for these monthly pier nights Kai insists on.

"I needed this."

"The night hasn't even started yet." Kai grins, guiding me through the crowds of tourists rushing to and from the bars and restaurants and shops that line the pier. Bursts of red and blue and yellow cast neon shadows along the pavement as we continue, the signs buzzing above each establishment.

We turn up a set of concrete stairs toward a building filled with shops and restaurants. He holds open the glass door for me, ushering me inside and into my favorite bakery.

"I hate that I'll be traveling the day before your birthday," he says as we take our place in the considerable line.

The rich wooden counter is split by a glass case, glittering with golden-rich caramel four-layer cakes, butter-yellow pound cakes, dark chocolate cupcakes, lemon éclairs, pies by the slice, turtle brownies, and more. Each delicious treat and confection beckons and sparkles under the lights. My stomach aches at the smells of sugar and bread and chocolate.

"But I'm hoping to catch the red-eye to get back in time for the apartment appointment," Kai continues.

"It's okay if you can't." I can barely sleep from the anticipation — that and Ray's nightmares have been more frequent recently. I've started leaning against her bed as she sleeps, hurrying to smooth my hand over her little arm whenever she starts to thrash. "You can always see it when you get back."

"I'm going to do my best to make it back," he says as we move up in the line.

"You always do," I say, smiling when it's our turn to order. A pretty girl with purple hair gathers our orders, sliding them toward us as Kai pays.

After receiving our box of treats, we head to a little table pressed against the wall of windows on the other side of the shop. It offers the perfect view of the water, an old-school ship floating just a few yards down the pier. The moonlight shines through the masts, creating an array of lined shadows on the pavement as pedestrians hustle up and down the pathway connecting to the water.

I pluck a chocolate cupcake, white crystals sprinkled on top, from the box, peeling back the white paper and dropping it onto the table.

Kai grins at me, shaking his head as he grabs his éclair.

"What?" I say around a mouthful of cupcake.

"You always go for the sparkly sweets," he says.

"It looks like stars," I say, as if that explains everything, and take another massive bite. The cake is moist and the balance of creamy icing is perfection. And the sugar is doing everything to soothe that undeniable ache in my chest that has taken up residence since earlier.

Kai finishes off his éclair and then wipes his perfectly clean hands on a napkin before leaning back in his seat. "This place is totally worth the hype," he says. "Everyone has been talking about it," he continues. "It'll be ten times busier the next time we come."

I take my last bite, then use four napkins to get all the frosting off my fingers. "Everyone?"

"Social media isn't the devil, you know."

"We'll agree to disagree on that." I never understand why he's so hooked on every page imaginable, always on his phone checking stats and news sites and gossip pages.

Though I suppose if my phone had unlimited data, I might check it out. I'm a total sucker for any dog videos he shows me on TikTok, but I don't like the idea of having my information so readily accessible. That, and the limited data plan I can afford.

Kai and I fall into an easy sort of chatter as we finish off the box of delights before us. So much sugar, my stomach hurts, but I never pass up an opportunity to gorge myself on the confections from this place.

"And then you decided to make friends with that beast of a dog," Kai says as we sip our soda waters in an attempt to rid our teeth of the sugary film sticking to them.

I laugh, fiddling with the paper napkin on the table. "He wasn't a beast!"

"He tried to eat me!" Kai laughs, the sound as comforting as the memory. "I can't believe I let you talk me into sneaking into that skate park after dark."

"It wasn't my idea!" I toss a piece of the napkin at him.

Kai tilts his head. "It absolutely wasn't *my* idea."

I scrunch my brow, thinking back on the memory. It was so long ago… "Oh right," I say, remembering I had been the one to suggest the skate park. "But *you* were the one dying to try out your new Rollerblades."

"I was ten," he says, tossing the napkin back at me. "Who wouldn't want to try out a new birthday present?"

"Me," I say, laughing. "Wheels attached to my shoes? Hard pass." I could just picture me flying down a hill and colliding head on with a parked car.

"Oh, come on," he says. "We could grab a pair right now. I can video the whole thing. I bet you'd go viral."

"*Never.* Anyway," I say, shaking my head. "I didn't know that stray dog would be there."

"But you still couldn't help petting it."

"I love dogs," I say. "They're loyal and strong and have awesome protective instincts."

Kai's smile fades as he nods. He fidgets in the seat across from me, something rattling inside those eyes of his.

"What's up?" I ask.

"I just…" He chews on his bottom lip, his gaze darting behind me to the confection counter. "It's nothing."

I arch a brow at him, then smile as I glance over my shoulder. The purple-haired employee quickly glances away, hurrying to wipe down the counter. I return my focus to Kai.

"Is it her?" I motion over my shoulder.

"What?"

I lean farther across the table. "Do you like her?" I ask, my voice a whisper.

His lips part as he shakes his head. "No."

"She keeps looking over here," I say. "You should go talk to her."

Something like defeat flashes in his eyes. "I'm here with you."

I shrug. "You're always with me," I say. "Don't let that stop you. You should go ask her for her social media page or whatever it is you friend people on."

Kai takes a long drink of his soda water. "I'd rather get out of here." The words are short, wiping the playful smile off my face.

"Need some air," he adds.

I straighten in my seat, nodding. "Okay."

He stands, his arm extended toward me as if I'll slide into it while getting out of my own chair. I study him with a questioning gaze, wondering why his mood shifted so quickly, but then shrug as we head out of the shop.

Something is off with Kai, I can feel it in my bones, and I need things to get right again.

CHAPTER TWELVE

"Want to stop in here?" he asks, nodding toward the place next to the bakery.

I snort-laugh. "The Fun House Maze? You're not serious."

Kai shrugs. "It's late," he says. "All the kids are in bed by now. It'll be fun."

I tilt my head, then wave him onward. "Sure, why not?" Anything to get that easy smile back on his face. I don't know what upset him, but it's seriously messing with my sugar high.

After Kai grabs tickets, I step through the attraction's doors first, Kai on my heels. He's right; this late at night there are only a few random people partaking in the ridiculous glow-in-the-dark fun house, and the vacancy of the place creates an even creepier aesthetic.

The door shuts behind us, immersing us in a near-pitch-black maze, the walls covered in splashes of glowing neon-green and orange paint that illuminate the space just enough to urge us forward.

"Whoa," I say, nearly tripping over my own feet as we walk down the hallway. "These walls are narrowing." I can touch either wall by sticking my arms out halfway. The hair on the back of my neck prickles, and I slow my pace as we near the apex of the hallway.

Kai's warm breath rushes over me from behind. "You're not scared, are you, Harley?" he teases, nudging me forward.

"Never," I say but swallow hard. My axis feels off as we turn left at the dead end of the dark hallway, passing under an archway and into another room.

This one is full of mirrors, and a strobe light flashes from somewhere above. My mind whirls from the effect, the bright flashes illuminating the warped mirrors, which make our bodies look elongated or wavy. I hold my arms out for balance as I try to get through the room as quickly as possible, disoriented from the lights and the eerie music that blares from the speakers through the entire place.

Kai is visible behind me in the glass, a small comfort as I try to find my way out of the room with no luck. I swear I walk in *two* full circles before winding up right back where we started.

"Want to help?" I ask over the music, and Kai laughs, his teeth flashing white in the strobe light. He points behind me and to the left. I spin around, hurrying toward that direction. I missed the exit because it's covered with a black curtain.

I peel back the curtain, stepping through it and into another room. This one is just as dark as the first but thankfully no flashing lights or mirrors. It's pitch-black except for the glowing red paint that's splattered over the walls, looking an awful lot like blood.

One step into the room lets me know the effect—the flooring is disproportionate, a contraption of ramps and dips, all painted black to make it nearly impossible to see. I try anyway, slowly walking down the first steep ramp and halfway up the next before I stumble and nearly eat the floor.

"If I break my ankle in here, I'm totally blaming you," I say, turning to glare at Kai.

Who isn't there.

I furrow my brow.

"Kai?" I shout over the music, scanning the room. There's no sign of him. I didn't see or feel him walk ahead of me, but now that I've made it farther into the room, I can't see the curtain that leads back to the mirror room. Did he stay in there?

Footsteps echo ahead of me, and I practically run down the second ramp, sprinting up the third. The music blares a pulsing rhythm that echoes off the glowing red walls, and my chest tightens as I hurry to reach Kai.

"Hey—" My voice stops short as I clear the third ramp. I fully expect to find Kai standing there laughing his ass off as I struggle through the fun house room. But it isn't Kai who waits for me at the top of the ramp. "Sorry," I hurry to say. "I thought you were someone else."

"Who are you looking for?" the man asks, two of his buddies flanking either side of him.

Is this part of the attraction? Do they work for the fun house? Because they certainly resemble those costumed actors who prowl haunted houses during Halloween—all towering and menacing in dark clothes, and their eyes…they look red, as if the paint on the walls makes them glow, too.

"My friend," I answer, telling my instincts to calm the fuck down. This is part of the maze. And Kai? He's just messing with me, or he got lost on the other side of the mirror room before I left.

"This one smells different," the man on the left says, spittle spraying from his lips as if his mouth uncontrollably waters.

I didn't shower after work, so I probably reek of the meats we put on the sandwiches, but *fuck him* for pointing that out. Still, I can't stop the sliver of shame curling in my stomach.

"I like it," the other one whispers.

Um, *ew*.

And just like that, panic flares at the base of my spine, locking my muscles when I most certainly need to keep walking. Either turn around and try to find the mirror room and Kai or push forward and find the damn exit to the place.

But if they work for the fun house, they aren't allowed to touch me, right?

"What are you?" the man in the middle asks. He and his buddies shift their weight, their boots scraping against the wooden ramp loud enough to be heard over the music, as if they can't stand still.

What am I? Did I suddenly fall into my own twisted version of Vampire Diaries and I need to choose a faction—vampire, werewolf, witch? If that's my current predicament, then I'm just a deli-girl and where the hell is my Damon Salvatore because *this* is some bullshit—

No, stop. It's so not the time to go down the Vampire Diaries train.

Fuck. I'm thoroughly creeped out, that's what I am. I spare a glance behind me, mapping out my route to go back the way I came—

Movement snaps in my peripheral vision, and I barely have time to turn around before the man in the middle has his hands on my shoulders. He presses me against the nearest wall, so fast that my brain barely registers the movement.

Oh God. They aren't part of the maze. They're creeps.

"You really don't want to do this," I insist, trying like hell to sound like I bite worse than I bark. I slip my hand into my bag, fist curling around the pepper spray Nathan bought me. I jerk it out, aim forward, and barely push the nozzle—

A half gasp, half growl tears from the man's lips.

His two buddies knock the spray out of my hands, the one in the middle reaching for my throat as the other two wrap meaty fists around each of my arms.

"Hey! That was a gift, asshole!" I choke out defiantly, my words strained from the tight grip on my throat. My struggle is pointless against their strength. My muscles ache with adrenaline, but they're weak, trembling, and goddamn my *useless* body. The man drags his nose along the length of my neck, and I recoil.

"What *is* it?" the one on my left asks.

"Take it," the other one says.

"No," the one in the middle orders as the other two have me pinned. "This could be the one everyone is talking about. We should take her. To Marid."

Marid?

No, I heard that wrong.

But whatever the argument, they're distracted, and Coach Hale taught me to take advantage of any and all weaknesses. I think through the moves in my head and then strike.

I circle my arms to break the hold of the other two while simultaneously kicking the one in the middle with the heel of my shoe. The middle one stumbles back and loses his footing. He falls down the ramp, growling.

The other two jerk back, gripping their hands and wailing as if I burned them.

Oh God, they're drugged out of their minds.

Whatever works.

I don't waste a second pondering the situation. I haul ass forward, trying like hell to watch my footing on the uneven floors as I search for the exit.

I barrel toward an opening illuminated by glowing green paint, propelling myself into another room that thankfully has even floors. Demonic faces cover the walls—all glowing with malicious grins, sharp teeth, and horned heads. I hear the men screaming in the other room, their wails angry and shattered and just wrong.

I twist and turn into another room, this one covered with strings of plastic glowing beads. I race through them and finally—

An exit sign glows over a doorway, perfectly normal and real. I barrel through the door, crashing straight into Kai, who's speaking with one of the maze employees.

He catches me easily, hauling me against him, his eyes flaring wide. "Harley?"

"Where were you?" I snap, shoving him off. I whirl around, half expecting the men to come crashing through the door behind me, but it remains closed.

"I was looking for you," he says, motioning to the concerned-looking attendant. "I was just asking—"

"There are three men in there," I cut him off, my eyes on the attendant. "Do they work here? Are they supposed to grab you like that?" I desperately want the attendant to laugh and explain the situation away.

She doesn't. She shakes her head, glancing between the two of us. "We have employees throughout the maze, but no one is allowed to touch you. Only jump out and give you a scare."

I swallow hard, ice coating my slick skin. "Are there other people in there, customers like us?"

"You two are the only ticket holders right now," she says. "I'll call security. We'll search the place."

"Good!" Kai snaps and tucks his arm around my shoulders. "You're burning up, Harley," he says, sliding his fingers along my cheek as he guides us outside and into the cool night air. "What happened?"

"Bastards cornered me," I say and breathe in the fresh air, sucking in a lungful to clear my head. "You were *gone*," I accuse.

"I lost you after the mirror room," he says, ushering me farther away from the maze and down the pier. "There's another exit in the room so I took that, thinking we'd meet back up in the middle for a laugh, but it led me through a few more rooms and then the exit."

I shake my head and flex my muscles, still trembling from the scare. Nothing is broken—hell, I don't even feel like I have a scratch on me except for the throbbing around my neck where he grabbed me. Pinned me to that wall—

"What is it?"

"Take it."

The men's voices echo in my head as my heart pounds against my chest. What the hell were they talking about? Why did I hear them say *"Marid"*?

"Let's get you back to Nathan's," Kai says, still guiding me toward the El that will take us back into town. "I'm sorry I wasn't there, Harley," he says after we board.

"It's not your fault." I blink as the event replays over and over in my head. "They caught me off guard."

Those creeps probably waited in there all day for an unsuspecting girl and found me instead—someone who took Krav Maga lessons from a damn master. They could *choke* on that and hopefully think twice before jumping someone in a damn fun house ever again.

I nod to myself, the memory of the man flying backward

down the ramp—from a blow *I* gave—filling me with a justified sort of satisfaction.

"Are you sure you're all right?" Kai asks an hour later as he walks me to Nathan's front door.

I wave him off. "Definitely. I'm not signing up for another maze run anytime soon, but seriously, Kai, I'm fine. It isn't your fault we got separated."

He purses his lips, and that weight from earlier in the bakery is back in his eyes. I reach out and squeeze his arm.

"I promise," I say, assuring him. "Sorry to kill the night so soon," I add, noting I'm two hours ahead of the midnight curfew I gave myself. "You should head back to the bakery, talk to that girl," I say, remembering the way the purple-haired girl couldn't keep her eyes off Kai.

Kai furrows his brow, his eyes slicing into me. "I don't want to talk to her."

"Okay," I say, taking a step back from his tone. "Why are you snapping at me because I suggest you talk to a pretty girl?"

Kai leans against the wall next to Nathan's door.

"Kai?" I ask.

"I don't want to talk to her," he says again, pushing off the wall until there is only an inch of space between us. "I want *you*."

My stomach bottoms out so fast, I can't speak, can't think.

No, no, no.

"Kai, you're my best friend—"

"I know that," he cuts me off. "But I want more."

I stumble back a couple of steps, shaking my head. "I can't—"

"Why? We're perfect together."

"I'm not," I say, my voice a whisper, as if the air is being choked out of me. "I'm nowhere near close to perfect, Kai."

"You're so much more than you think," he says. "Harley, you're everything—"

"I can't do this, Kai." I find the strength in my voice. "I'm not…" I shake my head as I try to pick the words to make him understand, shock and sadness storming my system. "I'm sorry, but I don't feel that way about you, Kai. You're my best friend. My *only* friend."

He visibly swallows, pain and a shade of anger coloring his eyes. He avoids my gaze as a muscle in his jaw flexes. "Right," he says, shaking his head. "Forget I said anything, okay?"

Anything else will just make this worse, so I say the only thing I can. "Okay."

He shrugs, finally looking at me again, his gaze an empty plate. "I'll see you when I get back from Oregon, right? If I can make that red-eye?"

I nod, wondering how the hell this night got so twisted. "You know where to find me," I say, the tension in my voice tight.

"Good night, Harley." He gives a half wave and hurries down the street, back toward the El that will take him home.

I stand outside Nathan's door, my mouth hanging open on a silent goodbye I can't utter.

CHAPTER THIRTEEN

"You're leaving?" I try and fail to keep the shock and excitement from my tone as I watch my father sling his duffel over his shoulder.

"Don't get any ideas," he warns, jabbing a finger at my chest. "It's only two days. Jerry has a new boat to test out. Don't even think about throwing a party while I'm gone…" He levels me with a stare, letting some of the monster beneath his mask show.

"Understood," I say, more than happy to be agreeable, compliant. Like I ever throw parties. God, he has no clue who I am. Who he turned me into—I was labeled *trash* my first day of high school. I only had three outfit combinations, and most of them had holes or stains on them. Hell, I'm the girl who graduated without a single friend.

Just Kai.

And maybe now Draven? We still haven't spoken, so I'm not sure if he qualifies or not. Probably not.

Dad's eyebrows crawl up his head. "I mean it, Harley," he says. "I catch you with anyone here—"

"Yes, sir," I say, shifting away from his jabbing finger.

He nods, then shuts the front door behind him.

I let ten minutes go by before I move from my spot in the living room.

And another five before I sink onto the threadbare couch.

I still have three hours before I need to pick up Ray from Nathan's house, so I decide not to waste it. I push off the couch and head into the kitchen, riffling under the sink for the minimal cleaning supplies we have. Armed with a fraying rag, some disinfectant spray, and a duster, I roll up my sleeves and get to work. It's impossible to clean this place when Dad is home. He makes a point to spill his liquor or knock things over the moment after I fix them.

I lose myself to the scrubbing process, working my muscles into a frenzy as I wipe and scour every available surface I can. My stomach turns and tightens as I carefully pick up Dad's gold rock paperweight on the shelf in the living room so I can dust beneath it. There's a drop of reddish-brown on one of its jagged points, glistening slightly in the light as I examine it.

Bile inches up my throat and I feel dizzy, but I set it down and out of my mind. Three whole days, and then it'll be my birthday. I'm almost free.

I hurry with the shelf, ensuring I return the rock to its exact position atop a black wooden pedestal—the only thing Father ever puts any value on. Not that I think it's worth money or anything, more like a trophy. Someone of importance gave it to him before I was born, and it happens to fit perfectly in his hand to hit me over the head with.

I shake off that thought by focusing on my best friend—the best friend who said he *wants* me. Ugh. I don't have those feelings for him, and I can't help or change that. Wouldn't even if I could. He's my safe harbor, and I wouldn't risk that for anything.

My phone buzzes on the counter next to me, and I scoop it up with a smile, expecting it to be Kai. I can't wait to tell him I have the place to myself for the weekend.

DRAVEN: Are you home?

The breath in my lungs catches, a zing of electricity racing through my blood.

ME: Yes, why? Need me to cover a shift?

DRAVEN: Not scheduled today. Can I drop by?

My lips part, my heart skipping a beat. My recently favorite and most infuriating distraction wants to come over? Here? I scan the trailer, my insides twisting.

DRAVEN: Nathan told me your address. I'm close. If it's all right.

Shit. He already knows, then. Where I live, what I live *in*. I could tell him no. Tell him to piss off. Could make up an excuse.

But I don't want to.

I'm curious about what Draven can possibly want with me, especially after he snapped at me yesterday. I type out my response.

ME: Sure.

I hurry to my room, slipping into a fresh pair of black cargo pants and my favorite hunter green long-sleeve thermal. Sure, it's hot as hell outside, but I'm used to wearing longer clothes to cover the scars that pepper my arms. A quick glance in the rusted mirror in our bathroom shows I still have a bruise on the side of my head, although faint, and I pull my hair down to cover it up as much as I can. There are still angry red marks on my neck from the man's hands at the fun house last night—

A knock on the door jolts me from the memory, and I smooth my red hair over my shoulders to cover my neck as well. As I head back to the living room, I take a deep breath to calm my pulse.

Then I swing open the door, and my jaw hangs open. Draven holds two large paper bags, the heel of a fresh loaf of bread sticking out from the top of one.

"Hello." He awkwardly waves one hand underneath the bags.

"Hi?"

Draven shifts on the rotting wooden porch that connects to our trailer, and heat blooms in my cheeks.

"You practicing for a cooking competition?" I ask, nodding toward the bags.

"No," he says.

"What's all this for then?"

"An apology."

I raise my brows, studying him for a minute. Genuine concern flickers there and something else. Regret?

"All right." I motion for him to come in. As he makes his way into the house, his eyes scan the interior like he's checking for monsters under the bed. For a moment, I worry about the threadbare couch with beer stains peppering the cushions, the worn carpet that snags in rough patches, the thin-as-paper walls that separate our meager bedrooms.

But he just lifts the bags against his chest and heads to the kitchen. "May I put these away?"

"What prompted you to bring two bags full of groceries?" I follow him into the small area, happy as hell that I cleaned Dad's crusty dishes from the sink earlier.

Draven sets the bags on the small counter space and starts pulling things from them. Bread, milk, and two cartons of eggs. Pancake mix and some bars of chocolate. A few frozen dinners and several bags of chips. Delicacies we aren't normally afforded outside of Nathan's home.

Emotion clogs my throat. "You didn't have to do this," I say as we finish putting everything away, Draven never once commenting on the lack of food there. "And you don't owe me an apology," I admit as he folds up the paper bags and leaves them on the counter.

"Yes, I do," he says.

"No, I crossed a line," I counter, waving him off. I need a task to ground my racing mind. "I'm just going to finish up what I was doing before you texted." I walk out of the kitchen and down the hallway to my room, straightening the comforter on Ray's bed.

"You didn't." Draven wanders behind me and lingers in the open doorway.

I glance up at him, moving in front of the small table I scored from a garage sale that's littered with Ray's drawings. I continue tidying her station even though it doesn't really need it. My fingers shake slightly, as if Draven's presence alone vibrates the entire room. "You don't have to hover there," I say, motioning to the neatly made twin beds on either side of the room. "You can sit."

He comes into the room but doesn't sit, instead electing to examine Ray's work hanging above the table I now clean. His eyes keep going back to her character Marid, a crease forming between his brows. He leans closer to the drawing as if the proximity will make something clearer.

"You've seen him before," I say, and Draven jolts slightly, eyes on me.

"What?"

I raise my brows, pointing to the art he examines. "Marid?"

His shoulders tense, his mouth pulling tight at the corners.

"He's Ray's character," I continue. "The one you meticulously taped back together?"

Draven forces a laugh. "Right," he says. "I must've not been paying attention."

I study him as I finish cleaning our room—is he nervous? But that doesn't make sense; Draven is never nervous. Surly, sure. Overly confident and mysterious most of the time, definitely. But never nervous.

After straightening everything I possibly can, I nod to myself. I'm a little flushed from the cleaning, so I fish a hair tie from my pocket and gather my strands, lifting them off my neck and securing them in a knot atop my head.

Draven tracks the movements, his eyes widening when his gaze zeroes in on my neck.

I swallow. Dammit. I forgot about the bruising there.

"What the hell is that?" he demands, his hand outstretched toward my neck but stopping just before he makes a connection.

My cheeks flush as I walk to the living room, needing the motion to stop my body from trembling. He follows me, silent and patient, waiting as I stop by the couch and shrug.

"Last night…" I cringe against the memory. "You know Kai and I went to the pier…" Draven visibly bristles at Kai's name. "And we ended up doing this fun house maze thing. Inside it, these three guys came out of nowhere." I trace a sore spot along the side of my neck.

Draven goes so still, I'm not sure he's breathing. "What did Kai do about it?"

His words are as cold as an arctic breeze, and I bristle.

"I can handle myself," I say with a little bite.

"Clearly." He draws out the word, his finger air-tracing the mark on my neck. I can feel the heat from his body, my heart racing with how close we stand without touching, but I don't move, don't dare reach out like my body *begs* me to. Not again.

"I don't need anyone to rescue me. You should remember that from the night we met." The words are no more than a whisper between us but land like a brick. The memory of our dance, of our bodies moving in perfect rhythm, has a craving thrumming beneath my skin. "Anyway, Kai and I got separated, but I managed to fight them off—"

"Without assistance." He doesn't pose the words as a question, but something flickers in his eyes—pride? He takes two large steps *away* from me, but his gaze remains on that sore spot.

"I'm a fast healer," I say, hoping to steal some of the worry from his features. "Always have been." And thank God for it. If I hadn't been, more people—namely teachers—would've noticed the array of bruises or cuts or burns throughout the years. And I wouldn't have been able to explain them all away.

"Interesting," he says, shoving his hands deep in his pockets like he needs to secure them.

"Draven—" A buzzing sounds from my room, and I hurry to where I left my phone on Ray's art table. I scoop it up quickly, worried it might be Nathan needing me to pick up Ray early.

My shoulders tense the second I read the text.

KAI: Made it to Oregon. How are you feeling?

I chew on my lip for a moment, my eyes catching on Draven as he follows me. He doesn't look at the screen of my phone, instead walks around my room.

ME: Fine. Glad you made it safe.

And I'm happy he's acting normal—he always texts me when he lands safe during his trips. Maybe last night was blown out of proportion. Maybe it really was the fear from the attack that made him say those things.

KAI: I'll text you when I know what time I'll land on your birthday, cool?

ME: Sounds good.

KAI: Doing anything fun right now?

I glance at Draven, who continues to peruse my shared bedroom, and swallow hard.

ME: Just cleaning. Have fun out there.

I type the response before I can think about telling him the truth—that I'm hanging out with Draven in my freaking bedroom. Not that I have anything to hide. Draven is a friend—maybe. Fuck, if Dad comes home early for some reason...

No, he's gone. I swallow the sliver of fear at breaking the rules.

KAI: Be careful while I'm gone.

ME: As much as I can.

I pocket my cell, hoping above hope that the normal vibe from him means we're back on the same page. The friendship one.

"What are you chewing on so hard over there?" Draven asks from near my bed, where he runs his fingers over a stack of books I left on my nightstand.

"Who says I'm chewing on anything?" I fire back.

He flashes me a look that screams as much. "I'll tell *you* if you tell *me*."

I purse my lips—an honest trade of truths. I've never played that game with anyone, even Kai. Because Kai never pushes, not like this. He lets me stew in silence and comforts me without explanation. But Draven? He seems content to scrape at all my scabs.

"Fine," I relent, crossing my arms over my chest like donning a sheet of armor. "I'm wondering what I can call you."

He arches an eyebrow. "I'm rather fond of hearing you say my name."

My lips part as my heart hiccups. Cocky deflection, a good mechanism to lighten the mood when things are turning serious. Too bad I can see right through it—once my heart calms down, that is.

"I mean...are we friends, Draven?" I drag out his name, just to toy with him, and by the way his jaw ticks, it works. "We had that moment at the concert. Then we've worked together every day since you started, even if half that time is either spent in silence or arguing. And if we're not working, we've somehow found a way to see each other," I continue, thinking of the bookstore and now today's gesture with the groceries. "Isn't that what friends do?"

"I don't have many friends," he says, something I can't identify coloring his tone. "*Astral Projection*, *Advanced Meditation*, and *Deciphering Dreams.*" He taps my books one by one as he reads off the names. "I'm thinking," he says, continuing his end of the deal, "that these books go beyond just a curiosity."

I swallow hard but remain silent as he turns to face me again.

"You read these, study these techniques, because of your restless mind. But also because they all represent ways to escape—the body, the mind, even dreams." His eyes churn with intensity as he takes a step closer to me.

"How do you know that?"

He stops a few steps away, gazing down at me. "I've studied them, too."

And there it is again, that simple yet vague acknowledgment of the connection we can't deny.

"You forgot another reason," I say, and he tilts his head. I wave my hand toward the pile of books, just nearly grazing his arm, but he moves out of the way so fast, I barely register it. "A lot of the techniques in those books help…"

"With?"

I shrug. "Panic attacks. When I was in school, there were lots of kids who had medication to help them calm down when they needed it."

"And you can't…" His voice trails off.

I shake my head. "I'll never admit that weakness to my father." He flashes me a pitying look. "Don't do that," I say. "It's fine. Really. Some kids have no idea if their parents love them or not—at least I know exactly where I stand. My flag is firmly planted in the *fuck him* side of things." I grin when his eyes widen. "And I wouldn't want anything slowing my responses more than they already are, either."

"What do you mean?"

I hold out my arms, shifting them back and forth, the motion jarring the bracelet on my wrist. "It doesn't matter how much I train," I say. "I don't get stronger. There is something… Something makes my muscles shake. Tremble. When I need them most." I drop my arms, wetting my lips against the dryness collecting in my throat. I've never admitted that to anyone. "Maybe it's the lack of regular food. I don't know."

Draven's eyes narrow, the line of his jaw going taut. "You train?"

I nod. "Krav Maga, mostly. With Coach Hale from my old school. Three times a week, sometimes more in the summer."

A silence settles between us, thick and tight.

"So," I finally say when it becomes unbearable. I take a step closer to him, arching my neck to meet his eyes. "Tell me."

"What?" he asks, his voice a whisper.

"Why you don't have many friends. Why you seem hell-bent that *we* don't become friends."

He looses a hand from his pocket, shoving it through his hair. "I tend to ruin things," he says. "Hurt anyone who gets close to me."

I know that feeling—but Draven can't break me any more than I already am. Nothing from whatever past he has can taint what is already pitch-black.

"I'm stronger than I look," I finally say. "Despite the weakness in my body."

Draven shakes his head. "You're not weak, Harley."

Those words sink into my core, the absolute certainty in the way he says them warming me.

"You have no idea how strong you are," he continues, his eyes roaming over my body like he can see through me. Then he meets my gaze. "I just wish you were smarter."

I recoil inwardly, my brow furrowing as I meet his stare.

A small, crooked smile shapes his lips. "Because if you were, you'd stay away from me."

"Oh, please." I roll my eyes. "You sound like one of those bad boys from a teen movie. Do better," I challenge. "Plus, you came to *my* house."

"Maybe I wish I was smarter, too." He shrugs. "It would save you in the end."

I lift my chin slightly, keeping my hands firmly in place despite their need to reach out and touch him. "Like I said before, I'm not a girl who needs saving."

Draven's eyes flicker from mine to over my shoulder, and I follow his gaze, noting the way he lingers on the artwork on the wall.

My phone chimes from my pocket, startling us both. Draven takes a few steps away, blinking as if he's shaking off a trance. I wave the phone at him as I silence the alarm. "Time to pick up Ray."

I gather my bag and head toward the front door, locking it behind us as we stand on the dilapidated porch.

"I—"

"I'm going to be *not smart*." I cut off Draven's words. "And ask if you want to walk with me."

A grin slowly lifts the corners of his mouth. "I've been known to be unintelligent from time to time."

I laugh, the sound real and not forced, surprising even me. I usher him to follow me, and we take the path toward the train, a comfortable silence filling those aches between my heartbeats.

Only Draven would ever understand how hard it is to let anyone through a crack in the walls I've built around me, day by day, brick by brick. The only people inside those walls were there when I first started building them, and I can't help but wonder if Draven is right—and letting him in might be the most foolish thing I've ever done.

CHAPTER FOURTEEN

"Tomorrow night," Nathan says from his spot behind the desk in his office. "You, me, and Ray. Sleepover party at my house for your big day?"

I snort, unable to stop the sound, the tension and excitement for my upcoming birthday instantly melting. "You know, under any other circumstances, it would be *super* creepy for a guy in his thirties—let alone my *boss*—to invite Ray and me over for a sleepover," I tease.

"Oh, for the love of God, Harley," Nathan groans, cringing as he waves me off. "Don't do that. Don't ruin it. You know I love Ray like she's mine—"

"I know," I say, shaking my head. "I'm only teasing."

"You don't tease." He eyes me up and down. "What's gotten into you?" There is a slight smile to his lips that I mirror.

"Nothing," I say, shrugging. "Maybe I'm just excited about turning eighteen tomorrow. Feels like I've waited my whole life for this day."

He wags his finger at me. "There is something else."

I shake my head. "I have to get to work now, *boss*!" I call over my shoulder, heading to my prep station. Draven is already in front of the register, and my heart does that hiccup thing again once I set eyes on him, and I know the exact reasoning behind my elevated mood.

Him.

On Saturday, we actually *laughed* on the train ride to pick up Ray. Laughed instead of argued, some switch flipping inside him and relaxing his normally stoic attitude. We had more getting-to-know-each-other convos between prepping sandwiches and checking out customers this afternoon, too. He told me about his favorite places in New York City, making it sound like a dream haven.

I told him more about my obsession with astral projection and meditation and the dream books that occupy the space beneath my bed. Explained that the dream books are for Ray—for the nightmares. Last night, she had one so intense, I thought she was awake. Her eyes were wide open, but she spoke in muttered, nonsensical words that crested to screams by the time I got her back in bed. A kind of living night terror that rendered her speechless and her body shaken.

Thankfully, I was able to calm her back into a soothing sleep, but the evidence still shows on her face. The purple beneath her eyes, the blue less bright in her irises.

"Do you enjoy art as well?" Draven asks.

"No way," I say, laughing. "Ray got every ounce of that talent. I mess up stick figures."

He chuckles. "How is that even possible?"

"Dunno, but somehow I manage to do it." I finish wrapping the four sandwiches for our most recent group of customers and slide them over to him at the register. He rings them up, processing their card, then returns focus to me once the group sits at a table across the deli.

"Her mother must've been an artist." It's what I've always thought, at least, because no way our dad has even an inkling of whimsy or beauty in him.

"You don't share a mother?"

I shake my head. "Just our father."

"Do you remember Ray's mom?"

"No," I say, straining my memory. "He never brought her around. Just showed up with a baby one day, grumbling about another woman who couldn't handle being a parent." My chest tightens, but I force myself to relax, a smile on my lips. "I remember when he plopped her in my arms." I blink back the tears threatening behind my eyes. "She was the most beautiful thing I'd ever seen. And so calm for a baby. Well, for me at least. Whenever Dad tried to hold her, she'd wail like a wounded cat." I huff. "But for me? She was still, wonderous. I knew that first moment I held her, I'd never love anything more. Or go as far to protect anything as much as her."

"Fucking hell," Draven says. "You were only what, ten?"

I shift on my feet, blinking out of the memory, and nod. "I felt a lot older back then."

Draven glances up, halting the convo for another wave of customers. We work in an easy, almost effortless pace that I've come to count on when we share shifts.

"The way you love your sister," he says after we hit another lull in the night. "It's truly amazing, Harley."

I swallow hard, unsure what to do with my face, my body, at such a compliment. "Anyone would do the same."

"No, they wouldn't." Something distant crackles in his eyes before it's replaced by a painful lightness that catches my breath. "My brother and I hated each other."

Hated. Past tense.

"Oh, Draven," I say. "I'm so sorry—"

"He's not dead," he says, though his words are heavy. "He's just… He left. I haven't seen him in a very long time."

I press my lips together, silent, listening.

"I'd do anything to get him back," he adds, almost to himself. "Despite the way we fought. The way we see everything differently." He visibly swallows. "I'd sacrifice anything if it'd bring him back."

"Do you know where he is?"

He blinks a few times, then turns to face the register as a new customer strolls in. I allow the deflection, knowing when to push and when to drop it. But the fact that he's opened up means we're so much closer to gaining some form of common ground for friendship between us.

And I can only hope it continues to solidify, because I know how it feels to be alone for so long. How consuming the loneliness can become. But when he walked into my life with an understanding only likeness could offer? It's *mended* some of that gaping hole in my chest.

I want to do the same for him.

"Okay, serious question time," I say once the last wave of customers leaves. We've already flipped the CLOSED sign, and Ray has crawled out of her art cave to help wipe down tables while Draven and I clean up the stations behind the partition.

Draven cringes, his eyes a solid wall as he stops wrapping up the leftover chopped veggies in their prep trays. "What?"

I grin at the panic in his eyes. "Do *you* have any special talents?"

He grabs the discarded plastic wrap and continues covering the individual bins. "What, like Ray?" His eyes flash to her as she wipes down a booth across the room.

"Yeah," I say. "We've already established I have zero."

Draven pauses, those amber eyes flashing to mine and back down in an instant. "I wouldn't say zero."

I tilt my head.

"You make a delightful pastrami sandwich."

I snort, rolling my eyes. "Yes, I'll go down in history for putting already prepared meat on bread and slathering it with condiments."

He hands me a few wrapped bins, and we walk together to the industrial fridge in the back of the kitchen. "That's definitely not true," he says as he puts the bins away. "You'll be remembered for much more than that, honey badger."

I furrow my brow at the name he says so quietly, I'm not sure I hear him correctly. He takes the last bin from my arms, ensuring not an inch of our bodies touches. "So?" I push. "Do you?"

He shuts the fridge door, wetting his lips as he contemplates. "Piano," he admits.

"You play?"

He nods. "Piano, for me, is therapeutic," Draven says, then rakes a hand through his hair.

"Anything else?" I ask.

"Music isn't enough?"

"Oh, it's more than enough. I can't wait to hear you play someday." I smile up at him. "Just…you being *you*…you seem to have a wealth of abilities."

He gapes at me. "How do you figure that?"

"Just a feeling, I guess."

Draven smirks at that, a wicked twist of his lips that promises mischief and a challenge. Heat flushes over my skin. "Well, I *can* do this one thing—"

A crash booms from the front of the deli, and Draven moves faster than I can blink as a tiny scream freezes the blood in my veins.

Ray!

I race after Draven, only to slide to a halt when I reach him.

Three men are in the deli.

Three men I *recognize*.

The same men from the fucking fun house—only this time the one who choked me has a gun.

And he's pointing it at my baby sister.

CHAPTER
FIFTEEN

"Leave this place," Draven says in a tone so lethal, chills race down my spine. His hands are palms up as he stands in the middle of the deli, eyes on the men herding Ray into a corner near the door.

Tears streak her cheeks as the leader grips her shoulder with one hand, pressing that gun to her temple with the other.

"Harley," she whimpers and then yelps when he tightens his grip.

Rage—hot and undiluted—roars like a living flame in my blood. The deli *trembles*, shaking the ground beneath our feet as if the El is barreling down our street.

Draven cuts his eyes to me for a moment, but I can't decipher his silent order.

"Let. Her. Go." My voice sounds like smoke and acid.

The lights flicker above us, and the two men on either side of the leader bare their teeth as they track the wobbling lights.

The leader shoves Ray in front of him, keeping a tight hold on her as he trains that gun on me now. A slight relief settles in my chest, seeing the barrel aimed at me and not at her little head.

How did they find me? What do they want? Kill them. Kill them. Kill them.

The questions and dark desires race through my mind. My body trembles, but a white-hot rage courses through me as I take a step toward them.

"Uh-uh," the leader chides, jerking the gun toward me and clamping his fingers harder on Ray. She winces, more tears sliding down her cheeks, and I immediately stop walking.

"You want money? It's in the register. You want me?" I ask, meeting his gaze. "Want revenge on me for laying your ass out the other night? Come get me." I give him a come-hither motion. "Let her go." This is what I was born for—to keep her safe, no matter the cost.

Draven eyes me again from my side, and I spare him a glance, nodding at his silent question. These are the men I told him about. Everything around Draven darkens, almost as if the shadows in the deli are rushing around him, making him look all the more menacing.

"Maybe I want you both," the leader snaps. He waves the gun at me, ushering me forward. "Come with us and no one will get hurt."

I easily read the lie in his eyes, and in this light? It's much brighter than in the dark maze where they attacked me. Each of the men has a bloodred tint to their eyes, likely contacts to intimidate helpless little girls like me.

"Let her go," I say again, taking another step closer to him. Draven matches my movements like we're puppets connected on a string. "And I'll go wherever you want."

The one on his left hisses. "Marid's Second only wants one. Not all."

Ray stares at him, the name registering on her face. Her *panic*-coated face.

I want to rip them apart with my bare hands. I want to sink my nails into their flesh and tear at them until they are nothing but blood and bone. I want—

"You made a mistake coming here," Draven says, and it's only the sound of his voice that alerts me to how close he is to the men. How did he move so fast? And so silently? Because now he's within an arm's reach—

The leader whips the gun toward Draven.

And my heart stops dead as the barrel of the gun presses against the center of Draven's chest. Flames of hate lick and rage beneath my skin.

But Draven?

He *smirks*—a grin so viscous, every fear instinct in my body screams at me to *run*.

"This doesn't concern you, Judge," the leader snaps, and I tilt my head at what he's called him. Is "Judge" the same thing as "sport" or "champ" or "ace" now? "Make a move, and I'll put a hole through your—"

The building wobbles again, harder this time, with enough force to knock me off-balance.

And the others as well.

Draven moves so fast, I can barely keep up, his hands locking around the leader's. He disarms him in a matter of blinks, and Draven tosses the gun over the partition, blocking a hit from the leader while the other two men draw their weapons. Blades instead of guns. Long blades that flicker in the light as they swing them.

I don't think, don't *breathe* before I run and slide to my knees, ducking under one swinging blade to wrap my arms around Ray's shivering body. I tuck her against me and propel us across the floor until we can stand. I shove Ray near the back of the deli, screaming at her to "go!"

Nathan's office has a lock, and he clearly hasn't heard the commotion.

"Get to Nathan," I say. "Call the cops. Lock yourselves in."

"Harley—"

I silence her with a look. She hesitates for a second before hurtling to the back of the deli. I scramble to my feet and race back to the scene—unable to leave Draven outnumbered, to leave him at all.

One of the men screams as blood pours from some wound in his gut. He holds it like his intestines might fall out, causing nausea to pool deep in my stomach; then he limps through the front doors, disappearing down the street.

Draven fights the two remaining men, dodging their attacks as gracefully as a dance until he latches on to the one with the blade and turns its point toward the man's thigh. A sickening sucking sound fills the room, followed by a harrowing scream that rattles my skull. Something smells like electrified flesh, and before I can move, the other man is running after his buddy through the doors.

"I told you," Draven seethes as he circles the leader. "You made a mistake coming here."

The leader spits. "Marid will be pleased to hear whose protection she's under."

The name jolts through me, but it ignites something in Draven. One second, he stands before the leader, and the next he grips his throat, hauling him against the wall so hard, the drywall cracks behind him. Draven growls as he shoves the man up and up as if he weighs nothing, until the man's boots dangle off the ground.

"He's trapped," Draven seethes.

Not, *What are you talking about?*

Not, *You're out of your mind.*

But: *"He's trapped."*

"He'll never get out without the Key," Draven snaps.

The man's eyes wane as his struggles grow sluggish. He glances down to me before returning hateful eyes to Draven. He chokes out a laugh. "This isn't over. More are coming for her," he says, his arms weakening as they slip from Draven's and hang by his sides. "They'll never stop."

Draven growls in response.

"Marid has plans, Judge. So many plans." The man's voice is softer, color leeching from his skin, his eyes, as if he is being drained of life. "His Second is seeing to all coming-home affairs."

"Tell this Second," Draven says, "to come *themselves* next time."

The man gasps as all color drains from his face.

Oh God, he's going to kill him.

And while I wanted that seconds ago, my mind is clear now that Ray is out of danger. Killing this person will only put Draven behind bars, and I'd seriously miss our verbal dances if he was sentenced to life.

"Draven," I say, but my voice is swallowed by the man's

choking. I breach the distance between us, reaching out to touch Draven's shoulder, to beg him to stop—

Draven whirls away from my touch, swinging the man so hard that his boot clips my chin before his body flies through the glass doors, shattering them. My spine barks as I hit the floor and slide a few feet from the momentum. I curl around myself, trying to work the air back into my lungs as I watch the man get up, shake off the glass, and stumble down the street.

"Harley," Draven gasps, taking two steps toward me but stopping himself once I manage to stand.

I swipe at my chin, a warm liquid itching my skin. The back of my hand is stained with my blood.

Draven's eyes flare, pain and anguish rippling through them.

"Draven," I say, reaching for him. "It's okay. I'm okay—"

"No!" he roars, scrambling backward toward the gaping hole in the deli's doors. "Don't you see?" The words sound like they were ripped from his throat, hoarse and tight. But he's looking at his hands. They're *shaking*.

"Draven, please," I beg. "Talk to me. How do you know them? What are they talking about? What do they want?" I walk toward him, hand outstretched. Like if I can just get ahold of him, he'll stay.

"Don't touch me," he begs, reeling from my hand. "Stay the fuck away from me!"

The bite in his words freezes me in place.

And then he turns his back on me and walks out the doors, the sound of crunching glass echoing in his wake.

CHAPTER SIXTEEN

"Why did that man say my character's name?" Ray whispers to me as I tuck her into my side, waiting as Chicago PD looks over the scene and speaks to Nathan.

"I don't know," I admit, wondering if I should tell her I've seen the men before. About the conversation between Draven and the leader...as if they knew each other.

Later. She's been through enough tonight.

"Maybe it's more common than we think," I suggest.

Ray chews on that thought, allowing it to sink into her mind enough to calm her face for a few moments.

I haven't let her go since I knocked on Nathan's locked door to tell them all was clear—after Draven and the men ran off.

After Draven snapped.

I stiffen, thinking about the anger, the power he radiated. How can one boy be so strong? So...lethal?

And why the hell do I like it so much?

Maybe because you envy the fact that he's not weak like you.

I do my best not to flex my fingers into fists, since I'm holding my sister's shoulders, but there is nothing more I want to do than track down those men and slam my fists into their faces until my knuckles break.

"No," Nathan says, raking his palms down his face before crossing his arms over his chest. "I didn't hear anything."

And he's beating himself up over it something fierce. I can see it in his eyes. He'll never forgive himself for this, despite it not being his fault. His office is all the way in the back of the building; he can barely hear customers come in day and night, let alone a trio of men after closing.

Nathan nods to Ray as the officer asks him another question. "Ray ran back to tell me what was happening; then we called you. I didn't get a look at the men, but Harley did."

The male police officer turns his attention on me, dismissing Nathan with a nod. His fellow officers—two females—are walking the destroyed front room.

"Which one of you is Harley?" he asks, his brown eyes glancing at me with a skeptical gaze.

"I am," I say, moving to step in front of Ray.

"I'm Officer Mason," he says, grabbing a pen and notebook from one of his many pockets. "Can you describe what happened here this evening?"

I recount the events of the night, and Ray trembles slightly against me when I mention the gun at her head. I shudder, too.

Officer Mason gives a few nods, his eyes on his notebook the entire time I'm speaking. When I finish, he glances around the room. "Where is this"—he looks to his notes, then back to me—"Draven? The one who helped fight them off?"

I swallow hard. "He's hurt," I lie. "He ran to an urgent care nearby."

Officer Mason arches a brow at me; then his eyes fall to Ray, and I bristle when he points his pen at her. "Is that true, little lady?"

"I was in the office," she says. "I didn't see him leave, but if Harley says he went to urgent care, then he went to urgent care."

I smooth my hand over her back, pride rippling through me. And shame, since I totally lied and my little sister just backed it up. But I'm not about to tell the cops that Draven showed a strength I can't wrap my head around and then a rage and devastation that makes every inch of me envious.

Officer Mason waves his pen between the two of us. "You're sisters?" he asks.

I nod.

"You don't look it," he says, and I furrow my brow. What the hell does that have to do with anything?

"What are your parents' names?" he asks. "We'll need to contact them—"

"I'm their legal guardian." Nathan comes to stand on my right.

Thank God I know how to school my features before ever showing any true emotion, because I would've been less surprised if he'd punched me in the chest. Nathan has always taken care of us, has a vague understanding of how disconnected our home life is, but I never thought he'd blatantly lie to the cops on our behalf.

Guilt, sticky and fierce, threatens to suffocate me. This is more than a meal or a place to crash—this is lying to the freaking Chicago PD.

"Is that right?" Officer Mason turns to face Nathan, but his eyes keep returning to mine as if he can smell the lie on us all.

Nathan gives him a firm nod.

I swear Ray's holding her breath next to me, and I keep smoothing circles on her back, trying to ease her strain.

"All right, then," the cop finally says, flipping his notebook shut and pocketing it. "We're good here. Turner, Anderson," he calls over our heads. The two officers nod and leave through the doors to wait outside near their cruisers, the red and blue lights flickering over the glass on the pavement. "In case you remember anything else," he says, then hands each of us a small white card. "My cell number is the second one listed." He taps the card in my hand. "Call me anytime. I recommend installing security cameras on all entry points. We'll be on the lookout for these three, but to be honest, the manner of these crimes has tripled in the last few months."

"Why?" I ask.

"Who can tell?" He shrugs, then smiles softly at me before he gives us all a wave. "We'll be in touch," he says before joining his partners outside the shop.

The three of us don't move until we watch the cruisers drive off.

I quickly turn to Nathan, my lips parting—

"Don't," Nathan says, his tone soft but his eyes serious. "Not tonight."

I shut my mouth, silenced by the plea in his words. I nod and mouth, *Thank you*.

"Come on," he says, his arm outstretched as he looks at Ray. "Let's go home."

I shake my head. "If we walk in this late..." Now that he's returned, there's a one hundred percent chance our father will be in a punishing mood. He normally doesn't care if we don't come home until morning because by then he's too hungover to do anything but sleep it off. Coming home mid–drinking binge? Bad news.

"I said *home*," Nathan repeats, and Ray shifts out from underneath my arm and slides under his.

I glare at Nathan, a rock in my throat. He can't say things like that. No matter how desperately I wish for them to be true. He *can't*. It will crush Ray that much worse each time she has to go back to reality—where food is scarce and fear is endless.

"Come on." Nathan jerks his head toward the back of the building. "I've already called my maintenance crew. They'll be here in an hour. I'll come back to help them settle things here once I know you two are home safe."

Each time he says the word, another match caresses the gasoline rushing through my blood. My rage tastes metallic and sharp on my tongue.

Ray deserves a life where she's loved and cherished and encouraged and nourished—a home like Nathan would've offered had we been born to him. A life where she spends her evenings with friends or doing homework in the comfort of her own bedroom, proudly decorated with art of her own making.

She deserves so much more than the life I've given her.

Tomorrow...I'll be eighteen tomorrow. I'll get that apartment. Kai's warnings about my father accusing me of kidnapping my own sister rush right to the surface, along with my rage. I take a step away from them, that scream building and rising so fast, I think I may combust right here.

"I'll be there in a little while," I say, and Nathan looks like he might argue. "I need to walk, Nathan. I have to clear my head after…"

"Okay."

"Keep her safe." I glance at Ray, who has nothing but exhaustion in her blue eyes.

"Always," Nathan says, then turns them toward the back of the building. I watch as they go, my head spinning with too many emotions to count.

My boots crunch on the glass as I step through the hole in the door, ducking so I don't slice any part of my body. I suck in a breath of Chicago's night air—a mixture of exhaust fumes and wet vegetation—and run.

I run until my lungs burn.

I run until the tears stop rolling down my cheeks at how close I came to losing Ray.

I run hard, as if I can catch those men who are certainly long gone and make them pay.

It isn't until a stitch screams in my side that I realize I've run all the way to my high school. It looks haunting in the middle of the night, no lights on, no sign of life. I sneak in through the side-door gym entrance—I discovered how to jimmy the lock two years ago when I'd needed a place to hide for the night. Chalk one up for the talents born of necessity.

I flick on the lights, the fluorescents buzzing to life and illuminating the basketball court half covered with the thick blue wrestling mats Coach Hale and I use to train. I walk to the center of the mats, my feet now heavy, my skin peppered with sweat, my lungs heaving after the run. Some of my rage has ebbed, but I can still feel it there—that same oily sensation I sometimes feel when I gain the upper hand on my father—the urge to kill. To hear a neck crack. To feel the warmth of someone else's blood pool in the creases of my fingers.

A cold shiver races down my spine, and I shake out my limbs, trying like hell to rid myself of the sick sensation, but it *fills* me. My skin is too tight for my body. The scream builds, the dark hunger consuming—

No, you're not like him.

Not like my father.

I'm good—or at least, I'm better than him. I don't want to hurt out of a need to inflict pain... I want to hurt as a result of retaliation, whether it be him or those men.

I sink on top of the mat until my spine hits it, and I stare at the ceiling high above. It doesn't matter how long or how many scenarios I run, I can't figure out a stronger plan to give Ray a better life. Even with my pending apartment, the family court checklist nearly complete for application for guardianship, the money in my savings account...even if all of that goes according to plan, I'll still be *me*.

Dark.

Broken.

Someone who dreams of causing as much pain as I've received over the years.

I'm not silly. I know the statistics for children of abuse, the cycle of abuse it creates. And while I can't imagine a world in which I would *ever* harm Ray, I also can't deny I would have killed those men tonight if I'd had the chance, would have danced in their blood.

Not for the first time, I wonder if maybe she really would be better off without me. Maybe everyone would.

A sweet, silky sensation slides over my body at the thought— death. How peaceful that darkness would be. How simple it'd be to slip into that midnight ether where pain doesn't exist or fear or loneliness. Just an eternity of nothing.

Sure, death may be a sweet, tempting exit, but I need to stay here if only to win the most fucked up—yet loving—sister award. I'm sure there is some kind of gold statue out there waiting for me.

I squeeze my eyes shut, forcing the twisted thoughts away, dragging up images of Ray. She's my reason. I'll never leave her to face this wretched world alone.

You have to have hope, some small, weak voice whispers in

the back of my mind. I don't recognize the bitch, but I hear her all the same. Maybe I don't have much of it, but for Ray, I can hope a little.

I glance at my phone to check the time.

12:01 a.m.

Happy birthday to me—

A metallic *thud* snaps me to attention, and I'm on my feet before I can blink.

The side door I came through is thrown wide open so hard, the brick behind it cracks. A group of people files through, their features gaunt as if starvation has eaten away most of their muscles. Their cheekbones jut at sharp angles, their limbs long and lithe, almost skeletal, and their dirt-sodden clothes hang off them like rags.

I back away with my palms up. "I didn't realize this spot was claimed," I say, my voice shaking. I know Chicago's homeless situation, and there have been plenty of times our principal caught a few seeking shelter for the night on school grounds, but that's usually in the winter when survival outweighs the consequences.

They fan out left and right, their movements jagged, their eyes all holding a glazed, vacant look.

"I'll just be going," I say, stepping back toward the door on the opposite side of the gym. "Space is all yours."

"No," a man in the middle says as he shakes his head.

Good God, will this night *ever* fucking end?

A woman to his left lifts her nose, sniffing like a dog on a hunt. Her lips twist into a smile, revealing blackened teeth, some chipped. Some missing altogether.

"Claimed," another man echoes from the right, causing a few others to growl.

"No, mine."

"I want the first taste!"

"Plenty to share. Don't waste it!"

The wall hits the back of my boots. They herded me into a corner, and the exit is a good four feet away.

Adrenaline floods my body, the sensation painful after being in panic mode all night.

They circle me, their eyes near black as they lick their lips.

Kai is right—the world is ending, and people are losing their fucking minds.

Mine races with everything Coach Hale has ever taught me, and I curl my hands into fists, shifting my feet for better balance.

They're thinner, frail-looking. Maybe I can fight my way free.

Or you can just let them kill you.

I crack my neck, effectively silencing that horrible voice in my head.

They come so close, I can smell them—sulfur and tar and something rancid that makes my eyes water.

I raise my fists.

Not today.

The man in the middle snaps his teeth at his pals, stopping their advance. "Everyone will get their turn. Just a taste. The boss wants her alive," he says. "But I'm first."

A collective roar erupts from the group, but they don't move.

Only him.

One.

I can take *one*. Shove him toward the group and run.

Ten steps away.

I steel my nerves, desperately trying to slow my heart rate as I focus on his approach.

Six steps away.

He favors his left leg—a previous injury? Doesn't matter. I'll exploit it.

Four steps away.

My body shakes, sweat popping from my brow as heat soars and swirls underneath my skin, the fire of my fight instincts making my muscles tremble.

Two steps.

The man outstretches his hand, his fingernails filed to sharp points and caked with a reddish-brown soot.

My surroundings slow like syrup coats everything. I cock back my fist, drawing his attention away from my right boot poised to snap at that left leg of his.

One step.

I unleash the strength I coiled in my right leg, jerking my boot down on the man's left. He wails a screeching sound that rattles my brain. Spit sprays my cheeks and *stings*.

But I don't have time to focus on that as the man rights himself and comes at me again. I use his own momentum to dodge several times, getting in a few quick jabs here and there as we dance on the mat. Well, I dance. He just sort of holds my gaze and circles me, taking the hits as though they were nothing more than annoying flies buzzing around his face.

Duck, jab, jab, dodge. Over and over. But he doesn't come any closer. Doesn't engage. Just circles me, arcing out a wide arm at me occasionally but otherwise remaining distant. It's not until I start to huff that I realize why. He was just wearing me down, waiting for me to weaken.

And then he attacks with razor quickness.

And damn, he's strong, so much stronger than he looks. I can hear the rest of his gang laughing manically as he manages to wrap his hand around my throat.

I flail my legs back and forth as he lifts me off the ground. The tension on my neck screams from his grip, and black spots burst along my vision. The gymnasium flashes from black to the cackling group to black again, in and out like a camera sharpening its focus and then not.

I swipe at his wrist, digging in my nails. I come back with strips of skin, but he doesn't flinch, and something like true terror tears through my chest, each slowing beat of my heart a prayer for air to fill my burning lungs.

Every inch of my body feels like it's on fire as he squeezes the life from me.

My muscles weaken, my fingers numb as I try and fail to dislodge his grip.

I'm sorry, Ray.

I can't believe I've waited years to turn eighteen, to finally get Ray somewhere safe, and now, only minutes into it, it turns out I'm going to leave her all alone anyway.

Life has always had a cruel sense of humor where I was concerned. No reason to change things just because I'm dying, I suppose. With that thought, I strangle on a laugh, the last of my breath gone, and do the only thing I can.

I raise my shaky hand and flip off the asshole who killed me.

CHAPTER SEVENTEEN

A streak of black flies across my vision, a *whoosh* of wind as something fast and huge leaps behind the man, the ground trembling beneath its feet.

Not something.

Someone.

Draven.

Instantly, the man drops me. My knees crack against the gym floor, but I barely register the pain as I gulp down lungfuls of air amid a coughing that shreds my throat.

Screams erupt behind me, seeming to come from everywhere at once, but I don't have the energy to look around yet. I've almost got my coughing under control, but the room is still spinning.

"On your left!" Draven yells as he fights three from the group, including the man who nearly killed me.

I drag my gaze to the right, blinking the fog from them.

Then I blink again.

Because surely I'm seeing things *wrong*—surely that isn't Coach freaking Hale fighting the other half of the group with... knives? Two six-inch blades that flicker in the light and spin in her hands like they're an extension of her body.

I shake my head back and forth, trying to reassemble my brain as I force myself to stand. Searing pain ripples up my legs, and I yelp through clenched teeth. The sound ensnares the attention of the man—the one who choked me—and he slips under Draven's outstretched arm, sliding on his knees across the floor to reach me.

Despite my entire body shaking with exhaustion and pain,

despite knowing I'm no match, I raise my fists and snap one across his jaw. His head jerks to the side from the motion, but I don't have a second to process where the strength came from. I only have time to ready my arm for another hit as he lunges for me.

He tears through my attempt to block him, and we crash to the ground, the back of my head bouncing off the floor so hard, I swear I hear it crack. My teeth rattle, and the sting of split flesh rips down my spine.

"Gonna enjoy draining you," the man says, his weight atop me much more than his skeletal appearance. The sharp points of his nails graze the edge of my neck as I struggle to work my legs beneath him. Just a couple more inches and I can use them to shove him off, but before I can gain that ground, those sharp points sink into my neck.

A wail rips from my lips, the pain like a thousand hot pokers penetrating my skin.

"Anka!" Draven hollers from behind me.

"Shit!" A succession of hisses and screams is silenced; then, in a blink, the weight disappears. The man hauled off me like someone lassoed him and *yanked*.

I yelp at the way his nails tear from my skin, and I cover the tiny wounds with my fingers as I hurry to my feet.

"Harley." Coach Hale kneels beside me, her eyes raking over my body quickly before I point behind her. "Just a second," she says, drawing those knives from the sleeves of her leather jacket, spinning around to face the man coming at her full speed.

In one smooth, fluid motion, she sinks the blade dead center in the man's chest. A *squelch* sound cuts off his scream, and he drops to the floor with a *thud* before his body convulses over and over again, each time his skin growing darker and thinner until it...

Crumbles.

Leaving nothing but glittering black dust on the floor where he just stood.

My eyes widen as silence fills the room, more piles of the black powder hitting the floor until there is no one left.

"Coach Hale?" I scramble backward, away from her, away from Draven, who has yet to turn around to face me.

She shifts to stand, spinning her knives back up her sleeves, then tilts her head. "You just saw me dust a Minion," she says. "Think it's fair to call me Anka."

I gape at her, then at the piles of black powder all over the floor, then back again.

A screeching metal sound makes me jolt, and Anka curses again. "Missed one." She glares at Draven as if it's *his* fault, then hauls ass across the gym, following the straggler out the door.

My hand itches with a warm liquid, and I wince as I move it off the wounds on my neck. Red fills the creases in my fingers, fresh trickles snaking their way down my skin. My stomach twists, the sensation of the ground tilting beneath my feet forcing acid up my throat.

"Draven?" I whisper, and he finally tears his eyes off the black on the floor.

I gasp at the way his eyes glow, almost like liquid gold churns behind them. He steps toward me, his boots silent on the gym floor.

"What's going on?" I ask, covering the wounds on my neck again. Every time I speak, I can feel the blood rushing from the cuts. "What were those things?" My voice shakes, weak.

Draven takes another step toward me, stopping an arm's reach away. Such pain and devastation and anger churns in his eyes, more so than when he snapped at the deli— God, was that mere hours ago?

"Tell me this is a bad dream," I beg.

A muscle in his jaw ticks as he shakes his head.

I swallow hard, my eyes scanning the piles behind him, the open and cracked door even farther away. "What do they want?" I force out the question even though my mind feels like quicksand.

Draven's eyes narrow on the hand covering my neck.

"What do they want, Draven?" The rawness in my voice is so loud, he flinches, but he doesn't answer.

Instead, he crouches and swipes his finger on the floor, standing as he rubs something between his thumb and forefinger.

I spare a glance down, the motion taking all my strength, and note the small splatter of red liquid there before meeting his gaze again.

"The same thing I want," he finally answers. "Your blood."

CHAPTER EIGHTEEN

I hear Draven's voice in the distance, but it's like I'm underwater and can't make out anything he says. My entire body aches as I shift against something soft, trying desperately to pry open my eyes.

The last thing I remember is passing out on the gymnasium floor. Not my finest moment, I'll admit, but the memory helps me waken enough to hear the conversation going on around me, at least.

"What's your stake in this?" Draven asks.

"Who says there is one?" Coach Hale meets him with equal venom in her voice.

The smells of citrus and cedar swirl around me.

"You're saying your involvement in her life is completely coincidental?"

A mute light illuminates half of the small room, the glowing embers of a few candles flickering atop shelves on the opposite wall. My head spins as my brain rushes to remind me of all that's happened.

Skeletal people, snarling as they tried to kill me.

Fights and screams and piles of ash.

"Please tell me you're not that naive," Coach Hale snaps, and my eyes clear enough to focus on the pair facing each other in the open doorway. She's a good foot shorter than Draven, but she stares up at him like she'll put him on his back if he *blinks* wrong.

Draven cocks a brow at her, glaring at her like *he* might do the same if she keeps running her mouth.

"Why are you here, then? Why'd you show up?"

"I smelled them."

"That's the only reason?" he challenges.

"I could ask the same of you, *Judge*." She draws out the last word.

I shift, wincing at the cut on my neck that now has a bandage over it.

Coach Hale's eyes snap to me and soften the second they lock with mine. "You're safe," she says.

Something about the assurance in those two words gives me the strength to push off the bed I occupy, a thick blanket sliding down my body.

I finger the tight bandaging on the side of my neck.

Coach Hale parts her lips, but a loud buzz cuts her off. She fishes her cell from her pocket. "Kaz," she answers. "Yeah. We need to talk." A pause before she huffs. "That can wait." She rolls her eyes. "Fine. As soon as you're finished." She hangs up the call, pocketing her cell as her eyes dart between Draven and me. "Looks like you two have some talking to do," she says, taking a step toward the exit and flashing a glare up to Draven as she does.

"I won't," he snaps at some silent question she poses.

She nods, then glances at me. "Meet me for training when it's daylight."

I tilt my head, my chest feeling heavy, my head splitting in so many different directions. She clearly knows way more about *everything* than I do. And part of me wants to rage at that, but she doesn't wait for me to respond before leaving.

And then I'm alone with Draven.

"How long was I out? Where am I?" I ask.

"Only an hour," he says. "And my place."

I swallow hard, heat sliding over my skin as I shift on his bed. Of course, that smell—*his* smell—drenches the covers that were over me moments ago.

"I passed out?"

He nods, crossing his arms over his chest as he leans against his doorframe.

I touch the bandage on my neck again. "Thanks for this."

"I didn't do that." His voice is as cold as his eyes. "Anka did."

I narrow my gaze. "What were those things?"

"Minions," he says on the end of a sigh.

I raise my brows. "Like the little yellow dudes in overalls with only one eye?"

He flashes me a look that shows just how much he appreciates my attempt at humor.

"Lower-level demons," he says once I've dropped the smart-ass grin from my face. Guess I'm not as clever as I thought.

"You can't be serious."

He cocks a brow at me. "I'm *dead* serious."

Ice water douses my skin, effectively squashing all the jokes when I see the sincerity in his features.

I swallow hard, remembering the way those people disintegrated into glittering black dust. The way their eyes hadn't seemed entirely human, nor their strength. Remember the men who attacked me, their eyes a glowing red.

"Demons are real," I say, testing the words on my tongue.

He just nods.

I shrug. "Okay."

Draven's lips part. *"Okay?"*

"What?"

"You believe it that easily?"

"Do you want to have a rousing debate about it?" I shake my head, glaring at him. Of course he'd rather debate it. Hash it out. Nothing with Draven is ever simple or easy. "It's kind of hard to deny what I saw tonight, what I saw when those men tried to take me in the fun house." I swallow hard. "Also, the world is shit. No wonder. Demons don't seem that far-fetched."

Draven shakes his head, his lips twisting like he's holding back a laugh.

"And Coach Hale—Anka," I say, wringing my hands. "She knows about all this?"

Another nod, his jaw tightening like he has to physically hold back answers.

Something tugs at the edge of my mind, something vital. I sift through the haze and chaos of memories. The last thing I remember was him saying something about my blood—

My eyes flare at the memory, my pulse spiking.

"Finally," he says, his eyes cold, hard. "You *should* be afraid."

I glare at him, forcing myself to stand. "I'm not afraid of you."

But I can see the fear in his eyes as I get closer to him. See the way his body tenses, a battle of corded muscle and willpower as I stop an inch away from him.

Draven lifting the armed man like he's nothing.

Draven throwing him through the glass doors.

Draven fighting off four people before turning them to dust.

All the logical reasons I should be afraid of him flash in my mind like a high-speed train, but all are countered by different scenes.

The way he always gets down on Ray's level to speak to her.

The destroyed artwork he reassembled just to make her smile.

The way he showed up on my porch with food and not a hint of judgment.

"I'm not afraid of you," I say again.

He draws his lips back, showing his teeth a bit, a flare of wickedness in his eyes. "Listen to your instincts," he says, a growl to his tone. "They'll tell you everything you need to know about me."

I search inward only to find the same satisfying heat I feel anytime Draven is near me.

"You won't hurt me," I say, proud my voice only shakes a little as I feel another crack forming in my walls.

He forces out a dark laugh. "I will. Unless…" He uncrosses his arms, examining his palms as he turns his hands over and back.

I shake my head. "You haven't hurt me yet."

"I haven't *touched* you," he admits. *"Yet."*

There. A sliver of icy-cold fear slides down my spine, but it's matched by the intensity in Draven's eyes. The heat thrashing through my blood the closer we stand.

Maybe I really am damaged beyond repair.

Because that thrill trickling in my veins? That hot, thumping *need* to cross that line of fear even if it burns me? I *want* it—that danger, that risk—I crave it almost as much as I crave food when starving.

"We danced—"

"I didn't touch your skin," he clarifies. "I barely touched you then. Merely moved with you."

I think back on that night, his fingers just slightly grazing my jeans, the sleeves of my shirt. I furrow my brow, thinking further, searching for an argument to prove Draven's statement wrong. Surely we've *touched* before. Shaken hands? Passed things in the deli?

But we haven't. Not once.

Every time I came close, he jerked away. I thought it was because physical contact was hard for him, but after everything I've seen tonight, I don't know what the hell to make of anything.

"You're not like those…*Minions*," I say, testing out the new word.

"No," he says, a crooked smirk shaping his lips. "I'm far worse."

Something new flares and trembles just beneath my skin, a delicious sort of ripple. I don't dare look away from him. "If you wanted me dead, I already would be."

"Half true," he says.

"And I wouldn't stand a chance at defending myself against you." I already feel helpless to fight the thrall he has on me, that connection I can't deny or shake. And part of me wonders why I like it so much—that feeling.

Because it makes you feel alive.

Draven's breath shakes as I take another small step closer to him, but he doesn't deny my words.

I reach my finger toward his hand—

"Don't," he says, tracking my movements like a hawk, the primal warning in his tone freezing me.

"I told you, I'm not scar—"

He growls. "You were attacked *twice* in one night. Do you have no self-preservation skills at all?"

I purse my lips but don't drop my hand. Instead, I get closer.

"I'm warning you," he says, his voice going lethally quiet. "*Don't* touch me."

I draw my hand back.

"Fine," I snap.

Confusion ripples in those amber eyes.

"*You* touch *me*, then. Show me what I'm supposed to be so afraid of," I challenge, my voice stronger than I knew possible. "Unless *you're* the one who is afraid?"

That muscle in his jaw ticks.

I stand my ground, chin raised despite the exhaustion traveling through my body. Soon, I'll wake up from this hellish nightmare and curse my overactive imagination. I'll roll my eyes at this twisted dream and get back to my normal twisted life.

"It's my birthday," I whisper, realization hitting me hard. I survived…I made it to eighteen. The overwhelming odds— especially after what's happened tonight, if I'm not truly dreaming— make a swirling sense of giddiness rush through me.

So much that a slightly mad laugh bubbles up from my chest.

Something glitters in his eyes, but he squeezes them shut, effectively blocking me out. He rakes his hands through his hair, his eyes snapping open to reveal some internal battle raging just beneath the surface. "You're eighteen," he says, another dark laugh ripping from his lips. His eyes scan the length of my body, his head slightly tilted. "How do you *feel*, Harley?" His tone is more devastated than concerned.

"Fine," I say. In truth, the cuts on my neck barely hurt anymore. It's hard to feel anything outside the rushing need flaring inside me.

"Fine? Nothing more?"

I swallow hard, my hand still extended between us in an offer. "Am I supposed to feel something more?"

He eyes my hand but doesn't move.

"Do you want to *make* me feel something more?" I challenge, a thrill rushing through me. This…this battle between us…the same one that started the second he stepped into my life, *this* is better than any adrenaline rush. Distracting and powerful and dangerous and all the things I know I shouldn't enjoy or want but can't stop. Not with him.

Something shifts in his eyes, dark and jagged, as he steps closer. "Do you trust me?"

"I rarely trust anyone," I answer. Then add, "But I trust you."

Draven tilts his head back, eyes on the ceiling as if he's silently pleading for help. Slowly, he draws his focus back to mine. "You shouldn't."

I turn my palm up and hold it between us.

A challenge.

A dare.

A question.

If he's so terrifying, I want to *feel* it. Want it to raze me to the ground until all I can feel is this sensation—this spark I've never experienced before.

"Show me," I say, and Draven flinches.

"No."

I keep my hand open between us.

His lips turn to a hard line, his eyes darting between my hand and my eyes and back again.

"Touch me, Draven."

His chest rises and falls quickly as he holds his hand over mine, hovering just an inch above my skin.

The battle is clear in the rigid lines of his body, the way his fingers shake.

But he spans that distance, the resolution clear enough in his churning eyes.

So I lift my hand.

Draven gasps as the pads of my fingers graze his skin.

Once.

Twice.

His eyes fly wide and expectant as they scan my body like he's searching for some kind of injury. After a few seconds, he grips my hand with a gentle strength that makes heat pulse beneath my skin.

"Harley?" He whispers my name like a question.

"Draven." I answer him, solid, calm, practically bored. "I'm waiting to be *terrified*," I tease.

His grip tightens.

I match that strength with my own, meeting him move for move as our hands interlock and unlace and graze over each other. My entire body is coiled like a spring from the innocent touch.

But touching Draven feels like taking a drink after dying of thirst.

His gaze roves over my body, searching, scanning until he chokes out another dark laugh.

"I'm trembling in my boots." I mock his assumption that one touch will kill me.

"It's not possible," he says, his eyes near-wild with wonder. He snakes his fingers over my wrist, yanking me closer. A flicker of fear flashes on my skin, but I go to him willingly. Our bodies nearly touch as he draws my wrist to his face, running his nose along its seam and inhaling.

My heart thunders inside my chest, a hunger for something I can't name growing inside me. I reach up on my tiptoes, instinct begging me to get closer. And I can feel an answering need in his gaze as well, but Draven goes absolutely still as my lips inch near his. I pause, silently challenging him as we've done so many times before in our verbal battles.

Draven's eyes flare, the gold blazing as he searches my face; then ever so slowly, he leans down.

He brushes the lightest of kisses over my lips, my eyes closing against the contact, the heat of it. The smell of him swarms my senses, spinning my head and filling it with a glittering fog that I want to swim in all day.

"Draven," I whisper against his lips, and something about the way I say his name snaps some leash he's held himself on. One second, I'm reaching up for him, and the next he hauls me up and up until I have to lock my ankles around his back.

He spins us until my spine touches the closest wall, and he

presses the warmth of his body against every inch of mine. His eyes look like liquid gold before claiming my mouth in a searing kiss that steals my breath. His tongue grazes over the edge of my lips, teasing. Infuriating. Electric.

More, more, more.

I open for him and moan at his taste—mint and spice and hot damn he's like the sweetest high, sending my mind soaring, flying as he claims my mouth. As he holds me against him with just enough pressure to sting in the most delicious way.

He explores my mouth with teasing flicks and slow grazes. His hands grip my thighs, and everything in me melts into nothing but living flame as he slants his mouth over mine again and again. I tangle my fingers in his dark curls, drinking him in, meeting him kiss for kiss until I'm a breathless, wild flame in his arms.

"Harley," he growls against my mouth.

My blood sings at the way he says my name. At the way his body feels against mine. At the way I feel in his arms—dangerous and strong and powerful. The feel of his kiss electrifies every inch of me, some lost inner piece of me sparking to life.

His lips move to the corner of my mouth, across my jawline, and back again, and my body tightens to the point of aching with each pass. And when he claims my mouth again, I tremble in his arms.

No, that isn't me.

It's the wall.

His entire room shakes like a train is rattling past it.

Draven tears his lips from mine, his eyes turning hard as stone as he sets me on my feet so quickly, my head spins. I brace myself with a hand on the wall.

"Draven?" I ask as the shaking in his room abruptly stops, the heat from his body still clinging to my skin.

Draven rakes his hands through his hair as he steps back toward his open door.

"Draven."

"You truly *are*… And I have to…" He shakes his head. "I can't."

Then he turns his back on me and *walks away*.

CHAPTER NINETEEN

"Didn't think you were going to show," Coach Hale says from her position on the mat in the gym.

I walk toward her cautiously, scanning every inch of the gym as if those Minion things will show up any second. The floor is a polished sort of clean, and the look on Coach Hale's face when I meet her on the mat? It's open and raw and just this side of terrifying.

"I thought about blowing you off," I admit, not bothering to hide the bite or exhaustion from my tone. After Draven ran off, *again*, I went to Nathan's and found him and Ray crashed out on the couch in front of the TV. I changed clothes and was barely able to stand the wait until I could take Ray to art and meet up with Coach Hale. "But it's my birthday and all." I shrug. "So I figure I'll give you the benefit of the doubt."

She flinches at my glare.

Good, she *should* feel the betrayal that stings every inch of my skin.

"All those lessons," I say, shaking my head as I face her on the mat and position my feet slightly apart, preparing for an attack. "All those hours we spent together, and you never once thought to mention..." I wave an arm toward the gym floor, as if those piles of glittering ash still remain.

"You're the one who asked *me* for help," she counters, sliding into her own defensive position. The move is so subtle, I wouldn't know to track it if we hadn't trained together.

"And agreed. *Instantly.* Why?" I once thought she took pity on a girl who wanted to know how to defend herself. Now? After everything I've seen? I don't know what to believe. And it hurts like hell to have someone in my life, someone I allowed *in*…to be hiding so fucking much from me.

Her dark eyes are hard as she scans me from head to toe. She juts out her chin. "If you want answers," she says, "you have to earn them."

A flicker of life sparks in my blood. She wants a fight? So fucking be it.

I lift my arms, my palms tight as I twist my body.

"Fair enough," I say, arching a brow at her. A new sense of strength radiates right alongside my normally trembling muscles. I feed off it, off the betrayal, as she launches herself at me.

I see the forward attack, twist on my toes, and lay a palm strike to her spine, sending her sprawling. I don't pull the hit, either. Not this time.

She flips on her feet in a flash, a grin shaping her lips. "Good," she says, circling me on the mat. "Your scent was faint." She never loses my gaze. "I didn't know if it would amount to anything. But when you came to me for help…I couldn't say no. Not with what you might be."

"Am I a demon? Like those Minions?"

She arches a brow at me.

I swipe out my right leg, attempting to knock my foot across her beautiful face. She catches my ankle with ample time, yanking it to the left. I soar across the mat. My skin thwacks against it, but I shove to standing quick enough.

"Land a hit," she challenges. "And I'll tell you."

I run at her full speed, my hands outstretched as I cut through the air near her face. Palm strike after palm strike, all my attempts are easily blocked by her superfast reflexes. Her grin deepens with each attempt, so I switch tactics, listening fully to my instincts and letting them take over my body.

I feign another strike before dropping to a crouch and landing a full blow to her left side. The air *whooshes* out of her lungs as she stumbles backward from the hit. A laugh slips past her lips as she holds up a finger to pause the fight.

I straighten, sucking in a heaving breath, fists still up.

"Nice one," she says, then lets her arms hang loose at her sides. "I don't know exactly what you are," she admits, her dark eyes scanning me as if she can see something crawling beneath my skin. "Just rumors. You haven't shown what you're capable of yet."

I shake my head, anger gripping my lungs. "Is there only one kind of demon?"

"Oh, honey," she says, flashing me a pitying look.

I grind my teeth.

Fine, maybe it's a ridiculous question, but my head is still spinning. She snaps her fingers, fight stance back in place.

"Right," I say, raising my hands like claws. "Do all demons look like those Minions?" They almost appeared human—run-down and starving but human features nonetheless.

Coach Hale lashes out with a palm strike that I barely dodge. "Do all humans look alike?"

"No," I huff, swinging a right hook and missing a connection.

She retaliates with a four-jab combo. I swing my shoulders, jogging backward to dodge the hits. Damn, she's been holding herself *way* back in our previous training sessions—the woman is beyond fast.

Woman.

I drop my hands, glaring at her. The betrayal slaps me all over again.

"Are *you* human?"

Coach Hale furrows her brow, pursing her lips as she drops her attack. "What does your gut tell you?" she challenges, extending her left leg backward, lengthening her arms in a move I recognize.

I adjust my stance for it.

A blink and she cuts through the air, her arms the force of propeller blades. I bounce on my feet, zigzagging out of her way, smacking away her attempts to chop me in half with nothing but the side of her hand.

"Are you going to tell me I shouldn't trust you?" I ask as she continues to come for me. "Like Draven did?" Though, to be honest, I wouldn't trust her again, no matter her answer. Not fully.

That knowledge hurts much more than I thought it would, and I'm already grieving the loss of someone I foolishly considered a mentor.

And yet, here she is, making me pay for answers that should be given freely—seeing as how I apparently am central to whatever the hell went down last night.

My anger rushes to a crescendo beneath my skin, and I land a hit to her chest that sends her backward a few steps. A delighted smirk flashes over her face before she tips her chin at me.

"Do you think a *human* could dust five Minions without breaking a sweat?"

"You know, I think I skipped that day at demon camp," I snap.

"The correct answer is *no*," she says. "Normal humans can't see them like we can."

"What would someone normal have seen if they walked into the gym last night?"

"Whatever their minds conjured to make sense of such a situation." She waves at the space between us. "You yourself said you thought they were homeless people seeking shelter."

"But *I* can see them…" The black eyes, the rotting teeth, the acidic spit, the inhuman movements in bodies that didn't fit the motions.

Coach Hale lashes out faster than a cobra, her hit connecting with my face so hard, I snap down to my knees. I growl, angry at being distracted enough to let the direct hit slip by.

"So I guess *I'm* not human, am I?"

"And *there* it is." She looks at her watch again. "Six hours before she starts asking the right questions."

No. No, no, no.

"There has to be some mistake," I say, looking at my palms as if the answers lay there. "I'm nothing. Nothing special. I'm *weaker* than most girls my age. I can't be—"

A soft popping sound cuts me off. Bursts of rose-and-currant-scented wind tickle my nose.

I stumble, barely catching my balance before I fall on my ass.

"What's the matter?" Coach Hale asks, a wicked glint to her eyes.

Heat prickles beneath my skin as I stare at her—she hasn't moved, but she's *shifted*. Giant indigo wings extend behind her back, the material like stretched rubber. Hardened scales link one on top of the other, outlining the finer material. A long, scaled tail of the same color swishes back and forth from her lower back, a gleaming point at the tail's end capable of skewering anything that dares step in her path.

She takes a calculated step toward me, those massive wings moving delicately with her. I stand my ground despite everything in my bones telling me to *run*. Her eyes are on mine, but I can't tear my gaze off her wings. Especially this close. They catch the light, the deep indigo color shimmering with bits of gleaming black.

"Only those who aren't entirely human can see through the veil," she says.

I force myself to focus on her face. "There has to be a mistake," I say. "I'm weak—"

"Your blood isn't."

Her words ground me like ice slicking over my skin.

"*What do they want?*"

"*The same thing I want. Your blood.*"

Then later with Draven, that kiss rattling in my head.

His lips on mine, his hands on my thighs, the wall at my back…

Nope. Not going there. Hell no.

"What's wrong with my blood?"

Coach Hale tilts her head as she steps closer to me, inhaling deeply. "I'm not certain," she says, her eyes fluttering a bit. "But it's incredibly potent."

I swallow hard, my heart sinking down to my stomach. All this time, my entire life I've felt wrong, dirty. I thought it was because of my father, of what he constantly does to me.

Maybe it's been something more all along. I really am as

bad as I always feared. I thought I was putting Ray in danger before, but now? Oh my God, what if she was with me when those Minions—

Coach Hale swipes a leg beneath my ankles.

My back hits the mat with a *thunk*, the air whooshing from my lungs as she pins me to the floor.

"There is nothing wrong with your blood, Harley," she says, easily blocking my attempts to throw her off. She pinches my chin between her fingers, forcing me to meet her eyes. "Except that you don't understand it. Don't *listen* to it." She narrows her gaze.

"Excuse me for not having a clue until now that I'm different beyond the normal shit in my life," I snap, still struggling to break her hold. "No one told me—"

"No one should have to tell you," she says. "If you weren't so busy listening to the poison your sack-of-shit father pours in your ear, you may have noticed it about yourself a long time ago. But no. You're content to think you're worthless."

Tears bite the backs of my eyes, but I shake them off and grip her elbow, twisting it until she hauls off me. I leap to my feet, glaring at her. "You have no idea what I've been through—"

"Because you never let anyone in, Harley," she cuts me off again as we circle each other. "You keep everyone shut out. Even yourself. That's why you have no clue who you really are. *What* you really are."

"Do you really not know what I am?"

"No," she admits, fists up as she watches me carefully. "But I sure as hell hope I'm around when you figure it out."

But will she be on my side when that happens? *If* that happens?

God, my mind is racing. I can't stop the thoughts coming at me rapid-fire, each hitting me like a bullet. I belong in a world of demons. I'm probably worse than a demon. Will Anka one day need to kill me, too? Is that what Draven meant by wanting my blood? Is it possible my shitty life actually just got shittier?

Anka drops the circling, drops her attack stance, and turns

around, exposing the backside of those wings. All scales and rubber and glittering indigo.

A vulnerable position, something I doubt she does often, almost as if she wants to give me the opportunity to return the knife to the back I felt the second I realized she'd lied to me for more than a year about who and what she is and why she's in my life.

I swallow hard, dropping my fists. "You're a demon." I don't pose it as a question.

She whirls back around, arching a brow.

"But you're not evil."

"Not all the time," she teases, and my instincts prickle with fear.

"Is that unusual?" I ask. "For a demon to be so…" I search for the right word. "Perky?"

"Ugh." She rolls her eyes like I mentioned eating maggots for breakfast. She points a finger at me. "I am *not* perky."

I bite back a laugh, the sensation clearing away some of my anger.

"Not to everyone, anyway," she says. "And no, it's not unusual. Are all humans wholly good or wholly evil?"

"Okay," I say, nodding. "I'm starting to get it. I think. But…" I stop myself, wondering if some questions are off-limits.

"Out with it."

"Aren't most of you supposed to be in *Hell*?"

A burst of laughter rips from her lips. "Some would say so, yes," she admits. "I have no desire to go back."

"How'd you get here?"

"There are ways," she says. "Less now than there were when I first escaped."

Which begs the question… "How long have you been here?"

She narrows her gaze on me but answers, "Much longer than you can conceive."

A cold shudder runs the length of my spine. How can any of this be real?

You once believed in a God; is it so hard to believe in Hell?

"And you're a high school gym coach."

"Don't knock the gig," she says. "I've been many things over the span of several lifetimes." Something distant flickers in her dark eyes. "I like being in a position where I can help younglings. Like you."

I want so desperately to believe she's here to help people like me, but I just can't. I trusted her once, and now here we are. Trusting her again would just be foolish. "And the fact that you think I have special blood? That has nothing to do with your *help*."

"I knew it from the second I smelled you," she says, shrugging. "But I didn't approach you for years. I don't care about your magical blood or what it can potentially do. I care about your safety—from enemies known and unknown. And now that you've come of age, your scent has heightened. More will be coming for you. Worse than last night."

I shake my head, denial rippling over my skin. "You've got the wrong girl. They all do." I can feel it in my muscles right now— that weakness that's left me near powerless against my father for years. If I'm some supernatural creature, you'd think I'd be strong enough to fight him off in the end.

"I wish that were the case."

I raise my brows at her.

"I wouldn't wish my world or the risks that come with it upon anyone, Harley."

My stomach turns over as my alarm chimes on my phone just off the mat. I hurry over, silencing it. "What about Ray?" I ask.

"I do not know," she says.

"We have different mothers."

Coach Hale nods.

"My father?" Pity flickers in her eyes, but I ignore it. "I have to get Ray," I say, but I have a few more minutes, since I'm already in the school building. "What is Draven?" I've been trying so hard to keep him out of my thoughts, but it's an impossible task. Not when every waking second, something deep inside me screams for me to find him—like a chain reaching through the ether looking for some latch to secure itself to.

Of course, I don't know if I want to punch him or kiss him, but I know without a doubt either one of those would be fun. Not that I should focus on having fun right now, but God, after everything? I crave his distraction more than ever, crave getting lost in that touch—battle or brilliance—if only to stop my world from spinning out of control.

"That's not my story to tell."

I press my lips together as I gather my things. "He says I'm not safe with him."

She doesn't try to deny that statement.

"They'll keep coming for me?" She knows who I mean.

"I fear this will get worse before it gets better."

"They mentioned a name. The men who tried to take me," I say. "Marid. They say he has a Second. Who are they talking about?"

A sliver of fear cracks in those dark eyes. "There are rumors in the world outside the veil," she says. "Rumors of a greater demon attempting to escape their cage. I'm hoping they are false, but the recent attacks…" She shakes her head, lost in thought.

"What can I do?" I'm not silly enough to ask how something like a greater demon can exist, let alone what it wants with me. Everything I've seen in the last few hours shouldn't exist. And now I may not be human?

Something fierce swirls in my gut, but I shove the sensation down.

"I'm working on it." Coach Hale clutches my shoulder. "Give me some time. And just…try to stay out of trouble meanwhile."

"It's not like I ever go looking for it." I roll my eyes.

She laughs. "You never do."

"You have my number," I toss out and head toward the exit. "But I'll be at Nathan's for the next few days." With everything going on and Draven going AWOL, I can't afford to push away my only connection to the shitstorm I'm swimming in. "I'll text you the address."

She nods, and I head down the hallways to pick up Ray from art.

Miller's is still under repair but set to reopen soon. I arranged for Ray and me to stay at Nathan's after last night's attack and the one that followed—frankly because it's the only place I feel Ray will be safe. I called Father and left a message, fabricating a story of Ray's art program doing a week lock-in without electronics in order to enhance their skills, and added that I picked up double shifts in order to bring home some more cash. The promise of money always softens his hand, which is all I can hope for when we return.

I'll tell him about the apartment after I sign the lease.

I glance at my cell, the appointment reminder scrolling along the bottom. I have a few hours until I need to be there.

"Mr. Harris used Marid as an example of original character style today!" Ray squeals by way of greeting as she bounds out of the art room, her backpack smacking against her spine as she hurtles for me.

I try not to flinch at *his* name and force a smile as I hug her back. "Of course he did."

"I was kind of embarrassed," she says as we walk toward the exit.

"Why?"

"After he showed it, I had to stand in front of the class and talk about where I got the idea."

"Oh," I say, totally understanding. "But there are tons of artists who get their ideas from dreams."

Ray nods. "That's what Mr. Harris said after a few of the kids laughed when I explained."

I clench my fists but force myself to let it go as I open the door to let Ray through. I can't stop every kid from hurting Ray's feelings—that's not how the world works. But what I can try to do is help her own her self-worth, something my father never attempted to do for me. When in doubt with this whole "parenting" thing? I do the opposite of what he'd do. So I stop her at the bottom of the stairs outside the school and kneel so I can meet her eyes.

"There will always be people who say you're different, Ray. I can't change that." She chews on her bottom lip as I speak. "But those people who laugh? Those people who tell you your art isn't worth it?" I swallow hard, remembering how Father tore up her piece. "They're terrified of you."

"What?" she gasps. "I'd never hurt anyone!"

"I know." She has a heart twice the size of mine and an endless well of compassion. I never want that to change. "They're scared of your talent," I say. "Of your light. They're scared because they can't fit you into society's standard one-size-fits-all box. You have the ability to create life out of a blank page. And you have dreams that are so real, entire backstories and motivations are shown to you for your characters. It's a rare gift. A beautiful one. And the passion you add to it?" I smile at her. "It's unmatched. Don't ever let anyone tell you otherwise."

Ray lifts her brows. "Jeez, Harley," she says, giggling a little. "You turn eighteen and suddenly you're so serious?" she teases but squeezes me in a tight hug. "Are you having a good birthday so far?"

I force a laugh as I release her. I'm being a little serious, but being attacked by demons that make monster movies look like a trip to Disney World will do that to a girl.

"The best, now that you're here," I say, swallowing down the dark truth at the edge of my words. I never keep anything from Ray, but I don't know how to explain what I can barely understand myself.

Compartmentalization.

That's what I have to do. Shove the supernatural world in one box in my mind and my real life in the other. Just because I know demons are real and want my blood—because *of course* they do—it doesn't mean the world stops spinning. I've been waiting for this day for eighteen fucking years. It's finally here, and I have important things to do. Things that revolve around my sister's safety—safety I may now be jeopardizing simply by being with her.

"This isn't over. More are coming for her."

The man's voice from the deli echoes in my head, and I cringe, scanning each random tree or corner we round on our way to the El. As if demons will jump out at any moment, and with Ray at my side…

Nope.

Not going there.

Two boxes, remember?

Ray yawns and stretches when we make it to Nathan's, my spare key easily letting us inside. Nathan calls a friendly greeting from the kitchen, motioning to the phone at his ear in apology as he speaks to someone on the other end.

"Tired?"

She nods. "Another nightmare last night."

I usher her to the large, comfy couch in the living room, sinking down beside her. I wasn't here to wake her up. No, I was fighting off demons, passing out at Draven's place, then arguing with him, kissing him…

"What was it about?" I ask.

"Marid again," she says. "Always Marid these days. He's been…a little upset with me."

"Why?" I smooth some blond hair from her face.

"He keeps demanding things. Things I don't want to do. And when I say no…"

A chill races down my spine. "What?"

She visibly swallows, shaking her head. "They're just nightmares." She rubs at her shoulder, almost absentmindedly. "They're not real. Just…I'm tired."

She looks it, her skin leeched of color, her eyes drooping. Did Nathan not notice this morning when he took her to art? No, she likely put on a brave mask. She'd never want to miss that class.

I grab the throw off the back of the couch and motion for her to lay back. "You should nap," I say.

"It's your birthday," she argues. "I don't want to nap."

I arch a brow at her, and she reluctantly lays back. I settle the throw around her tiny body, wishing like hell I could offer her more protection than a warm blanket. I hate that these nightmares bother her so much and that they've gotten worse lately.

"I have an appointment anyway," I say. "You rest, and I can tell you all about it when I get back."

"Can I at least give you your present now?" she asks, her blue eyes so hopeful that I nod. She grins and shifts a bit, grabbing something from her pocket. She presses a tiny square of pink tissue paper into my hand.

I unwrap the paper and blink.

"I thought…" she says, pointing to the thin, braided string in my hand. "That since yours is getting so old, you could have this one. That way if it ever breaks, you'll still have the one I gave you."

I swallow hard, immediately slipping the bracelet right atop the one I never take off.

"Red for passion because you're so strong," she says, pointing to each color of braided string. "Yellow for happiness because you need more of it. Blue for calmness because you definitely need a chill moment in your life." She laughs, then continues. "And black for power because you're the most powerful person I know." My eyes widen at her explanation, but she falls back against the pillow. "I wanted to buy you something," she says, chewing on her bottom lip. "But I didn't want to ask for money. I borrowed the string from the art room and made it myself instead."

My heart melts. I hold up my wrist, the two thin bracelets contrasting—one pure black, the other a rainbow of braided colors. "It's officially my favorite bracelet in the universe." I manage to choke out the words, my throat tight.

Ray's eyes light up. "Really?"

"Really," I say, lowering my wrist to settle my palm against her little chest. "I don't know how I got so lucky to have a sister like you."

Ray smiles. "I'm the lucky one. You're the best."

My heart sinks. Am I the best for her? With everything…

"You should sleep," I say instead of responding. "Thank you so much, Ray. Seriously. Best birthday gift ever."

"You'll be back soon?" Her lids flutter closed.

"Yes," I assure her.

"And we'll have cookies?" Her voice is soft, barely a whisper.

"Absolutely." I tuck her in more securely, patting the edges of the blanket under her chin. "Now, get some rest, Ray. I love you, you know that, right?"

"More than I'll ever know." She repeats the correct answer, a slight annoyance to her tone. "You tell me, like, a zillion times a day."

"Just want you to remember it," I say, rising from the couch. The weight of that truth hits me in the chest as I back toward the door, silently motioning to Nathan, who's still on the phone, that Ray is already asleep. He nods and waves at me as I hurry through the door.

My phone buzzes in my pocket before I make it two steps off the porch, and I have the silly rush of hope that it's Draven.

KAI: Flights haven't been delayed. Should be able to meet soon. Where will you be in an hour?

ME: The apartment

I type out the answer quickly, my mood lifting at the idea that Kai might make it back in time to look at it with me. Just as fast, those hopes are slapped down.

One more person I have to lie to. About who and what I really am...whenever I figure that out. What if he'd been with me that night in the fun house? What if we hadn't gotten separated? Whatever my scent is, whatever attracts these things, it would've put him in danger, too.

Fuck.

I need to be careful. Maybe I should text him back and tell him not to bother.

I glance around, realizing I'm still standing on Nathan's porch. Panic tightens my skin. Is merely standing here putting them in danger? Is my scent *that* strong?

Anger thrashes in my chest at my lack of knowledge. Coach Hale should've told me more. Draven shouldn't have run off.

Someone should've—

Stop, stop, stop.

I hustle toward the El, telling myself I can't have a full-blown panic attack right now, not when I'm so close to getting a safe haven for Ray.

The supernatural answers will just have to wait.

But I *will* get them, even if I have to hunt Draven down to do it. Of course, there are a lot of reasons I want to find Draven... What did that kiss mean to him? Nothing? Sure didn't feel like nothing. Do I care either way?

I resist the urge to groan out loud on the train. Of course I care, and the fact that I do bothers me more than anything. I can't afford to be attached to anyone else. Not now. But Draven...he's this perfect distraction, this mind-boggling mystery, a challenge and thrill in every single way. It's impossible to think about anything past that delicious *alive* feeling he gives me—whether we're arguing or kissing.

I shake my head as if that will clear the sensation, the chaotic thoughts storming my mind, and hop off at my stop. I kill an hour at Myopic Books before walking the few blocks south to the complex I've had my eye on for months now.

I glance at my cell while I wait in the lobby, but there's no text from Kai yet, and my shoulders sink. He probably got stuck on his flight.

"You must be Harley," a sweet older woman says as she walks across the lobby toward me, hand outstretched.

I shake it twice. "I am."

"Wonderful," she says. "I have the keys here; let's go take a look." She tucks a blue folder under her arm as she walks me through the lobby and to a back door that opens into a small common area bordered by a well-maintained flower garden. Wrought-iron chairs and tables scatter throughout the community space, empty as we pass them and head up a set of concrete stairs leading to one portion of the apartment's building.

She passes four royal-blue doors, the paint chipped and

peeling at the corners. She stops in front of the one labeled with a silver-plated number 6. "Here we are," she says, sliding the key in and jiggling the handle a few times before the door gives. She forces out a tight laugh, motioning me inside.

I step under the threshold, scanning the small vacant space. I've seen pictures on their website, but nothing can compare to the reality. A tiny kitchen sits directly to the door's right, barely big enough to turn around in, the fridge taking up most of the space. To the left lays a sprawl of gray carpet, oil stains peppering it in random places. A sliding glass door opens to a small concrete balcony, the edges of which are caked with dirt. A few roaches skitter in and out of the cracked corners.

"Bedroom is this way," she says, waving to the lone door on the other side of the confined living room. She swings open the fading white door, revealing another room lined with stained carpet. A small bathroom that's definitely seen better days tucks into the far right corner.

I nod, returning through the living room and to the kitchen, where I run my fingers over the chipped countertops. A small alcove tucks into the opposite side of the fridge, a cracked counter hanging between the two thin walls—a desk, of sorts.

"We'll give the carpets a good cleaning before you move in," the woman says, chewing on her bottom lip as she gazes at the oil stains.

I smile at the little desk, picturing Ray drawing or doing her homework there. Grin at the kitchen where I'll prepare her breakfast and lunch and dinner—stretching our grocery budget so she'll never have to go hungry again. Nearly cry when looking at the open bedroom door, knowing it won't have to be barricaded to keep our father out.

"I can throw in a deep clean of the bathroom, too—"

"It's perfect," I say, cutting off the woman's worries. Her eyebrows shoot up. "I'll take it." I extend my hands, eyeing the blue folder.

She hustles to the nearest kitchen counter and lays out all the paperwork for me. I fill it out while she takes my ID to make a copy in her office in the lobby. By the time she's back and I return it to my wallet, I've signed the lease.

"When can I move in?" I ask.

"Once your deposit clears," she says, tucking the folder and my paperwork beneath her arm, "I can have the keys ready for you day after tomorrow."

I beam at that, swallowing back tears of relief. A couple of days and step one will be done. I'm so, so close.

"I'll be eagerly awaiting your call," I say by way of goodbye as we walk toward the lobby again. I motion toward one of the empty tables in the outdoor common area. "Is it all right if I hang for a bit?"

"Of course," she says. "I'm always saying tenants don't take advantage of the outdoor area nearly enough. And it's a beautiful night out."

Yes, yes it is.

I settle into a chair as she disappears around the corner and through the opposite building back to her office. I breathe out the deepest sigh. Ray and I will have a life here. I'll do everything in my power to ensure that.

I can't shake this sinking feeling in my gut, though. Even as I scoot back in my chair and stretch my arms in an attempt to rid myself of the sensation. The absence of someone to share this moment with is paramount. My mind tortures me with *what-if*s—my mother helping me unpack boxes, a smile on her lips—if life were different. But I don't live in a fairy tale, so I push the unwanted vision away.

Walking through the courtyard, I head toward an iron gate situated between two of the concrete buildings that leads to the main street on the opposite side instead of having to go through the lobby again. I want to get back to Ray and see if she's feeling better after her nap.

My phone buzzes in my pocket, stopping me just shy of the corner of one building, and my fingers shake as I fish it out. I can't wait to show Kai—

KAI: I'm stuck in a traffic jam. Meet you at Nathan's for birthday cookies instead?

Disappointment unfurls in my chest.

ME: Cool

I shove my phone back in my pocket, glancing up to continue toward the gate. I round the corner, the area a bit darker, since it's so far away from the complex's outdoor lighting, and I swear something moves from the corner of my eye.

The hair on the back of my neck prickles as I slow my steps, the space between the buildings suddenly feeling too small, too quiet. I listen, barely breathing as I strain my ears for anyone, anything. I glance to my right, to the wall closest to me. The same cracked concrete as the rest of the buildings but—

It *ripples*.

Like something prowls beneath its surface.

My eyes widen as fear becomes a living, pulsing thing in my veins.

Not again. Not again.

The wall ripples a second time, a section of it detaching itself and coming toward me—

No, that isn't part of the wall.

I almost swallow my tongue.

The color changes—shifting with cracks and snaps until a half-canine, half-human-looking thing towers over me. Its skin color shifts with each step, flickering from one background to the next—the gray wall behind it, the iron gate, the trees off to the side.

Camouflage. But it can't do anything to hide the elongated snout jutting from a bulbous face. Or the serrated teeth glistening and dripping with thick green saliva as it licks its chops, sniffing furiously at the air as it heads toward me.

I scramble back, and my spine smacks against the wall behind me, the space too narrow to gain any upper ground. The *creature* blocks my way back to the courtyard, so I spin on my heels and race for the iron gate—

A sharp-clawed hand wraps around my ankle and yanks me back, and my chin hits the pavement, the air *whooshing* out of my lungs. I flail, rolling to my back as I kick at the beast that's most certainly not a man or a dog.

Demon.

Fuck my life.

CHAPTER TWENTY

The beast growls and warm, thick spit sprays my chest as it hovers over me. Its massive maw pulls open, teeth gnashing as I throw my hands up to stop it from chomping at my neck. Its skin is rubbery and slick against my fingers, strong muscle flexing underneath as it snaps at my neck.

Panic claws up my spine. I lift my feet, trying like hell to kick it off, but my muscles, goddamn them, they are useless. All my strength focuses on stopping those rows of sharp teeth from tearing my throat open.

It roars, its huge, clawed hands shaking my shoulders, hitting my spine against the pavement over and over again. Trying to knock me out. To make me drop my grip on its neck.

Fuck, fuck, fuck!

I scream, rage and fear coiling together into one loud screech I hope to hell someone hears. I don't want to subject any of the innocent people in this apartment complex to this monster, but holy *hell*.

White-hot pain lances my shoulder as it digs its claws into my flesh, roaring right back in my face, but the pain sharpens my senses, cools my panic, and sets my rage on fire.

I can feel it burning beneath my skin—no, *outside* of my skin.

The demon yelps. Whimpers this sharp sound as smoke curls around my fingers. The smell of sulfur clogs my nose, the thing's skin giving under my grip in a way it hasn't before.

Another clawed hand swipes at my forearms, slashing my flesh.

I scream again, willing any strength I have left into the hold on its neck. I shove at it with all my might, all my anger, every ounce of hate I have in my blood. I use it to lash out, and something tears through me despite my weak muscles, despite the exhaustion begging me to lose consciousness and let this thing take me. A blazing heat, so hard and fast it burns and burns and—

An earsplitting wail threatens to burst my eardrums as the canine demon scrambles off me, its massive, muscular body hunching over as it claws at its own neck.

As it tries to smother the collar of black flames searing there.

I stumble backward, trying like hell to regain my footing to run. But I can't tear my eyes away from the sight, even as I manage to stand. Even as the demon's wails stop, its body going rigid and black until...

It dissolves into a pile of ash on the pavement.

My chest heaves, the wounds on my shoulder and neck pulse, but the heat on my fingertips? That makes me forget all about the blood gushing down my shoulder, about the spinning in my head that threatens to send me to the pavement again.

I forget everything outside my hands.

Because they're on fire.

Glittering *black* flames dance atop each fingertip like old friends winking in the night. A shimmering glow around the flames lights up the darkened passageway with flickers of midnight silver.

I gasp, my blood singing at the wonder in the flames—

My muscles shake, my entire body trembling like something is lassoing this newfound strength and yanking it back, back, back.

The fire winks out.

And I'm once again left in the darkness of the night. Perfect... so I channel my inner evil Captain Marvel and I can't control it for more than twenty seconds?

It takes me a solid five minutes to move again, but eventually I walk on shaky feet toward the iron gate, pushing through it until I'm on the crowded sidewalk lining the main street again.

"Harley?" Kai's voice sounds from my left, and I whirl toward the sound. He hops out of a cab that has barely slowed to the curb. "What the hell happened to you?"

I furrow my brow. "I thought we were meeting at Nathan's?" I ask like I'm not currently covered in my own blood.

Kai rips off his blue blazer, tossing it over me. "Traffic cleared, and this is on the way. I saw you and told the cab to pull over—" His eyes widen at the cuts on my shoulder and forearm. "We need to get you to a hospital. What the hell happened?" he asks in a panic as he motions me into the waiting cab.

"No hospital," I say. "I'm fine. Just take me to Nathan's. I can fix myself up." The last thing I need is to go to a hospital and have them test my blood or something. Who knows what they'd find?

"Harley—"

"It was just a stray dog," I lie through my teeth. "I got too close—"

"Jesus, Harley," Kai says, then gives the cab driver Nathan's address. "Why? Why does this stuff always happen to you?" he asks like it's my fault while still holding me against him. I don't have the energy to argue with him.

We make it to Nathan's, and Kai quickly hustles me into the bathroom without anyone noticing. I definitely don't want Ray to see me looking like I went ten rounds with Cujo.

I settle onto the side of the bathtub, wincing slightly as the move jostles my right arm.

Kai scrambles, searching through the cabinets beneath the sink, sighing as he pulls out a first aid kit. He kneels before me, gathering supplies from the kit and laying them out on the tiled floor.

He eyes me in question before he shifts my shirt at the shoulder, enough to expose the full length of the wound. "How big were its teeth?" he asks as he presses an alcohol-soaked piece of gauze to my skin.

I wince at the sting, but it quickly cools. "Big."

"Obviously," he huffs, hurrying to continue cleaning my wounds. He is surprisingly gentle and fast and before I know it, he's bandaged my shoulder and forearm with the precision of a first responder. A stray drop of my blood lingers on his index finger. He stares at it so long, I worry he'll puke all over Nathan's bathroom floor, but he blinks a few times and hurries to the sink. He quickly washes his hands.

"Thanks." I sigh with relief to have clean skin again. I shift my shirt back to cover the bandages as I look up at him. "Lucky you came along," I say. "I doubt I would've thought to hail a cab." I usually avoid them. Cabs are much more expensive than the train.

Kai barks out a laugh, shaking his head. "No, you would've bled out on the El." He shakes his head. "I'm beginning to think I need to stick to you like some detail on royalty. Be a bodyguard—"

"I managed fine alone," I argue. I certainly don't need him deciding to follow me around every waking second. Especially since I barely ventured out on my own tonight and another fucking demon tried to take a bite out of me.

Shit.

I have to hunt down Draven. I need answers, need to know how much danger I'm putting Ray in just by being with her. Is it only because I've been out in populated areas that something happens across my scent? Is it more contained here, in Nathan's house? Is there any form of safety or am I doomed to deal with this the rest of my life?

Ice-cold panic settles like a rock in my stomach.

"Clearly," Kai interrupts my thoughts, standing there staring down at me like he might haul me over his shoulder and lock me in a padded room just to keep me safe. "I don't…" He visibly swallows, tossing the empty bandage wrappers in the bin next to the sink. "I don't want what I said that night to push you away, Harley. If I could take back those words, I would. I don't want to lose you."

I push off the edge of the tub. So much has happened since that night, I'd almost forgotten his confession—that he feels more for me than I do for him.

"I don't want to lose you, either," I admit, my voice cracking.

"You won't."

"But, Kai, I want things to go back to the way they were *before*." In so many ways. Not only to when I never thought he would think of me that way but before I knew about…everything.

Demons.

My blood.

The dark flames that danced from my fingers earlier.

Kai's lips are a firm line, the disappointment in his eyes clear, but he doesn't say anything.

"I want my best *friend*. The boy who would stay up until two a.m. playing Betrayal with Ray and me because we couldn't sleep. The boy who held my hand when I was terrified to go on the Ferris wheel at Navy Pier but knew I had to because Ray wanted to ride it so badly." I fiddle with the bracelet on my wrist, Ray's colorful braid above it.

Kai forces out a breath, a muscle in his jaw ticking as his gaze lingers on Ray's gift so long, I fear he may be searching for the words to tell me he doesn't want to be friends anymore.

"I'm still that guy," he finally says. "I am. I messed up, in more ways than you realize," he adds as he looks up at the ceiling, and I furrow my brow. "But I want to make it right." He glances back down at me, his eyes *so* green in the near-blinding light of Nathan's bathroom. And the way he looks at me…

It should be easy to fall for him. He's handsome and caring and we have history. I should feel that ache in my heart for *him*. Not for a boy who gives me verbal whiplash and then constantly disappears on me. Kai is *here*. Kai shows up when I need him to, whether he knows it or not.

Kai reaches for my hand, his eyes gauging my reaction, and I nod. He grips my hand in his. The motion is effortless, normal, and no zing of electricity shocks my system like it did when Draven and I finally touched.

No, Kai's touch is comforting, protective even.

"Who gave you this?" he asks, eyeing the braid above my bracelet.

"Ray," I say. "My birthday present." I smile, glancing down at the colorful, thin string. Beyond relieved it didn't get torn in the attack.

"I like it," he says. "Much prettier than your other one."

I swallow hard. He's not wrong, but I can't help but shake my wrist, my sleeve coming down to cover the two bracelets. Some protective instinct in me wants to keep them all for myself.

"I know we don't have much time left," he says, his voice heavy, and I tilt my head.

He clears his throat, still staring at my hand. "Until we have to put on normal faces for the birthday celebration like you weren't nearly mauled by a wild dog," he hurries to say, his eyes flashing to mine. Kai wets his lips. "I'll take whatever pieces you're willing to give me, Harley. Just please don't shut me out for what I said. I have to...I *need* to be in your life."

I shift until I wrap my arms around his neck, resting my head on his shoulder like I've done a hundred times. This boy has spent a lifetime earning my trust, and I can't let one slip of the tongue ruin that. Besides, he'll realize soon enough that he deserves far better than I can ever possibly give him. One day, he'll see that.

He holds me for a few moments in the bathroom, and I sink into that normalcy, that comfort. The events of the past few days sit on the tip of my tongue—I want to tell him everything, but the fear for his safety slams a door over the words ready to fly from my mouth. That, and the worry he won't believe me.

Because who would believe demons—both good and evil—prowl our city, some of them desperate for my blood?

So I muster up the bravest and fakest mask I can. "Come on," I say. "Ray will be waiting for those birthday cookies."

"You sure you're good after—"

"A freak accident," I cut him off, jerking open the door. "Nothing I haven't dealt with before."

And will likely deal with again.

That truth haunts me like a dark cloud the entire night—throughout the joyful birthday celebration in Nathan's kitchen and well after Ray has fallen sound asleep in the bed in Nathan's guest room. It even follows me into my dreams, creating restless worlds of shadows and smoke and flames and ash, all burning and searing as if my soul itself is on fire.

ME: I need to talk to you.

I send the text the next morning after I peel back the bandages and find nothing but fresh skin where gaping wounds should be. I've always been a fast healer, but this? Whole other level.

ME: I was attacked again last night

I send *that* text a few hours later when Draven seems content to ignore me.

DRAVEN: Meet me in an hour.

He texts an address and tells me to meet him outside. After making sure Ray is good for the night, I don't wait one second before I hurry out of Nathan's and hop on the train.

The weight of the past few days crashes over me as I ride, so many thoughts racing in my mind that I feel dizzy.

The attacks.

The demons.

The idea that I'm not human.

And Draven.

Always Draven, his name pulsing like a beacon in my mind. Maybe it's a wicked coincidence, but my world started to crumble on its already unsteady foundation the minute he danced into my life.

The ache of an unfinished task taunts me, begging—no, *demanding*—answers. Some inner sensation eases knowing I'm headed toward him, like once I make it to him, everything will click back into place, make sense, settle.

But how? He's refused to answer me before, so why do I think now will be any different?

Maybe because you were attacked. Again.

Maybe I'm walking into another battle, seeking Draven out like this.

But that instinct roaring inside me? The one that feels as hot as the sun and as searing as a white-hot poker? It cools the minute I stop before the address he sent me. An ancient brick building downtown, one I've passed a dozen times before. I *swear* it was abandoned.

Now colored lights pulse from the cracked windows, a thumping base vibrating through the brick. I turn, stepping down the stairs that lead to the entrance, to a gleaming black door with a rose-gold insignia of a bridge that sits above an eye slat. I try the handle, and though the door doesn't give an inch, that pulsing something inside me swirls and tugs. Instead, I rap my knuckles against the door.

The slat slides open with a swish. A set of yellow eyes narrows on me before the slat swishes closed again.

I wait, contemplating trying one of the windows on the street level, but then a loud groan echoes, the door hauled open to reveal a tall, lithe woman with fur instead of skin. Those same cunning yellow eyes look me up and down as she holds the door open. My eyes widen as I realize a pair of cat ears sticks out on the top of her head amid her long golden hair that hangs in massive curls.

She's beautiful. Terrifying but beautiful.

"Well?" she hisses, waving her hand at me. "Are you coming in or would you prefer to stare at me all night?"

I school my features, forcing my mind to accept the sight as I pass her. She snatches my hand, and I nearly hit her with a palm strike before I see the stamp between her fingers. She presses the ink on the back of my hand before releasing me. "Enjoy," she says with a cackle as I hurry farther inside the building.

The stamp is in the shape of a bridge—the same as the insignia on the door—the ink a bright pink that shimmers beneath the pulsing lights hanging high above a massive dance floor. A square bar sits dead center, neon lights illuminating shelves upon shelves of glass bottles, the liquid inside varying from clear to amber to pink and green and blue. The place is packed, people writhing on the dance floor, the music loud and pulsing and hypnotic. A sparkling fog swirls around the floor, snaking through boots and stilettos and…hooves?

A club? Draven asked me to meet him at a club?

Does he want to recreate the night we first met? The notion almost makes me laugh, but I resist the music begging me to hit the floor. Instead, I hurry to claim an empty barstool, telling my fight-or-flight instinct to quieten as my eyes adjust to the pulsing lights—to who or what is really surrounding me.

Demons.

Hundreds of them scatter among the dancing crowd or line the bar. All shapes and sizes—some with horns, some with purple-scaled skin, some with tails, and some with feathers.

None of them glances my way. None of them acts suspicious of the human who has wandered into their club.

And I swallow down the certainty in my blood doing its best to scream the answer at me as to why.

Because you aren't a suspicious human. You're one of them.

That chant inside me demanding answers settles to a calm sort of feeling, loosening the tightness that's pricked my muscles since Draven bolted.

I'm in the right place *somehow*. I know it in my bones. A good place. The demons here? They aren't clambering over themselves, snapping teeth and claws to try and get me. In fact, they ignore me almost as much as everyone else does.

And besides, Draven wouldn't invite me to this club if it would put me in danger, right?

I scan the room a few more times, searching for Draven's eyes, then pull out my phone, sending him a quick text to let him know I'm here early before pocketing it again.

"Looking for someone?" a sensual masculine voice says from my right, and I jolt a bit at the male's sudden appearance. He wears a white button-down shirt and black slacks, human in body, but his face? All sharp angles, too beautiful to be human, his eyes a sapphire blue that matches the four horns poking from the brown hair atop his head. He swirls a red drink in his hand, the contents threatening to spill over the lip.

"I am, actually," I say, mustering confidence I don't feel into my tone.

"It looks as much," he says, his voice calm, charming even. "Lucky for you I know everyone who steps foot inside this club."

"Do you own it?" I ask, my muscles relaxing, my mind fuzzing at the edges. I haven't taken a drink, but it *feels* like I have. Maybe those instincts telling me this place is safe are also calming my usual anxiety. I sigh at how wonderful the relief feels, the near-constant panic I've had practically my whole life just evaporating.

"Not exactly," he says, shifting closer. He smells sweet—like the red-flavored syrup on shaved ice. "Who is it you're looking for?" he asks, the warmth from his body a welcome delight as he draws closer.

"Draven." His name slides off my tongue slowly, like honey dripping off a spoon.

I blink, my eyes heavy.

"Ah, I know Draven," the man says. "He's in the back."

My heart soars at the notion, but I can't get my legs to hop off the barstool like I want.

"Let me take you to him," he says, and I nod, finally able to move after he has. He leads the way through the crowded dance floor, weaving in and out of the gyrating bodies. I'm suddenly *desperate* to dance. I must tug my hand—which has somehow wound up in his—in that direction because he coos, "Later, pet," and hooks his arm through mine.

"Where are we going?" I ask, my thoughts drenched in that too-sweet syrup.

"I'm taking you to Draven," he says.

Oh, right. "Thank you."

"My pleasure." He stops before a door at the back of the club and swings it open, motioning me inside.

"It's dark," I say but step inside anyway. If Draven is here, then that's where I need to be. Something tickles the back of my mind, but I catch that syrupy scent again and the feeling disappears.

"Here," he says from behind me.

A shimmering blue light illuminates the room. Black leather couches line the wall opposite where I stand, a few chairs of the same kind scattered about, and a smaller bar hugs the wall to the right. The door snicks shut behind me, and I manage to slowly turn around.

"Draven's not here," I say, my tongue thick, heavy.

The man smirks, his lips pulling back to expose rows and rows of razor-sharp teeth that *totally* weren't there a second ago. "No, I'm afraid not," he says.

I back away as he approaches, my legs like lead. "Is he going to meet us here?"

The man laughs, his eyes trailing down to my throat. "Oh, I certainly hope not, pet."

"But you sa—"

The man snaps his hand out with a speed my eyes can't follow. He ensnares my wrist and hauls my back against his chest. I struggle to break his grasp, my movements slow and sluggish as I look up at him over my shoulder. "What are you doing?" I slur, somehow shocked by his sudden shift in mood. Why? Why am I surprised—

He opens his mouth, razor-sharp teeth gleaming in the blue light.

"You're allowed to scream now, pet," he says, as if he has the power to tell me what to do. "No one will hear you back here. And it makes your blood so much sweeter."

CHAPTER TWENTY-TWO

I scream.

But not because he told me to.

No, the minute his teeth graze the edge of my neck, the world snaps into a sharp, brutal focus.

Anger and rage—both at myself for the stupidity of coming here and at the demon for believing he has the right to do this to me—sear like acid in my chest. The syrupy fog that slows my judgment and mind vanishes, the situation crystalizing before me in a cold reality.

The music thrumming beyond the walls of the room swallows my scream, so I stop.

No one will hear me.

No one is coming to save me.

I have a choice—give up or fight back. Just relax into his hold—or reach deep inside me and latch on to that well of anger that never quite disappears and unleash it on this demon for doing whatever he did to my mind.

Faster than I think possible, I spin in his embrace and dart my forearm between us, hard enough to snap his jaw shut before he can sink those glistening teeth into my neck. He grumbles, but I don't let his irritation slow me down as I pivot underneath him.

He didn't anticipate me fighting back. *That* much is clear from the shock in his eyes as I manage to hit him with a right hook that sends him whirling. His head bounces like a basketball off the wall, and he roars through gritted teeth, loud enough to shake the room.

My muscles tremble, but I launch for the door. My fingers are slick against the iron handle—

I fly backward, my stomach smacking against the floor as he yanks on my ankles, dragging me back to him. I claw at the floor, but he flips me onto my back, and true terror licks up my spine at the weight of him on top of me. Suffocating, powerless. I claw at his face, tearing three lines of skin from his left cheek. He bats away my second attempt, and it feels like an anvil pins me to the ground.

He secures my wrists with one hand, his grip like a vise as he uses his free one to wipe at the dark-blue blood leaking from where I scratched him.

"How'd you break my hold, bitch?"

"No more '*pet*'?" I seethe, baring my own teeth like some sort of trapped, feral animal. Maybe I am. Because I feel exactly like that—something building, writhing, *burning* beneath my skin. I felt it yesterday at the apartment complex with the beast-man-thing…

Only this time, I'm not afraid of it.

He smirks, trailing one finger down my jawline. I recoil from the touch. "Oh, I'm definitely going to make you my pet," he croons. "Pity," he continues, leaning closer to my face. His weight is crushing. "I had planned to kill you quickly. You should've played nice."

"Because you certainly are." I choke out each word.

I flail and fight and push and pull, but I'm no match for his strength.

Weak.

"Get up!" My father screams as he kicks me in the stomach over and over again. I curl into a ball in an attempt to block another kick. "You're so weak!" he yells. "You've always been weak. Worthless." Another kick, this one to my head. "No one will ever love you. Ever think you're worth the trouble that follows you like a dark cloud."

Stars burst along my vision, the room blurring.

"Maybe you should let me do that," Kai says, stopping me as I reach for a heavy box in the deli. "Wouldn't want you to tip over," he jokes, but the words hurt like hell. My own best friend thinks I'm incapable of holding my own.

Heat surges in my blood, my body roaring at me to fight. To do something as the demon drags a pointy nail along the inside of my forearm.

"You should smile more," my ex-coworker says. He grins at me like he would a child, as if I need a demonstration on how to be pretty.

The demon's sticky, rough tongue drags along the slash he makes in my arm. He growls. "What *are* you?" His sapphire eyes roll back in his head.

"Know your place, Harley," Dad says, my cheek stinging from the backhand he delivered. "You don't get to question me. Ever." He raises his hand again, and I flinch.

"What are you? What are you?" The demon repeats the question over and over again as he laps at the blood welling on my arm.

Angry.

I'm fucking angry.

At the world.

At my father for keeping his boot on my chest.

At my friend for thinking he knows what is best for me without any regard for my own desires.

At Draven for avoiding me and not giving me answers.

At all the men who decided I'm just a girl who doesn't have or *need* any choices. At this demon, who feels entitled to my body, my blood, just because he views me as weak. Lesser.

Not today.

The decision not to die—*again*—clangs through me like a bucket dropping in a well. The determination and rage bursting through some inner barrier causes heat to swirl and swell to the point of searing.

Sweat beads along my skin, the droplets stinging the cut on my arm before something seals the pain and shifts solely to…power.

And then the demon screams, a keening sort of wail that rattles my skull.

The smell of seared flesh—like the burned pork shoulder ends

Nathan sometimes serves as a special at the deli—clogs my nostrils. The demon scrambles off me. Sweet, beautiful air fills my lungs in great gulps, clearing my mind, sharpening my focus, my senses.

There, right next to my usual flight-or-fight instinct, writhes the same sensation from last night.

And this time, I grin at the pulsing anger that manifests as black flames on the tips of my fingers. Glittering obsidian with flecks of silver flicker as I manage to get my feet underneath me, my eyes wide with awe as I stare at the flames dancing on my fingertips.

The demon backs away, howling as he bares his teeth. "You have the dark flame."

I cock a brow at him, my blood flooding with power, with a strength I've never known. I can *taste* the fear rippling off him— tangy and slick on the back of my tongue. I step closer, my head soaring with the way he flinches.

Flinches. Because of *me*.

"How does it feel?" I seethe, drawing closer, the fire on my fingers pulsing. "To be scared?"

He growls. "I'll shred you and collect your blood in bottles, bitch." He slices those sharp nails through the air, their tips slashing my cheek as he backhands me.

I suck my teeth, righting myself as I raise my flaming fists. His eyes flare with panic at the sight of my dark fire. "Doubt it," I snap right back.

He lashes out again, this time tearing at my other arm, but the move costs him. I wrap my flaming hands around his throat and squeeze.

I grip him so hard, he can't scream.

So firm only a silent, gaping gurgle rattles from his lips as he tries desperately to pry my hands from his sizzling flesh.

He can't.

Just like the beast-thing couldn't.

Neither a match for the strength of the fire.

Stop.

Some voice in the back of my head warns, soft and soothing. "Harley." Someone calls my name.

But I ignore it and squeeze harder. Squeeze until my fingers push through sticky, melted flesh and interlock—the demon's eyes flying wide before he bursts into a glittering pile of ash that dusts my boots.

My chest heaves as the roaring in my ears slowly dies.

"Harley?"

I spin around at the sound of Draven's voice, the tone slicing through the flames.

He gapes at me from the open doorway, his eyes glowing from the black-and-silver fire still crackling on my fingertips. He takes a step toward me, then another, as if he approaches a wild animal.

I stare at my hands—beneath the flames, my fingers are drenched in dark-blue blood.

The demon's blood.

My stomach rolls, acid clawing up my throat, and an icy wave douses my insides, the heat in my body ebbing as the flames flicker out.

"I killed him." I spit the words as tears bite the backs of my eyes. "I killed him," I say again as I watch that demon die by my hands over and over and over in my mind.

"You had to," Draven says. "He would've drained you without a second thought."

"He almost *did*," I say. "But that doesn't mean…" I shut my eyes, the clarity of hindsight wrecking my brain. "I could've run. I could've stopped him and then run—"

"You could've not been back here in the first place," Draven snaps, and I flinch.

"You told me to meet you here—"

"I told you to meet me outside!" He runs a hand through his hair. "Not venture into a demon nightclub without protection."

"Clearly I don't need a ton of protection," I challenge, despite my stomach still rolling from what I just did.

I pace toward the door of the room, all at once wanting to

bolt but not having the power to take that step away from him. Now that I found him, that aching, pulsing chain in my soul has gone taut.

"I told you to stay away from me," he says as if that explains away my current ailment.

"And I told you that's bullshit."

He narrows his gaze, extending his strong arms to encompass the room. "Don't you get it?" he asks. "Don't you see what my world will do to you?"

"Obviously it's *my* world, too." The truth hits me like a sledgehammer to the chest.

I denied it before, my weak body allowing me an excuse to pretend like my ability to see demons was just a fluke, that I wasn't some supernatural creature.

But now? After the fire has saved me twice? The same soft roaring I can feel prickling just beneath my skin? I can't deny it. And something in me dies at the loss of normal, despite how dark it's been—it's been *mine*.

Now I don't have a clue who or what I'm supposed to be.

Draven's eyes fall to my fingers as he reaches for me, his hand hovering over mine enough for me to feel his heat but not enough to graze my skin. "How many times have you summoned the flames?"

I roll my eyes. "Oh, dozens of times. It's a hidden talent, of course. A fun party trick for all my friends."

Draven cocks a brow at my sarcasm, but a hint of a smile dances at the corners of his mouth.

"First time was last night," I relent. "When this dog-beast-looking thing came after me at the apartment complex."

"Your birthday," he whispers, a shudder racking his body. "A Cannis," he continues. "Nasty half-breed. Intelligent to a degree, but mainly they give in to their baser instincts."

"Which equated to smell me and kill me." I swallow hard. "It seems to be trending," I add, glancing down at the pile of ash.

Draven rakes his hands through his dark curls, the motion

so natural, it makes me blink a few times. God, how can he be this gorgeous, even when he's clearly irritated with me? His black T-shirt hugs his muscled chest, and a pair of black jeans tucked into even darker boots completes his *fuck-off* look. And then there's that smell, somehow magnified in this room—cedar and amber and citrus. Intoxicating in an entirely new way.

"You need to explain everything to me," I force out, somehow managing to focus on what is important.

"Why me?" His voice is rough, tight. "Anka could—"

"I want you," I say as heat blazes on my cheeks. "I mean," I continue, scrambling, "I need you." I squeeze my eyes shut, shaking my head. God, this is mortifying. "I managed to punch some answers out of her," I say, finally recovering. "But she was very clear that there are answers only you have."

Draven drags his palms over his face, and I step closer to him, the heat from his body buzzing between us. He drops his hands but doesn't back away. His golden eyes are liquid as he gazes down at me, his fingers moving to hover just over my jawline.

"Are you saying you're here to *beat* the answers out of me?" There is a hint of humor in his voice, right next to a great deal of challenge and mischief. That same confident and yet wrecked tone I've grown used to since he entered my life. The same infuriating yet enticing sharpness I haven't been able to stop craving since he first opened his mouth.

"If that's what it takes," I say, holding out my arms to either side of me. I can feel the heat sizzling in my blood, the tiny trail of fire begging for release, just as easily as I can feel that invisible *something* holding it back. Is it my own fear? My own lack of understanding, like Coach Hale mentioned?

"As inviting as sparring with you sounds, Harley," he says, arching a brow at me, "I'm not ready to kill you just yet."

"It appears you'll have to wait in line." I laugh, a dark sound.

"But what if I was here first?" He narrows his gaze.

And damn it, that sizzle turns to a full-on *roar* as I hold his gaze, as I don't dare back away from that challenge.

He groans at my obvious lack of fear, and something breaks in his eyes.

I reach upward, my heart thundering in my chest, a plea to get closer, closer, closer. Like an insect drawn to the pretty blue light, I can't stop wanting to cross that threat of danger he clearly draws between us. I want to feel the sting, *his* sting, more than any other.

He doesn't move away.

Doesn't lose my gaze.

"Honey badger," he whispers, his breath warm on my face.

"Why do you call me that?"

"They're fearless. Recklessly so," he murmurs. "But amazingly strong. Like you."

Some coiled part of me goes tight and loose at the same time.

"Maybe I like feeling like this," I say, an inch from his mouth.

"Like what?"

"Alive," I admit, pulse soaring the closer our bodies are.

"Will you say the same thing if I hold a knife to your throat?" he challenges, his lips grazing mine with a featherlight touch that makes warmth dance over my skin.

"Are you saying touching you will make me bleed?"

"Eventually," he growls, and his eyes shutter as he stares into mine.

So many shades of gold swirl in his irises—honeys and metallics and deeper hues.

"Do your worst," I say, his scent filling my head, making it spin almost as much as it did with the demon earlier. Only this time, I'm fully aware it's my own cravings, my own desires shaking me to the core—

His lips crush against mine, not gently, not timidly. No, he claims my mouth with all the power and hunger that radiates from his skin. He cups my face in his hands, slanting his mouth over mine. Again and again. Drinking me in, devouring my kiss like he can't survive without it.

More, more, more.

I need more. I fist his shirt, yanking him closer, giving back everything he delivers, relishing the bite at my bottom lip as he presses me against the wall. Danger and desire soar, stealing the breath from my lungs as we crash together.

That taut chain inside me ignites, flames swirling around it in powerful spirals. I don't know if that internal flame is trying to protect me from him or bind him to me, but either way, it feels so. Damn. Good.

The searing mounts inside, threatening to burn us both to ash.

But I don't stop.

Can't stop.

And he doesn't, either.

"**O**h, god*damn* it," Draven growls and rips out of our embrace, taking my breath along with him. "I can't—"

"Don't you *dare* run away again," I snap, reading the flight instinct in his eyes. "I still need answers—"

"You seem hell-bent on avoiding getting them," he argues.

I glare at him, watching as he takes another step away from me, hands sliding effortlessly into his pockets.

"Didn't hear you complaining a second ago," I say, darting my tongue out to wet my lips, where I can still taste him. And that quickly, I want *more* again, but I shoot down the need and focus. I point toward the pile of ash. "I'm pretty sure I'm in just as much, if not *more* danger when you're gone."

A harsh, dark laugh. "I suppose I can't argue that. But this"— he motions between us—"can't. Happen."

I swallow hard, rejection a bitter taste on my tongue, but remind myself he sure as hell didn't kiss like he wanted nothing to do with me.

In truth, I don't need this complication, either—this insatiable need for him. I have so much more to deal with. The last thing I need is…whatever *this* is.

I steel my spine, nodding. "Fine. Just don't disappear again. I'd rather not *guess* at why suddenly everything wants to eat me."

"Fair enough," he says. "But promise me you won't go looking for trouble on your own instead."

"I wasn't looking for trouble," I say. "I've been looking for *you*."

He cocks a brow at me as if to say there is no difference between the two.

I roll my eyes. "A promise for a promise?"

"I can't promise I won't have to leave again," he says. "But I promise I won't leave without letting you know first."

Well, that's something.

"Fine," I say. "I won't be the one to act on whatever it is between us—and you won't leave me to figure out this other mess on my own. Deal."

He opens his mouth like he wants to argue the wording of my first point but then nods. We just stand there staring at each other, not knowing where to go from here, as the music filtering from the still-open door fills the space between us.

"Why did you want to meet here?" I finally ask.

"This is the place to be if you're looking for information."

"In a supernatural nightclub?"

"The Bridge has been the perfect source of valuable information for centuries."

"The Bridge?" I scoff.

"What?" Draven tilts his head.

"Shouldn't a supernatural nightclub have a cooler name?"

"Such as?"

I open and close my mouth a few times. "I don't know," I say. "Like Mordor's or Wolfsbane or something."

Draven bites back a laugh. "So you read fantasy and paranormal along with your astral projection and meditation books?"

I smile. "Maybe."

"Well, I hate to be the bearer of bad news, but nothing in the real world is as black-and-white as those books."

A cold shiver runs down my spine. "There's so much I don't understand." Like why my blood is different, why everyone seems to want it, and why black fire shoots out of my fingertips like the most natural defensive mechanism in the world. The questions are endless, and Draven holds up a hand as if he can read them in my eyes.

"This isn't the place," he explains. "There are too many gossip-hungry demons waiting to spread something juicy."

I raise my brows. "Am I that kind of news?"

"Maybe," he says. "I'm just glad I found you when I did." He fishes his phone from his pocket. "There are rules," he says as he dials a number. "For this club. And you've broken at least four of them."

"It's not like I was handed a rule book at the front door!"

He holds the phone to his ear, a crooked smile shaping his lips. "Where would the fun be in that?"

Fun? Fighting for my life? Killing a demon? Is that his idea of a good time?

From the adrenaline crackling in my veins, is it *my* idea of a good time? God, I don't know who to trust or what to think anymore.

"Kazuki," he says, pacing. "Draven. Yes, we've had a little incident." A pause. "Chicago. Yes, I know the rules. She doesn't—" His eyes flare at whatever this Kazuki person says on the other end of the line. "No. No one saw. Back room. Yes, the blue one." A muscle in his jaw ticks. "Have I *ever* been able to guarantee that?" He nods at something the other person says. "Understood. We'll be here."

Draven hangs up the phone, and I wait for him to deliver some sort of supernatural sentence.

"We have to wait for the club's owner," he says. "I'm sure Kazuki just wants to give us a little lecture—"

"Wait," I say. "That's it?"

Draven grins. "Were you expecting a jury of Hypnos to pass judgment?"

I furrow my brow. "Did you just say hippos?"

"Hyp-nos." He annunciates the word before glancing at the pile of ash in the corner. "That's his breed. They have incredible thrall powers. Usually once a victim is under their hypnosis, they're unable to snap out of it. They can get them to do whatever they want them to do—dance to their death, leap off skyscrapers. Some turn their victims into blissfully ignorant slaves." His eyes scan the

length of my body. "Not surprised you broke the hold."

"Why?"

"Even the honey badger withstands the venom of the world's most deadly serpents," he says, humor coloring his tone. "And yet science marvels at how unexplainable this resistance is."

I give him a side-eye. "You keep comparing me to a honey badger. Are you saying—" My eyes flare wide. "Omigod, am I some sort of twisted half-breed—"

Draven's laugh, full and booming, breaks across my panicked words.

"Of course not, Harley. There are no known honey badger half-breed demons that I'm aware of. I'm merely making a comparison—"

"To a *honey badger*?" I cross my arms. "Seriously?"

He shrugs, those hands still secured in his pockets. Like he's scared of what he'll do with them otherwise, and warmth dances along my spine at the thought, but I force it down.

"Do you deny your innate ability to face situations head-on that most would flee from, *honey badger*?" He takes a step closer to me, his voice a caress around the nickname I'm suddenly in love with. The way he shapes the words has everything in my nervous system firing up again—sharp sparks of heat that make my legs tremble.

"No," I whisper.

And I can't deny it. My whole life I've run into danger instead of away from it, but that's because of my father, what he conditioned me to do. I would much rather it be me than anyone else getting hurt.

Draven's lips soften, all the mischief dropping from his face as he shakes his head. "You think so little of your own life," he says, and I glare at him. There is no way he can read me that well. No. Fucking. Way.

"How long are we going to wait for—"

The blue wall to our left *moves*, effectively squashing my words.

An invisible door swings open and fills the room with the loud bass of music that thumped against the walls moments ago. Something in the room shifts, some atmospheric pressure practically buzzes, as a man saunters into the room.

Tall, with broad shoulders, yet lithe in an almost feline way. He wears a suit of deepest green, his hair sleek and black, and a neatly trimmed beard lines a wide, strong jaw. He grips an ebony cane between his fingers, an emerald the size of an egg, smoothed to a polish, resting atop it. The steel tip clanks against the marble floor as he stops before us.

And behind him follows another male, this one a few inches taller, his skin golden dark like Draven's, with eyes of liquid silver. They shimmer like a light flickers behind them and—

Wings.

He has obsidian-colored wings, thousands of feathers flaring out behind him like blots of ink, but he keeps them relaxed even though they almost touch the opposite walls with their expanse.

The man in green taps his cane against the floor and the wall seals shut, the blaring music muting once again.

"Cassiel?" Draven growls, and I instinctively take a step back as Draven stops an inch shy of the two.

Power crackles in the room. I can taste it on my tongue, feel it in my bones. The breath halts in my lungs as the winged one— Cassiel—and Draven stare each other down. The man in green watches the silent exchange with a feline smile on his lips.

"Draven," Cassiel says, his silver eyes narrowing as they glance from Draven to me and back again. "Looks like your plans... changed." He tilts his head, a predator sizing up prey. "And you've gotten yourself in a bind again. I'm sad to say I'm not surprised."

My hands curl into fists at my sides, instincts flooding my body to prep for a brawl.

"Quite," the man in green says, his cane poised between his feet as he leans slightly against it. His eyes are the shade of light lavender, the color so starkly bright in the room as he glances to the pile of ash in the corner. "You know the rules, Judge—"

"It was me," I say before he can continue. No way in hell is Draven getting in trouble because of a choice *I* made.

All three of the men turn their gazes on me.

And damn it, my knees *shake*. The three of them, the power radiating from their muscular bodies, the distinctive gorgeous qualities, the cunning and ancientness about them…they practically suck all the air from the room.

But something stirs in my blood. A swirl of power, the same one that defended me moments ago. It writhes in their presence. An answer to a silent challenge. I can feel it there, itching for escape.

The man in green steps out of the trio, sliding up to my side. He inhales deeply. "Anka told me about you," he says as he circles me. "I thought you'd be more…"

I glare at him as he stops in front of me.

"Well-fed," he finishes.

I resist the urge to laugh. That makes two of us.

"How did a tiny little thing like yourself manage to vanquish a Hypno?" he asks.

Cassiel arches a dark brow at Draven, who dips his chin in answer.

"I don't know," I answer honestly. "He attacked me. I chose not to die."

The man in green turns to smirk at Cassiel, whose feathers ruffle as he tries not to laugh.

"Fascinating," he says.

"What are you doing with Kazuki?" Draven asks Cassiel. "Catching up on old times?"

"*You're* Kazuki," I say, eyes widening at the owner of the demon nightclub.

He takes a dramatic bow before righting himself. "Myth *and* legend, darling."

"It's a long story." Cassiel answers Draven's question, and I finally notice the ease in which Draven stands at the winged male's side. Arms loose, a half smile tugging at his lips. He trusts him.

"The Hypno broke the rules first, Kaz," Draven says.

"Oh, I have no doubt." Kazuki winks at me, his eyes lined in a dark green that matches his suit. "They're nasty little creatures," he continues. "But I don't discriminate. Anyone who seeks The Bridge's offerings may partake. When they break the rules…" His eyes narrow on me. "All bets are off."

Again, that power writhes in my blood, the sensation so new and confusing that I can barely stand up straight.

All three of them tense, shifting their stances ever so slightly as if I might combust at any second.

God, am I capable of that? The fear is enough to yank back the fire in my blood.

"I'll atone for the mistake and accept the punishment meant for her," Draven says.

Cassiel and I are mirror images as we both stare at him.

"No way!" I snap, and Kazuki raises his brows as he glances between us. "*I* did it. I broke your rules."

Kazuki tilts his head. "You would take the punishment? Though he offers? You don't even know what I'd sentence." His eyes glitter, and a chill skates along my skin. "I've been known to be very…*creative* in my punishments."

Cassiel hisses. Draven flinches.

Me? I don't even blink. I have zero doubts about the power Kazuki radiates or what he's capable of. But it doesn't change things.

"Yes." I answer without hesitation. "I'm responsible for this. No one else."

CHAPTER
TWENTY-FOUR

K azuki points at me while turning toward Draven. "I like her. She's got *spark*," he says and laughs.

Cassiel rolls his eyes, his wings extending outward another few inches.

Draven shakes his head. "What's it going to be, Kazuki?"

He spins his cane in his hand, his lips pursed. "I suppose I could ask you two sexy beasts to spar," he says, a devious grin shaping his lips. *"Shirtless."* He clanks the cane against the floor. "I can have oil here in a snap."

I smirk at him, unable to withhold a laugh of my own.

Draven flashes me a chiding look, but I merely shrug. Maybe I'm not human, but I can certainly appreciate Kazuki's imagination. Who *wouldn't* want to see Draven shirtless?

"Keep dreaming, sorcerer," Cassiel all but growls, the deep, primal tone firing up all my protective instincts again—as if his voice alone is a weapon that can slice me in half if he wishes it.

Kazuki kisses the air in Cassiel's direction. "Fine," he says. "I'll let you off with an official warning. Don't do it again and all that. How dreadfully *boring*," he nearly whines.

"The night is still young," Draven says, his voice light, almost playful. "I'm sure you'll round up some entertainment—"

"You've got that right," a screechy voice says from the doorway on the other side of the room.

I barely have time to turn and seek out the source before Draven is in front of me, herding me backward without touching me. I peek over his shoulder to see why.

Not one or two but *three* Hypnos stand in the doorway—

distinctive in the way the other was, all hooded eyes, slick features, and four horns glistening through their hair. Each of them seethes as they push into the room and seal the door behind them.

"Which one of you killed him?" the one in the middle growls.

Cassiel's wings flare outward, blocking me—and the blue blood on my hands—from sight.

"Oh, you've got it all wrong," Kazuki says, his fingers tight on his cane. "Pain games are in the red rooms."

"We felt it," the one on the left says, ignoring Kazuki completely. "We know someone in here shed our kin's blood. Blood for blood is *due*."

I part my lips, but Kazuki stops my confession with a raise of his hand. "I have the culprit at hand," he says. "And I've ruled it as self-defense."

A succession of snarls erupts, and suddenly the room feels ten times more crowded.

The shadows seem to peel from the corners of the room and slither around Draven, their cool forms closing in around me, too.

"Pussy," one snaps.

Kazuki takes two graceful steps toward the three, those lavender eyes searing. "You mean the chalice of all life?" He scoffs. "If you're going to be bold enough to insult me in my own establishment, *do* try to be more clever."

Cassiel coughs a laugh.

I'm not sure Draven is breathing.

And all I can do is stand there and try not to faint—there is *that* much power flying around the room.

A blink, and the three lunge for Kazuki. He taps his cane on the floor, and they fly past him as *dust*. Black joins the pile I already established in the corner.

The shadows lift, and blue light illuminates the room once again.

Cassiel tucks in his wings, and Kazuki swipes at some stray dust on his immaculate suit.

"Shame," he says, flicking his wrist as if he's swatting away a fly. "I bet they left an enormous tab behind."

Draven laughs, the sound soothing along my frayed nerves.

Kazuki's gaze meets mine, then flashes to Draven's. "They weren't wrong," he says. "The breed can scent the kill of their kind. More will come for her."

Great, like I don't have enough demons lining up to slaughter me.

"But you knew that already, Draven," he says, drawing out his name. "Didn't you?"

Draven nods. "Kazuki," he says, his voice lower, almost imploring as he turns to the sorcerer. "Harley needs answers. I don't have all of them—"

"And you think I do?" Kazuki cuts him off. "How *flattering*." He glances at me, raising his brows at Draven. "Want me to take a peek?"

Draven turns to me, eyes wary. "Kazuki is an incredibly powerful sorcerer. He can slip into your mind, your blood, and read it. Listen. Look for the truth."

I swallow hard, mentally constructing a steel wall around my brain as if that can somehow keep him out.

"If he sees something of importance, we might be able to understand why every demon within a mile radius of you is trying to kill you."

Cassiel clears his throat, casting a confused glance at Draven.

"Without any *doubt*," Draven adds, his eyes silently combating Cassiel.

"I need permission," Kazuki says, and I relax a fraction. "I don't enter where I'm not wanted unless lives are at stake."

"Mine is," I answer, shaking my head. "And I have people who depend on me. Important to me." Ray firstly, Kai secondly, not that he depends on me really, but I'm certain he'll be upset if I die. I inwardly sigh. "Do what you have to."

Kazuki steps toward me, and I retreat, his powerful gait eating up the space in the room until the backs of my knees hit the leather sofa. I sink onto it, and he follows, unbuttoning his suit jacket as he settles next to me. He rests the cane across his lap, raising his hands to either side of my face, his nails a polished glittering blue.

"Close your eyes," he says, his voice soft as silk.

I spare a glance to Draven, who stands next to Cassiel, some battle raging in his eyes, his muscles taut like they might snap at any minute. I slowly close my eyes, black filling the space behind my lids.

"Relax," Kazuki coos. "Feel me there?"

A small pressure nudges against my mind, the sensation like being lightly tapped on the shoulder when you think you're alone in the room. I nod in answer, suddenly unable to work my voice.

The pressure intensifies, and the fire in my blood prickles at the intrusion—consensual or not.

"Easy," he warns. "This is my favorite suit. If you scorch it, I'll be rather put out."

I swallow hard, doing my best to relax those instincts thrashing inside me.

Flashes burst behind my lids—images and memories swirling and shifting as quickly as they come.

Me as a child. Can't be older than three. Sitting in the middle of our threadbare carpet, crying, screaming. My father yelling at me from the kitchen to shut my mouth.

My mother, her red hair framing her face. She leans down and secures the bracelet on my wrist, repeating over and over again to never take it off. To let the wish do the work. Tears streaming down her cheeks as she rushes out the door.

My heart clenches, but the pressure mounts.

Fire, blazing and hot and all-consuming. It fills every corner of the jagged pieces of my soul. The dark flames dance there, swirl around those jagged edges as if they can put me back together.

Wetness tickles my cheeks, and the image changes.

The back of a man, tall, lithe, dressed in all black. He stands in an empty room that looks like it's carved from obsidian. He holds a crystal glass with amber liquid in it. He shifts as if to turn and look at me—

My chest tightens, stomach bottoming out.

Blood leaks from a wound on my wrist. It splatters the walls of my home, of our shared room. Peppers all the artwork Ray has worked on so tirelessly. Marring it. Dirtying it. Ruining it. All those images of Marid laugh. *Laugh and move as he walks through the papers on the wall, swiping at the blots of blood with his fingers.*

My entire body trembles; I can sense myself shaking against that leather sofa, but my mind…it feels so far away.

A rippling mound of earth, dirt and grass churning and cracking, spreading into a wide, gaping black pit. Clawed hands glistening with blood grip the edges of the earth. Snakes, hundreds of black snakes slithering over the lip of the dirt—

"Kazuki." A warning word from Draven, but it sounds like he's calling from the end of a long tunnel. "That's enough," he growls.

Darkness swirls around me until it becomes a living, breathing thing hell-bent on suffocating me. I feel the mass, pushing and pressing against me. Heavy and thick like dirt on a coffin. I mentally snap my fingers, a lone flame of midnight and silver glowing just enough to light the space before me…where I stand in an endless stream of darkness.

The air shifts before me, the figure of a man taking shape, but his skin…that isn't skin. It's snakes. *Hundreds…*thousands *of black snakes slithering over one another to create the body, his face. His eyes and mouth endless black pits.*

"I see you." The voice is a hiss and a growl. "I see you, Key—"

"Kazuki!" Draven snaps, and I'm shoved over the lip of the edge in that darkness.

Free fall down that terrible night, away from that horrifying thing—

"Harley." Draven's voice is softer, coaxing. "Open your eyes."

I do, slowly blinking away a heavy fog like I've been asleep for days.

But Kazuki sits next to me, lavender eyes wide and concerned as he shifts off the couch and straightens his suit jacket. "You didn't tell me she has the dark flame," he whispers.

"What does that mean? What did all of *that* mean?" I ask, standing on wobbly feet. The memories, the visions...they cling to my lungs like I inhaled sand.

Kazuki glances to Draven and they lock gazes, holding some damn silent conversation I can't follow. "You saw what I did, Judge?" he asks, and I turn to Draven.

He dips his head, visibly swallowing.

Kazuki returns focus to me. "Those are pieces of your soul," he says as casually as if he's explaining the plot of a movie. "I can't control what we see, only what the soul presents of itself. Those things you saw are pieces of *you*."

I tremble—the blood splatter, the darkness, the man in the black room—

"Not *all* of you," Draven hurries to add, but I can barely hear past my own spiraling panic.

"What does that mean?" I ask, slightly frantic. "That creature, Kazuki..." I shake my head. "He said he could see me. Who is he? Am I supposed to let him come after me? Let them kill me?" *All that blood and darkness from my soul.* "Is the world better off—"

"No," Draven says sharply, and Cassiel's wings rustle behind him as he steps next to his friend.

"It means you're ancient," Kazuki says, eyes scanning the length of my body. "Something the world has been anticipating for as long as I can remember." He grins like a cat who's just caught a mouse. "And I have a vast memory." He tilts his head as if he's playing out a hundred different scenarios in his mind. "More are coming for you," he says a bit reluctantly. "Not just the Hypnos because of the kill, but others. Your coming of age and powers surfacing may as well have shot a beacon into the sky announcing your arrival."

"The snake guy," I say. "Who. Is. He."

Kazuki glances to Draven, then back to me. "Marid." He says the name, and I about lose my shit. "One of the most feared greater demons this world has ever known. A Serpent Whisperer. His powers are endless—"

"He's locked in Hell." Draven crosses his arms. "He can't come after her."

"Marid has Minions spread over all the planes, Judge," Kazuki says. "You *know* that. His network is intricate; the ability to penetrate the minds across planes is his livelihood. There is no telling how many he has constantly working for him. And now that *she's* surfaced?" Those lavender eyes cut to mine. "He'll stop at nothing until…"

I glance at the three of them, eyes widening. "Until what?"

Kazuki tilts his head left then right, spinning his cane in his hand. "Until you free him."

My lips part open, a silent cry choking the sound from my voice. "I won't—"

"No," Kazuki says. "Of course you won't. But his spies? They will stop at nothing to use you to set him free."

"How?" I ask at the same time Draven says, "The demons before, they mentioned his Second. That's who's sending everything after her. If we can track down who it is, we can stop Marid's network?"

Kazuki purses his lips. "I can't see who that is, but I can feel the power." He cranes his head to the side. "It's bigger than those who've already tested her. It's controlling them somehow, the lower-level demons," he says, his eyes distant like he's seeing into a misty future. "Find the Second," he continues, "and you should be able to cut off Marid's main ties to this realm."

I rake my palms over my eyes, swiping at the tears that stained my cheeks when Kazuki exposed those pieces of my soul.

And Marid. A tremble racks my body as if his snakes slither in the crevices of my mind.

"We need time," Draven says. "To hunt. Kaz…" His voice trails off, a silent question in his eyes.

The sorcerer raises his brows. "You know that comes with a price—"

"I'll pay it," Draven says, and Cassiel flinches behind him, as though Draven just promised his soul.

CHAPTER
TWENTY-FIVE

Kazuki turns to me. "Your choice, darling," he says.
  I glance between the two. "My choice *what*?"

"Draven here wants me to place a spell of protection upon you. One that will hide your powers from Marid's Second on Earth."

"I can pay for it," I say, finally catching up. "Draven, you don't have to—"

"Oh, but he does," Kazuki says. "As of now, you don't have the capability of paying me." He purses his lips. "Though I do hope you seek me out when you're fully in control of your powers." Those searing lavender eyes look up at Draven, another silent conversation expanding between them before Draven finally nods.

"How long does that buy me?" Draven asks.

"One week," Kazuki answers, tapping the end of his cane against the floor. Green sparks light up on the other side of the room, and a table appears out of thin air, mortar bowls and colorful glass vials atop it.

Kazuki strides to the table in a flurry of graceful movements, popping the corks on the vials and delicately pouring blue and white and green powders into the stone bowl.

"Your blood, Judge," he says without taking his eyes off his mixing.

Draven meets him at his side, exposing his wrist—

"What?" I snap, crossing the room to them. "No, you're not paying in blood—"

"He's not," Kazuki says, pricking Draven's wrist with a needle. He guides Draven's wrist over the bowl, drops of red splattering the fine powders within. "I deal in favors. This?" He squeezes

Draven's wrist a bit harder, more blood dripping into the bowl. "Is what strengthens the protection spell. Blood of the divine. Quite powerful, too. Hence, the week it's affording you." His eyes widen, a spark swirling behind the lavender as he releases Draven and continues mixing. "Sit down," he says, motioning me back to the couch.

I obey, the words choking my throat, stealing my voice as I try to silently convey my thanks to Draven. He merely blinks, holding the wound on his wrist without even flinching.

Kazuki settles next to me, bowl in one hand, emerald-topped cane in the other. A quick snap of his fingers and the blood clinging to my hands disappears. I sigh at the clean feeling. He scans the length of my body. "Where do you want it?"

I stare at him.

"The tattoo," he says. "The blood and ink brands the spell on your body."

My lips part as I shake my head. I extend the underside of my right wrist, my left occupied with the bracelets from my mother and Ray. Once again, I'm thankful the attack left them intact. I roll back my sleeve, exposing the skin on my free wrist.

Kazuki sucks his teeth. "So many scars," he says, eyeing the array of lighter, puckered skin from my past injuries.

I shrug. "What's one more?"

"A grain of rice weighs nothing," Draven says, glancing at me. "Collect a crate full and it's heavy enough to stop a heart."

I swallow hard, but Kazuki rolls his eyes. "Such dramatics, this one," he says, then locks gazes with me. "This will only take a minute." He sets his cane on the couch, retrieving the needle from earlier. He dips it into the bowl, and I turn my head away as he touches it to my skin, my eyes connecting with Draven's.

The sting is warmer than I expect, a delicious burn as I feel the liquid mixture from the bowl pierce my skin. A crackling buzzes the air as Kazuki retrieves his cane, green sparks circling us both before a searing heat blazes on my wrist.

I hiss, and my skin tingles with a cooling sensation.

"All done," Kazuki says, tapping his cane on the floor once more and the table, bowl, and supplies all disappear.

I tear my eyes from Draven's, examining my wrist. I gasp at the detailed artwork now decorating the small underside of my wrist. A delicate vine—no more than two inches in length—with intricate green leaves curling upward at the ends. And in the center where the tiny vine dips, just above the greenery, is a vivid black flame, four sharp tips nearly crackling with life, they look so real.

"It's beautiful," I say, awestruck.

"I'm a sorcerer of many talents," Kazuki coos. "One week," he adds. "The color will fade to black, and then it will merely be a regular tattoo, not a spell."

"Thank you," I say, glancing from him to Draven. Cassiel stands behind him, a curious yet hard gaze trained upon his friend.

I have a week to hunt down this greater demon's Second. To stop the onslaught of demons who keep coming after me. That will *keep* coming until we stop the Second.

But what about my apartment? My safe haven for Ray? My plea to the family courts to gain guardianship—

"The spell hides you from the Second. They won't be able to touch you or sense your power," Kazuki says as he stands. "Nor will the Minions who work for them. But the Hypnos? They will still be able to sense their kind's blood on your hands. So stay sharp." He turns to Draven, an eyebrow raised.

Draven holds his gaze for a few moments, then shakes his head. "I'm staying."

Cassiel's silver eyes widen at this, his lips parting as if to argue—

"Come, Cassiel, darling," Kazuki says before Cassiel can get a word out. "We have our own pressing matters to attend to."

Draven steps into Cassiel's path, stopping him from following Kazuki. "You're helping the sorcerer?"

Kazuki laughs from his spot by the doorway. "Goodness, no," he says. "I'm helping *him*."

Cassiel grimaces. "It's a long story, brother."

Brother? Draven spoke of his brother before, but—

"Does it involve a girl?" Draven challenges, his eyes narrowing as if he's sifting through Cassiel's thoughts.

"Stay out of my head," he says, but the command is playful. "Lest I ask you about—"

"Fair enough." Draven nods at him. "I've missed you."

Cassiel dips his head. "We'll catch up," he says. "After... everything."

Silence stretches between them as the two appear to hold some conversation without speaking, and then Draven nods.

"As delightful as the bromance reunion is," Kazuki says, "pressing matters and all that." He bows to me. "Lovely to meet you, Harley. If you survive what's coming, be sure that the next time you visit, you try the dance floor. *Way* more fun than killing things."

"Speak for yourself," Cassiel grumbles before stepping past Draven.

I try to make myself as small as possible as the duo leaves the room, their power radiating off them in waves that threaten to suck me under like a riptide.

"Is he the brother you spoke of?" I ask after the door seals shut again.

Draven just stares at me. "The most powerful sorcerer in existence just gave you a battle-to-the-death warning, and you ask if Cassiel is my brother?"

I raise my hands before letting them fall between my knees as I shift on the couch. How can I possibly voice the panic racing through my head? That all the plans I had of freedom, of a life of safety for Ray, have just popped like a fleeting soap bubble.

"No," Draven finally answers when it's clear I can't...*won't* voice the terror filling me. "Not my brother. Not in blood, anyway."

"So Cassiel is the best friend you spoke of before. The only one."

"So easy to tell?" Draven smirks at me.

"Not a hard guess."

"We need to leave," he says, motioning for me to follow him.

I reach for his hand so I won't lose him in the crowd just outside the door, but he shakes his head.

I drop my hand and stay on his heels as we weave through the throngs of demons still dancing on the floor. The music thrums and pulses, the colorful lights illuminating each creature we pass in bursts of reds or blues or greens. And without the sluggish mind I had earlier, I see them with a degree of terror I didn't before.

But there is also such beauty in the way they move—some graceful and some primal. Some with wings or talons or claws. Some with skin or fur in varying shades of purple or orange or pink.

"Ray would lose herself in here," I say, awestruck by the scene as we make our way toward the exit.

"She'd need a hundred more sketchbooks," Draven calls over his shoulder.

Something warms the center of my chest at his instant understanding of my statement. At how well he knows Ray. How he's managed to get a sense of both our personalities in such a short time.

And yet…what does it matter now? When the Second Kazuki spoke of—the big bad who hunts me like a shadow in the night.

We clear the exit, climbing the steps to the main street, my thighs trembling from the exertion. "You know," I say as Draven turns in the direction that leads to the train. "You'd think if I'm so damn *special*, I'd get the perk of having some physical strength."

A crease forms between Draven's brows, and I have the ridiculous urge to smooth the tense lines with my fingers. His eyes scan my body as he slows our pace. "Are you injured? Normally Kazuki's efforts don't exhaust the person."

I lift my sleeve, showing him the cut the Hypno delivered, the space just above the tattoo. I gasp when I see the pink line of healed flesh where the cut had been. "It was bleeding." I state the obvious, since dried blood decorates the fresh skin.

"The flames accelerated the healing process."

A throbbing at the back of my head aches, and I rub at the spot.

"What else hurts?" he asks, tracking the movement.

"Everything," I admit. "I've never been strong, Draven. That's why when Coach Hale told me I had something special in my blood, I swore she was wrong. I told you before, my muscles are weak. My body...I've always been weak."

Draven abruptly stops our pace, stepping in front of me. "You are *not* weak."

"I think *I* know my body a little better than you do."

"Up until tonight, you had no clue your body could create fire," he challenges.

True. "But I can *feel* my muscles right now."

"Describe it."

"Like dried rubber, ready to crumble at any minute. Or like that moment between sleeping and waking, where you can't quite get your hand to close or your legs to move without an effort."

"And it's like that all the time?"

"I fight through it every single day. Coach Hale has been working with me for more than a year to build up my strength."

"Has it helped?"

"With the instincts? Yes. With my actual muscle capacity? No."

Something churns in Draven's eyes, a question and answer both out of reach.

"Does it mean something?"

"I'm not sure," he says, continuing our walk. The sidewalks are peppered with late-night bar goers, hustling from one to the next, giggling and carrying on, not a care in the world. "With the power...you should feel the strength in it."

Just one more thing I can't control. "Did you know that would happen to me?"

"I suspected." He doesn't need me to clarify that I was asking about the flames, and I'm growing oddly used to his uncanny ability to understand me when I can't make sense of things myself.

"How?"

"What I do," he says. "What I am...I'm sometimes assigned to monitor people of interest."

I force a laugh. "Like an undercover agent."

"Something like that."

"Wow." I shake my head. "By who?"

"A select group of ancients," he says, but the answer is strained, the tension in his broad shoulders tight.

Touchy subject. Got it.

We make it to the train and hop on, riding in a silence I desperately want to break. But the late-night crowd sits or stands all around us, so I can't risk it. And I keep darting suspicious looks at each passenger, wondering who is human and who is demon. Wondering if one of them could be the Second Kazuki spoke of. The one who controls all the rest of the demons chomping for my blood.

When we come to the stop that will take me back to Nathan's, I'm beyond grateful when Draven follows me off the train. I half feared he'd leave me to walk home alone with nothing but a mind full of questions haunting me.

My body aches with each step we take toward Nathan's. The effects from the fight or the power or Kazuki's trip into my mind? And the protection spell tattoo. All of it ripples through me like little pinches over my body.

As we come to Nathan's porch, I lower my voice to a whisper.

"I saw what Kazuki saw…" The darkness, the blood spatters, the rip in the earth and the demons coming out of it, the snake creature. Nothing *good* or *pure* could come out of it. Out of *me*. My chest tightens as the images replay themselves over and over in my mind.

Draven rakes his fingers through his hair, causing the dark strands to fall in this perfectly messy way that has me suddenly forgetting every question I have. Right now, all I want him to do is press me against the nearest wall and make me *forget*.

Make me forget my blood is dark, dirty.

Make me forget the demons who attacked me.

Make me forget that an all-powerful sorcerer just told me I have a week left to live.

Because sure, he said I can hunt down the Second and stop

him before he finds me, but with the way my body feels? The weakness I always live with? There is *zero* chance I'll win against something *worse* than what has already come after me. I've been lucky these last couple of times. And in my experience, luck never lasts.

"My blood," I say instead of finishing my earlier sentence. "You said you wanted it, too."

Draven visibly swallows. "Because you're powerful." The words come out in a struggled rush.

"And these ancients who sent you to watch me...they wanted proof?"

He dips his head, just barely.

"How powerful?" I ask.

"Endlessly."

The weight in his answer settles heavily over my heart, and from the way my body shakes as I try to hold myself upright outside of Nathan's front door, I know I can't handle one more thing tonight. Does that make me weak? Maybe. But I don't fucking care.

"You've told me multiple times to stay away from you, yet you told Kazuki you're staying," I say, my voice soft. Is he staying to stand with me against this unknown evil? Or is he merely staying to fulfill some supernatural mission he's been assigned? "I have an endless well of questions rattling in my brain right now. Most importantly, how we're going to hunt down this Second." Draven's face softens with pity, making it pretty clear how accurate the sorcerer is. "I can't make a solid plan if I don't have the full picture."

"I agree," he says. "Once you know everything..." He shifts his weight. "You can make the right choices." His eyes scan me from head to toe. "But you won't be able to listen to me for more than a few seconds, it looks like." He blinks a few times, taking a step away from me. "We can speak more after you sleep."

I turn, keys in hand.

"Draven?" I ask as I unlock the door.

"Yes?"

I wet my lips, tracing my fingers over the delicate leaves of my tattoo, the dark flames above it. "Thank you," I say, glancing up at him. "For this. For the blood you gave for me."

A mischievous smirk shapes his lips as he backs off Nathan's porch, but his eyes? Those eyes churn with such devastation, it makes emotion clog my throat.

"What's a few drops of mine…" he finally answers, hands in his pockets as he lingers on the sidewalk near the street. "When *all* of yours is at stake?"

A warm shiver dances down my spine as I graze that spot on my wrist—the one mixed with his blood and magic and power. "Everything," I say. "It's everything."

"Careful, Harley," he warns. "You're dangerously close to sounding like you still trust me."

I swallow hard. "And what if I do?"

That grin deepens. "Then you're much more fond of fire than I gave you credit for."

My lips part, a rush of electricity dancing across my skin.

Then I watch in awe as shadows peel from the street, gathering around him like sheets of black silk, until he disappears entirely.

So that's how he does it.

As I stumble inside and plonk down on the extra bed in the spare room beside Ray, I'm asleep almost as soon as my head hits the pillow. Draven's grin as he disappeared wraps around me like a warm blanket, and my last thought before I sink into oblivion is what he will do if I can't keep my side of our deal. Because *not* acting on that connection between us suddenly seems harder than surviving the big bad coming for me.

CHAPTER TWENTY-SIX

I always forget how bad our house smells until I've been away from it for a while. Mildew and the sharp smell of alcohol. I cannot wait to finally escape this place.

We came home from Nathan's yesterday, me armed with a handful of cash that I "earned" from working doubles. Or at least, that's what I told my father when I handed it to him. It's worth dipping into my savings—I can't take another beating. Not after the attacks, the long night of endless questions. The ticking clock now hovering above my head, each heartbeat counting down the seconds until the bomb blows and I'm nothing more than a horrid stain on the pavement.

Dad pocketed the cash like a thief and left for the bar within five minutes of us returning home yesterday. A small mercy, since he's now sleeping off that celebration in his room and no threat to anyone.

And me? Well, I'm hiding out in the bathroom while Ray is conked out in our room. I can't sleep, too many thoughts whirling in my mind. I have to either figure out a way to survive the upcoming supernatural shitstorm blowing my way, or more realistically…figure out a way to take care of Ray after I get my ass kicked for good.

For a girl who's spent her whole life waiting for the day I could get Ray and me out of this hellish place and actually have choices for once, I've somehow managed to end up leaving anyway, but with even less control over my life. And no, it doesn't escape my twisted sense of humor that I've traded the constant threat of one person beating on me for what could possibly be an entire supernatural stadium taking a whack.

Irony, you are a wicked, wicked bitch sometimes.

But I don't have time for tears or fist waving. I've got plans to make, so the pity party can wait.

Miller's has been repaired and cleaned and opened again, but Nathan told me to take the next couple of days off, somehow noting the exhaustion I wear like a heavy coat.

"You're much fonder of the fire than I gave you credit for."

Draven's words haunt me as I think of that snake creature and cringe. The darkness and the blood...

What does that make me? And why the hell does everyone want my blood?

Well, screw that. I sort of need that liquid.

I texted Draven earlier, setting up a time to meet so we can talk—strategize—and glance at my phone's clock, willing it to be an hour later, when I'll see him again.

Because I've worked my entire life to get to this point—to get my own place and gain custody of Ray. If I'm not going to let my abusive father stand in the way, then I sure as hell won't let some goddamn demons, either.

I just need to practice drawing out my dark flame, but as I stare at my fingers held in front of me, all I can feel is icy doubt and fear. *Come on, Harley. Focus.*

Right. Kick-ass flames. I've got this.

I glance at the door I left slightly ajar in case another nightmare wakes Ray and hear Father's snoring from his room. Good. He should be out at least a few more hours. So I focus on my hands again, knowing if I have a chance in hell at surviving whatever is headed my way, then I need to get control of this shit real quick.

I close my eyes, searching inward, focusing on that instant awareness in my blood—a crackling heat itching to be played with—and then I mentally grip the flame, hold on to it, coax it out to play. Fire blazes from my fingertips so fast and harsh, a soft roar fills the bathroom—like lighting a gas pilot to full blast.

I startle, backing up until my spine hits the wall behind me, and the fire disappears.

I'd think it was gone for good, but the skin of my fingertips prickles with heat, like the living flames have only slipped beneath the surface, waiting and ready. I take a steadying breath and try a softer inner coaxing.

I smile as one flame snakes out of my pointer finger, dancing lazily with only the range of a lit candle. I wave my hand before my face, mesmerized by the unique color—midnight black with sparkles of silver. I'm awestruck by the obvious heat pulsing from my body, and yet, it doesn't sear my flesh. I've been burned before, but still, I don't fear *this* flame. In fact, I *love* it. There's no other way to describe it. For a girl who's rarely felt any real power herself, I've instantly become addicted to it. Because that's what this flame is.

Power. My power.

I'm just about to light the rest of my fingers when it dawns on me that the trailer has gone eerily silent, and my heart stutters, killing the flame instantly. I jump when something moves just outside the bathroom door, then swing it open, finding my father standing there, eyes wide, a manic smile shaping his lips.

"You're awake," I say, my voice cracking. I draw my hands behind my back, despite the fire being gone, and he tracks the movement.

"It's my house," he says. "I can wake up when I want." His tone doesn't hold the usual bite, which scares me more than if he outright started a fight.

"I just didn't hear you," I say, shifting on the balls of my feet.

His eyes fall to where I hold my hands behind my back. "I need biscuits and gravy. Get your sister up, and I'll take you both for breakfast."

My stomach bottoms out, and I swallow hard. "I have to get her ready for art," I say, the words more question than a statement as I try to walk that line between being too ungrateful or too thankful. One toe over that line, and I'll be fighting my way out of this bathroom.

I could burn him.

The whispered knowledge turns my blood cold, a shiver skating down my spine.

"Okay," he finally says. "More for me, then." He turns down the hallway, but not before glancing toward me again with a look I can't place. One I've never seen before that seems dangerously close to…pride?

I shake my head, tossing the thought from my mind. The only thing Dad is ever proud of is the sound of his fist hitting my flesh.

CHAPTER TWENTY-SEVEN

An hour later, I hug Ray before she heads into the school building, then hurry back to the train to head toward where I'm supposed to meet Draven in thirty. I practically sprint inside Myopic Books, waving to John without stopping as I head for the stairs.

Today is not a day for lingering in the stacks, leisurely strolling and soaking up the relaxing comfort the bookstore offers.

No, today I need answers I can't get from a book—or at least, no book I know about. I need them from the infuriating boy who sits in the corner seat in the basement, my seat, waiting for me with a sad sort of smile on his face. His eyes meet mine the instant I round one of the stacks as if he sensed me coming, and I can *feel* that answering chain buried in my soul, the one constantly reaching for Draven like the edge of a dream I can't quite remember.

"Thanks for agreeing to meet me," I say as I sink into the plush chair next to him.

Draven raises his hands from the armrests, shrugging. "I promised you answers in the hope you make the right choices."

"What's the right choice, in your opinion?"

"For you to stay as far away from me as possible."

"Well, since I've only got six days left to hunt down a demon doing a greater demon's bidding or die…" I can't hold the snark from my voice, but as Draven flinches, I reel back the bite and hurry on. "Maybe we can agree to stand each other for that long?" He narrows his gaze. "Either way," I continue, "you're here. *You* came into my life, not the other way around." Not that I want him to leave, but he doesn't need to know that. "And you're the one who decided to stay, to give your blood to this protection spell." I hold out my tattooed wrist. "You should at least admit you're being frustratingly contradicting."

"No, I *have* to be here." A muscle ticks in his jaw as he shifts in his leather chair. The movement causes his scent to crash over me, and my eyes close for the briefest of seconds, everything in my head emptying except for that smell. The need to get closer to him, to drown in it, disappear in it—

Draven clears his throat, and I blink a few times, cheeks blazing. He's worse than the Hypno when it comes to stealing my focus.

A small smile turns up the corners of his mouth, but it's gone before I can appreciate it for long.

"Who ordered you to watch me? Why?" I finally grasp a few floating questions in the endless stream trickling in my mind.

"A high council called The Seven," he says, his voice low. Luckily, we're the only two down here, and the risk of being overheard is incredibly slim. "And I told you, I'm sometimes asked to watch people of interest."

I smooth my fingers over my palms, back and forth, the friction crackling with the barest of flames before returning to normal. Draven's eyes flare at the small show, and he cocks a brow at me. "You've been practicing?"

"Failing is more like it," I say, settling my hands in my lap. "I can't get ahold of it. It'll either come out too powerful or too weak or not at all."

Draven tilts his head.

"And why is it black?" The Hypno and Kazuki had called it *"the dark flame."* "Is that normal?"

"No." He rubs his jaw. "Prophecies have been written about people who possess the dark flame, but as far as we knew, they were fairy tales."

I raise my brows. "Do I look like Little Red Riding Hood to you?"

Amusement flickers in the golden depths of his eyes as he cocks one eyebrow. "You *do* have a knack for drawing out the wolves."

The breath catches in my lungs, and I try to remind myself to focus.

"I haven't come into contact with many people like you." He doesn't seem especially happy about that fact.

Still, I perk up. "So I'm not the only one? There are other people out there who can control fire? They could teach me?"

Draven shakes his head. "No, I've never met anyone who can manifest flames, let alone the dark ones."

"But you said—"

"Recently," he clarifies. "I once heard of a girl who can create ice."

I raise my brows. "Okaaay." I drag out the word.

"It's rare in our world, to be able to control the elements."

"It means something." I don't pose it as a question.

"Yes."

"What?"

"Kazuki said it himself," he adds, waving a hand toward me. "Your blood is something ancient—"

"But I'm only eighteen," I argue.

"Your blood isn't, nor the power it holds."

"Okaaay." I draw the word out again. "So what now, then? How do I stop this Marid and his Second from coming for me *and* stop all the other demons, too?" God, how many are there? Are any of them still trapped in Hell or is there a big, gaping hole in the world unleashing all these creatures like ants from an anthill?

"Anka is helping me hunt for someone who knows the Second's identity," he says, though he doesn't seem pleased with the answer. "Either we find them first or they'll show their hand soon and then—"

"I'll die."

He flinches. "You don't know that."

"The odds are against me."

"Haven't they always been?" he challenges, and the tease in his voice snags on that internal chain, tugging us closer.

"I'm not very good at waiting," I finally admit.

"If I knew who the culprit was, honey badger, I would've already ended them."

Awareness blooms beneath my skin, warm and tingling at the use of the nickname he gave me.

"Why?" I tilt my head. "Honestly, why are you here? Beyond watching me. It's clear I am what everyone thinks I am. This ancient temptress flashing my potent blood all over Chicago. And now with what's probably an amphitheater of demons wanting to end my life…why would you stick around for that? The risk?"

"You…should not be forced to face this alone." He grinds out the words as if they physically hurt him to admit. "You didn't ask for this—"

"Neither did you," I counter.

"I am a part of the Darkness, not you."

I swallow hard. "Darkness," I say, shaking my head. "I have an endless well of it inside me." The admission sits like a whisper between us, and I can't help but look away from the intensity in his gaze. "I saw it when Kazuki traipsed through my mind."

Draven shifts on the seat, leaning his elbows on his knees as he draws closer. "You also saw a light."

I snap my eyes to his.

"Barely," I argue. "Hell, you said it yourself—my flames are *dark*."

Draven holds my gaze. "Even an ember of night can be a beacon in the darkness."

My stomach tightens, rebelling at the hope in his words. "Too bad I didn't light it up enough to see his Second."

"Nothing is ever that simple," Draven says.

"What are you exactly?" I ask after a beat. "Kazuki called you a Judge. Said your blood is divine." Clearly, he's powerful; I can feel that in the electricity buzzing against my skin. But…how does he know about the images I saw with Kazuki?

Draven's jaw juts out just a bit, his eyes narrowing as he stares at me. A heavy silence settles between us, and I shift closer to him until our legs almost brush, but he quickly jerks away.

"I am called a Judge, as Kazuki said," he finally relents. "A divine solider drafted by the Creator and ordained with powers in order to vanquish evil that threatens the human world."

"The Creator," I say. "Like…*the* God? No way."

Draven laughs. "You handled the existence of demons without a blink, but you struggle with the possibility there's a Creator?"

"It's easier to believe bad things exist." I regret the words as soon as I say them.

"And who says God is good?" he challenges.

"Every religious person *ever*." I eye him. "Am I wrong?"

Draven leans back in his chair. "I've never met the being," he says.

"But you don't like it…" I study the tense set of his features. "Do you?"

"I was enlisted in a war I didn't know existed. My brother and me. We had no choice. No say. And now my brother suffers—" He cuts himself off, shaking his head as if he didn't mean to say that.

"But if you're part of"—I wave my hand in the air—"the whole biblical stuff, why aren't you mentioned in the bible?"

"Judges *are* in the bible. It's a watered-down version of what we truly are, but there is an entire book dedicated to them."

He says the statement with such a *duh* tone that I can't help narrowing my eyes and firing back, "Well, not all of us had time for Sunday school when we were kids."

He winces at the reminder of my shitty home life and has the grace to duck his head.

"You said you're worse than a demon, but it turns out you're divine…" My brow furrows as I try to put all these pieces together. "If God chose you, how can that be?"

"I'm hated among my kind." He fiddles with the peeling leather on the chair. "Frankly, I think they're surprised *and* disappointed that I've survived this long."

"Why?" I ask the question through clenched teeth, and a small, soft crackle sounds between us, flames kissing my fingertips in a succession that jolts me in my seat.

Draven smirks but doesn't comment on the fire I attempt to extinguish by cupping my hands. "My powers, for one." He shrugs a wide shoulder. "And the fact that I don't see all demons as evil and in need of vanquishing."

"Like Coach Hale," I say, finally managing to coax the flames beneath my skin.

He nods.

"What can you do?" I ask.

He raises a haughty brow. "The better question is what *can't* I do."

I tilt my head, not playing into the cocky deflection. The severity in his eyes tells me enough about this topic—painful. An old hurt, one I'd bet my savings he doesn't speak about often.

"I'm a Siphon," he says, and my eyebrows shoot up in question.

On a sigh, he extends his hand between us, those strong, lithe fingers reaching toward me. "Anything I touch, I *drain*."

My lips part with a small gasp. "Drain of what exactly?"

"For supernatural creatures—demon or divine—one touch and their power belongs to me. Stronger beings will be restored after some time, depending on how long I touch them. But for me? I'll never lose the power once I've gained it."

I swallow hard. "And if you touch a human?" Ray's face flickers behind my eyes.

"I'll kill them if it's more than a few minutes."

Emotion clogs my throat, my heart breaking over what he's endured. No wonder he's so adamant about not touching me.

"And once you have their power, you can wield it whenever you want?" I ask, my own fire inside me shivering at the mere idea of it being taken so easily.

"Yes," he says. "I can conjure any power I wish, but I can only hold it for a short period of time." He sighs. "Having this many powers…it can be exhausting. If I try to use any of them for too long, I will drain my control—and then there's no telling what would happen. If I'm lucky, death before I take innocent lives." He notes my wide-eyed stare. "Everything has its cost, Harley."

"Damn," I say, shaking my head. "And I thought weak muscles and a ticking time bomb over my head was bad."

"You should run," he says, ignoring my attempt at dark humor. "Like everyone else. It'll only be a matter of time before I either drain the life from you or drain your power for—"

"Draven." I simply say his name, but that one word holds so much more than either of us will ever admit, and he looks away. So I shift off my seat, kneeling before him so I can catch the gaze he keeps on the floor. "I'm sorry."

A crease forms between his brows. "You're *sorry*?"

I nod, wetting my lips as I search for the right words. "You were dealt the absolute worst hand in the supernatural deck. You had your freedom stripped from you in an instant and were given possibly the worst power I've ever heard of." Granted, I've only heard of superpowers in books and movies, but still. "You got the rawest deal," I continue, holding his gaze. "And I say that fully aware of the shitstorm I'm in." I shake my head. "Yet you still somehow have such a kindness to you."

His gaze narrows like he's about to deny it, so I rush to continue before he can get the chance.

"You do," I say. "You go out of your way to make Ray smile. You show up to make sure I'm fed. You gave up your *blood* to protect me—"

A low growl rips from his chest, and he jumps from the seat so fast, he nearly knocks me over. I'm on my feet in a second, watching him pace before the shelves next to us.

"I *am* a monster, Harley," he says. "You should not pity me—"

"I don't—"

"Or applaud me," he continues, turning to face me. "You should *fear* me. Fear me just as much as every other demon out there who wants a taste of you. Wants to use you—" He cuts his words short, his lips tightening in a firm line.

Then he lifts the palms of his hands, curling his fingers—and chains of liquid silver dart past me. The ends hook onto the chair behind me, and he yanks, the flowing silver jerking the seat against me so hard, I fall into it with a *thunk*.

The silver disappears, shadows gathering around his body like wisps of smoke. The well-lit room suddenly darkens, and his features blur from sight as the darkness swirls around him.

"This power…" His voice comes from behind me now, and I jolt in my seat, disoriented in the darkness. "Has taken *everything* from me."

Electricity snaps around me, and my eyes widen when a burst of white light zigzags along the shelves. My instincts roar, my blood searing at the display of power as books rise from the shelves. They whip past my face but never make connection as they fly on their own in a circle around me.

I will ruin you.

His voice caresses the inside of my mind, and I go absolutely still at the feel of him there. A different kind of pressure than Kazuki's presence was. Draven stepping into my mind does not feel like an intrusion. That searing blood inside my veins? It does not thrash out at his power; it does not cower.

It *sings*.

It curls around his presence, soothing it, greeting it, welcoming it like he's always belonged there.

The breath *whooshes* from my lungs as I feel his mental retreat, that place now a tiny spot of empty space I want to fill with everything that's *him*.

And then I remember something—Draven and I have kissed and touched, and though they were brief, he did *not* drain me.

No, our kisses did nothing but make me crave more. More of that feeling, that sheer *alive* feeling his touch sparks in my heart.

And knowing that, I step through the darkness, through the tornado of books, through electricity snapping along the shelves. I close my eyes and focus on that connection between us, and when it blazes behind my closed eyes, I lash out.

My hand grips Draven's wrist so quickly, the darkness immediately evaporates.

The buzz of electricity halts.

The floating books fall in thuds to the floor.

Draven's eyes are a churning liquid gold as he gazes down at me, at the touch where I hold his wrist.

"I am not afraid," I say and draw him closer.

His eyes blaze for a beat, maybe two, and then his free hand comes up to grip my neck. He crushes his lips on mine, and I whimper from the intensity of his kiss. The taste of it.

I yank on his shirt, drawing him down to my level so I can push back, give him everything and take it at the same time. If we're nothing else, we're *this* to each other—an addiction and a distraction from the constant stream of people who want us dead. Mirror images of the same ruined and broken person. People hate him for his tragic power, and demons want me dead for just the same.

He snakes his arms around my waist, his body pressing into mine until I hit the shelves, books toppling to our feet.

His tongue teases mine, tracing along the edges until every inch of my skin tingles. Until my heart beats in time with his, and I want nothing but to drink him in, breathe him in, devour him.

Draven groans, tearing his lips from mine, his eyes dropping to where my hands glow a white-hot onyx and silver at his hips.

I jerk my hands away as he takes a step backward.

"I'm sorry!" I gape at the holes in his black shirt, a perfect fit for my fingertips, and the red marks on his bare skin beneath.

A wicked, delighted, almost manic grin shapes his lips, his eyes still blazing, churning as he gazes down at me. And then he *laughs*.

"What's funny?" My cheeks warm from the utter mortification of it. I can't control my power, but embarrassment seems to work as the flames wink out.

Draven continues to laugh, those eyes of his wild and open and delighted in a way I've never seen. "I had a suspicion you were hot for me, Harley," he says through his laughter. "But I didn't realize I could make you *burn*."

The raspy way his voice shapes the words makes everything inside me melt, but I snort, rolling my eyes. "That's so cheesy," I say. "Way less cocky or philosophical than usual."

He shrugs, his chest rising and falling as quickly as mine.

I eye the piles of books scattered around the floor, biting my bottom lip. "We made a mess."

Draven doesn't move, doesn't even blink, and those books lift off the floor, floating gracefully back to their proper places among the shelves.

Fire pulses in my blood, banging on some inner door, begging for release.

I take one step toward him, then another, sighing slightly when he doesn't retreat. I lightly graze my fingers over the inside of his palm as I look up at him.

"I can touch you," I say.

His brow furrows, a battle wrecking his liquid eyes. "And you feel nothing?"

I press my lips together, still feeling the heat on my cheeks. "Obviously I feel *something*." I draw my hand back the second I sense the flames slip through that inner door.

Draven hovers his hand over the tiny flames, and my entire body tightens and coils.

"Do you?" I ask, a whisper between us. "Feel anything?"

"You *know* I do," he says, raising his free hand, flexing his fingers. "But I didn't take your power."

"What does that mean?"

"It shouldn't be possible," he admits, dropping his hand over mine.

I flinch, but the flames extinguish immediately, leaving nothing but his hand in mine. "Probably not as pressing as the threats at hand, though, right?" I ask, cold reality dousing my delightful moment of distraction.

Draven nods, the light glowing behind his eyes dulling back to normal.

"Definitely," he says. "We should—"

My phone buzzes in my pocket, cutting him off, and I flash an apologetic half smile as I fish it out. I can't ignore it when Ray is in school, in case she needs me.

KAI: What are you up to today? Want to grab a bite?

ME: Sorry, I can't. @ Myopic with Draven. Heading to pick up Ray soon. Rain check?

KAI: Sure. Text me when you're free.

I'm relieved when Kai's response comes quickly and effortlessly. Maybe our talk at Nathan's truly made a difference. He seems almost back to normal, and not even a snide remark about hanging with Draven? That's a huge high five in the best friend column.

"Everything all right?" Draven asks as I pocket my phone.

"Just Kai," I say and furrow my brow. "Why were you a bike messenger in New York a few summers ago? Or was that just a cover for another Judge mission thing?" I wonder if that's why Kai disliked Draven so much. Maybe he got a bad vibe from him during the job, as any normal human would with the way Draven keeps people at a growly distance. For their own safety, from *him*, I now know. God, to go through life worrying that one touch would kill the other person? What kind of havoc would that wreak on someone? And to know that those same powers would consume you if you push it too far?

I shake my head. I may have a death sentence hanging over me for whatever darkness snakes through my blood, but Draven got the worst end of this supernatural world.

"Bike messenger?" He arches a thick brow at me.

"Yeah, when you worked with—"

A booming crash swallows my words as an entire bookshelf flips over and slams against the concrete basement floor, and then the stairwell exit door bursts open, splinters from the force of the hit flying in all directions.

And four demons funnel into the room in a succession of eerie clicks and scrapes that makes my skin crawl.

Draven and I shift automatically into defensive stances, my heart pounding in my chest. "What in the blue hell are those? And how the fuck did these assholes find me? I thought the tattoo was supposed to mask my scent."

The creatures push farther into the room, close enough now that I can tell they have slits for nostrils and milky white eyes that are much too big for their pointed heads. Grayish, sickly looking skin covers pounds of corded muscle, their elongated bodies tapering off to four pillar-like legs with six glistening black claws on each foot—like some ancient dinosaur.

"Aspis demons," Draven answers as he scans the room. "And I have no idea."

"They're not the good kind of demon, are they?" I ask, desperately wishing they were just here to find a great book.

"Not even remotely," Draven says, never taking his gaze from our unwanted visitors. "You wouldn't know another way out of here, would you?"

"Behind them," I say. "The door they blew open is the only way out of the basement." Otherwise, we'll have to make it to the stairs to the upper levels and risk leading these creatures to the innocent customers and employees above.

Their hissing mounts as they claw their way to us, those sharp talons gouging marks in the concrete with each step. The one in the middle clambers up and over the fallen bookshelf, its claws digging into the books beneath it.

"Hey!" I snap, fire curling around my fists. "Mind the books, assholes!"

"Seriously?" Draven chides.

The milky eyes of the demon on the fallen bookshelf narrow at me, a forked tongue lashing out of its thin lips.

"That's the one," a low, seductive voice says from behind the group of Aspis demons, and five more men stroll in as casually as if they'd come to browse the store.

No, not men—*Hypnos*.

"Ah," Draven says. "*They're* the assholes who found you."

My stomach bottoms out as I remember Kazuki telling me how Hypnos can track someone who has killed their kind.

I'm not safe. I'll never be safe again.

Each demon has that same sensual air about them as the one from The Bridge, the auras around them buzzing with sugary scents beckoning my mind to lapse, to relax until I become nothing but a willing victim who dances to her death.

"Guessing these guys didn't drop by to chat?" I whisper to Draven.

"For the sake of time management," Draven says through clenched teeth, "let's just assume everything here wants to kill us."

I give a firm nod, the fire in my blood mounting with each pump of adrenaline. My eyes dart from one creature to the next as they fan out, creating a half circle around the area—*herding* us toward the back corner.

"She killed Phenton," one of the Hypnos with shoulder-length blond hair says, pointing at me. "And Sal, Bruiser, and Thane."

I gape at him. "To be fair," I say, tilting my head. "Those three got themselves killed. I had nothing to do with it." Not directly anyway. It isn't my fault the trio challenged Kazuki—even I'm not that foolish, and I barely have an ounce of understanding of this world yet. But I know enough not to challenge an ancient sorcerer.

The Hypno curls his lip back before glancing at Draven. "Leave now, Judge, and we'll spare you. You have no role in this restitution."

Blinding, icy panic claws up my spine. He can leave. He *should* leave. This isn't his fault. He isn't the pulsing beacon in the sky calling all the demons toward him like the Pied Freaking Piper.

Draven's lips shape into that mischievous smirk I can't resist. "A sound plan," he says, his voice like liquid steel. "But since I'm already here…" He shrugs, hands casually at his sides as if he doesn't have the faintest clue that we're surrounded by demons blocking the only exit from the building we can take. "Since when do Hypnos employ Aspis to do their dirty work anyway?"

The blond flashes his teeth, then clicks his tongue at the four

Aspis who hold steady ahead of him and his friends. "A temporary alliance," he says. "For a common goal." His glittering blue eyes flash to me.

A low growl rumbles from Draven's chest.

"Can't you feel it, Judge?" the blond coos. "He's changing everything. All the rules. Flipping them." He arches his head back, cocking it slightly as if he's listening to something in the air. "Nothing will be the same now."

"Enough chatting," his Hypno friend to the left snaps. "I don't care what the order is. She has our blood all over her hands. We kill her. Now. Slowly."

I flash a look to my hands, half worried I'll find them caked in the blue blood of the Hypno I killed at the club. They're clean, but gritty guilt clings to me—self-defense or not.

The blond purses his lips, those blue eyes contemplative. "Quite," he finally says. "What the boss doesn't know won't enrage him."

"I would tell you to inform your boss he should come himself next time," Draven says, staring down the blond. "But you won't be alive long enough to deliver that message."

One second.

That's all it takes to burst the banter bubble we stand in.

One second after the words leave Draven's lips, a collective roar rumbles the room.

The blond clicks his tongue again, and the four Aspis bolt toward us. Two on either side of the room leap to the walls, running sideways across them, their claws gouging the concrete and propelling them toward us with a higher-ground advantage.

"On your left!" Draven hollers before spinning to his right, ensnaring the two Aspis with those same ropes of silver liquid I saw only minutes before.

I pivot toward the oncoming demons, flames engulfing my hands easily as the panic mounts inside me.

One demon leaps and lands atop me, wrestling me to the ground with the weight of a fucking truck. Jesus, what do they *feed* these things? Bricks? I pound against its hard chest with my fists, and the flames scorch its slippery gray skin, but it doesn't budge. It digs its claws into the concrete above my shoulder as if it can shove me through the hard floor if it can just gain the right purchase.

And holy hell, my bones feel like they might snap from the pressure, my lungs aching for air, but still, I hold my flaming hands against its rubbery skin and grit my teeth.

Its forked tongue darts out, its breath hot on my face as it snaps its teeth, and real panic starts to set in. I need to get this bastard *off* me. Now.

The flesh beneath my fingers sizzles, but I'm clearly not hurting it. With a shallow breath, I shift enough to lift my hands up and dig my thumbs into its milky eyes instead.

It hauls off me, roaring and shaking its head back and forth as black flames engulf its head entirely, and air *whooshes* back into my aching lungs. I scramble away, gathering my feet beneath me—

But something jerks me from behind, strong fingers digging into my shoulders like knives. I spin around, drawing my fist in a hook as I do.

It connects with the Hypno's face, leaving a black scorch mark along its perfectly smooth skin.

"Go ahead and fight," the blond says. "It'll only make you taste that much better."

"Taste me and you'll regret it," I snap.

A sharp crack along my left cheekbone sends me flying backward, and my spine slams against one of the shelves. Books topple to the floor around me, my head spinning from the impact. The Hypno is on me in a blink, fisting my hair and hauling me up by the roots.

"Look at me!" he growls as he grips my neck with his other hand.

I claw at his wrist with flames that flicker in and out, that same invisible something in my blood drawing my power back until the sparks wink out entirely.

"*Look* at me," he drawls, and I focus anywhere *but* his eyes.

I glance behind him, where Draven fights the remaining demons—his powers crackling through the room. Searing ropes of silver liquid, shadows in the form of axes and swords, and his hands…his bare hands as he reaches and grips and lashes at anything brave enough to come within touching distance.

His shoulders bow slightly, his face strained in concentration. He told me there's a limit to his endless well of power, and I can see it on his face, see it in the way his speed slows as he blocks a taloned hand from the Aspis in front of him.

The fire in my blood screams against whatever holds it back. My muscles tremble as the Hypno strengthens his grip, the air slower and harder to get to my lungs.

Books and wood scatter along the ground, flying this way and that during the battle. My store…my favorite place in the city. They're *destroying* it.

"Look at me, pet," the Hypno says, and with the rage boiling in my blood?

I do.

Those deep blue eyes look like some undiscovered gemstone with flecks of glittering silver bursting across the iris. His lips are sensuous as he shapes them into a devious smile, delighted with his own power to enthrall me.

I drop my hands from his forearm. Go weak and pliant in his hold.

Because that's what I am, right? Weak. Worthless.

I make sure he sees that in my eyes.

"Ah, good girl," he coos, and my stomach turns acidic. But he loosens his grip, and it takes every ounce of willpower in my arsenal to not immediately lash out. To will that glazed look into my eyes.

Because I've been fooled once before, and there is no way in hell I'll be fooled again. That's how my mind has always worked—one chance, that's all you have with me. Betray me? I'll never forget it.

He lifts my hand to his face, his nose skimming along my wrist, and I will my muscles not to recoil from the intimate touch. He bares his sharp, ultra-white teeth. "I could make this painless," he says, glancing at me, then back to my wrist. "But you deserve to hurt."

No shit. Haven't I always deserved it? Isn't that what my father tends to tell me while he's kicking me when I'm down?

That fire inside me pounds against the invisible barrier in my blood, thrashing and screaming as the Hypno's needle-sharp teeth sink into my flesh. I grind my jaw to keep from wailing at the searing pain that shoots through my arm.

He moans as my blood pours into his mouth, staining his lips red. He closes his eyes with the delight in it—

And I pounce.

Wind my fingers in his long hair and twist until his head jerks back. Until that fire breaks free of the restraints once again and blazes so hot and so fierce, he doesn't stand a chance.

"I warned you," I practically growl.

One second he screams; the next he's ash.

In a blink, I leap toward Draven, using the momentum to jump on the back of an Aspis dead set on sinking its teeth into Draven's thigh. The creature screeches and thrashes beneath me, but my flames hold strong. Hungry, consuming, they raze the creature until I fall atop another pile of ash.

But there are so many more, and the gaping wound on my wrist and the blood pouring out of it turn my vision foggy.

"We have to run," I say as I make it to Draven.

The two remaining Aspis linger near the exit, blocking the door as Draven holds the Hypnos back with his shadow weapons.

"I have minutes left," Draven says, his voice weak, exhausted.

For a split second, I contemplate grabbing him and risking the stairs to the main level, but I just as quickly dismiss it. I won't put innocent people in danger, and if we run? These demons *will* follow us.

"Drop your powers when I say," I whisper, internally holding on to my flames with a viselike grip. Even now, I can feel it waning, feel it being hauled back by those invisible chains, but I think I have enough in me for one last blast. "And stay on my heels."

Draven doesn't argue, for once.

I shift on my feet, angling for the Aspis guarding the door. I dig my mental claws into my flames, holding on to the power for dear life as I say, "Now!"

Draven's shadows disappear, and I shoot a quick ball of fire at the Aspis, who dodges it with ease—as I expected—but now the door is left unprotected.

I sprint toward the exit, pushing past the pain, the trembling in my legs, and launch over the threshold before the Aspis demon can turn around. I propel myself up the concrete stairs that lead to the main-level street, not even pausing to see if Draven is with me or not. He is. I don't know how I know, but I do. So I keep pushing, keep climbing until we break into a run down the sidewalk lining the shops on the street.

"This way!" I shout, finally glancing over my shoulder. Draven hauls ass behind me, the Aspis and Hypnos clambering up the stairs farther back. The surprise of us darting out the door only lasts for a second, but at least we gained a small head start. And those creatures are out of the bookstore, a bonus.

"Want to let me in on your brilliant plan?" Draven huffs, keeping step with each of mine as we run and dart down an alley to the right. The demons screech and roar behind us, but I keep pounding the pavement. I wonder what the veil has every human on the street seeing as we flee for our lives from these creatures— regular, common thieves? Burly cops chasing down two delinquent teens? No, not the time to think on that. Right now, getting us to safety is all that matters.

"I know this city better than anyone," I answer through heaved breaths. I take a sharp left down another back alley, flying past the sides of restaurants and shops until we clear the buildings and turn right, heading toward an abandoned building not far from Miller's. I used to go here to clear my head on breaks. "Almost there," I say, glancing behind me to ensure the demons are still on our tail.

They are, and I have no fucking clue if this will work, but we're out of options. I'm bleeding heavily, and Draven maybe has one burst of power left in him from the look of his ashen eyes.

"Here!" I crouch, barely slowing my speed as I duck through the street-level broken window into the abandoned building. Dust-covered papers and crumbling debris litter the concrete floor—the place was once a printing press, I think. Old machinery, half decayed and rusted, is scattered throughout the dark room, filling the place with an industrial scent that tastes metallic on my tongue.

"Trapping us in *another* building?" Draven growls. "That's your brilliant plan?"

"I didn't hear you spouting off any gems!" I snap back, hustling to the other side of the room just as the demons crash through the windows we came through, shattering them completely.

"Clearly I wouldn't have suggested *this*," he says as the snarling demons make it to the floor.

I glance behind me, to the opened steel door I know from memory. And the small room behind it. A brick storage room with no windows and no other exits.

"You're dead," one of the Hypnos says. "And I'll make it last an eternity."

The remaining Aspis snap their teeth.

"Do you trust me?" I whisper, glancing up at Draven.

His eyes flare, his lips parting for a moment before shutting.

Fuck my life.

I roll my eyes. "Make us disappear when I say," I demand, knowing he can easily accomplish that with his shadows. I don't wait for him to agree. "Then you'll have to come and get me," I snap, raising my bloody wrist toward the Hypno and flicking the fresh blood across the concrete floor.

The demons roar and shake with the scent so close to them. I spin on my heels, sprinting into the back room. I race through the open doorway that looks like another way to exit, as if I'm about to lead them on another chase through the city.

The floor trembles from their advance, the pounding of shoes and claws behind us as Draven sticks to my side and we bolt into the room.

Each demon scrambles in after us, barreling over one another to get to me. To get at that gaping wound in my wrist.

I reach for Draven's hand, clasping it as hard as I can. "Now!"

All the light in the room winks out.

The cool, almost smoky caress of Draven's shadows engulfs me, teasing my hot skin as the demons growl and spit from the sudden darkness. I silently and swiftly navigate us back through the door.

"Harley," he whispers as we clear the open doorway. "I don't have much—"

The sight of my black-and-silver flames stops his near-breathless words as I propel every ounce I hold into that room. The ball of fire cuts through his shadows so quickly and enormously, they evaporate just in time for the demons to jump back from the flames now igniting every scrap of paper piled in the corners of that room.

I shove against the old steel door, pushing with all my weight. Draven slumps against it, pressing with his back, sweat beading on his brow. The metal groans but gives, and it slams shut just as an Aspis barrels into it.

I jerk the massive lock into place, cringing against the keening wails and roaring flames that sound from just behind it. The agonized screams mount, the pounding on the other side of the door enough to rattle my bones as I keep my body flung against it. As if that alone will be enough to keep it in place.

After a few seconds, silence. Except for the crackling of burning paper.

My knees buckle, smacking against the concrete as I slump before the door.

Draven slides down it, his arms heavy at his sides. He lolls his head to the left, those golden eyes of his nearly leached of all color as he looks to me.

A sharp laugh rips from his lips.

I blink at him, wondering if he's lost his mind.

"Mind…" he says through his laughter. "*Mind the books*?"

My lips pop open, and then I clamp them shut. "They were destroying them," I argue but can't hold back a laugh, too.

His eyes drop to my bloody arm, the flesh on either side ripped and stinging. Thankfully—or magically—the wound sits above the tattoo, not coming close to damaging it.

The fire healed me at The Bridge, but now? I continue to bleed and burn with no sign of it stopping. Maybe I used it all. It certainly feels like I depleted every dreg of power in my blood to set that room on fire.

Draven shifts, wincing as if his limbs weigh two tons. He rips at the hem of his T-shirt, tearing off a long strip before securing it around my wound. "Demons chomping for your flesh," he says, tying off the fabric around my forearm. "Demanding your death," he continues, his head falling back against the steel door like he may pass out any second. "And the honey badger worries about the books." He shakes his head, the motion sluggish.

But he grins at me, that same mischievous grin that makes my legs weak.

"Books have value." Duh.

He furrows his brow. "And you don't?"

I shrug, wincing from the movement that jars every inch of my aching body. I need a nap. A shower and a fucking nap. *Maybe a brownie, too.*

"Even the darkness has value to those who seek its shelter," he says, his voice soft, low.

But how can I just go home and rest, I realize, knowing those Hypnos dicks could find me there at any time? Find *Ray* there? I swallow hard, panic and anger and worry swirling in my chest.

Just then, an alarm chimes from my back pocket, causing us both to jump at the sudden sound.

"Ray," I say, silencing the alarm. I shove to my feet, every one of my muscles screaming. "Can you walk?"

His face says he'd rather sit for a few hours, but he pushes off the floor, limping toward me. He shakes his head as we carefully climb out the windows, slowly walking down the street toward the El.

I do my best to tuck my sleeves over the wound, Draven watching me intently as we take the train closer to the school.

"If these creatures can find me just by knowing my usual haunts, is anywhere safe?" I wonder quietly. "Can I even go back to work? School? The trailer?"

"Not all of them can find you," he says, lowering his voice. Luckily, no one is close enough to catch our conversation.

"I know Kazuki said that the Hynpos could sense me, but the others? Like the Aspis?"

"Not all demons are created equal," he says, raking his fingers through his hair. "I'm sure you've heard theories about Hell—that there are nine levels?" I nod. "Each level is a home to numerous types of demons. The outermost levels are the birthing grounds for the sentient demons…like the Hypnos or the Dracos, like Anka, or the half-breeds consummated from interbreeding."

I swallow hard. "Okay," I say. "So that means the closer the levels get to the center of Hell, the worse they are?"

"Yes," he says. "Like the Aspis or the Cannis you saw. Those are baser-level demons who are more animal than intelligent. Those make up many of the Minions the Second recruits."

I scrunch my brow. "What about those Minions in the gym on my birthday? They looked like people…skeleton-zombie people but still. They *spoke*."

"Those were half-breeds from the outer levels."

I trace the edges of the tattoo.

"We were attacked today, honey badger, because those Hypnos knew you were marked. Blood for blood. Kaz warned us to stay sharp. I should've listened better."

I purse my lips at him. "It's not your fault. I've never been one to hide from a fight." I sigh. "We need to find this Second. ASAP."

"I know," he says. "But it seems to me this is going to get worse before it gets better." His words sound almost like an apology.

I swallow hard, that anger inside me solidifying as I nod. "Story of my life, Draven."

By the time we wait outside the school for Ray, my body feels like it's been run through the garbage disposal. Draven and I used the rest of the train ride to make ourselves appear presentable enough—though we both look like we've pulled an all-nighter in a fire sale and could fall over at any second.

He stands more than an arm's length away from me, such a drastic change from when he'd pressed me against the stacks earlier, kissing me until I literally burned. Or from when we fought side by side, in sync as if we'd been doing it our whole lives.

I would've rather spent the time pressed against the stacks, learning the curves of his mouth, instead of fighting for our lives against demons out for my blood...*again*.

God, this *is* just the beginning. They'll keep coming until we find the Second and stop them. But that asshole doesn't seem inclined to show their face, and I don't have a clue where to start looking.

I scan the area near the school, my senses on high alert. Is another attack waiting around the corner? Maybe I shouldn't even be here, picking up Ray. But who else is there? Certainly not our dad. I'd rather face down every demon on this whole godforsaken planet than subject Ray to an assault by him.

Draven seems to be chewing on something similarly troublesome, silent and brows furrowed, arms crossed over his chest. Likely wondering how the hell he got stuck with me as an assignment—a demon magnet, not worth the hell that continues to rain down on me.

Still, he hasn't disappeared yet. And I can't deny how damn *good* he looks when he wears that serious gaze—like he can master the problems of the world if he merely thinks hard enough.

Hot and cold.

Cold and hot.

A thrill rushes through me at the spark his mood swings leave on my skin. I *like* the push-pull; I *enjoy* the blistering sting and the searing relief when he finally crosses that line we've drawn. I relish that bite of distraction, that free-falling sense of oblivion that happens whenever his lips are on mine, his hands on my skin. And I don't know what the hell that says about me, but I have much bigger things to worry about right now.

Like the fact that we have six days until the spell wears off, to find the Second before they find me. Not to mention all these demons hunting me down.

Or the many questions I still have regarding this new world I've been shoved into.

And, most importantly, how I'm going to protect Ray from it. Because she's shown no signs of supernatural abilities, and hopefully it will stay that way. She doesn't need to add demons to her already full list of worries.

"Hi!" I wave to Ray as she bounds down the steps, a smile on her lips as she clutches a rolled-up white piece of paper to her chest. "How was it today?" I ask after she grips me in a side hug and flashes a smile at Draven. One he returns in full. He may be able to be indifferent and snappy to me at any given moment, but he's never been anything but kind to Ray.

"So awesome!" She bounces on her feet as we walk, rattling on about the color scheme they're using as we make our way onto the train. "Here," she says once we score a few seats.

"What's this?" I ask, slowly unrolling the paper.

"We played with fantasy elements today," she says.

My entire body freezes as the drawing reveals itself with my last tug at the paper. "That's me." My words are thick as I spare a glance to Draven on the other side of her. He blinks slowly, his eyes churning.

Ray's drawn me with incredible detail. A perfect rendering where I stand in a wide-open field of green grass, trees bordering the background, water lapping just at the edges...

And black flames engulf my hands as I hold them aloft with a sly grin on my face.

This accurate depiction of me, as well as her using the same name for her character as the greater demon who currently pulls the string of countless demon puppets on earth? How can this be a coincidence? How can I explain it away?

At least she's never drawn *her* Marid with snakes making up his entire body, but—

"My teacher loved it," she says, breaking up my thoughts. "Harley?" Worry creeps into her voice, and I snap out of the terror racing through me.

"It's incredible, Ray," I manage to say. "I love it."

She blows out a breath. "Thanks!"

"Where did you get the idea?" I ask, gently rolling up the paper.

"I had a dream about it last night," she says, her voice light. "Weird but super cool, right?"

"So cool," I say, but my stomach drops into an endless well. I tuck an arm around her, hugging her close.

My mind begs for this to be a coincidence, but my heart breaks with the odds that it's not.

CHAPTER
TWENTY-EIGHT

DRAVEN: Meet me outside Miller's.

I read the text twice before I respond.

ME: Just dropped Ray off at art. Be there in twenty.

My sneakers hit the pavement of the school steps as I up my speed toward the El. I don't bother asking Draven why he wants to meet up on our day off—after what happened yesterday at Myopic, I'm more than ready to see that he's fully recovered.

"Hey," I say, stopping in front of him. "Are we here to cover a shift or…" I let the sentence hang there as I scan him, some inner part of me relaxing at the sight. He leans against the brick building just beside the entryway doors, his golden eyes bright, those lips turning up at the corners.

"Are you always so eager to work?" he asks, pushing off the building to stand within inches of me.

"No," I say. "Want to let me know what I'm doing here?"

He hesitates, that inner battle I've seen far too many times flashing across his face.

I sigh. "You asked me here," I remind him. "Not the other way around."

"Admit it," he says, all smirks again. "You're happy to see me."

I purse my lips. "Happy to see you're still alive. You looked half dead yesterday."

"You weren't far behind me, honey badger."

I glare at him, despite the warm shivers dancing along my skin.

"Fine," he says, nodding to himself like he's just lost the fight. "I have a lead."

Apprehension and hope burst in my chest. "On the Second?"

He dips his head. "Ray is in art for a few hours, right?"

"Yes," I say, smiling at the fact that he knows her schedule.

"Good. We can get this done and still have time to pick her up." He turns, heading in the opposite direction, but glances over his shoulder when I don't instantly follow. He blinks at me. "Unless you don't want to go on the hunt with me," he says, doubt creeping into his gaze.

I hustle to stand beside him. "Oh hell no, I'm going," I say and match his pace as he continues to lead us down the sidewalk. "I was just momentarily shocked."

"By?" he asks, dodging a few people rushing past us.

"That you'd include me," I admit way too fast. I swallow the mortification like a too-big bite of meat.

Draven's eyes fall on me, even as he navigates the busy path, and I instantly regret my no-filter mouth around him. "This fight is more yours than mine," he finally says as we round a corner.

And isn't that the damn truth? Without him, I wouldn't even know where to look for this Second who wants me dead. Now we might be headed straight for them. Something sharp and fierce grows inside me, so fast that my hands tremble and those flames beneath my fingers itch.

"You're right," I say with more seriousness. "If we find the Second, I'll make the kill—"

Draven jerks to a halt, eyes wide as he looks down at me. "You'll make the kill?"

I move into a small alcove connected to the shop we stand in front of, and he follows me. "Yes," I say, lowering my voice. "I'm the reason all this is happening. It's not your responsibility—"

His dark laugh stops me.

"What?" I try to snap, but his laugh is infectious.

"Honey badger," he says, folding his arms over his chest. "You truly believe you can simply take out something as powerful as the Second with a snap of your fingers?"

I don't. Not really. But I have to at least *pretend* like I can, right? If I want to keep Ray and Draven and everyone else I care about from ending up as collateral damage. And the idea of ending this…within *hours*? It sends excitement and anticipation barreling right down my spine. But instead of admitting any of that, I simply lift my chin.

"Does it bother you, Draven? My confidence?" I ask, stepping an inch closer. *Why* does he have to smell so good?

"On the contrary," he says, his voice low and scratchy. "I find it absolutely…"

My breath tightens in my lungs as I wait for him to finish, his eyes scanning every curve of my face and lower until heat floods my body, and it has nothing to do with the flames inside me.

He blinks a few times, taking a quick step away from me. "We need to hurry," he says, folding himself back into the foot traffic on the sidewalk. I hustle to keep pace with him. "And besides," he says after a few too-tense moments. "Today is not about killing."

"What's it about, then?" I ask, the bite totally gone from my tone. Back and forth, hot and cold, flirting and pushing away—that's Draven's and my signature dance, but goddamn, it's exhausting sometimes.

"The place we're going is a likely place for the Second to visit, but I doubt they'll be alone. We need to play this smart. Gather information so we can strike when the Second will least expect it," he says, and I try to bite back a groan but Draven senses it nonetheless. "You don't like my plan?" he asks, turning down another street, leading us toward a back alley I vaguely recognize.

"I told you I'm not good at waiting," I say. "I'd rather get it over with. Hell, those Hypnos demons tracked us to Myopic yesterday. What's to stop more from finding me wherever it is we're going?" Which, I realize, he has yet to tell me.

Draven stops before a wrought-iron staircase that is half hidden behind two large green dumpsters in the alley. Cracked stone stairs lead to the lower level of the brick building on our right. "Kazuki told you the Hypnos can track someone who has killed their kind."

"Right," I say. "But the tattoo?" I raise my wrist, showing off the pure art that also happens to give me a handful more days of protection. "Are you sure you want to test its strength by taking me with you?"

Draven's eyes churn. "Kaz's spell hides you from the Second and their Minions. Though I would never admit it to him, Kaz is the most powerful sorcerer I've ever met. Besides, I wouldn't have invited you if I didn't think you could handle yourself, Harley," he says, and my heart skips at the way he says my name.

I smile because I can't stop it. I think it's the first time anyone has ever said anything like that to me before, and it warms every inch of my skin.

He jerks his head toward the stairs. "We're here," he says, arching a brow at me. "Do as I do. Don't draw unnecessary attention to yourself."

My lips part open. "Do I ever?"

He sucks his teeth, shaking his head. "You draw attention even in your sleep."

"It's not *me*," I say. "It's whatever the hell is in my dirty blood—"

"Don't." He's in my space within a blink, his body a breath away from touching mine. I swallow hard but don't lose his gaze. "Don't ever call your blood dirty."

"But—"

"It's powerful and endless and..."

I furrow my brow, scanning his face, the sharp angles that seem so damn tortured in this moment. My fingers tremble, aching to reach up and smooth away the worry lines, but I know better, so I hold still.

"Beautiful," he finally whispers, then swallows hard as he turns on his heels without another word and descends the stairs.

Whiplash. Maybe that'll be the nickname I give *him*.

I resist the urge to flip off his back and instead follow him down the stairs and through the door he opens.

Four steps into a long, narrow hallway, and a metallic smell clings to the air, combined with sweat and beer. I almost gag, the stench amplifying as we clear the hallway, stepping into a packed room about the size of a basketball court. Only this is no high school athletic game packed with students and staff.

Draven ushers us to the right, weaving through the crowd of demons standing and shouting in a wide circle around something I can't see. A small wooden bar is tucked in the farthest corner of the room, several demons with wings that almost look like Coach Hale's crowding it. And the more we move around in the room, the more I realize he's right about the tattoo—not one demon is looking my way. If Draven really believes the Second is here, I have no doubt the demons pressed together in the room—at least some of them—know the Second or work for them. Still, the relief is only a small release as we push farther into the crowd.

I keep my hands plastered to my sides as I follow Draven—the last thing I need is to accidentally touch a back of scales, an arm of fur, or that stinger that looks like a scorpion tail. But somehow, the throngs of demons shift or shuffle just out of reach of Draven like they can sense his power and know to stay the hell away.

I can't help but study each one we pass, wondering and assuming which level of Hell they descend from—the more animalistic ones have to be from the deeper levels like Draven and I talked about, but the ones with cunning eyes and almost human movements? Those are the ones that send terror licking over my skin. The flames beneath my skin writhe in warning, and yet they all...

They all seem completely *normal* here...cheering and throwing their fists—or claws—in the air. But at what?

Draven climbs up a few steps of wooden bleachers, stopping us in a small pocket of space. He situates himself a few feet away from a massive demon whose rocklike skin stretches tight over so much muscle, he may as well be the Hulk.

I try not to tremble as I take the spot open on Draven's right, sitting close enough for our thighs to touch but somehow managing not to, and then I gasp. Because from this seat, I can now see what the crowd is hollering about.

A giant circle of sand makes up the center of the room, splotches of red and blue and green mudding it up in areas. Two demons face each other, each one sporting freshly torn skin and swollen lips. One is shirtless, the oxlike chest covered in coarse fur that seeps green blood. The other is fully clothed in what looks like yellow spandex, stained blue across the abdomen, and one of its six horns lays broken on the sand.

Something rolls through the crowd as they charge each other for what is surely not the first time. This isn't like The Bridge where demons gather to drink and dance and escape.

No, this looks a hell of a lot like a fight club—if Brad Pitt and Edward Norton had been creatures straight out of a horror film.

"This is a Belluk den," Draven whispers in my ear, and my entire body reacts to his breath on my skin. I mean, seriously? With the smell and the blood flying and *still* I can't resist him?

God, you really did twist me up when you made me. I pair the mental accusation with a mental middle finger, then focus on what Draven is saying.

"A demon fighting ring," he clarifies, and I shoot him an *obviously* look. "Definitely a place where a Second to Marid would hunt for recruits."

I flinch at the sound of bones cracking—the ox-looking demon overtaking the one in yellow for a moment. "How will we know if…if who we're looking for is here?" I whisper back.

Draven scans the room in slick sweeps, and the lethal concentration he holds sends goose bumps over my arms. "Someone that powerful?" he asks, leaning closer. So close, in fact, all it will take is a simple turn of my head and my lips will brush his. Not that I'm thinking about doing that, of course. "I'll sense them."

I lick my lips, my mouth suddenly dry as I try like hell to follow his gaze over the crowd. "Is that something I can do?" I ask, grateful for the roaring crowd making it super unlikely that we'll be overheard.

He draws his eyes from the thrashing throng of demons,

looking down at me. "I think there is a great deal of things you can do," he says, eyes falling to my lips for a moment before he looks back out at the crowd. "Once you accept what you are and gain control of your power."

My lips part, but I quickly clamp them shut. How can he possibly compliment me and insult me at the same time? "Let me get right on that," I say with as much sarcasm as I can muster. "You know," I continue, nodding toward the mass of demons jostling near the fighting ring. "Once I handle everything else on the *don't die this week* to-do list."

Draven barks out a laugh, shaking his head. "Not what I meant."

I ignore the way his laugh fills my heart with a lightness I barely recognize. "It might help if you told me a little bit more about what I am," I say. "Maybe if I understand better, then I can control it better."

He dips his head, contemplative.

"Kazuki called me a Key. Said my blood was ancient," I add, hoping to goad him into opening up. I get having walls, but this is sort of life-and-death. At least for me, anyway.

"You are," he says, eyes still searching.

"Am I the first?"

"No," he says, a muscle in his jaw ticking. "There have been other…Keys. Others who have come into existence over the centuries."

My blood runs cold. "Where are they?"

"Dead." He doesn't trip over the word.

"Fuck. Well, that's comforting." I roll my eyes.

"They weren't…complete," he says, his brow furrowing like he's searching for the right words to explain. "None of the previous Keys worked. Their blood never had quite the right potency."

"Worked…" I chew on my lip, digging inside for the courage to finally ask what I've been avoiding since the night at The Bridge. "What were they supposed to open?" I jerk back as the crowd shifts, rolling toward the benches as they catch the ox-looking demon and shove him back into the ring. I don't understand how either one of them is still standing. "What am I supposed to open?" I ask when the fight resumes.

That muscle in Draven's jaw ticks. Fear and anger curl against my chest.

Don't shut me out. Don't lie to spare my feelings—

"You heard me speak of Marid," he says, still not looking at me. "You heard me say he's trapped in Hell."

I swallow the rock in my throat. "Yes."

"The Key…when used at the right time and place, it can open Marid's door. Allow him to return." He turns his head fully away from me, and under different circumstances, I might think he's hiding something more from me…but we *are* here trying to sense out the Second. That's the only reason he isn't looking at me.

My stomach churns as my mind conjures pictures of a black door in Hell, holding back the snake creature I saw in my mind when Kazuki walked all over it.

"And these other Keys were hunted? Like me?" I manage to ask.

Another nod.

I shake my head. "Figures." I almost laugh, but it comes out more like a choked groan.

"What?" He finally brings his eyes to mine.

I shrug. "That all these demons are tripping over one another to kill me, thinking I'll finally be the one to open the door."

He raises his brows.

"I'm just another broken Key, Draven," I say as if it's the most obvious thing in the world. "Every time I've been attacked…" I bite my lip to try to find the right words. "It's like the flames work on their own—protecting me. Only when I'm an inch from death have I ever felt like I have any control over them." Like when we trapped those demons behind the steel door. "It's almost comical," I say, a painful sense of irony washing over me. "Even if they win. Even if the Second finds me and tries to use me. They still won't be able to bring back Marid."

Shadows cling to Draven's golden skin, and I tilt my head at the sudden darkness hovering around him. He shakes his shoulders, and the shadows pull back. "You don't know that," he says, his voice a whisper among the roaring.

"Sure I do," I say, and a sliver of relief pools in my stomach. If anything, at least I can die with the satisfaction that they won't get what they want. Because no way in hell am I the Key that's finally going to be "complete." I haven't felt complete once in my life—my skin always too tight for my body, the breath in my lungs never enough, my restless and unsettled mind a constant churning thing.

No. I may be a Key, sure. The fire proves that. But I'm not exactly what they're looking for, either, and there is some kind of solace in that.

"**D**amn it," Draven says more than an hour later. "I sensed the Second's presence lingering earlier, but they must've left minutes before we came."

My heart sinks. "Should we wait?" I hate the strain in my bones. I wanted this over with, wanted this to be my chance to take back my life.

"No," he says, rising from the bench in one graceful move. "The lingering power is gone."

I may have whined or demanded we stay just a bit longer if it wasn't for the lethal anger in his eyes as we descend the benches. I follow him down the steps and through the demons hollering for a new set of fighters who step into the ring.

We make our way back outside, and I gulp down the fresh air as we head up the steps—sure, it's tinted with dumpster smell, but it's a thousand times better than the decay that clung to that place. I glance at my cell as we clear the alley, heading back in the direction of Miller's.

"At least we have solid proof Kazuki's tattoo works," I say, aiming for that silver lining. "None of them paid any attention to me."

Draven nods, his eyes still distant, calculating, as we walk.

"I have an hour until I need to get Ray," I say, trying to break the icy silence that settles over him. "Draven?" I say when he still gives no response, barely even blinking as we walk down the sidewalk lining shops and restaurants and bars.

"Hmm?" He blinks out of his thousand-yard stare. "Oh, right," he says. "Do you want to play with fire until you have to go?"

Anticipation soars at his offer. "Yes," I say, then arch a brow. "Is there somewhere you know we can do that?" I ask, gesturing to the people walking the sidewalks around us.

"I think I might. But, Harley," he says, slowing suddenly. "I *am* sorry that the source was wrong about that place."

I tilt my head, wondering if it's the first time he's ever apologized in his life. "It's not your fault," I say, resuming our pace. "As much as I would've loved for the Second to be there," I say, my body itching with disappointment. I should know better—nothing worth it is ever easy. "Without you, I wouldn't even have a clue where to look anyway."

"Even so," he says, turning left down another street. "I didn't mean to get your hopes up."

A real laugh rips from my lips, and his eyes flare. "Sorry," I say, reeling it in as he makes another turn. "Just the idea of me getting my hopes up to stalk the demon that wants me dead?" I snort. "Really puts my whole life into perspective." I glare at him when he turns again, stopping in front of a familiar building. "*Really*? Here?"

"Why not?" he asks, ducking through the same cracked window of the abandoned printing press that we had yesterday. "You've already proven it can withstand your fire," he adds as I follow him inside. "That way if anything happens…" His voice trails off as he comes to a stop in the center of the room.

"You mean if you piss me off so much that I set the whole building on fire?" I tip my chin up, my eyes sliding behind him to where the steel door remains sealed, the ashes of the demons from yesterday inside.

The power in my blood rumbles at the memory, at the knowledge that *I* did that. Does that make me the Key that could truly open the door and release Marid? Nope. Not even going there.

"Oh, I'm counting on that," he says, rolling his neck. He shifts his stance, a defensive position I easily track, then curls his finger at me.

A warmth spirals down the center of me at the motion, and my eyes widen at him. "You're not suggesting I actually try and fight you, are you?"

"Haven't we always done that?" He cocks a brow at me. "Why would this be any different?"

I scoff. "As much as I'd love turning you to ash, I actually need you. Tracking the Second, remember?"

"Scared?" he teases.

"Never," I fire back, shifting my stance. "What about the whole *no touching* thing? Fighting me will kind of break your number one rule, won't it?"

"You won't get close enough to touch me, honey badger," he says, and the confidence in his words, in his smirk, makes those flames prickle right beneath my fingertips.

"Want to bet?" I ask, heart pumping with the challenge.

"*Let's,*" he says. "If you touch me—flames or skin—I'll answer a question."

I roll my eyes. "You sound like Coach Hale."

"And yet you're practically glowing," he teases, scanning the length of my body.

"I am not." I totally am, but only because I'm excited to punch the smirk off his face. "And if you win and I don't touch you?" I ask.

He shrugs.

"What do you want?"

"I'll get creative." The way he shapes the words has more than my adrenaline pumping, and I nod as I slowly approach him.

"Fair enough," I say. I haven't trained with Coach Hale since her betrayal, and while I've come to terms with her secrets, I haven't had a second to think about asking to start up the sessions again. If anything, this will be good practice.

I swing, lashing out with a fast right hook.

Draven dodges.

I keep my momentum, rushing him with a jab-hook combo Coach Hale drilled into me.

He evades, his moves so graceful and elegant, I want to scream.

I glare at him, faking another hook, then dipping down to swipe out with my leg. I barely clip his ankle, but the connection feels like a victory.

"Ask," he says, dancing away from me.

I stand in place. "Did all the other Keys," I say, breath heaving, "the broken ones. Did they have the dark flames like I do?"

"No," he says, holding his fight stance but never once reaching for me. This isn't about him fighting with me; it's about me gaining control and using him as my own personal punching bag. Pretty selfless when I actually think about it. "It's been millennia since another possessed the dark flames like you have. And that legend is so ancient, many believe it to be myth."

I chew on that, bouncing on the balls of my feet to stop the icy fear from settling in my gut. Just because none of the other Keys had this power doesn't mean I'm the special one. I can't be—

"Should I turn on some music?" Draven asks, drawing my attention. "Bishop Briggs, perhaps?"

My cheeks flare. "What?"

He motions to my bouncing. "Don't get me wrong—I'd love nothing more than to watch you dance all day." He flashes me that wolfish grin, and my breath catches. "But it would be nice if you could control your fire even a little bit. Big battle coming and all that."

I narrow my gaze, biting my lip so I don't laugh, so I don't run and tackle him as a thank-you for making light of a hellishly dark situation. How is it that his twisted sense of humor matches mine?

Jab-jab-hook. I shift, lowering myself and throwing an attempt at a kidney shot.

He dodges everything, making me think he *let* me kick him before. That pisses me off even more, enough that those flames creep from my fingers, slow and steady as they wrap around my fists.

"Ah," he says, golden eyes widening. "I wondered when you'd *actually* use your strength."

"I didn't want to beat you too quickly," I say, curling my black-and-silver-flamed fingers toward him. "Wouldn't want to wound that ego of yours."

"You're more delusional than I thought," he teases, "if you think you can put a dent in that."

I laugh; I can't help it. His stance drops just a fraction, like the sound surprises him.

I flick my wrist, the tiniest of sparks from my fire spiraling through the air.

He hisses, flinching as it lands on his exposed forearm.

"I'm—"

"Ask," he says, his eyes all wonder and pride now.

The battle between feeling bad for singeing him and celebrating the win makes me scramble in my own mind.

"When did this all start for you?" I ask, suddenly wondering how long he's been doing this enlisted service thing.

Draven shifts his weight, not dropping his fighting stance. "The Calling happened when my brother and I turned nineteen."

"Wait, your brother is your twin?"

He nods, and I quash the urge to ask if he's an identical twin. I know it's a sensitive subject, that he hasn't seen or spoken to his brother in years. But something else doesn't add up.

"So you've only been doing this for what? A couple of years?" I ask. He doesn't look a day over nineteen, but he could be twentyish.

His eyes trail to the side.

"Draven?"

He brings his attention back to me, something wary in his

eyes. "I was Called five hundred years ago." His voice is low, his eyes never leaving mine. "And my brother...well, I haven't seen him in almost as long."

Shock slides cold and icy over my skin. I hold up my hand as if I need an invisible wall to keep me upright.

"You're *five* hundred years old?" I whisper. "That's... I can't even..." I'm unable to form words.

His lips twitch, an apology flickering in his amber eyes. "I haven't technically been alive that amount of time."

I blink once.

Twice.

"The Seven only awaken me from the divine sleep when they need me." He shrugs, but I see the anger churning in his eyes.

"Divine sleep?"

He visibly swallows. "I'm a weapon for them," he says. "They may be terrified of me, but they won't ignore what they have in their arsenal. After my Calling, after they realized what I was, they put me in the divine sleep. It's hard to explain, but I simply *cease* to be...until they need me."

A knot forms in my throat. "Draven," I say, shaking my head. "How many years pass when you're like that?"

"It varies," he explains.

"What was the longest?" I ask, even though I'm afraid to.

"A couple hundred years, give or take." He says the words so casually, but I can sense his powers roiling from the conversation.

Anger licks up my spine, causing my flames to roar a bit harder. "And they can do this to you whenever they want?" Does that mean that at any second, he could disappear? Evaporate into a plume of smoke and never return? The notion is enough to make my legs go weak.

He smirks, gaze scanning the way my eyes are narrowed. "Worried about me, honey badger?"

"Can they, Draven?" I ask again.

"No," he says, sighing. "All Seven have to agree to put any Judge into the divine sleep. And of course, the Creator can overrule the decision any time they wish."

I shift my weight, needing to feel the solid ground beneath my feet, our training and fight totally forgotten. The power the Seven hold over the Judges seems…so incredibly wrong. "But they've done it to you enough that…" I shake my head. "How long have they allowed you to *live*?"

"I suppose that depends on your definition of living," he counters.

"Days, months, years…doing things you love?"

"In that case, I had nineteen years on this earth as a free human." He folds his arms over his chest.

"And everything after?"

"Pieces. Fragments. Missions. And then…" His eyes go distant.

"And then *what*?"

"I don't know how to put it into words."

And from the pain in his eyes? I need to accept that. It's easy enough to tell he can't or doesn't want to talk about it, and I… *Fuck*, I wouldn't want to, either. It's not like I'm an open book about what my father has done to me my entire life, but Draven? Not having any agency over his own life—when he's present and when he's…what, just gone? Why is every layer he reveals to me worse than the last? And why isn't there a clear way to help him, to ease some of that strain?

I lighten my expression, shoving down the anger at the sheer *wrongness* at what's been done to him, knowing if our situations were reversed? I'd be more than uncomfortable with the heavy topic and be internally begging him for something, anything else.

"You're like Bucky Barnes," I say, grinning up at him.

He does a double take. "The Winter Soldier? Really?"

I shrug. "I'm guessing you caught the Marvel trend, what with your Doctor Strange reference to me at Myopic."

"I managed to catch it this time," he says. "But this isn't a movie."

"I know."

If it was? We would've already solved the mission and been

on our way to eating shawarma. Something else totally awkward hits me over the head, and I try and fail miserably to hold back a laugh. It's so loud and sudden that Draven jumps.

"What's so funny?" he asks, his eyebrows near his hairline now.

"I…" I *can't*. "I've made out with an *old man*." The image itself, the true one, is enough to make me tremble, but the idea of making out with a five-hundred-year-old? It's creepy as fuck and yet makes another fit of laughter escape my clenched lips.

"I just told you I haven't actually lived that long," he says, but there is laughter in his voice.

"Oh, I totally get it," I say, reeling it in. "But you can't blame me for the logistics around the explanation." In truth, nothing is funny about what he's endured over his long—or not so long?— lifetime. But there is light in his eyes now, the ghosts of the past free from his features.

And his past, what he's told me, the knowledge settles in me like an anchor in a stormy current. And it doesn't change that ignited chain inside me, the one that goes taut and uncoils at the same time.

Draven rolls his eyes. "You're impossible."

"Why?" I breathe deep, sliding into that comfortable balance between heavy and light that we like to dance in.

He steps closer, the sudden nearness sobering me up quick. "I tell you that I'm ancient, and you…"

I raise my brows as his eyes scan every inch of my face, something flickering behind them.

"You *laugh*," he says.

"What am I supposed to do?" I challenge.

"Run in the opposite direction. Quiver in disgust. Accuse me of lying to you."

I purse my lips. "All viable options," I tease. "But, you're not *truly* ancient, although I'm sure what you've seen in your brief missions is enough to make you feel like it." No wonder he speaks with such eloquence sometimes—being human five hundred years ago and then only waking up a few times to defeat some demons and going back to whatever the divine sleep is… Once again, I question the Creator's intentions when making lives like ours. "Or…" I hurry to continue. "I could not judge you on anything other than the way you treat me. Treat my sister. The way you make me *feel*." I glance down at his now lowered hand and trail my flaming finger just above it. "Everything else seems…insignificant."

He shudders at the almost touch before stepping away from me, a warning in his eyes. "I've never met anyone like you, honey badger." He raises his fists again, ready to resume the training.

"I know," I say, mimicking his stance. "You've told me before. I'm annoyingly stubborn—"

"Infuriating," he says.

"Same to you." I hurry to swing while he's still so focused on our conversation, and I just graze his shoulder.

"Cheater," he teases, but waves at me as we dance around each other again. "Ask."

"The other Keys," I hurry to say. "Were you assigned to each of them, too?"

"In a way," he grinds out.

I tilt my head, my chest suddenly feeling like an anvil sits atop it. I drop my fists, their warmth buzzing against my jeans as I stand up straighter. "You…when you were awoken…you had to watch them all die?"

Draven visibly swallows, then shakes his head, a predator's gaze crinkling his eyes. "Don't do that," he all but growls.

I bristle at the tone, taking another step toward him. "Did you, Draven?"

Tension coils his muscles the closer I get, but he doesn't retreat. And I can see it there, just behind the steel door he keeps over those golden eyes—maybe I really am a powerful Key, because that door is cracked…for *me*. I can see inside—the pain, the memories that haunt him—fuck, I can almost feel the gritty weight of it inside me, settling over that chain I can't explain connecting us.

"I hate that for you," I say, and he tilts his head.

"What?" he rasps.

"Five hundred years—shattered by the divine sleep and robbing you of any true life in this fucked-up world—and you've suffered more than I can even fathom." Watching the people he was assigned to as they die over and over again only to be forced into nothingness until he's needed again? Not being able to touch anyone without worrying about killing them? Losing his brother? "I thought my life sucked," I say, shaking my head. "But you totally win." I try to lighten the mood.

"Good," he says. "I like winning."

I reach up, the flames still dancing on my fingertips, hovering an inch away from his cheek. He watches me, never taking his eyes off me, never flinching from how close my fire is to him. Almost like he *wants* to burn, like he thinks he deserves it. And my foolish heart breaks for him all over again.

"Do it," he says, challenge coating his tone. "Claim your win." He extends his arms horizontally, inviting and intimidating at the same time.

But I'm no longer thinking about our bargain, the fight, or the need behind it. I'm not thinking about the power I have to master or the countdown over my head.

All I can think about is him—this powerful and broken being before me. A mirror to me in so many ways. That chain between us pulls taut, causing my insides to go tight and loose at once.

A thought, that's all it takes to snuff the flames and touch his cheek.

He gasps at the contact, at the feel of my skin against his, no barriers between us. His eyes go molten and churning as he lifts his hand to my face, his fingers shaking before he grazes one over my jaw.

"Honey badger," he whispers, and I part my lips, fully prepared to tell him I'm not afraid of him, but he steals my words with a kiss.

I whimper from the power behind it, the surrender in the way he gently cups the back of my neck, drawing me to him in one smooth move. I part my lips under his, opening for him, and his tongue slides against mine, all mint and spice and *Draven*.

His fingers dive into my hair, and he grips it, tilting my head back to give him a deeper angle. He claims my mouth with deep, sweeping strokes, ratcheting up my heart with each pass. I arch into his body as his free hand slides around my hip, holding me to him.

Warmth coils low in my belly, a hunger blooming as I dig my fingers into his back.

"Harley," he growls, drawing back enough to look in my eyes, and his are blazing. He yanks me against him, planting his lips along my jaw, down the seam of my neck, raising warm shivers everywhere he touches. I gasp, craning my head back to give him better access as he drags his teeth just above my collarbone. Awareness ripples throughout my body, tendrils of need racing to every nerve ending as he playfully nips my skin before soothing the small hurt with his tongue.

My skin flushes, my pulse racing as he works his way back to my lips. He slants his mouth over mine, and I take what he gives, give what he takes, until I'm trembling in his arms—a coiled spring of need ready to snap.

This is real fire.

This is exquisite torture.

This is *living*.

"More," I sigh between his lips, my mind hazy with need and bubbling with want.

A ringing from my back pocket shatters the moment as I jolt in his arms, and he's releasing me before my brain can connect with my body.

"Time to get Ray," he says, his voice hoarse.

I touch my fingers to my swollen lips before nodding. "Will you…" God, what did I want to say? *Come with me*? *Text me later*? What could I possibly say to make whatever is happening between us make sense?

"I'll see you soon," he says, and before I can respond, he becomes a shadow, disappearing through the window.

"Show-off," I snap before climbing out the window so much less gracefully.

CHAPTER TWENTY-NINE

"How much stronger is this lead than the last?" I ask after Draven and I have cleared the steps away from Nathan's after dropping off Ray. I love the way he never misses an opportunity to keep an eye on her.

I just wish the reason I gave him for me *needing* him to watch her was true—that Draven and I are going out tonight. Just a totally casual, super-fun Saturday night out on the town—if hunting down an immensely powerful demon who wants me dead is casual.

"Hey." Draven's voice is lighter than I expect based on what we're about to do, but then again, I've come to expect the unexpected with him. I mean, we left things on such a heated note two days ago, I'm honestly shocked he even reached out. "It's not my fault the last source sent us to a Belluk den." He casts me a sideways glance as we board the El, snagging some empty seats near the back. "Which, like I mentioned, *is* a place I imagine someone like Marid's Second would pass the time. You saw the fighters; they're chosen for the pits for a reason. Ruthless, strong, exactly the kind of demons this Second recruits."

I somehow manage not to shiver at the mention of the faceless demon we now hunt. I shake my head, the memories from two nights ago churning my stomach. "I still can't believe there are underground clubs where demons are pitted against each other for money," I whisper.

"Really?" Draven asks, eyebrow arched. "After everything you've already seen?"

"I know," I say, sighing. "Nothing should surprise me at this point. But come on, that place reeked." And the scent *lingered*—sweaty flesh, a variety of blood splashed upon the sandy floor of the club, making it look like multicolored mud.

And yet, somehow I'd still followed up that gruesome and horrible letdown of an experience with the one and only thing that can erase every single worry from my mind—Draven's mouth on mine.

His strong hands in my hair.

His teeth teasing my neck.

A tremor rolls through my muscles, delicious tremors dancing up my spine.

"Harley?" Draven says my name like he's called it more than once. I blink out of the haze the memories threw over me, jolting a little to see him staring at me from the opened doors of the train. "This is where we get off."

My jaw about comes unhinged as I hurry toward him, my cheeks no doubt flaming with red. God, the way he says things drives me absolutely wild.

A hoarse chuckle rumbles behind me, and I cringe at the sound. He *knows*.

I whirl on him once we clear the other foot traffic. "Stay out of my head," I demand, and he raises his hands like I pointed a loaded gun at him. Like that would do any damage to him anyway. I can *feel* the power rolling off him in staticky waves that raise the hairs on the back of my neck. My dark flames whisper to the tips of my fingers in answer.

"Trust me, honey badger," he says, dropping his hands. "If I'm in your head, you'll know."

I straighten. "Then how…" I stop my words with a huff.

"You're very easy to read," he answers anyway, grinning as he motions to the left, leading us toward Washington Square Park.

"Only to you," I say, shoving my hands into my jacket pockets. It's not cold by any means, though the early evening air is less suffocating than during the day, but something about the motion helps me feel contained when being with Draven on another hunt is completely chaotic. Everything inside me is a battle—my need to breach his walls and unearth the source of the connection between us I can't deny versus my need to stay focused and survive the damn week.

Right. Survive. Kick ass. *Then* internalize dramatically about the ancient boy who gets under my skin in the most delicious way. Priorities.

"Truly?" he asks, mimicking my stance as we walk—hands firmly tucked inside his leather jacket pockets. And damn, could he look any better? He probably isn't even hot, either. Some ancient power where he's immune to the elements along with so many other things. "Not even Kai?"

I raise my brows at the mention of him. Draven isn't usually the one to bring him up. "Even with him," I admit, following Draven as his pace slows and he turns down another busy street. "He knows not to push me," I try to explain.

"Or he simply doesn't bother to look," Draven counters.

"Maybe," I say, shrugging. "But that's only because he's dealt with me longer," I add, trying to lighten my voice. "Talk to me in a decade and we'll see how much you can read me." I nearly stumble over my words, reality catching up with me.

I'll be lucky to be here in a few days, let alone years.

"It may not matter anyway," I hurry to say before he can give voice to the strain etched in his face. "I haven't been able to see him much recently, and with everything that's happening, he's safer the less time I spend with him." Something eats at my chest, knowing what a terrible friend I've been lately, but I've been a tad preoccupied with…the world crashing down around me.

"That's my line," Draven says, his tone softening as he stops on the outskirts of the lush green trees bordering Washington Square Park. And I *want* to say I'm sorry that he knows what I'm feeling. Sorry that he's experienced it far longer than I have, but I know that he'll brush it off, just as I would, so I try to focus on what's in front of us.

"Um, Draven?"

"Yes?" he asks, his eyes scanning the building across the street like he has X-ray vision. I guess he *could* have that power and I wouldn't know. It's not like he came with a codex or anything—at least, not one that he's offered up to me.

"Why are you staring at the Newberry Library like you're trying to move it with your mind?" My eyes widen. "*Are* you trying to move it with your mind?"

His head snaps in my direction, a rough laugh tumbling from his lips. "You think I can do that?"

I shrug. "I feel like I haven't even learned half of what you can do."

He presses his lips together, the laughter leaving his eyes. "That's true," he says, motioning toward the library. "What do you see?"

I scrunch my brows but figure I better indulge the random question anyway, seeing as how things with Draven are rarely random. I turn, shifting so my back is to the trees and I fully face the building.

Evening is transitioning to night, casting the sky a stark indigo behind the sand-colored stone building. White lights illuminate the carved arches over the library's entrance, and two large trees nearly as tall as the building itself stand guard just outside it. Countless windows and more stone detail round out the rest of the library, the glass of the windows reflecting the indigo color of the sky.

I spare a glance to Draven, who isn't looking at the library anymore but at *me*. I take a deep breath, realizing from his look that I'm definitely missing something. I focus on the building again, this time opening my mind I keep guarded out of sheer habit.

My senses ripple like a rock thrown in a river, the sensation strong at first, then spreading out wider and wider until my entire being feels the warning.

"Something is in there," I gasp.

Draven nods, his golden eyes flickering with pride. "What kind of something?"

"Powerful," I whisper, my insides thrashing as the flames gather and swirl near the surface of my hands.

"Good," he says.

"This? This is where your source told us to look for the Second?" I ask.

"Indeed," he says, eyes narrowed as he surveys the library again. "I was skeptical at first, but it actually makes sense." I tilt my head for him to elaborate. Draven shifts back toward the trees a bit more, moving us off the sidewalk and out of earshot of anyone passing by. "The library itself has been here since 1893, and structures like this, ones preserved and protected by time, are often locations with underground ties to our world."

The way he says "our world" without hesitation fills me with a wave of warmth. Because it truly is my world now, and while I've accepted that, hearing it from *him* makes it seem all the more real. Important.

"A library," I say. "That's where the Second is hanging out?"

Draven's lips turn up at the corners. "Where would you like the Second to be hiding? Under a bridge? An abandoned warehouse, perhaps? Or maybe in a cavern complete with brimstone and dark deeds?"

I flip him off. "I *get* it," I say, laughing as I shake my head. "Nothing is as it seems in *our world*. Ever. You don't have to be an ass about it."

He shrugs. "It's what I'm good at."

"You're good at more than that," I mumble under my breath. Like winding me up so much, I can barely think straight.

"What was that?"

"Nothing," I say, nodding toward the library. "So, do we head straight to the horror section or…?"

Draven closes his eyes, tilting his head toward the sky like he needs the moment for patience, and I can't stop another laugh. He glares down at me. "For someone with so much riding on finding this Second, you're awfully *joyous* tonight."

Omigod, he's right. But it's one hundred percent *his* fault. I laugh more when I'm around him—his dark humor matches mine. And with the creepy internal warning I felt when I reached my senses out to the library? How can I *not* try and focus on literally anything else than the truth that pulses from the power in the building—the Second is likely in there, and that means it's time to take a swing.

And I'll never admit it out loud, but I'm terrified it'll be the last swing I take.

All my laughter and jokes are swallowed up by the unknown, and I manage to shrug instead of actually responding to Draven.

He must understand, or maybe he's reading my mind again, who knows, but he nods and turns to face me. "Just like the Belluk den," he says. "Do as I do. Tonight isn't about a direct attack—"

"But I only have three days left," I say, raising my wrist for emphasis. "If not tonight, then when?"

"I don't know yet," he says.

"When will you know?"

"After we see what all is in there."

"Then what are we waiting for?" I place my hands on my hips, showing that my patience filter just went up in smoke.

"Honey badger," he says, sighing, as he crosses the street without another word.

I follow close behind, mimicking his casual yet stealthy steps as he enters the library as easily as if we're really there to check out a few books. I can't help but sigh happily as the smell hits me, that signature scent of weathered pages and leather spines is so damn comforting. Books have always been my escape from my home life—until more recently, when an infuriating, ancient boy managed to help me escape with nothing more than a brush of his lips over mine.

Instead of heading toward the main floor, Draven turns left, aiming for the stairs. I run my fingers over the wooden railing, appreciating the carved pattern as we descend the stairs. I try and fail to make my sneakers as silent as his boots, but it becomes clear that it doesn't matter the farther down we go. Chatter echoes off the walls, bounding up toward us and practically vibrating the air.

"Aren't libraries supposed to be quiet?" I whisper at Draven's back as he stops before a door that is half blended into the wall to our right when we reach the last of the steps. The frame of the door shimmers slightly like heat waves, and I gulp around the knot in my throat.

"No one can hear that," he says. "No one human anyway. Veil, remember?"

I nod. "Right. Just like I'm sure no one can see this door?"

"We can," he says, anticipation lighting up his eyes. He draws a finger to his lips, giving me the universal *shush* sign as he lays his other hand flat against the shimmering door.

It silently slides to the left, and Draven darts through it.

I hurry to follow him, the door sliding home behind me.

Our shoes are quiet against the carpeted floor, but I mimic Draven's crouch as he stalks to the right. The light is darker in here, as if this section of the building is closed this time of night, but I quickly realize we're somehow a floor *above* the actual basement because there is amber light leaking over a wide banister several feet away from us.

All the chatter I heard moments ago is coming from whatever rests below that banister, and it no longer sounds like an overzealous group at a private event.

Nope. It sounds like a chorus of growls and screeches, grunts and clacks, and other hissing languages I can't even try to understand.

Draven slows, creeping in that crouched position as he nears the banister—it can't be more than three feet high, so he's practically crawling. I follow him, my heart in my throat, that internal awareness thrashing the closer we get. The pressure in the room mounts like bricks against my skull, and everything in my body is begging me to run. The flames at my fingers are pounding against my skin, demanding release, but I mentally shut a door on them, knowing now is so not the time to blow our cover.

Draven settles against the banister, one shoulder pressed

tightly against it as he carefully, slowly lifts just enough to take a peek over the lip.

He drops below it immediately, going so still, I'm not sure he's breathing. Something like defeat and anger flashes over his face, and it's that look in his eyes that makes me unable to wait. I mirror his earlier move, glancing over the lip of the banister and looking down.

Terror freezes me for seconds, heartbeats. I can't tear my eyes off the scene happening a floor below us—the amber light drenching the demons below.

Hundreds of them.

Some I recognize—Hypnos and Aspis and Cannis.

But the others? My mind can barely focus on one before my eyes are panic-darting to the other. They line tables, cards sprawled among some of them and what looks like maps among others. Some chug thick green liquid from goblets while others pace the wooden floor like they're guarding a perimeter.

My blood turns to ice as my gaze hangs on a demon in the farthest corner of the room, sitting alone at a small round table, an ancient-looking book opened before him. He wears a red velvet suit, a black tie tucked beneath his pristine jacket, but his style isn't what has the breath in my lungs seizing. It's his skeleton head—some hybrid between man and beast—the bone bare and bleached until it meets with three giant branches shooting from the top of his skull. Twisting and sharp with tinier branches jutting out and down, protruding from his spine and disappearing beneath the suit. Eyes of pure black yet somehow still seeming so very *deep* as they watch the room, the book before him forgotten.

Draven's hand on my jacket is the only thing strong enough to draw me out of that all-consuming panic. He tugs me down, and I go willingly, our eyes locking in matched looks of shock. He gives me another *shush* signal, and I roll my eyes, feeding off the irritation to root me in the present and out of the panic.

He moves then, the same slow crawl toward where we came in. We're a few steps away from the door when Draven stops so fast, I nearly plow into him face-first. And since we're *crawling*, I stop just shy of falling right into his muscular back—

The door *swishes* open, and Draven rolls on the carpet, taking me with him as he darts behind one of at least fifty shelves in the darkness. I hold my breath as he tries to melt us into the back of the shelf, my eyes widening as a dozen little creatures scurry from the door. No bigger than a Scottish terrier, the demons are covered in fuzzy black fur with pointed ears as long as a rabbit's. They almost look *cute* waddling on all fours as they head toward a spiral staircase on the other side of the room—

One stops, whipping its head in our direction. Its eyes are a searing, glowing red, and a lipless mouth reveals a permanent smile shaped from serrated teeth.

Fuck me, not cute! Not cute!

Draven's arm bands around my chest, holding me so tight that I think my ribs might break. Nice to know his *no touching* rule disappears under life-and-death threats.

The scurrying sound of its paws against the carpet is slow as it draws closer. Somehow I can feel Draven's irritation all the way in my bones, but I don't have a second to think on it, because one breath he's squeezing the life out of me, and the next shadows caress my skin.

Luckily, I'm too terrified to scream or react in any way, my mind swarmed by a disorienting sensation. A soft clicking sounds, another wave of movement, and then the click again. The shadows disappear, and I gasp.

No longer pressed against a bookshelf, Draven and I are in a small closet. There is just enough light filtering under the door to make out that it's filled with rows of plastic tubs sitting atop tall shelves. Storage, old books, whatever the closet is for, I'm grateful.

"Fucking hell," Draven whispers, raking his hands through his hair. "That was too close."

"Where are we?" I keep my voice just as quiet.

"The first confined space I could find," he says, settling next to me. "Those Parvosses are curious little creatures. I couldn't risk them finding us, tattoo or not." He eyes my wrist. "I managed to slip us two floors above that one."

"Wait, what?" I shake my head. "Can't we just leave, then? If we're in the main part of the library?"

"We're not," he says. "We're still in the veiled portion of the building, simply two floors above."

"How long do we have to stay here?" I ask, eyeing the tiny room.

"Until I can no longer hear the thoughts of the Parvosses scurrying about below us."

I tuck my knees against my chest, hating the tremble I can't stop from shaking my body. "That guy in the corner," I whisper, eyes on the tubs across from us as I try not to rock against the wall. "The skeleton dude with branches on his head and an abyss for eyes?" I clarify, and Draven nods. "That's the Second, isn't it?" I shiver. The demon felt powerful when I looked at him— endlessly so.

"No," Draven says, and I meet his eyes. He leans against the wall next to me, forearms resting on his knees. "That's a Malus," he says. "Extremely powerful, but not as much as the Second will be. Plus, their species isn't one to strategize like Marid's Second is required to do. They're more stab first, think later."

"Not the Second," I manage to say, the tremble in my bones ramping up. "Did you sense them, then?"

Draven shakes his head, disappointment churning in his eyes. "But this is the place," he says with certainty. "I may not have sensed the Second's presence, but the demons? Their thoughts were all clear—obey orders and get infinitely rewarded."

"Any of them happen to *show* you a mental image of what their leader looks like?" My teeth are literally chattering now. What the actual fuck?

"No," he says, shifting as he pulls off his jacket. He drapes it over my shoulders, careful his fingers don't touch any of my skin. "Breathe, Harley."

I release a tight breath, sighing at the warmth of his jacket over me, and quickly tug it around myself. It's big, almost tucking around my knees I have against my chest, and it smells like him. It's enough to fight off the shakes just slightly.

I open my mouth to say thank you, but no words come out. I shake my head, unable to form a coherent thought. All I can think or feel is the sight of all those demons, so many kinds, so many working for the Second. Each one would likely drag me straight to the Second—or do the job of killing me themselves—if the tattoo didn't hide that I was here.

"So damn many," I finally say minutes later, the warmth from his leather jacket calming my muscles enough to speak. "Hundreds, Draven."

"I know."

"And they all want me dead."

"Yes," he says.

"I…" I choke on a dark laugh. "Like, I joked that there was a stadium full of demons coming after me, but *fuck all*, there are literally hundreds down there just waiting to slaughter me." It feels like a cement blanket sank over me, threatening to crush the breath from my lungs. "How can I… I can't possibly…"

"Look at me, honey badger," Draven says, his voice a primal whisper I can't ignore. I draw my gaze to his. "This changes nothing."

"It changes everything."

"Nothing," he says, eyes blazing. "We're smarter than all those creatures combined. We will watch this place and wait. We'll strike when the Second least expects it."

I nod, letting his confidence chip away at the heavy weight trying to choke the life from me.

"Can we leave yet?" I ask, my body itching to move, to *run*.

"Not yet," he says, eyes scanning my face.

"Tell me something." I tug his jacket tighter around me. "What?"

"Anything," I say, giving him a pleading look. "Dogs or cats?" I ask when he doesn't immediately speak.

"Dogs." He stumbles over the random question.

I nod, relaxing against the wall a bit more. "Chocolate or strawberry?"

A small smirk shapes his lips. "Both," he answers.

"Tacos or burgers?"

"Trick question," he says, and it draws a smile from my lips. But the image of those demons still clings to my skin.

"What power is your favorite?" I ask, reaching for something deeper, something strong enough to take my mind off how close I am to death.

"No one has ever asked me that before," he says, eyes on his hands.

"I bet I can guess," I say.

"What do you want if you're right?" he asks, tone lighter.

Butterflies flap around the panic sitting heavy in my stomach. "I'll tell you if I guess right."

"How will you know?" he asks. "I could simply lie to you."

The bite in his tone hits something deep inside me, but I brush it aside. "You wouldn't," I say. "Because I can read you as well as you can read me."

"You think so?"

"I do," I answer, totally focused on him now.

"Then what is my favorite?"

I bite my bottom lip, thinking over every power he's revealed to me. While all are equally amazing and this side of scary, my mind snags on one over and over again. "The shadows," I finally answer.

His eyes crinkle around the edges for the briefest of moments, and I know I'm right.

"Why?" he asks instead of denying me.

"Because you believe you belong in them," I answer honestly, and while I should probably feel bad for drawing out that truth, I don't. He laid me bare in Myopic before I even knew what I really was, so tables turning and all that. "You relish the ease in the darkness, the weightlessness in becoming something everyone overlooks. You'd rather go unnoticed than feared."

Draven's eyes stray from mine as he rubs his palms together. "You're right," he says, finally turning to look at me. "Except for one thing. There is nothing weightless about the dark." I part my lips, but he hurries to continue. "Still, you guessed right. What prize do you want, Harley?" He leans an inch closer like he can *sense* what I want, what I can't deny whenever we're together.

"I—"

Draven's eyes snap to the door, something lightening their previously hooded gaze. He moves to the door, peeking out of it, closing his eyes as he breathes deep. He motions for me to follow him, and I slip my arms through his jacket as we rush on quiet feet through the room.

We clear the library, but I don't stop walking until I'm in the heart of Washington Square Park. The moon is high, casting the green trees in a silvery glow, and we're nearly alone. Draven stops before me, looking very much like he wants to say something but doesn't know exactly what.

I wiggle out of his jacket, handing it back to him now that I'm free of the power roiling in that building. The power, and the overwhelming odds that just slapped me in the face like a proverbial hand.

"Now what?" I ask, drawing in lungfuls of the Chicago air. "We strategize? Formulate a plan to come back and—"

"What do you want as your prize, Harley?" Draven asks me again, this time taking a step toward me.

I crane my neck to meet his eyes. "That's not important now."

"Yes, it is. A deal's a deal, and I'm not one to be in anyone's debt."

"Like I'd ever hold you to it," I say, and he cocks a brow at me. "Fine." I shrug. "Distract me."

"What?"

"That's what I want. To be distracted," I say. "I want to disappear, if only for a few seconds. Want to escape the fate I don't know how to beat." I raise my hands like I can encompass the entirety of the world. "Can you give me that, Draven?"

He slides into his jacket, focusing extremely hard on the movements as if he needs them to help him think. And once it settles over those broad shoulders, his golden eyes meet mine. "A deal is a deal," he repeats, a whisper of a smirk on his lips.

And then his mouth is on mine.

I sigh at the contact, at the instant connection that blazes to life between us. Sigh as I fall into his kiss like diving into the deepest pool of warm water. Here, his lips on mine, his tongue caressing into my mouth, I'm not a Key. Not a girl from a broken home. Here, I'm nothing but *this*…this wild, aching thing he turns me into. I'm the girl who draws out the growl coming from deep in his chest, the girl who he breaks all his own rules for.

His hands trail down my arms, stopping at my hips as he hauls me against him. He's so damn warm against me, and he smells so good. I want to drown in him, want to lose myself entirely to this writhing need thrashing inside me. The taste of him makes me gasp, and I meet him stroke for stroke, our tongues exploring and dancing like we've done this a thousand times.

Each graze from his fingers down my spine has me arching into him.

Each playful nip of his teeth on my bottom lip has me gasping.

Each growl from him has my head soaring with the power in it.

I tangle my fingers in his hair, silently urging him for more. To kiss me harder, to hold me tighter, to take away the ache that's been building and climbing in my soul since the day I met him.

"Draven." I sigh as he hooks his hand behind my knee, drawing it up and over his hip. His hard body aligns with all the soft parts of mine, and every thought and worry empties from my mind. Nothing exists outside of his lips, the way he feels pressed against me, that inner chain yanking tight. *So* tight it feels like a bridge between us, something I can easily walk across and settle right into him forever—

Draven goes deathly still, and my heart plummets to my stomach as I feel him pull away before he ever physically moves.

"Draven, no," I say, my voice a plea as he releases me, taking that damn graceful step away from me that I knew was coming.

"I can't," he whispers.

My shoulders drop, and I remind myself this happens every. Single. Time.

But something about the hard set of his jaw, the coldness in his eyes replacing the liquid gold that was there seconds ago...

It feels different than the other times.

"You can," I say in case he needs the verbal consent I thought I made crystal clear when I asked him to distract me.

A tremor rolls through his body. "I'll kill you."

I sigh, making sure I catch his eyes. "Funny enough," I say, stepping away from him like I know he needs me to. "People keep trying to do that and find themselves...disappointed."

Another step, and my body mourns every inch of space I put between us. But I know a wall when I see one, and the one he's just thrown into place? It's not the same as his others, and I hate the doubt creeping into my chest, whispering things I *don't* want to hear.

Things like Draven is hiding more than I think, which means he doesn't trust me.

And when he's the sole ally I have in this overwhelming doomsday battle? That's more tragic than knowing I've stirred up the supernatural world, my blood planting me with a mystical bull's-eye, making them all believe I'm something I'm not.

CHAPTER
THIRTY

"I didn't hear from you for a few days," Kai says as we walk the crowded streets of downtown. We just finished a pleasantly normal lunch, and my stomach twists at his turn in conversation.

"I was slammed every day. Between three shifts and securing the apartment and dodging telling my father..." My voice trails off.

It's not a lie; I *have* been busy. I just leave out the part where I watched a demon fight club, saw an entire fucking demon army at the library, and still managed to meet up with Draven every day after work to play with fire. He's helped me understand it more, helped me learn to conjure it at will instead of just when my life is in jeopardy. Still, he doesn't have an answer to why something constantly feels like it's yanking that power back, or the fact that according to him, I *should* be able to do far more damage with a simple flick of my wrist. *Incinerate with a blink* were his exact words.

Like, of *course* I can't. I keep telling him, I'm not the complete Key. I'm just one of the defective ones. But he refuses to listen, and I can't really blame him. If I'd spent centuries watching potential Keys die? I wouldn't want to believe it could happen again, either.

Thankfully, we haven't run into any more demons since the bookstore—thank you, mystical tattoo—but I know even now, my odds of dying are close to fifty-fifty, based more on steering clear of my typical spots and keeping my location under wraps. Can't wait to up those odds to a whopping one hundred percent once time runs out and I'm demon fodder again.

And while I miss my best friend, I didn't text him because I didn't want to put him in danger. Just the same as I'm keeping as much distance from Ray as I can without throwing up any warning flags. It's killing me inside, but I have to keep them safe.

Luckily, nothing interrupted my and Kai's lunch or the easy stroll we take now—no attacks or awkward confessions, but he seems to be leaning toward the latter, and I legit *can't* right now. I hate lying to him, but with his life on the line? Time to suck it up, buttercup.

I got the keys to my apartment yesterday, though the accomplishment feels hollow. The clock is ticking on the Kazuki countdown, but we have a plan. Anka has been watching the library when Draven and I can't, and in a couple of days, hopefully, we'll make our move. But a couple of days feels like a damn eternity, and my patience is so, *so* thin. Waiting around and watching the days of my life wind down like sand through an hourglass isn't my idea of a good start to being eighteen—which is almost as frustrating as not being able to shut off my cravings for Draven during training.

"I get that," Kai says, drawing me back to our conversation. "Has Ray been to the apartment yet?"

"Not yet," I say. "I haven't had time to even buy an air mattress to set up for her. Plus, I've been trying to find the right time to bring up the idea to my father…about her staying with me for a while." And I don't plan on doing anything until after I get this demon mess over with once and for all. I can't risk bringing Ray anywhere near it. I have to beat this, have to survive. There's no other option—Ray needs me, and yes, the whole apocalyptic army is terrifying, but for her? I'd burn the world to the ground if it meant keeping her safe.

"You think he'll go for it?" Kai asks as we board the El.

"Honestly, I'm going to offer to keep paying rent on the trailer if he'll let her stay with me. There's not much he won't do for drinking money." It'll be tight, paying rent in two places, but if we budget our money right, I think I can just swing it.

"I hope it works out," he says. "But I don't want to see you crushed if it doesn't."

I rub the bridge of my nose, a headache forming behind my eyes. Too many things happening at once. I'm on constant alert now, always worrying if merely being out in public with Kai or Ray or Draven will result in an attack.

Not that it would be terrible with just Draven and me. Though we barely scraped out of the last attack, we'd at least faced the fight together.

Ray and Kai wouldn't be so lucky.

As the train pushes on, Kai shifts the conversation to normal small talk, telling me about how his parents are planning a trip in the next month or so and how he can't decide if he's going with them or not.

"Why wouldn't you want to go? It's Europe," I tease him as we get off the train and head toward school to grab Ray.

My chest tightens at what drawing she might bring home today. Draven and I have talked a couple of times about what it means that Ray dreamed about my fire and Marid and agreed that odds were, being half related to me, she has some demon blood in her, too. Thank God that blood seems to be benignly focused on art.

"I've been a dozen times," Kai says, drawing me back to the present.

"Does it ever get old?" I ask, always a healthy level of jealous at his family's ability to travel anywhere at the drop of a hat. He's headed somewhere this week, too—Ohio? Oregon again? I can't remember, and I chalk that up to the demons having an anxiety party in my head twenty-four seven.

"It does if you have more important places to be."

"Like where?" I ask, my boots scraping along the pavement as I stretch out on the steps. "I've never left Chicago. I'd kill to take Ray to Japan." She's always wanted to go ever since she learned her favorite anime artist resides there.

"Here," Kai says, his tone switching to serious. "It's important for me to be here."

"Why? It's summer. We've graduated. You're taking a year off *to* travel." And he doesn't have a job because his parents won't allow it. Claimed it would detract from his grades. Couldn't really deny it, since I struggled with the deli's hours during school and the amount of homework teachers piled on me each week. It was a never-ending balancing act that I couldn't ever quite master. But I'd done enough to graduate with an average GPA.

"*You're* here, Harley," Kai says, and I snap my eyes to his.

"We've survived tons of trips," I say, keeping my tone light. He'd be gone weeks at a time sometimes, and while I always missed him—sometimes so much that I asked him to stay—we always went back to normal when he returned.

"That's different."

"How so?"

"Because things were different when we were younger." He stares straight ahead, the line of his jaw hard. "And something is happening. You're…different." He points to my tattoo. "You didn't even bother to tell me you got that done. Something that huge? You always tell me everything."

I furrow my brow, my lips clamping shut. I want to argue, to tell him I haven't changed, but I have.

Infinitely.

"Talk to me, Harley," he says when I remain quiet for too long. He reaches for me, then jerks back quickly, as if I sting him with my look. *"Please."*

"We're talking now, Kai."

"Not what I meant." He rakes his fingers through his hair. "You're hiding something."

I feel his disappointment like a punch to the chest, and I can't even fault him for noticing. He's been my best friend for years, so of course he can tell when I'm not being myself. But as badly as I want to tell him the truth, I can't risk it.

"I can't talk about it." There, I didn't lie; I just didn't give him the whole truth.

"You can't talk about it or you can't talk about it with *me*?" He shifts to face me.

"Both."

"Since when have you ever kept a secret from me?" he challenges.

I never have.

"Try."

"Kai," I groan. "Please just leave it alone."

"That's not fair," he says, a pleading in his eyes. "I can see something is hurting you. Bothering you. More than usual. I can't help you if you don't talk to me."

"I don't need your help," I say, softening my tone so it's not as harsh.

Kai flinches regardless. "You don't need *me* is what you really mean, isn't it?"

"That's not what I said."

"Pretty much." Anger tightens his voice, and I hate that I put it there.

"Look…" I sigh and run a hand across my forehead. "I'm sorry, but I can't talk about what's going on. I'm dealing with some things that I need to handle on my own—"

"You need someone to help you through this," he insists. "Whatever it is. I've always been that person."

Not just him but Ray and Nathan, too. Coach Hale—before I stopped our training sessions because of her betrayal. Time has cooled my anger over it—plus her willingness to help watch for the Second—but I still can't get past the fact that she knew for years I was different and never once thought about clueing me in.

"And I appreciate that, Kai," I say, my eyes pleading with him to understand. "You *know* how much our friendship means to me. But there are some things I need to handle by myself."

"You shouldn't do everything alone."

I narrow my gaze, suddenly feeling like his *shouldn't* sounds a whole lot closer to *can't*. Like he doesn't believe I can handle what life throws my way. "You know what?" I say, anger rising in my chest, "if it bothers you so much that I can't talk about this one thing out of *all* the things I've ever shared with you my entire life, then maybe you shouldn't hang around me anymore."

Kai gapes at me, his brow pinched. I hate the hurt in his eyes, the betrayal, but if I have to push him away to keep him safe, then that's what I'll do. Besides, how many times should I have to say no before he hears that I mean it?

Guilt, sticky and heavy, slides through my chest.

Kai pushes off the steps, pacing the space before me. "I'm trying, Harley," he says. "I'm trying to save you from…from what's eating you from the inside out. I can see it on your face, in your eyes." He shakes his head. "But you're shoving me away."

"I am not!" I say, standing as well. "I'm here. And I don't need you to save me—"

"It's Draven."

I do a double take.

"What?"

"It's Draven." Kai stops pacing. "You've been seeing him more and more outside the deli."

I open and close my lips a few times. I've been totally honest with Kai whenever he texts and I'm with Draven. I just never say we're training with flames and fighting.

"We're not *seeing* each other. We're friends." At least, I think we're friends. I honestly don't know what the hell we are. One second, we can't keep our hands off each other and the next, we stay three feet apart because we're terrified one will kill the other. It's been days of this push and pull, and honestly, I'm just as frustrated as Kai seems now.

"Damn it, Harley!" Kai snaps, his voice so harsh, I flinch. "I *told* you to stay away from him. He can't save—"

"God!" I cut him off, exhaustion and anger sucking the air from my lungs. "I'm so tired of men telling me what to do! I'm so fucking tired of you or Nathan or Draven or any man thinking he knows what's best for *me*!"

At least when Coach Hale and I trained, she never demanded anything of me and let me make choices that were best for *me*, despite the lies. While Nathan always means well, sometimes he can't see past me as a little girl in need of help.

And Draven? Well, he affords me more choices save for one—the one where he keeps telling me he is dangerous right before he steals my breath with a searing kiss that has me dancing on the edge of a blade.

And Kai. Maybe he thinks he's helping, but in truth, he's driving me further away by assuming he knows better.

"You don't have to protect me," I say, calming a little. "I can take care of myself. I can make choices for myself."

Kai scoffs. "And what *choices* you make." Sarcasm drips from his tone, and tears bite the backs of my eyes. "He'll ruin you in the end. Where I would elevate—"

"Stop." I raise my hands, focusing like hell not to let my fire slip. "Stop. Kai, we've been over this. You're my best friend, but I can't...I *can't* be what you want me to be." Can't he see that? Sense it? We're so wrong for each other, I can't even picture it in my mind.

Kai narrows his gaze. "He's changing you."

"What?"

"I waited too long." He shakes his head. "If I would've told you the truth a month ago..." His voice trails off, his eyes going distant.

"This has nothing to do with Draven," I say on the end of a sigh.

"This has everything to do with that waste of breath!" Kai shouts, and fire thrashes in my blood.

I close my eyes, cooling it mentally.

"Careful," I warn once I manage to open my eyes without bursting into flames. "Careful how you talk about him."

Kai's eyes widen, shock coloring his features. "You've known me"—he huffs, his hand on his chest—"your whole life. You've known him for all of two seconds, and you would choose him over me?" His shoulders drop.

"I'm not *choosing* him," I snap. "I'm stopping you from saying things you have no clue about!"

"No clue?" His voice grows deadly quiet. "You... Harley, you're the one who is clueless."

I gasp, my eyebrows shooting up to my hairline in disbelief.

"Are you calling me stupid now?"

The stairs vibrate beneath our feet, the motion trembling up my legs, and I glance toward the street on the other side of the school, wondering if a parade of semis is about to head our way. Kai tilts his head at the shaking ground, eyes snapping to mine after a few seconds as if I have all the answers.

"You should go, Kai," I say once the ground stops shaking.

He stumbles back a step, then another, as if I physically pushed him away. "You're asking me to leave?" His eyes rake over me from head to toe, looking as if he's never seen me before in his life.

And maybe he hasn't—not like this. Because I've never once asked him to leave. I'm always the one begging him to stay anytime he has to fly off with his family.

"You keep pushing me away, Harley…" he warns in a low voice, pointing at me. "One day, I won't be there to save you."

"Save me from *what*?" I practically growl.

Pity flashes in his eyes, piercing my body like a thousand knives, but he doesn't answer. He just turns his back on me and walks away, disappearing around the side of the building.

I reach up and scrape off the wetness on my cheeks. Kai and I have had fights before, but not like this. Not about something as serious as his faith in me. My stomach is churning by the time Ray comes skipping out of the school, and for once, the smile on her face doesn't chase away my fears.

This time, all I can think about is if that's the last time I'll ever see Kai again.

CHAPTER THIRTY-ONE

I sink atop my bed, dragging my astral projection book into my lap. The chaotic state of my mind, which leaps from demons, to my father, to the fight with Kai earlier today, to how close Draven and his contacts are to finding the identity of the Second, to the insatiable desire to seek out Draven and have him help me forget *all* of it are exactly why I'm preparing to meditate now.

I close my eyes and empty my mind of every thought except *sensation*.

The feel of each muscle in my body—one by one uncoiling and settling into a deeper state of relaxation. I lock on to the sound of Ray's charcoal scraping against the thick card-stock paper, the steady *swish-swipe* a beacon to anchor my mind to the present while my physical body sinks further into relaxation.

Mentally, I picture a rope hanging above me—just like the book instructs—but mine glows a bright white instead of the book's more traditional beige. My breathing evens, my body a heavy thing threatening to suck my mind down, down, down.

Swish-swipe.

Swish-swipe.

The sound helps my mind stay afloat, and I mentally reach for that rope, grasping it with fuzzy fingers. With one hand, then another, I pull my mind from my body, leaving that heavy, scarred, anxiety-ridden thing behind, and breathe deep. Such a sweet breath, outside the physical anchors that prickle and sharpen with each inhale in the real world.

A light, bubbly sensation tickles all over as I climb that rope and glance around our room. I remain seated on my bed, eyes closed, that book still in my lap. Fresh bandages cover up the wounds of the last attack at the bookstore, that once-gaping injury now sealed shut and nearly fully healed.

Elation threatens to shake my focus as I realize I've never made it this far all the times I tried deep mediation before. I want to high five myself for finally achieving astral projection after all the times I wished and begged and *prayed* to be anywhere else in any given moment. To shed my body and not feel the pain anymore.

Here, there are no demons or bigger evils chasing me. On this plane—I'm free. It's almost as liberating as when locked in Draven's embrace.

My eyes shift to Ray, the room slightly blurring at the edges as I smile down at her. She works on her character Marid, this time placing him before an ancient building, arms raised like he's trying to lift it with his mind.

The walls beyond her are peppered with Marid drawings, dozens of them. They've been there for months, but as I look at them now…

They *move.*

Like they did when Kazuki slipped into my mind, and we saw my blood splattering these works of art.

In some, he waves at me, a primal smirk on his lips. In others, his indigo eyes glow like the silver in my flames. And in the one she works on now? He glances over her shoulder at me, peeling his lips back to bare his teeth like a hungry, cornered animal.

"Doesn't she look tired?" Marid's voice is scratchy and deep as he looks from me to where Ray guides the charcoal over the paper.

My stomach drops and his words echo in my mind.

"Do you want to know why she's barely sleeping, Harley?" Marid growls my name, and all the sweet, blissfully free feelings evaporate.

I try closing my eyes, but I can't, not in this form. Not this deep in the meditation—have I gone so far that I fell asleep?

"You," he hisses, pointing a long finger at me. He then directs it toward Ray's temple, and that fire inside my blood roars as he

sinks it two inches beneath her skin.

Ray winces, her brows pinching as the charcoal pauses, and she rubs at the spot he currently touches.

"Stop!" I try to shout, but it comes out a whisper. This can't be the same Marid Kazuki spoke of, right? The one I saw is made of snakes and pure evil... This character is a creation of my sister's mind—

"You're hiding from me," he whispers, not budging an inch. *"But I'm coming for you. Even if I have to tear through her mind to get you to listen."* He shoves his finger farther into her temple. *"Ready or not—"*

A pounding sound jolts the center of my chest.

Ray jumps, dropping her charcoal as her head jolts to the left.

A sharp hook yanks my middle, hurtling me backward so fast, I gasp as I pry my eyes open. Tiny pinches of pain radiate along my skin and muscles, like when your leg falls asleep. I shake out my hands, jostling when the sound happens again.

A knock on our front door.

"Are you okay?" I ask Ray, slightly frantic as I kneel before her, smoothing my hands over her face.

She furrows her brow, nudging me off. "It's just a knock on the door," she says, looking at me like I've grown a few extra arms.

"Does your head hurt? Did you have another nightmare?" I ask just as another knock sounds.

Ray sighs. "Sometimes I get headaches when I draw," she says, motioning to her work in progress. I resist the urge to rip the piece to shreds like my asshole father did. "It's not a big deal—lots of artists do. And yeah, I had another nightmare last night." She motions to the drawing like that explains everything and goes back to her work. I remain there by her table, staring at her, then the drawing, then back again.

Did I fall asleep? Did I create my own nightmare? A combination of what I saw with Kazuki and my own powerlessness to stop Ray's nightmares that have kept her exhausted these last few weeks?

"Are you going to get that?" Ray asks when the knock sounds again.

I blink out of my panic as I study her drawing. Sure, she makes it look real, almost with a haunting quality. But it isn't the greater demon I saw. It *isn't*. It's just my overcrowded mind, the exhaustion clinging to my bones from everything that's happened recently.

"Yeah," I finally say. "Stay here, okay?" Not that a horde of demons will knock, but I'm not taking any chances. I hurry down the hallway to our front door.

With each step, my muscles awaken a little more, the world snapping into focus as my mind and body come together once again. And even though the meditation was only minutes, it feels like I slept for an hour. Slept…and dreamed.

I spare a glance through the windowpanes in the front door, instantly swinging it open.

"Draven," I say, slightly breathless.

He raises his eyebrows at the exertion.

I wave him off, not wanting to talk about what just happened yet, but I step to the side, silently extending an invitation inside.

Cedar and amber and citrus invade my senses as he walks in, and a restless sort of swirling prickles with awareness.

"What's up?" I ask, my voice low. I don't particularly want Ray to overhear anything supernatural. Not yet. I plan on telling her; I just haven't figured out the best way to do it yet. Plus, there's that nagging, gnawing fear that she might be afraid of me after I show her what I can kind of do. "Did you find something?"

Draven shakes his head, his hands deep in his pockets. He looks…nervous, which ratchets up my heart rate. "The Second has yet to reveal themselves at the library," he says, the line of his jaw hardening. "Anka is taking over the watch tonight."

"She's still helping?" I raise my brows, unable to stop wondering when she'll bow out. It's not her fight, but then again, it's not really Draven's, either. And as much as I hate that Draven is only allowed awake status for random missions, part of me is glad he made it to mine. "But we're stuck in a holding pattern?"

Draven nods.

"More training, then?" I ask, eyeing his clean black jeans and boots, the soft black T-shirt he wears. If we spar again, I'll ruin his clothes like the last time, or we'll end up in another lip-lock that leaves me more confused and frustrated than before. The walls he hides behind are still there, but I swear I was getting so close to slipping through those cracks. One step forward, two steps back. I wonder if we'll do this dance until one of us...

Nope. Not going there.

"Actually," he says, his voice soft. "I wanted to see if you'd accompany me on an outing tonight. I regret never celebrating your birthday like we should have." He clears his throat, his voice so hopeful, I have to bite back a smile. The boy has been nothing but confident bordering on arrogant since I met him, and with good reason—he's gorgeous, super powerful, and has put up with so much shit all his life.

"My birthday is what started this whole mess," I say, rolling my eyes. "You don't need to feel obligat—"

"I don't," he clarifies.

I chew on my bottom lip. The tattoo still has two days—well, one and a half, seeing as it's almost dinnertime—of protection left, but should I really be going out and acting like I'm not about to have the *literal* fight of my life?

"We can't let fear steal your chance at living..."

While you can.

He doesn't speak the words into my mind like I know he's capable of, but I hear them as clearly as if he did.

"You want to take me out?" I ask, and my heart hiccups a little in anticipation.

Hell, he's right. If I only have a little more than a day left to live—which I refuse to believe on stubborn and likely foolish grounds—then I might as well make the most of my time.

"Yes," he says, almost timidly.

"What happened to staying away from each other unless we're on the hunt or training?" Or fighting for our lives from demons.

He takes a step toward me, not enough to touch but enough to brand me with that golden gaze of his. "I can't," he says, the words strained. "I *physically* can't do it anymore."

A warm thrill rushes through me before my shoulders sink. "I can't." I motion down the hallway toward Ray. "My father left for the night, so he'll be out late, but I'll never leave her here alone—"

"I made plans for all three of us," he says, stopping my ramble.

"You did?"

"Of course." He eyes me like it's the most obvious thing in the world. And I swear in that moment, I feel him slide through my veins, settling in all the jagged pieces inside me.

"And you're confident we can keep her safe if something happens?" I don't want to let fear control me, but when it comes to Ray—

"I'd never let anything happen to that girl." He says each word as though it were wrapped in iron, and I can't help but believe him.

It takes me a few minutes before I realize I'm staring up at him with a likely goofy and embarrassing grin on my face. And he seems perfectly content to let me do that forever. Heat blazes on my cheeks, and I blink the stars out of my eyes.

"Ray," I call out, and she hurries down the hallway.

"Draven!" she squeals, and the two proceed to do some choreographed secret shake that consists of a few air fist bumps and air high fives. I watch it with wide eyes. "I have a new piece I want to show you!" She urges him to follow her.

"When did you guys come up with that?" I whisper as we follow her to our room.

"While you were doing inventory with Nathan."

I shake my head in wonder as he catches up with Ray at her sketch table. I lean against the doorway, my skin tightening the closer I get to all the drawings of Marid.

It's just part of the meditation. Some deep, dreamlike state.

It isn't real.

"So many of Marid," Draven says, almost struggling over his name as he shifts a stack of papers on the corner of her desk and draws one out of the pile. His eyes not so casually find mine as they drift from the drawing and back again.

"Yeah," Ray says, one knee balancing on her chair. "He's all I dream about lately. Well, him and Harley, of course."

His eyes remain locked on the most recent image, the one that came to life and lifted off the page to threaten my sister moments ago when I…fell asleep.

And a cold chill races along my skin.

"It's beautiful," he finally says. "You've been busy." He traces a finger over the rest of the work she shows him, such pride in her eyes. "I don't really believe it," he says, and all my pride shifts to worry in a blink.

"What?" she asks.

He kneels to her level, studying her face. "That you're only seven years old. Someone with this extraordinary talent?" He tilts his head. "You must be *at least* thirty-two."

Ray bursts into a fit of giggles, shaking her head, her blond braid flying back and forth. "I'm *almost* eight," she says.

"You sure you drew these?" he teases, standing again.

"I'm sure," she says. "I just put the ink to paper. The rest sort of just happens the way I see it in my mind."

"That's how it is with a piano for me." Draven nods. "But I've tried to draw before. Trust me, it's not like that for everyone."

Another smile from her, and my freaking knees wobble.

"I have a serious question for you, Ray," he says, and my stomach drops. Good God, he's the master of whiplash, and I swear if he asks her about her dreams in correlation to the drawings, I will lose my shit. I don't even want to think that she may be seeing something real out there, real and terrifying and part of *my* world. Not hers.

"Okay," she says, shifting so both her feet plant on the floor, her shoulders square. I don't think she even notices the movement, the need to face any serious situation head-on.

"Would it be all right if I take you and your sister out for the evening?"

"Oh, is that all?" She gives him a big, toothy grin.

Draven chuckles. "What did you think I was going to ask?"

Her blue eyes flicker to the wall where Marid's image covers the space. "Nothing," she says a little too quickly. "Where are we going?"

"That's a surprise."

Ray claps. "Let's go!"

As we both grab our things and head out, I realize I never even asked where we were going.

CHAPTER THIRTY-TWO

"**S**hut. *Up!*" Ray squeals a half hour later as Draven stops outside of Rotofugi—one of Chicago's coolest sources for anime toys and merch. "Draven!" she says, bouncing in her sneakers.

"You think we can find something you need in there?" he teases as he holds the door open for us.

"I'll be happy just looking." She grins as she walks inside, me following her.

"No way," he says. "You have to get something—"

"I can't," she says, chewing on her bottom lip as she glances to me. "I don't actually need any of this stuff. We have to save our money for necessities, right, Harley?"

A rock lodges itself in my throat. That's been our motto—food, clothes, running water, they all trump luxuries. But I try to afford her some fun whenever I can—manga, paints and sketchbooks, and art supplies.

Draven kneels to her level again, drawing her gaze. "This is my treat," he says. "As a thank-you."

"For what?" she asks, scrunching her brow.

Draven glances up to me and then back to her. "For being my friend."

She snorts. "You don't have to bribe me to be your friend, Draven. You're funny and smart and you're a really good listener. It's *easy* to be your friend."

Draven visibly swallows, and I can read it in his eyes—that hasn't always been the case. "You too," he says, his voice tight. "Now, please? Let's get you something *cool*." The way he says the word has me biting back a laugh for some reason. It sounds foreign coming from him.

"I don't know…" Her voice trails off as she takes in the massive store filled with all the things we can never afford—Funko Pops, *tokidoki* Unicorno series toys, colorful candies in pretty packaging, plush characters, neon puzzle boxes, shirts with anime covers on them, and tons of bags and backpacks and wallets.

Draven glances up at me, a plea for help, but I can only shrug. It's her choice, whether she accepts his generous offer or not. "Tell you what," he says, returning his focus to her. "Would you be open to a trade?"

"I'm listening."

"I'll let you pick any three items in this store," he says, "as a form of payment for that drawing of Harley you showed me yesterday. The one where she has that black fire on her hands."

Her eyes light up, her pink lips parting on a gasp. "*Three? That's too much, Draven.*"

He scoffs. "For that drawing? I'm practically *stealing* it from you."

She chews on the offer for a few minutes, and I can tell the moment she acknowledges the worth in her hard work. It makes my heart ache and swell at the same time. "Deal," she says, extending her hand for him to shake.

A cold dread swirls in my stomach, but she blinks and shakes her head.

"Oh, duh," she says, rolling her eyes at herself. "My bad." She curls her hand into a fist, and Draven air-bumps it. "Can I go look?" She turns to me. I nod and she hurries off, her sneakers squeaking on the slick floor.

Draven and I fall into step a few paces behind her. "What did you tell her?" I whisper, eyeing his hands.

"Germaphobe," he says.

I snort at the prospect. Draven, a boy with an endless well of power, afraid of germs? Yeah right.

"More believable than you'd think," he says, our conversation hushed between the two of us. "It's always worked for me."

"Every time you're allowed to be...awake?" I say, that same hurt clogging my airways every time I think about his life.

"Well, not *every* time, I suppose," he says, eyes going distant. "I can't actually remember when germs became a perfect excuse for no contact..." He shrugs. "When I was human," he says, his voice a whisper. "People were more concerned with conquering than germs, though plagues *were* a thing."

I try to school my features, but I can tell from the smirk on his face, he's enjoying my blatant shock. He lived in the sixteenth century, for Christ's sake, and then in brief spurts until now. "How the hell do you keep track of it all?"

"With difficulty," he says. "Memories from that time...it's like looking through a thick fog. It's easier to remember my more recent..."

Missions? Awakenings? I don't know what to call it, either, so how could I expect him to?

"Is it weird?" I ask, fascinated despite myself. "Waking up and everything's changed so drastically? Like, suddenly cell phones are a thing?"

Draven smiles. "The Creator takes care of that. I'm essentially... downloaded on modern society before I show up."

"Wow," I say, nodding. "Divine Wi-Fi is a thing. Good to know." He laughs softly. "So, then do you have a favorite awake moment?" I ask, wanting to shift things to something happier.

"Besides this one?" he asks, and my heart does that damn hiccup thing. "When I had enough time to learn the piano," he says, his fingers hovering just an inch above my cheek.

"I'm still dying to hear you play." I so desperately want to lean into that touch, but I know better.

"Let's...get through the next couple of days," he says. "Then I'll play you whatever song you wish."

Right. Because tonight, this special outing, could be our last.

"Harley!" Ray calls, and I blink out of the warm haze that covers my body, my mind. "Check this out!"

I break Draven's gaze and head toward her, my body tingling from his almost touch.

I'm not sure how much longer we can dance around this fire between us before it engulfs both our walls. I just hope I'm still alive to see what happens next.

CHAPTER THIRTY-THREE

A few hours later, Draven walks Ray and me to our door, a *tokidoki* unicorn mini backpack on Ray's back, with some fizz candy and a Creepy Kawaii Edgehog plush toy tucked safely inside.

I gently swing the plastic bag full of our leftovers from dinner back and forth as we linger outside the trailer door. "I don't know how to thank you enough for all this, Draven," I say, my heart begging me not to let the night end.

"You have no need to thank me." He shoves his hands in his pockets, shuffling one boot against the ground.

I do, though. It's been perfect, from the anime toy store to dinner and dessert, where we all laughed and joked and just hung out like we were regular friends. I've never had a better night. A blissful kind of normal, beyond the few snippets of supernatural conversation we had in the store. And maybe that was Draven's goal all along—to give me one perfect night before all hell breaks loose.

Which means... My lungs tighten. *He truly doesn't believe I'll make it.*

"Keys," Ray says with a giggle, her eyes not at all hiding her mischievous look. "I'll give you two a minute."

I drop my keys into her hand, laughing softly as she unlocks the door and steps inside.

Draven's jaw goes tight as I step toward him, my eyes narrowing as I prepare to tell him exactly all the reasons I will survive tomorrow when the spell wears off and long after—

Crash!

The sound jolts me out of the verbal battle I almost unleashed just as Ray screams. Faster than I can blink, I'm inside the house, my chest heaving.

And the world slows.

Father's home early. And he holds Ray by the shirt, the toes of her sneakers dragging across the carpet as he moves.

"Where the fuck have you been?" he snarls, his speech slurring. "And where did you steal this from?" He jerks on the little backpack secured at her shoulders, and she yelps.

"I didn't steal it!" Ray cries.

"Of course you did, Harley! You're a worthless little thief," he snarls.

Oh God, he thinks she's me.

"Stop!" I scream, barreling for him, but it's like my legs are dead weights.

He throws her across the room, tossing her like she's nothing more than a bag of garbage.

I hear the sickening *crack*.

See her head bounce off the wall.

Watch her little body crumple on the floor.

And I slam into my father hard enough to tackle him to the stained carpet.

All I can see or taste or feel is red.

CHAPTER
THIRTY-FOUR

"Harley!" Draven yells as he encircles my waist, tugging me back and back until I can only land a quick kick to my father's side.

"Who the hell is this kid?" Father snaps, scrambling to stand.

I thrash against Draven's hold.

"Harley! Ray needs you!" He has to shout to break the roaring in my ears, despite holding my back against his chest.

But those words change *everything*.

I forget my father, forget the rage. Think of nothing else but getting to Ray. Draven releases me, feeling the shift in my priorities, and I skid on my knees to her side.

"She's breathing!" I glance over my shoulder at Draven. "But she's not waking up!" I try to rouse her, but her little head only lolls to the side at my gentle nudging. Then I see the blood on the wall: a little smear of red where she made impact. I softly tuck my hands beneath her head, my fingers coming back stained with crimson.

My entire body shakes, rage a white-hot roar in my blood.

"I thought she was you." My father blinks over and over as if he can clear the film from his eyes. "She's fine. She's fine, she's fine," he repeats like a scratched record. Like it's only now catching up to him what he's done. Hurt his perfect daughter. The good one. The one worth everything.

He starts to stumble over to Ray, but Draven's fist jabs at Dad lightning fast, snapping back his head with a loud *crunch* before he falls to the floor with a satisfying *thud*.

"It's a twenty-minute train ride to the closest hospital," I say.

"Will an ambulance make it here quicker?" he asks.

"I don't know!" Panic sets my whole body trembling as I hold Ray's limp hand. "Draven, she's not waking up. Why isn't she waking up?" Tears race down my cheeks, the air coming too harsh, too fast in my lungs.

Please be okay. Please.

All my fault. All mine.

Draven sinks by my side. "Do you trust me?"

"What?" I snap. Now is *so* not the time—

"Just close your eyes, Harley."

"But Ray…"

He pulls down his sleeves to cover his hands, then scoops her up against his chest. "Close your eyes, Harley." There is a primal command in his tone I can't ignore.

I squeeze my eyes tight, tears still trickling out the sides.

A whirring sound fills my ears, soft at first, then louder and louder. A cloudlike caress encircles my body, smoothing over my skin in spiraling whirls until I feel weightless. A floating sensation makes me dizzy, but I keep my eyes sealed shut. Draven's scent drenches the air around me, thick and swirling with the faint hint of smoke.

Unable to stop myself, I peek open my eyes and gasp.

Thick black smoke fills my vision. A constant spiraling movement that snakes between my arms and legs and around my core. And Ray—the smoke crisscrosses over her body, bands of shadow creating infinity loops around her as she floats, her blond braid lifting toward the sky. I reach out, my fingers filtering through the smoke, a sweet softness to the texture—

And then my boots smack against pavement, jarring every sense in my body.

The shadows converge to a central point, spiraling until Draven stands at the epicenter, Ray still cradled against his chest. The shadows dissolve, a bright-white light illuminating the surrounding area.

"Omigod," I breathe, then take no time at all to grab Ray

from Draven's arms and rush through the emergency room's doors. "Help me!" I scream so loud, I scare the receptionist, who immediately launches into action.

Within minutes, I hustle alongside a gurney, Ray atop it, while a nurse fires questions at me.

"My father threw her against a wall," I blurt as we turn into a private room. Shit, I'm supposed to lie. I'm supposed to *lie* to ensure they don't take her from me. But she's hurt this time, not me, and I can't lie. Won't hide what he's done to her.

Another nurse hurries in behind us, checking vital signs. The one with the questions pushes me out into the hallway. "You need to give us space," she says, her hands before me like she'll tackle me to the floor if I try to get in that room.

"That's my baby sister," I cry, my chest caving inward.

"I know," the nurse says, lowering her arms. "And you have to let us help her."

I nod too rapidly, my mind dizzy with a loop of her hitting that wall, her tiny body limp and motionless. "She hit her head," I say, not sure if I mentioned that. "She was bleeding."

"They're going to do everything they can, ma'am," she says, moving her head to tear my attention off the closed doors. "I need you to come to the waiting area. Did someone drive you here? Someone who can sit with you?"

I shake my head, having sense enough not to explain how I managed to get to the hospital so damn quickly.

Draven. Where is he?

"Ma'am," the nurse says, ushering me down the hallway. "Is there someone you can call?"

I swallow hard as she situates me into an empty chair in the waiting room near the receptionist desk. "Yes."

"Good. Make that call," she says. "I'll bring you news in a minute."

I nod, fishing out my cell and hitting the name on autopilot.

He answers after one ring. "Harley?"

The sound of his voice, the instant concern, shatters whatever little control I have. I sob into the phone.

"What's wrong?" His voice is panicked. "Where are you? I'm coming." I hear a shuffle on the other end of the line. Keys jingling.

"Northwestern Memorial," I manage to choke out.

"I'm on my way." I hear the car door slam, the engine rev.

"Nathan," I blubber. "It's Ray."

A cold, dreadful silence.

"I'm coming, kiddo." His voice tightens like he's trying not to crack.

I nod and hang up the phone, letting my head sink into my hands.

And I weep.

CHAPTER THIRTY-FIVE

"Harley," Nathan says a half hour later, smoothing his hand over my back. "Officer Mason is here. Wants to ask you a few questions. Are you up for that?"

I blink the haze out of my eyes, scraping my long red hair off my shoulders. The waiting room comes into focus—Nathan at my left, concern coloring his features. A police officer, the same one from the night of the break-in at the deli, stands looking down at me, a slew of accusations on his face.

I clear my throat, scanning the rest of the room.

No Draven.

"Um," I say. "Sure."

Officer Mason pulls a free chair from behind him, positioning it right in front of me. "Where were you this evening?"

"We took Ray downtown," I answer. "Then went out for dinner." It feels like a dream world—the beauty and happiness of the simple night. And then the fresh hell of reality that slapped that dream into a million jagged pieces.

I turn to Nathan. "Did the nurse tell you anything?"

He presses his lips in a line. "She won't release the information to me, since I'm not family."

"She hasn't been back…" Each ticking second feels like an hour.

"When you say *we*," Officer Mason continues, drawing my attention back to him. "Who does that include?"

"My friend Draven, myself, and my sister, Ray."

"Draven?" Officer Mason says his name like he recognizes it.

"He works for me, too," Nathan says.

"Where is he?"

"I took off," I say. "I needed to get Ray here."

He makes a few notes in his pad, then looks up at me again. "Okay. So you got home from your night out at what time?"

"I don't know," I say. "Nine thirty-ish."

He tilts his head, but that police officer's hat doesn't dare budge. "And what happened then?"

"Ray went in first." My chest cracks. "And I heard her scream." My head has cleared enough to turn off the default-lie filter when speaking to authorities. Father crossed his hard line, and he will rot for it. "I ran in after her, but he already had her in his grip. Threw her across the room and she hit her head on the wall. She slid to the floor and didn't move again." I sob on the last part, still seeing her lifeless body in my head.

"Draven did?" the office asks.

I jerk my head, scoffing. "What? No. My *father*. He's the one who did this."

"I thought you were the legal guardian?" he asks Nathan.

"It's almost finalized," Nathan says, and I'm too numb to even pretend to be surprised at his lie.

My cell buzzes, and I jump a little, not realizing I still have it in my hands from when I called Nathan. My mind is jumbled and frantic while not being able to do a damn thing but sit still.

DRAVEN: I'm outside the building, recovering.

The text flashes over my screen, and I furrow my brow. Right, flying us here...shit, did it push his powers too far?

Officer Mason slides out of his chair, pushing it back. "I have to speak with the doctor regarding the injuries," he says. "But I'll get a crew over to your residence within the hour." He hustles through the restricted doors, the receptionist waving him in without a second glance.

Anger itches in my chest, though I know it isn't his fault. Police officers have access to all kinds of things, but I'm her sister, damn it.

I turn to Nathan and say, "I should be back there with her."

"I know," he soothes, his hand a warm comfort on my back.

"But these doctors know what they're doing. She's in good hands. It's going to be all right—"

"Harley Ward?" a nurse calls through the open double doors, and I bolt out of my seat, Nathan on my heels.

"You can come back now," she says, waiting for me to follow. She leads us into the room. "She's stable," she explains as we head to Ray's bedside. "The doctor had to give her ten stiches to seal the head wound. Her fourth rib on her left side is cracked, and she's got a nasty concussion, but she should be all right now."

I choke out a sob, taking Ray's hand in mine as I gaze down at her. She looks so peaceful sleeping there, the little rise and fall of her chest.

"The recovery will be tough—cracked ribs always are. But she'll be back to normal soon enough." The nurse glances at Nathan with a questioning gaze. "Who are you to these girls?"

Nathan clears his throat, flashing me an apologetic look as he motions to Ray. "I'm in the process of legally adopting Ray Ward."

My mouth drops open. Why is he keeping up the lie when the truth about my father has finally been revealed? And with that truth, the family courts have to grant me guardianship, right? Not that I ever wanted it to happen this way…but they can't possibly deny me now. Not with what he's done.

"Do you have the paperwork?" she asks, and I cringe. I don't want him in any more trouble than he'll already be for coming back here.

"I do," he says, retrieving a rolled-up chunk of papers and handing them to her. "My lawyer has already received approval by the family court judge pending the biological father signs over his rights to me on the set court date."

The ground trembles beneath our feet, the lights flickering as the building groans. Nathan's hand darts out to grab my elbow, the nurse holding Ray's bed rails to keep it steady.

I suck in a sharp breath, forcing my mind to focus on one thing at a time. And right now, all I can do is thank God Ray will be okay. That she'll wake up. She'll recover.

The trembling stops, and Nathan drops his hold on me.

The nurse continues to thumb through the paperwork before nodding and handing it back to him. "It's not official yet, but it's enough to afford you visitation. I won't be able to release her medical records to you until this is signed, though."

"Understood," he says, giving her a soft smile as she heads toward the door.

"I'll be back in fifteen minutes to collect you. Visiting hours are over at nine, but given the circumstances, I wanted you to be able to see that she's okay."

"Thank you," I say, my voice hoarse from screaming earlier.

The door shuts behind her, and I whirl on Nathan. "How could you not tell me?"

"I didn't want to get your hopes up—"

"My hopes up?" I snap, dropping Ray's hand to stalk Nathan across the room. To his credit, he backs up until he can't anymore. "You can't take her from me," I practically growl, my heart shattering. How could he? After all this time, all his kindness and generosity—

"I'm not taking her from you, Harley—"

"What do you call this, then, huh?" I smack the papers in his hand. "When did you even start this process? Why—"

"The day you showed up with another bruise and lied to my face about how it got there." He shakes his head. "I hate that I've been so naive, Harley. I knew life with your dad was bad, but I never thought he crossed the physical abuse line. You were always so good at hiding it, but then that day you told me you fell down the stairs at the El…" He sighs. "I saw through it. Saw the pain there. Knew there was no way you were telling me the truth."

I swallow the jagged pieces of glass scraping my throat raw. I trusted Nathan, counted on him, and now he went behind my back to take her away.

"*I'm* applying for guardianship," I snap, my insides shattering. "I've got the apartment. The money in my savings. All I need is a couple more paychecks to prove my financial stability. Need to convince my father to sign over—" I stop dead, my blood running cold. "How did you get him to agree? *When?*" I tilt my head, my entire body shaking with adrenaline.

"I *love* you girls," he says, and a rock lodges in my throat. "You know that. It's not a secret. And…" He shakes his head, his eyes going distant. "When I approached your father, I honestly thought he'd throw me on my ass—"

Cold dread snakes into my blood.

"But I asked him what it would take for him to sign his rights over to me for the both of you. And to not lay a hand on you while the process happens."

"And?"

"He wanted money."

I swallow hard. "How much?"

"Harley," Nathan chides.

"How much, Nathan?"

"He wouldn't even entertain giving me you," he says instead, a crease between his brows. "Which doesn't make any sense, since you were a few days away from turning eighteen—I still tried because I want you both. I want to legally be bound to you both so you know you can *always* count on me. But no matter how much I offered, he wouldn't take it. Said *you* belong to him."

"And Ray?" I nearly choke on the question. "How much did he want for Ray?" And somehow I know his answer is going to break me all over again.

"Ten thousand."

The words hit the bottom of my stomach like cement. "Ten thousand dollars." Tears well in my eyes, a blistering rage clawing beneath my skin. "Ten thousand dollars," I repeat, my hands trembling. The ground vibrates beneath my boots again, and Nathan braces his hand against the wall.

"That's all she's worth to him?" I rub the back of my neck, my breaths coming too quick.

The building shakes harder, the lights flickering above our heads.

"She's worth a million times that!" I gasp, the air in my lungs tightening. "She's worth more than money. She's worth more than my life!" I yell, pacing the length of floor before Nathan.

He sold her. He bartered her *life* like she was nothing more than a used fucking car.

He didn't know a thing about Nathan. He could've been a monster for all my father knew. And he *sold* her without a second thought.

The equipment by Ray's bed shakes and smacks against the wall nearest her because the building won't stop shaking, and something in my blood snaps to attention. Oh God, this has been happening every time I'm overly emotional—Draven and my first kiss, the fight with Kai, now...

I go very still, focusing on that inner rage, that power thrumming right alongside the flames in my blood, and beg it to quiet.

The shaking immediately stops.

"Why the hell does that keep happening?" Nathan groans as he releases the wall.

I don't have the energy to even entertain the reasoning behind it.

"You paid him?" I ask, my voice quiet, deadly calm.

"I'm supposed to meet him tomorrow morning. He gets the check. I get the signature and a promise he'll show up to the court date next week."

"Then what?" Maybe that's why he was so plastered tonight and thought Ray was me. Too busy celebrating the money he's about to get, drinking until he couldn't see straight.

"I was going to ask you two to stay the weekend, like usual," he says. "I was going to talk it over with you after Ray went to sleep."

"You should've asked me *first*."

Nathan sighs and runs a hand through his hair, his shoulders sagging. "I know. I should have. Harley, I honestly thought you'd be thrilled, but I didn't want to tell you until I was certain. Until he had signed over the rights to me, and you and Ray were free.

I would never *take* her away from you."

"Isn't that what you're doing?" I challenge. I don't know if my heart can break any more than it already has. He lied to me. Withheld something so important from me. Him, Coach Hale, my father…who's next? Why do I keep letting people in only for them to crush me in the end?

"No!" He shakes his head. "God, no. Like I said, I wanted you to have options. I'm not naive, Harley. You're eighteen now. I knew you'd petition for custody just like I knew he'd fight you on it. Now you won't have to. Now you have the option to be a *kid*, not a parent."

I gape up at him. How could he guess my shameful wish?

"I *know* you," he says. "I even have a savings account in your name so you can use it whenever for your own place."

"What?"

He shrugs. "What do you think I've been doing with all those phone payments you've made?"

"Oh, I don't know, *paying the phone bill*?"

"I've put it into a savings account and matched it every month."

"Nathan," I say. "I've been paying that bill for four years."

"At first, I did it because I hoped to give it to you as a college present. Then, as time went on, and I got to know you…" He sighed. "When I realized you didn't have a desire, or more likely, thought you *couldn't* go to college, I decided I'd give you the money when you turned eighteen for whatever you needed to use it for. But then I finally woke up and saw what was really happening, and I knew I needed to do more." Another shrug. "I'll never take her from you, Harley. I *promise*. I just want you both to have a safe place to land. If you want. I want you to have the pressure taken off you—the fear that made you too terrified to tell me the truth about how bad things really are." He lifts the papers in his hands. "This will fix that. This will allow me to help with Ray's college, and yours if you want. With all of it. But it's still your choice." He clears his throat. "She'll be safe now."

"She'll be safe." I repeat the words, more to myself than

him. Through all the blistering hurt, the betrayal, and anger that threatens to set my hands on fire—I feel it. That small coil of relief and certainty.

Nathan will keep her safe. He always has.

Especially if something happens to me. If I'm truly not strong enough to survive what's coming.

Nathan nods at me. "Yes, Harley. She's safe now. I promise. No one will be able to get to her. Not after I meet with him tomorrow morning. And after the judge finalizes the paperwork, your dad will have no legal right to come near her again. I'll even file a restraining order, if that helps."

I walk to the side of the hospital bed, gazing down at Ray. I hear his logic, his reasoning, but too many emotions swarm me.

"This is my fault," I say, motioning to her on the hospital bed.

"Hey," Nathan chides from where he remains standing across the room. "No. It isn't."

"It is," I say. "*I* let her go in first. I didn't check to see if he was home. He thought she was *me*. And I wasn't in there to stand between them."

"Don't do that," he says. "Don't go there. Put this blame where it belongs. *He's* the asshole."

I nod before I lean down to plant a kiss on Ray's forehead. "You're right." I cross the room, taking the papers from Nathan's hands. "Stay with her, please?"

"Where are you going?" he asks as I head toward the door, papers in hand.

"Tomorrow isn't soon enough." I hold up the papers. "I'm going to get you that signature."

"Harley, don't," he says, his eyes widening.

"It's okay," I say, a lethal calm slicking my insides. "He can't hurt me anymore." I spare a last glance at Ray, wanting to remember this when I set eyes on my father again. I shut the door behind me and sprint out of the hospital.

And crash into a hard chest, strong hands steadying me before I topple to the pavement.

"Harley?" Draven releases me quickly.

"Oh, good," I say. "You're here. Now we may actually beat the cops." I have less than an hour, and I sure as hell don't want them delaying the rights being signed over to Nathan, even if they won't be technically official until the court date. Despite the pain that he's lied to me, went behind my back—I know Nathan loves her. Know he'll take care of her if something happens to me. And with my whole world turning into a demonic sideshow, I can't really ask for more. Even if it hurts like hell.

"Wait, what?" He follows me as I storm around the building to a dark corner.

"Do your shadow thing."

"My shadow thing," he echoes.

I sigh, my head whirling, my chest aching, the power in my blood screaming. "I need to get home. Now." I hold up the papers. "Ray has a chance at freedom. Safety. As pissed off as I am about Nathan going behind my back, I can't deny her this. And it can't wait a second longer." I have other motivations for needing to get home so quickly, but he doesn't need to know them.

"I…" Draven struggles, some inner debate raging in his eyes.

"Draven," I say. "Please."

Something in my tone makes his entire body shift, and he gives me one solemn nod. He opens his arms, and I step into that embrace, noticing for the first time the purple smudges beneath his eyes, the drained, dull look like the amber has been leeched of color and light.

"This won't kill you, will it?" I whisper as he snakes his arms around my waist, hefting me against him.

"You aren't that lucky," he says, his entire body shaking as he tries to muster that mischievous grin of his. "Close your eyes."

I shake my head. "I want to see."

His eyes turn black, and then nothing but shadows swirl around me, lifting me higher and higher, propelling me toward the monster I no longer fear.

It's over in mere seconds, and my boots hit my front porch, the abrupt shift hard enough to knock me over, but I steady myself on the railing.

Draven leans his hands on his knees, his breath heaving.

"Are you all right?" I ask, reaching for him.

"I'm fine," he says, waving me off. "Do what you need to do." Each word is an effort from his lips, but I nod and barrel through the door.

"Where are you?" I scream, noting my father isn't on the floor where we left him. I prowl through our small house, a girl on a mission, stopping in the living room when I come up empty.

A creak sounds behind me, the smell of sweat and alcohol overpowering before his hand clamps on my shoulder. I grip his wrist and shoot forward, propelling him over my back to smack on the floor.

"Bitch!" he roars, shoving against the floor to regain his footing, but I'm faster.

I shove my boot against his neck with all the pressure I can without snapping it. His eyes fly wide, and I wave the papers in front of his face. "Sign these," I say, smacking the signature page atop his chest along with the pen I stole from the receptionist at the hospital. *"Now."*

"You don't call the shots," he spits, his voice gurgling from my boot at his throat.

I narrow my gaze, applying a little more pressure. "Sign it."

"Not until I get my money." His hands shove at my ankle.

Seconds.

I have *seconds* before my strength will give, and he'll overpower me.

He'll win.

Not today.

I lean down, my hand before his face, and snap my fingers.

A midnight flame dances over the top, causing my father's eyes to bulge. A hint of madness and delight flashes there. "Sign it. Or *burn*."

He stops pushing against me and scoops up the pen, scrawling his sloppy signature on the blank line, then initialing on the next one.

I double check the papers with my free hand, then stick them in my back pocket.

"Let me go," he says.

I withdraw my boot, stepping only a foot away as he stands to face me. His eyes track my fire with a glinting hunger.

"She's worth more than that," I seethe, the unfiltered rage coloring my tone.

"You think I coulda gotten more than ten for her?" He laughs. "Maybe I can squeeze some more outta your boss. Should I ask for twenty?"

Adrenaline soars through me, the image of Ray hitting that wall to my left, the image of her sleeping in that hospital bed fueling the fire inside me.

He flicks his eyes to mine, icy fear coating them as both my hands become an inferno of pitch-black and flickering silver.

"You won't—"

I lunge for him.

Wrap my hands around his throat.

And squeeze.

CHAPTER THIRTY-SIX

*K*ill him. Kill him. Kill him.

The jagged voice in my mind whispers, the soft hiss joining the sound of sizzling flesh.

"Harley, no!" Draven yells just before he hooks an arm around my waist and yanks me off my father.

"Why?" The word tears through me, half scream, half sob as he hauls me back.

My father leaps to his feet, rushing to the kitchen. He practically dives under the faucet, shoving his neck beneath the rushing water.

"Stop. Fighting...me." Draven has to force out each word, and I stop trying to dislodge him. He loosens his grip, and I turn to face him.

"He deserves to die!" I yell, pointing behind me. "He's *worse* than a demon. He's a real monster with no excuse for what he does to people!"

A loud, manic laugh splits the room, and I whirl. My father comes out of the kitchen, holding a wet cloth to his neck, the fabric spattered with pink.

The fire at my fingertips blazes at that laugh, at the malice in his eyes. I want nothing more than to shoot those flames at him. Fully consume him until there is nothing left but a pile of ash.

Father claps slowly, pursing his lips at me. "There. It. Is!"

A cold shiver snakes over my skin.

"Finally!" he continues. "I was beginning to think you'd never show that power."

The ground trembles, causing our tiny home to quake. It

throws him off-balance, but he manages to grab the nearest wall, that laugh rising.

"You knew?" I gasp, desperate for control. I curl my flaming hands into fists, soothing that inner rage enough to speak.

The shaking stops.

"Knew?" He glares at me, pointing at his chest. "They *gave* you to me. Paid me to turn you into what your blood demands."

"They"? My lips part, and he nods as he dabs at the ring of bubbling flesh around his neck.

Me. I did that.

Acid churns in my stomach, threatening to bring everything up right here on the carpet.

"Turn me into what?"

"Something stronger," he says. "Better. More powerful. A monster that can't be broken." He shrugs and spits on the floor.

I whirl, eyes on Draven, barely drawing the strength to ask, "Did *you* know?"

Draven wobbles on his feet, and my entire being tracks the movement. I reach out to help steady him, but he hurries past me, positioning himself in front of the door where my father inches closer. The amber in Draven's eyes barely glimmers now, and he bends slightly at the waist as if his legs might give out any second.

"You didn't think I was your real father, did you?" Those words, his laugh, cut into me like a white-hot blade. I step closer, glaring up at him with every ounce of hate and hurt that rushes through me. *"Idiot,"* he spits, not backing away from me a step. "You have too much of your mother in you."

"My mother?" Hot tears well behind my eyes. The bracelet she'd given me—the only memory I have of her—is icy cold on my wrist. Ray's rainbow braid is a warm beacon above it.

"Yeah," he says. "They had to pry her away from you. Must've offered her a boatload more money than me to get her to dump you here."

All at once I feel the thin foundation I live on crumble. I shake my head, swallowing the rock in my throat.

"They told me they didn't care what I did with you, as long as you didn't see a day of joy." His eyes scan the length of my body, his lip curling. "How much do you think they had to hate you to ask me to do that, ya think?"

I know what he's doing. He's trying to tear me down, like he always does, and he thinks some mystery parents who didn't want me are going to do that. But he's forgetting I've felt that way my whole life because of him. Who cares if my piece-of-shit dad is really him or not? Different dad, same shit. "You're not my real father," I say, needing to hear the words out loud before I never think of this asshole again.

"No."

"And Ray?" My voice breaks on her name.

"They told me I had to take her, too."

"Who are *they*?"

"Some group of old power," he says. "Call themselves The Seven." I glare at the sound of the name—the same beings who hold power over the Judges? The ones who keep Draven locked in unconsciousness for hundreds of years at a time? He smirks at my pain, leaning down to hold my gaze. "They also told me she's not your real sister. Your parents are completely different. You've been protecting someone who isn't even your *blood*."

I slap him with a fiery palm, and his head snaps to the left.

The bloody cloth falls from his hands to the floor before he backhands me. Pain bursts beneath my left cheek, my vision blurring as I stagger back.

"Bitch," he spits, stepping toward me with his fist raised. "Worthless—"

Draven blocks his path and presses a single finger to his neck.

And the man I've believed my entire life was my father, a father who could never love me, crumples to the ground, his knees cracking against the floor. His mouth hangs open, an agonized scream splitting the air.

A fingertip.

That's *all* Draven has on his skin.

Color drains from his face, his scream turning into a whimper as tears stream down his cheeks. *Tears*...I've never seen him cry once in my life. I didn't know he had a soul capable of weeping.

"Don't. Touch. Her." The demand in Draven's voice chills the marrow in my bones. He jerks back his hand, slumping against the door, and my father falls face forward on the carpet, his body twitching sporadically.

I marvel at the display of power even when Draven is so weak. The sheer exhaustion on his face seems more than his spent powers—much more than when we fought off the horde of demons at the bookstore. "What's wrong?" I ask. "Is something else hurting you?"

Is he sick? Disgusted by everything he's seen tonight?

Draven shakes his head. "Get your things."

I blink out of my concern, nodding. He's right. I'm never coming back to this place. And neither is Ray. After everything that asshole told me tonight, he has no grounds to come after us, either.

It takes a mere ten minutes for me to stuff everything we own into two large duffel bags—Ray's artwork and supplies fill one, the other full of our clothes, shoes, and a few books.

I drop them on the front porch, returning to the living room to kneel next to my father. His eyes are wide open and full of hate, but he can only manage a weak groan at the sight of me.

"Finish it," he growls, his body twitching like he's trying to wake it up. "Kill me. Get it over with."

I want to feel his neck crack beneath my fingers.

Want to snake my flames over his body, watch the skin crisp and peel back in layers as black as his soul.

The urge is a calling—pounding to the beat of my racing heart.

I bring my lips to hover over his ear. "You don't tell me what to do anymore," I whisper. "You get to live with yourself. Live with the fact that you failed in your mission. *Ray* beat you. She gave me light when all I had was smothering darkness. She gave me joy." I flick my fiery fingers over the back of his head, just close enough for the smell of singed hair to clog my nostrils. "But if you *ever* come looking for me or for Ray? If you don't show up to that court date with whatever bullshit documents you have? Don't legally sign Ray over to Nathan? I'll fucking *end* you."

I stand and spin around, my head held high.

Walk out the front door.

And don't look back.

CHAPTER THIRTY-SEVEN

We make it a few blocks away before I drop my bags and whirl on Draven, his lie of omission burning through my chest like acid. "You should've told me."

Draven has finally caught his breath, but he seems ready to fall over any minute. "I wasn't sure—"

"Are you sure of *anything*, Draven?" I cut him off. "For the guy with all the wise pieces of advice, the answers you give me are always so fucking gray. I don't know what to believe. It's like you're keeping me in the dark on purpose," I challenge. Fuck, maybe he is. I kept brushing it aside every time he pulled away from me, combating those instances with every time he let me in. Like tonight, when he told me about The Seven and what they do to him, or like at the Belluk den when he told me about all the broken Keys he's had to watch die.

But maybe *everyone* in my life is keeping secrets from me. Maybe my father has succeeded in one thing—I can't trust anyone. Ever.

"Don't," Draven warns, and I glare at him. "Don't push me on this—"

"Or what? You'll kill me? Get. In. Fucking. Line!"

Something flickers in his near-colorless eyes, something that prickles the back of my neck. And just like that, I know. I cannot go another day with the people in my life lying to me. It's hard enough for someone like me to trust—do they not get that their lies are just as much a kick to my gut as my father's boot?

I step closer to him, scanning his face. "You've got more secrets than anyone I've ever met." I shake my head. "They're eating you alive; I can see it. I've always seen it. And yet, you tell me to not push you?" I scoff at him, raking my fingers through my tangled mess of hair.

A muscle in his jaw flexes. "Harley," he says, his voice weak. "You…"

I want to know what's hurting him beyond his use of power. Want to know why he's still keeping secrets from me—even after we shed blood together, fought and nearly died together.

But I'm so damn tired of people not telling me the truth. So beyond exhausted. From the fighting, from the not knowing, from the realization that I spent my entire life taking beatings from a man I believed to be my father. Took that abuse because he made me believe I deserved it. Took it, because if he was beating me, then he had no reason to even think about going after my sister. Worked these last few years to save and plan and prepare to gain custody of her—to give her a better life than I had.

Now, I doubt he ever had legal rights to us anyway. How powerful is this *Seven* if they can fabricate a father? A life? And pay someone to tear me to pieces…over and over and over again.

"Never mind," I say. "I'm done." I scoop up my bags, ready to hop on the train and get back to Ray. But as I turn my back on him, something inside urges me to turn around, not to leave him like this, secrets or no secrets between us.

I plant my feet, sighing up at the night sky before I glance over my shoulder. Draven still looks like one good punch will send him to the ground.

"Can you make it home on your own?" I hate that I need to know, even after everything.

"I'll make it." His voice is raspy.

I give him a nod and leave him there.

I don't need him. I don't need anyone. And I sure as hell don't want Draven's death on my hands—which it would be if he stayed with me any longer, as weak as he is now. No, the only thing I need to do is go see Ray, make sure she's okay, and make a solid plan before my tattoo finally wears off and I go face down a mob of rabid demons.

Alone.

The way my life was always going to end, I suppose, although I fully plan on taking those assholes out with me.

CHAPTER THIRTY-EIGHT

I sink onto an empty seat on the train and let my head fall in my hands. I give myself the full twenty-minute ride to have a little pity party for myself. Grieving all the things that may have been different, if I were born something else.

But once I step off that train, I steel my spine.

The past doesn't matter—not anymore.

The only things that matter are the actions I take moving forward. And right now, all I want to do is see my baby sister.

"Harley!" Nathan meets me with open arms in the waiting room. He clutches my shoulders, scanning my body like he's looking for injuries.

"I'm fine," I say. Physically, sure. Emotionally? Yeah, right.

Nathan tilts my chin up, noticing immediately the red spot on my cheek from the backhand.

The last one I'll ever get from that man. That's some consolation, at least.

"I'm fine," I say again, tugging out of Nathan's touch.

"You scared the hell out of me," he says. "Please don't ever do that again."

Knowing what I know now about how different I am? I doubt that will be possible. "I'll do my best." I reach into my bag and pull out the roll of papers, put them in his hand.

Nathan's eyes go wide as he leafs to the signature page.

"He'll show up at the court date," I say, swallowing hard. I have no doubt. He won't risk me coming for him, not after what I've shown him tonight. The monster I can be, the one he wants me to be. "Keep your money," I say. "She's worth more than that anyway." I move toward the receptionist area, and the nurse must see something in my eyes because she opens the double doors for me despite it being past visiting hours.

Nathan stops me just as I head toward them.

"I would've paid anything, Harley," he says. "I would've given him Miller's if he'd asked."

I swallow the lump in my throat and nod. I know he's telling the truth, and it crushes what little heart I have left. Shatters it—a blow of betrayal and hope. He went behind my back, but he also gave Ray something I never could.

A future. A safe spot to land.

I dreamed of giving her that with my apartment, with the Hello Kitty stuff that awaits her, but who am I kidding? I have demons chomping at me left and right, and something even worse is eventually going to catch me. What life can I possibly offer her with all that surrounding me? "You shouldn't have had to offer anything," I say, and I meet his eyes, a silent sliver of gratitude leaking behind all the cracked bits of betrayal.

He nods as if he understands and motions down the hallway. "Go be with her. I'll stay here until you're done."

He'll stay. He'll be here.

And he always has been, no matter how much I try to hold him at arm's length. To not allow myself to get too close, too dependent on his kindness. Something builds in me, sweeping and solid, as he steps out of the way of the automatic doors.

"Nathan?" I say as they start to close.

"Yeah?"

"I—" I've never spoken the L-word to anyone except Ray. Because "love" is a dangerous weapon in any form—familial, friendly, or romantic. It has the power to crush a soul, and mine is hanging on by a thread. But I can feel it there, that kernel of love. Maybe that's why it hurts so fucking badly that he went behind my back. Maybe that's why I can't squeeze out the truth, even now. "Thanks," I mutter and spin around before he can say anything.

I slip into Ray's room as quietly as I can in case she's asleep, but I stop two steps in at the sight of the boy in the chair at her bedside.

His green eyes meet mine, and he stands up, hesitant as he waits to see what I'll say. And in that moment, I forget about the fights, forget about the heavy words still lying between us.

"Kai, you're here," I whisper, stopping on the other side of Ray's bed, my eyes locking with his.

"Of course I'm here," he says. "Nathan called me."

"*I* should've called," I say. "But—"

"No." He shushes me. "You had so much to deal with. I understand. I had to practically bribe the receptionist, but I'm here for you. Always."

And after everything that has shattered in my world—my father not being my father, my power, the secrets Draven has, Nathan working behind my back for the rights to Ray—Kai feels like the *one* constant from my former life I can hold on to. Someone solid, someone I can trust despite the arguments lingering between us.

"How is she?" I ask, finally pulling myself together enough to look down at her. She's still sleeping, but the sight of her with an IV in her arm and leads underneath her gown monitoring her heart makes me crumple inside.

"The nurse told me she was up an hour ago," he says, and I cringe at the fact that I wasn't here. "She said she had a nightmare, so they gave her something to calm her down, get her back to sleep."

I close my eyes, my tight chest cinching another inch.

Kai moves to settle in the chair next to me as I sit at her bedside. Silently, he reaches for my hand but draws his back at the last minute. He wrings his hands between his knees instead.

After a minute, he points to the black cord on my wrist. "You ever going to tell me what you wished for?" he asks, likely trying his best to distract me from the heaviness that clings to this room like a dark cloud.

"Never," I say, a broken smile forming on my lips. "Then it

won't come true."

The truth is, I can't remember what my four-year-old self wished for all those years ago when my mother fastened the thing around my wrist. Only the memory of her face, her making me promise never to take it off. But as I grew older, the only thing worth wishing for was to survive long enough to get Ray out of that house. Get her away from our father.

And with everything Nathan has done...maybe the bracelet really will break soon. Because sure, it's silly to believe in bracelets that grant wishes, but I recently discovered that demons exist and I'd been given to a monster of a father in an attempt to—

Actually, I have no idea what their plan was. Just to cause me pain, I suppose. I shrug. So in the grand scheme of things, my bracelet finally breaking seems like a real possibility.

Kai grins down at me, and I almost lean my head against his shoulder but force myself to remain strong. To keep upright all on my own. To not be weak.

The thought propels me to worrying about Draven, his exhausted powers—

No. Not going there.

Because even the *thought* of Draven stings my chest, and I don't have an ounce of strength left in my body to survive the hurt.

So I focus on Kai and hope like hell he doesn't ask me any more questions I can't answer. I want just one good night with both of them before I go do what my blood has wanted me to do my whole life...to beat on someone else—and a few thousand demons ought to be enough to finally work that kink out of my neck.

CHAPTER THIRTY-NINE

"I was under the impression you lost my number," Coach Hale says by way of answer.

I press my phone to my ear, my chest tight.

"I need a favor," I say instead of addressing the fact that I've ignored her calls and texts. Still hurt over what she kept from me after I thought we'd grown so close.

"I'm listening," she says, chatter and car honks creating her background noise.

I chew on my lip. I've walked the main pathways downtown for hours now, aimlessly wandering until finally breaking down and calling her.

Ray is sleeping soundly in the hospital, and I managed to drop our things at Nathan's before hitting the streets. Dawn is about to break on my last day of the protection spell, but sleep is the furthest thing from my mind.

My phone vibrates against my ear, and I don't need to look to know it's Draven—he's texted and called a dozen times since I left him hours ago. I've ignored him, too.

I know we need to talk. But as hurt as I am that he could be just another person I let behind my walls who lied to me, I know that's not really why I'm avoiding him. As strained as things are between us, I've calmed down and realized it was wrong of me to expect him to open up and tell me everything. We don't really know each other. Not really. And if I understand anything, it's that we all have a right to our secrets.

The real reason I'm staying away is to protect him. Somehow, he worked his way past my defenses, and of all the things I'm about to lose in the coming fight, I don't want to add Draven to that list, too.

"If you were an all-powerful Second tasked with killing someone like me for one of the greater demons, what would you be the most afraid of?" I ask, cringing at the absurdity of the question.

"If I knew the answer to that, don't you think I'd already be exploiting it?" Coach Hale huffs on the other end of the line.

I continue my walk, ensuring I don't bump into any of the other pedestrians as I hold the phone to my ear. A cab honks to my left, the sound ringing over the line.

"Where are you, Harley?" she asks, her voice suddenly tense.

"I'm downtown. Walking."

"Where?"

"I don't have much time left," I say. "And I can't risk Ray getting hurt again. I need to do something now, to stop hiding."

"I'm digging your determination." She sighs. "But it isn't that simple."

Nothing ever is.

"I've been charming and beating my way through the underlings dwelling on this plane, looking for a weakness in the Second," she continues. "Met with my top sources…"

"And?" I press.

"Rumors and whispers. They're terrified to talk even when I give them a little sharp incentive."

I flinch, remembering how easily she wielded those blades of hers. "Why are they so scared of the Second?"

"They say the Second has the power to *control* them. To take over their minds, render them mere puppets."

"Shit. No wonder I've had so many attacking me." The Second is controlling them. And Marid is controlling *them*. "They have to have some weakness," I insist. Everyone does.

"I would bet my knives on it," she says. "And I've had them for more than a thousand years."

I swallow hard, nodding. "Okay," I say. "Then I just have to find out what it is before they find me."

"We've all been working toward that goal, Harley," she says. "But the demons I've wrestled with either don't have a clue or they'd rather die than cross the Second."

I slow my pace, the defeat sinking in my chest as I turn around and start heading back the way I came. "You really have no tips at all? Something, *anything*? I'll take even the most ridiculous of ideas." Take those ideas straight to the library and call the Second out like I've given up on our game of hide-and-seek.

"If I did, I would tell you. I promise," she assures me, her voice growing softer. "You're not alone in this, Harley. Draven and I won't let you face this alone."

"Thanks," I manage to say. I miss our lessons. Miss the female companionship.

"Where did you say you were going?" she asks again when I fall silent, letting Chicago's city streets fill the noise on the line. "You're not going to do something ridiculously bad, are you?"

"Not yet," I say with a snort. But I plan to soon. "I'm heading back to Miller's." I don't have a shift, but I agreed to meet Kai outside the deli in a little over an hour. Earlier, in the hospital with Ray, I wasn't able to tell him everything I needed to. I'd been too focused on assuring myself Ray would be okay. I want to set things right with him, say goodbye even, before I figure out my next move. Just in case. I need to do the same with Ray once she wakes up, but that thought is so painful, I shove it away.

"Good," she says. "I'm still working on it. And I have eyes on the library now. Lots of movement but no sign of the Second yet. Draven is still hunting, too. Even Kaz is listening to the air. We're trying, Harley. I promise. If I find something, you'll be the first to know."

"I appreciate it," I say, my throat tight. "All of it," I add for good measure, thanks to that nagging sensation in the back of my mind—the one telling me to try and mend things with anyone I need to because I may not survive long enough to do it later.

"I'll be in touch," she says, then ends the call.

I pocket my phone, sighing as I slow to a stop before the deli, the early-morning dawn casting the sky in a rich blue. I slip into the connecting alleyway, since it isn't open yet.

I lean against the exterior brick wall of Miller's, my head tilted back and eyes closed. I need to do something, need to move, to act, *anything* other than wait—

A gentle tug of awareness ripples down that chain I can never ignore, and I don't need to open my eyes to know who's entered the alleyway.

"You don't have a shift today," I say without opening my eyes. "And it's about two hours before opening time if you came here for food."

"You know why I'm here," Draven says, and the sound of his voice washes over me like a warm breeze. Something internal sighs at the smell of him, all cedar and citrus and amber. I curse my body for being so weak. To allow him to have such an intoxicating effect on me.

I finally turn to face him.

Goddamn him. He wears a tight black T-shirt, the fabric stretching over his muscled chest. His black hair is perfectly messy, and his eyes are that golden amber color again. No purple smudges, no pained expression.

"You look better," I say.

"I'm hard to kill." That crooked grin shapes his lips, and my traitorous heart stutters at the sight. "Just needed a few hours to recharge."

"Needed to plug in your power source, Winter Soldier?" I try to tease, but my energy is sapped, and I feel hollowed out after everything that's happened. "You can relax," I say when he purses his lips at my joke. "I haven't been attacked in the whole eight hours we've been separated." I raise my brows at him, waiting for the relief to cross his features that the spell has held up in that time, but he doesn't look surprised. "You knew that already, didn't you?" I tilt my head.

"After I recovered from the trips we took, did you think

I'd let you wander about alone? Though I think even an hour without an attack is impressive given your track record for demon provocation."

"I don't *provoke* them. They come after me. There's a difference." I arch a brow at him. "And I thought we already talked about how stalking is creepy."

He takes a few steps toward me, drawing his face closer to mine. "I *am* watching, Harley. Because I want to help you through this." Genuine concern churns in the depths of his eyes.

Damn it, how is it that we had a fight mere hours ago, and I missed him? Missed this verbal battle, the craving, the thrill of testing his limits and mine in a dance that's electric. And now that he's standing only a few feet away? Something springs to life inside me. Some white-hot inner current begging to be played with.

I hold his gaze, tension rippling beneath my skin as he doesn't dare tear his eyes away from mine. Secrets and darkness and the threat of death all loom between us, but I *relish* this feeling. All the warm sensations spiraling down my spine, the anticipation flooding my lungs and stealing my breath.

Maybe that's why I ignored all his calls and texts—I knew I'd fall right back down this dark tunnel of need and want.

The corners of his lips twitch into that mischievous smile as if he's reading my thoughts, savoring the competition of who will break first as much as I am.

Stay out of my head.

He cocks a brow. *But it's such an inviting place*, he teases. The words are like silk shadows caressing the interior of my mind.

I hold my ground—

Until the buzzing in my pocket jolts me, and I break our gaze to fish it out.

I win. Draven's voice curls inside my mind, and I flip him off before grabbing my phone.

KAI: We still good to meet up at Miller's?

ME: Yeah. I'm here now.

KAI: I'm wrapping up some things at home. Will be there

in like thirty. Cool?

ME: Cool.

I pocket my phone, returning focus to Draven, who hasn't moved an inch. "Why are you here, Draven?" I ask, dropping the games.

"You know why," he says, eyeing the tattoo on my wrist. The color has almost faded entirely, the dark-black lines overtaking the design no less beautiful. "I know what you're planning on doing—"

"The same thing I was planning on doing yesterday—nothing has changed." Yet everything has. In the span of a night, everything has changed. Ray is in the hospital, Nathan one court date away from being her guardian. She'll be taken care of, which means I can do what I've needed to do since this mess started.

"I can't stay away," he admits.

A thrill rushes through me, but I shove it down. "You can't say things like that."

"Why?" He leans against the brick wall, one boot tucked up against it, his hands shoved deep in his pockets. If I had any of Ray's talent, I would lose hours of my life drawing him. Trying to capture the way the sun at dawn illuminates his dark skin, the way his eyes seem to glow.

"Because," I say, pacing in the space between us. "I have to do this alone." Everyone I've ever trusted has kept things about my life from me, important things, but despite that, I wouldn't want any of their blood on my hands.

"You don't have to do anything alone," he says, irritation coloring his tone. "And beyond that, you *shouldn't* do it alone." I stop pacing, glaring at him. He raises a finger. "I didn't say *couldn't*, honey badger. Shouldn't," he clarifies. "You have barely begun to understand the depths of our world. The different levels of demons, the source of your power—"

"You've helped me enough," I argue. "And I imagine taking down the Second will be just like any other demon I've turned to ash."

"It's nothing like that," he says, sounding exasperated. "Harley, we haven't been able to nail down the Second's identity, let alone a weakness to exploit."

I shrug, hating the worry in his eyes, the genuine concern over what will happen to me. "We know the library is where the Second will show up. I'm going. They won't be able to resist if I call them out."

"Seriously?" He shakes his head. "*Here I am, come and get me*? *That's* your plan."

"Yep," I say. "I'm done waiting to be picked off like a cow in the slaughterhouse. I'm *done*. And I'm doing it alone—"

"Then your father wins." He cuts me off, and I gasp.

"What?" The question is a whisper.

He shrugs. "If you do this alone, he wins." I swallow hard as Draven pushes off the wall and stops with only inches separating us. "He beat you. He made you feel like you were worthless. Why?"

"Because some assholes paid him to do it."

Draven shakes his head. "Because you're easier to control, to take down, if you feel alone."

I grind my teeth, forcing back the tears trying to gather in my eyes. I've had hours…*hours* knowing my father isn't really my father. That everything he did to me, my whole life…

Making me believe I'm worthless.

Weak.

Something so awful and ugly that even my own blood couldn't love me.

"Why do you believe him?" Draven asks. "Why are you letting that piece of shit win?"

A tear slips free, rolling down my cheek, because damn it, Draven's *right*. Yes, Nathan and Anka and even Draven himself have kept secrets from me, but I've done the same thing. I've kept the darkest parts of myself hidden and protected, even from Draven. And isn't that everyone's right? To have secrets, to have the choice of when to let people in or not? How can I possibly hold that against them?

And if I do, it'd be taking the easy way out. Because all my life, it's been *easy* to push people away because who would ever want to get to know me — the damaged, dirty thing my father made me believe I was?

"It's always been a thousand times harder to believe I'm worth the trouble I come with," I admit, and Draven leans down enough to catch my gaze.

"That's your father speaking," he says. "Not you."

"What makes you say that?"

"The honey badger I know?" he says, a grin shaping his lips. "She'd use everything in her arsenal to take down whatever bullshit is hunting her. Because she'd be damned if anyone else is going to make her choices for her for one second longer."

A choked laugh rips from my lips, and I swipe away the traitorous tears.

"What's it going to be, Harley?" He gives me a challenging look. "Will you let him win?"

I shake my head. "Everything in my arsenal, huh?" I ask, my eyes scanning the length of his body. "Are you calling yourself a weapon?"

"Everyone else always has," he teases, and I press my lips together. I can't hide the gratitude swelling in my eyes. Draven *wants* to help me, even if he has secrets. And hey, hanging around long enough to earn some more of those secrets is a pretty strong motivation to accept his help and put an end to this *Second out for my blood* nonsense.

And in those moments he holds my gaze, the silence and tension tightening between us, I realize with sudden clarity how close I was to letting my father win. How close I was to forgoing Draven's help, Anka's help, Nathan's…everyone's, just because I believed the words of a man who never loved me a day in his life.

How could I have been so naive? My anger at myself, at the situation, amps up —

The ground trembles beneath our feet, so fierce that the a few people walking at the cusp of the alley squeal and hurry past as if they fear the building will topple down on them at any second.

"Damn it," I say, shifting my feet for balance. "That keeps happening—"

"Harley." Draven's voice laces with power, a soothing sort of calm that jerks every one of my senses to attention.

The shaking stops, and my eyes track his every move as he kneels before me. He spreads his fingers on the ground, looking up at me from that position at my feet. My blood is suddenly on fire in a way that has *nothing* to do with my power.

"Try to focus," he says, motioning me to him.

I mimic his stance, my fingers shaking as I lay them against the pavement.

"Just like the flames," he says. "Seek it out in your blood. See if the earth responds."

I chew on my bottom lip but close my eyes, searching inward like I have so many times before. There, next to the fire in my blood, lays another door of power. This one heavy, thick, and interconnected across an endless plane. I mentally open it, coaxing it to come out and play.

My fingers tingle, and a crumbling sounds in my ears. I open my eyes.

Beneath my palm, the pavement *vibrates*, and cracks spiderweb under my fingers.

The wet dirt rumbles up from the splits in the rock, the soft earth meeting my skin with a jarring cold.

I jerk back my hand, gasping as the trembling stops, my eyes on Draven's, which churn with amazement and fear.

"Is that normal?" I ask. "For a potential Key? Two powers?"

Draven shifts to stand, pacing the small space between the buildings.

I stand, too, staring down at my hands. "Fire," I say, moving my left hand. "And earth." I rotate my right hand, my blood pounding with the power, thrashing against that weight holding it back. The leaves and flames of my tattoo practically sing with acknowledgment. Kazuki—he saw more than he let on.

Draven freezes before me, visibly swallowing as he holds his hands an inch above mine. The heat pulses between us, and every piece of me wants to breach that distance, but before I can move, he steps back. He fishes his cell from his pocket, firing off a fast text.

"Draven," I say with more demand. "Is this normal?" I realize suddenly that nothing has been *normal* since the moment he walked into my life.

He wets his lips, pocketing his phone. "For a working Key…" He rakes his hands through his hair. "Yes."

"You really believe I'm…complete? A real Key?"

Something like devastation flickers in his eyes.

"You can't break what's already broken, Draven," I say, my words a whisper between us. "I can handle it. Just tell me the truth."

"Yes," he finally answers. "This additional power means you're everything we ever assumed."

Fuck, fuck, fuck.

"If I'm a Key, one that can *actually* be used, then that means I can open Marid's door…" A tremble rocks the ground beneath us, but just as quickly, that inner something yanks it back, stilling the ground once again. Great, another power I'll have to battle with to try and get it to work properly.

Draven stops pacing, and I stare up at him with a million silent questions. "We can't let them use me," I say, my voice a whisper.

"We won't." His voice is pure gravel.

"Tonight," I say, my mind whirling. "We have to go tonight. To end this." I need to say goodbye to Ray. Need to tell her everything so she fully understands, just in case…

"Harley," he says, and I focus on him instead of the thoughts racing through my mind.

"What?" I ask, my brow furrowing.

"You said 'we.'" Something shifts in his eyes, some kind of solidarity as he reaches for my hand. I sigh at his touch, at the way he reached out for me this time. He runs a fingertip along the tattoo on my wrist, and everything narrows to the feel of his skin on mine. He moves closer so there isn't an inch of space between us.

"Together," I say. "We end this."

CHAPTER FORTY

His eyes shutter, his lips parting. "There's more," he says, still holding me.

"Of course there is," I say.

"You're not just a working Key, Harley," he says. "You're *the* Key. You and you *alone* have the ability to bring down the veil between our worlds." He pauses, and I try not to gape up at him. The veil that shields humans from the truth of demons among them? The one Coach Hale told me about? "And not just open any door," he continues before I can say anything, "but *all* the gates of Hell."

I freeze in his arms. The second he speaks the words, it's like the power in me sighs at the truth.

"They want to use me to open *everything*," I growl. "No, I can't. I won't."

"I didn't want it to be true," he says, his grip gentle on my wrist. "I've never wanted to be wrong more in my life."

"They'll use me to destroy the *world*—" A harsh laugh escapes my throat. They don't just want Marid, which is bad enough, but *everything* in Hell. "In the end, no matter what I do, I'm going to end up bringing as much evil to this world as my father. The cycle complete."

"Stop!" Draven's voice is lethal as he shifts to grip my shoulders. "You are not going to destroy anything." The determination in his words lashes and binds every trembling piece of me. "You're strong. You will survive this. You will—"

I span the distance between us, stopping his words with my lips.

I can't hear them, not anymore.

Can't stand here and listen to him spout false hope in the face of all this *horror*.

"*Harley,*" he growls between my lips, his gravelly tone doing everything to stop my thoughts. Everything evaporates beyond the feel of his tongue, the thrill as he slants his mouth over mine.

His fingers are frantic as they graze my shoulders and slide down to my hips. He grips me there as he walks me backward until my spine presses against the brick wall.

Searing heat zings beneath my skin, and I sigh between his lips. His kiss is consuming, his hands are magic, and the scent of him swirls and shakes my senses until nothing exists outside of *this*. This pure carnal need I have for him, for his ability to eddy every thought from my head, every fear—

"*No.*"

The word is a cold slice of ice from the other end of the alley.

Draven jolts at the voice, ripping his lips from mine.

"Kai," I say, my voice cracking on his name as I unhook myself from Draven. I completely forgot he was meeting me here. That we were supposed to have breakfast together—

"*Him?*" he seethes, betrayal coloring every single one of his features. "After everything between us…" He shakes his head.

"Kai," I plead. "Listen—"

"You have no idea what you've done."

Tar, sticky and hot, chokes my breath. He's *never* looked at me with such…disgust.

Draven slides his hands into his pockets, glaring at Kai with a steeled sort of silence as I rush toward him.

Kai backs away from me, his entire body shaking, the line of his jaw so hard, I think he might break his teeth. He slices a glare behind me at Draven. A look that chills me to my very bones.

"Kai, please," I beg, hating the accusation on his face. The betrayal. We'd talked about this. I told him I couldn't be what he needed me to be. And he promised me we were fine. "You have to understand—"

"You're dead"—the words nail me to the spot—"to me." He spins around and hurries toward the main street, leaving me there with my mouth hanging open.

How can he say that? After everything...*this* is what he'll end our friendship over?

No, no, surely not. He's pissed. Fine, I can accept that. But he'll calm down. He'll cool off when he remembers I'm not right for him. Remembers how I told him straight-up when he showed feelings for me that I didn't feel the same. *Can't* feel the same. He'll understand, after some time. He has to, right? This can't be, *won't* be the thing that drives him out of my life.

He'll be safer for it.

I swallow hard against the truth that filters through my mind.

"Harley," Draven says, his tone soft, beckoning me out of the panic about to swallow me.

I spin around to face him, my lips parting, but I choke on all the words I can't say. The emotions storm me—the knowledge that everyone around me is in even more danger now that I know what I can do, what I can bring to the world. Maybe I should do the world a favor—

"Don't you *dare* think like that," he growls, eyes blazing as he steps up to me.

"Stay out of my *head*." The anger over everything puts a bite to my words. Good. It feels good to release it somewhere.

And Draven? He doesn't flinch from my harsh tone. Doesn't cower from what I am. What I can do to the world.

No, he stands before me, a mirror of the darkness inside me.

And he does not look away.

Not like Kai...

"It's impossible for me to stay out of your mind when your emotions are this high," he says, apology flashing in his eyes. "They sweep me in like a current. And you can't think like you just were—"

"I *can't* let them use me," I say on a whisper, the admission tearing through me.

"We won't," Draven says, his hand grazing my cheek. "You are not alone in this."

The determination in his words scrapes against that hollow pit in my soul, the one threatening to swallow me whole. And I lean into his hand, into his touch, and let it quiet my mind.

CHAPTER
FORTY-ONE

"Will there ever be a moment where nothing shocks me anymore?" I ask Draven an hour later as I sit at the small table tucked near the window in his kitchen. I called Nathan, managed to keep the tears and panic and grief from my voice long enough to check on Ray. He assured me she was still sleeping, getting the rest she needs. I told him I'd be by later, once I worked up the courage to do what I needed to do—to tell her goodbye, just in case the worst happens tonight.

"I certainly hope not," Draven says, standing before his open fridge as he pulls out different containers.

"Why?" I ask, sliding my hand over the sleek wood of his table.

"Because the minute you stop being surprised, the minute you let down your guard, that's when this world will deliver a blow you can't come back from." He speaks like he has experience with that. He doesn't meet my eyes as he spreads the open containers along the table.

Crackers and cheeses and fruits and sparkling water. We munch on the makeshift breakfast in silence, the weight heavy between us. The food does little to soothe that ache in my gut. The one that tightens every time I think about what's to come.

The battle I have yet to face.

I can only hope I won't hurt anyone else when I meet it.

"I'm tired," I admit after we finish the food. "I should go back to my apartment for a power nap before we do what we have to tonight." Go to the library, call out the Second, and hope like hell I'm strong enough to stop them before they use me to end the world.

"Or you can stay here," Draven says, and I blink.

"Are you sure?" I ask, and Draven dips his chin, leading me to his bedroom. The same bed I woke up in after the first demon attack. That feels like months ago, not just a week.

"You're safer here," he says as I settle back on his bed. "You can nap knowing that, at least." He turns in the open doorway, his back to me.

"Draven?" I ask, unable to stop his name from leaving my lips. He pauses, pivoting to face me. "Will you stay with me?" I scoot over on his bed.

He visibly swallows but bows slightly before almost timidly crawling next to me.

I settle my head against his pillow, and he turns on his side to face me. Inches of space separate us, but I can feel the heat coming off his body in waves.

"Tell me something," I whisper.

"What do you want to know?"

"Anything," I say. "Distract me, please. My mind…it won't stop racing with all the horrible things—"

"I know," he says.

"Right." I sigh. "You can read minds."

"One of the many powers I've siphoned over time." Draven taps his temple. "I try not to, you know…unless I absolutely have to."

"And now? With me?"

"I told you, it's harder to turn off with you sometimes," he admits, raising a finger to trace the corners of my face.

My eyes widen, wondering what all he's heard me *think*.

He drops his hand, his eyes burning into mine with a sincerity that shakes my insides. "You often say exactly what's on your mind anyway," he says. "One of your many endearing qualities, honey badger."

"You have so many powers. Tell me something about them. How you earned them," I say, needing more. More of him, his past to distract me from my present.

He arches a brow. "Earn?" I nod against the pillow. "Where to start?" he asks, almost to himself. "I have so many."

I roll my eyes at the way he cocks his brow, the confidence radiating in his eyes. "Tell me about the one that scares you most," I say, wanting to see the dark parts of him, like he's seen mine.

He hesitates, that inner battle raging on his face.

"You don't scare me, Draven," I remind him for the umpteenth time.

"Let's see if we can change that," he says, and he tucks an arm beneath his head.

"One of the times The Seven awakened me, they sent me after a female greater demon," he says, eyes distant as if he's back in time. "I'd been on a few quick missions before, and even though they were blinks in time, I'd already siphoned off more powers than The Seven had ever seen before. They knew if any Judge had a chance at stopping the female greater demon, it was me. And if I died? They'd be rid of the weapon they feared they couldn't contain."

I furrow my brow, hating the way The Seven treat him. How they kept him in the divine sleep when they didn't feel like they needed him. All because they were terrified of what he could do. His power.

Bullshit. Draven is good; he should be allowed to truly *live*.

"It took me weeks to track her," he continues, shaking his head against the pillow. "And I still to this day don't know how she escaped her cage in Hell."

"Wouldn't she need a Key, like me?" I ask.

"Back then there were more ways to slip through the cracks," he says. "I believe that's how Anka escaped, too, but she didn't draw the attention of The Seven because she came to this world with no evil intent. The greater demon?" He sucks his teeth. "She thrived on chaos and lived for malice. She didn't just want to create her own havoc, either. She wanted to open all the gates." His focus comes to me, and a tortured smile shapes his lips. "You would've been her prime target."

I swallow hard.

"Her powers were unlike any I'd faced before. A source of pure evil matched in strength I could *taste*. I knew the second we started to fight that her power would consume me. Rip through everything good in my soul and leave me a husk of what I once was." His eyes trail to the side. "But I also knew she couldn't be allowed to live. She'd killed so many innocent people in her search for the Key. To open the gates and set everything free." Chills race across my skin. "So," he says. "I killed her. And her power crashed into me like the source of a thousand suns. Heavy like the plagues I used to fear as a child. Endless like she hadn't been born a greater demon but rather, *she* was a creator in her own right." His eyes close. "I don't know how long I lay there, absorbing her horrible power, the endless well of it. Don't know how long I struggled against it or when my mind and soul decided to fight it." He shrugs.

"How did you survive it?" I whisper.

His eyes find mine, and for once there are no walls over them. "At some point, I realized that despite The Seven's fear of me, despite their need to keep me locked in divine sleep when they had no use of me…there *was* a use for me. That everything has to happen for a reason, and there had to be a reason that, out of all the Judges and divine creatures in existence, *I* managed to stop her. And if I could hold on to her terrible power, then that meant I would have need of it someday. That when that day came, I'd unleash it and *then* it would end me, but it would be worth it."

I sat up a little on the pillow. "Using her power will…kill you?" I can barely say the word out loud, the idea of him dying—not being forced into a sleep but truly dying—terrifying me.

Draven reaches across the small distance between us, grazing a finger over my cheek, down the line of my jaw. "Worried about me, honey badger?" He smirks, and I narrow my gaze at the question he loves to pose.

"Will it kill you?" I ask again.

He nods, lowering his hand to the space between us.

"You can't ever use it, then," I say.

His brows raise. "I don't take orders from you."

"You should," I reply, forcing the tease into my tone to erase the fear rippling inside me. "Apparently I'm wicked powerful, so yeah. I'm going to go ahead and ax that as an option for you."

He laughs a rough laugh, shaking his head. "It's not like I want to use it," he says. "But if the need came? I wouldn't hesitate."

"What need could possibly be worth it?" I shake my head, quickly deciding that there isn't one.

"Oh, I don't know," he says, raising his hand to slide his fingers down my arm. "Closing a gate...or thousands."

My lips part. "You... Her power could do that? Then why didn't she just open them herself? Why would she need a Key?"

"Because it would've killed her," he says. "And greater demons aren't too big on self-sacrifice. She knew if she got her hands on the true Key, she'd be able to have her cake and eat it, too."

I blink a few times, marveling at how he could be so casual when talking about a power like that. One with the ability to destroy him. "Wait," I say. "That means if something happens to me..."

"*Nothing* is going to happen to you." He finishes the sentence I can't.

Damn straight, nothing is going to happen to me. I can't lose this fight, can't put the world at risk because I've allowed myself to believe I'm weak, thanks to my father. No, I have to beat him. Beat the Second, beat the fucking world, because there is no way in hell I'm losing the freedom I've found. No way I'm losing Draven, either.

"Scared of me yet?" he asks.

"Never," I say, and he sighs. "Tell me another."

And he does. One story turns into two, then three, and before I know it, I've lost count. Of his stories from his brief moments awake over the years, of how many powers he's siphoned, of how many innocent yet infuriating touches he's given me while talking.

A couple of hours pass, and though his stories have tapered

off to a comfortable silence, sleep still evades me, holding me in that fuzzy sort of in-between exhaustion and wakeful feeling. I laugh softly, his last story still filling my head.

"What's funny?" he asks.

"You," I say. "Your best friend *would* be an angel of death."

Draven grins, wide and unhindered for once. "I tell you of the time when Cassiel and I had to fight off a hundred Arachnes demons—one of them poisoning me to the point where I thought I could fly without any powers—and your takeaway from all of this is that my best friend is an angel of death."

I shrug. "What? You're obviously alive. And Cassiel looked more than capable of handling himself that night at The Bridge."

A muscle in his jaw ticks. "You noticed," he says, the words almost clipped.

I side-eye him. "You can't possibly be jealous—"

"Of course not," he denies, though his clenched jaw says otherwise. "But Cassiel could freely touch you without the fear of siphoning off your essence, your power, your life." He shakes his head.

"I'm not inviting Cassiel to touch me, so no. He can't." I plant him with a deadly serious look. For all the shit I've been handed in life, he has his own share. A life devoid of human contact, of physical touch, due to the powers he never asked for. "And you've been touching me this whole time," I say, motioning to the hand that has grazed mine, my arm, my face so many times during his stories. Did he not notice? "I think we've settled that your touch doesn't harm me," I say for the hundredth time. "Whatever I am, it must be immune to your siphon charms."

"Just because I haven't hurt you doesn't mean I won't in the end," he says, and there's something in his hushed tone, in the way he's holding my gaze, that tells me more than his words that he truly believes this. Believes he will one day hurt me. And my heart aches for him.

Because I know exactly how he feels.

I sink deeper against the pillow drenched in his scent, studying his features. The strong line of his jaw, the dark skin, the amber eyes. Today, he's opened up, taking me on a journey through his past, enlightening me to just how damn big the world truly is. Properly distracting me.

And in each story, an unspoken weight clouds his memory. Something heavy and dark he never addresses. Something missing I can't put my finger on. But one thing has been clear with every illumination…The Seven, his high council, from the moment they started training him, they hated him because of his power. Because of the threat he posed with it. If he wanted, he could drain them of their ancient divinity, could suck the supernatural world dry—one of the main reasons they control his life, the times he's allowed to be awake in this world. He's *that* powerful. Of course, those powers can just as easily consume *him*, creating a dark, bleak balance that tips on the edge of the sharpest blade.

"Anyway," he says, clearing his throat. "Cassiel is the only one who gave a damn to give me an assist with the Arachnes."

I swallow hard. "Did you call for help from someone else?"

He nods. "Oh, I alerted The Seven. Told them of the Arachnes nest so near an innocent village."

"And what did they say?"

Darkness flickers behind his eyes. "They told me I was strong enough to face it alone. And if I wasn't, the Creator clearly didn't wish me to live anymore anyway." He forces out a dark laugh.

Something breaks inside me, the way The Seven's words echo my father's. The way each has tried their best to grind Draven and me down to the very basest level of existence. Alone and worthless.

The reason he keeps himself so shielded from everyone, even me. *Especially* me. The same reasons I have trouble trusting anyone.

I shift, scooting closer to place my hand on his exposed cheek.

"I see you, Draven," I say. "*I* know what true monsters look like, act like. You're not one of them."

His eyes shutter. "I kill things," he says, finally opening his eyes. "It's all I know. All I'm asked to do when I'm…awake."

"Not with me." My body tingles with the need to make the inches separating us disappear. And if what I am grants me this, gives Draven the ability to touch me like he hasn't been able to with anyone before…then maybe there is some *good* in the power after all.

I move my hand from his cheek down his neck and his chest, resting it over his heart. It's pounding, and my entire body reacts to the feel of it thumping against my palm, at what my touch does to him.

He inhales deeply, gold lighting up behind his eyes as if he can smell and sense it. Sense that every response is for *him*.

My bottom lip trembles on a ragged breath as his fingers hover over my mouth.

"Draven." I say his name like a plea. "If you don't kiss me, I may burn your house to the ground."

That confident, wicked grin shapes his lips at my tone, but he draws his hand back. I almost whimper at the loss of warmth. "We should be resting—"

"We should." I scoot closer, my knees nearly brushing his. "But I can't sleep like this. We have hours, Draven. That's all we have left in this bubble of quiet that has settled over us. A few more hours until we take the fight to the Second. Until we make our stand. Until…"

I won't be a player in this game anymore.

A muscle in his jaw ticks, the gold in his amber eyes blazing.

The battle between what he wants and what he knows he needs to do to keep us both safe rages on his face.

"Please," I say, *beg*.

The word cracks something in him. And in the span of a breath, his mouth is on mine. That chain inside me flares to life, pulling taut with each sweep of his tongue against mine.

He growls against my mouth, his hands fisting the fabric at my hips. He yanks, bringing our bodies flush.

I tangle my fingers in his hair, pushing back against him, taking and giving, relishing the feel of him, the taste of him. His hands are strong as they explore my body, slipping beneath the hem of my shirt to slide up my back. The calluses on his fingers are rough against my skin, sending chills shooting over my body in every direction.

More, more, more.

The need becomes a chant in time with my pulse.

I can't feel him enough, kiss him enough, drown in his scent enough.

"Harley," he growls against my lips, drawing back to catch my gaze. His eyes are glazed as he trails his fingers toward the waist of my pants. He arches a brow in question, his hand stilling there with hesitation.

I arch up. "Touch me, Draven," I say, not wholly recognizing the need in my voice.

His pupils blow out, eating up every bit of amber as he slants his mouth over mine again at the same time he plunges his hand under my clothes.

I gasp under his kiss, the feel of his fingers between my thighs coiling my insides like a hot spring. He's gentle and teasing, sliding through the center of me. Instinct has me arching up and up, greedy for his touch. His tongue moves against mine, in time with the rhythm of his fingers, and I can't breathe from the aching need coursing through my veins.

He swirls and rocks against me, his thumb teasing some sensitive bundle of nerves. Sparks dance beneath my skin that have nothing to do with my power. Tiny bursts of electricity awaken every piece of my soul.

Draven breaks our kiss, the pace of his fingers increasing as he catches my gaze. His eyes ablaze as he watches me, wonder and a satisfied smirk shaping his lips.

"Let go, honey badger," he says, teasing that sensitive, swollen area. "I've got you."

I arch off the bed, my body needing more pressure, more of his touch, his scent, his words.

And then he slides a finger into me, then two, as he pushes

down on that bundle of nerves—

"Draven!" His name tears from my lips as my entire body shatters around his touch. A million eruptions dancing over my body, unraveling the tightest parts of me, flooding me with heat, racking my body with delicious tremors that push me over an edge I never knew I had.

He claims my mouth, kissing me, devouring my whimpers as I tremble against him.

Gently, he draws his hand back, settling it on my hip as he brings me flush against him once more. "Beautiful," he says, his voice like gravel as he looks down at me.

"More," I beg.

With the whole world collapsing around me with the likelihood of death, this...*Draven* makes me feel alive.

"Harley..." He says my name almost like an argument.

I reach for him, rolling until we're chest to chest, nose to nose, a knee on either side of his hips.

He grins, his eyes wild as he looks up at me. I rock against him, sighing as I lean down for another kiss. Another taste.

Draven slides his fingers in my hair with one hand, the other smoothing down my arm, my ribs, my hip. He clutches me there as his tongue flicks over mine. I grab his hands, intertwining our fingers as I pin his hand above his head—as he *lets* me. He's so much stronger than I am, but here? In this undeniable need for each other? We're equal.

A low growl rumbles from his chest as I nip at his bottom lip, drunk on his kiss, on what he's done to my body, on what crackles between us.

The power in my blood surges with my growing hunger. It pounds against the iron door holding it back, screaming to get out.

My muscles tremble, my hands growing too heavy as I try to stay steady atop him. Draven tears his lips from mine, his eyes a blazing gold.

"Harley?"

The breath stalls in my lungs, too thin to grasp. "I'm fine," I say, reaching down to kiss him again, but he reads something—either in my eyes or in my mind—and unhooks me from his body, gently settling me back on my pillow across the bed.

He backs up to his side, devastation dulling the gold in his eyes.

"It's not you," I say, my voice weak. The power roils in my veins, the fight draining me to the point that black spots burst behind my eyes.

A crease forms between his brows.

"I can feel it. Always feel it. Every time my power surges, there is something there, yanking it back. It's…exhausting." The words are harder to force out. "I promise, Draven," I say. "It's not you."

"You *can't* know that."

"I know my body," I challenge, my eyes heavy. "And what you just did to me? It has nothing to do with your power. Go ahead," I say with a smile. "Try to make fire."

"What?"

"If you think you siphoned from me, try it." I know it isn't him. This *trapped inside my own skin* feeling, hindered by my useless body, is normal for me. I've felt that my entire life.

Draven raises his hand. Flexes it, his brow furrowed in concentration.

Nothing.

"Told you," I say, reaching for him. "Now, hold me."

"Harley." His tone is a warning.

"I need you," I admit. "I feel stronger, more alive when you're touching me. Please."

A heavy sigh, then the mattress shifts beneath me, my body rolling into his weight as he settles next to me.

"Just…don't kiss me," I say, a teasing to my tone. A delicious soreness throbs between my thighs, and I curse whatever is wrong in my body that we couldn't keep going.

A shock filters through me at the fact that I *wanted* to keep going. But how could I not? After everything we've been through, after he opened up to me tonight, after what he drew from my body…

"Why is that any different than this?" he fires back.

"Because when your lips are on mine, my power surges, and whatever is beating it back surges, too."

Draven tucks me closer. "Okay," he says. "No more kissing."

"Don't say it with such finality," I whine, and he chuckles beneath me.

He strokes my hair in gentle, easy passes until my eyes shut and sleep settles over me like a heavy blanket.

"I'm sorry," he whispers, so far away in my mind, I'm not sure if I'm dreaming or not. "I'll find a way to stop this."

CHAPTER FORTY-TWO

Citrus and cedar and amber swirl in the peaceful darkness of my mind as if someone is slicing fresh oranges on a cedar block on a warm summer day.

Slowly, I rise through that darkness, the scent beckoning me to open my eyes.

The setting sun peeks through the wood-slatted blinds in Draven's bedroom, the rays sliding over the cushioned chair and nightstand in the corner of the room and lapping at the bed we occupy.

Heat flares along my skin as I shift to feel his strong body curled around my own. A protective embrace, Draven's muscled arm hooked around my middle as if he feared I might disappear. My spine presses against his muscled chest, the steady vibrations of his even breathing settling something inside me.

It couldn't have been more than a couple of hours' rest, but my body and mind feel refreshed, the power in my veins stretching wide with a deep, contented sigh. Heat floods my cheeks at the memory of earlier, of how he touched me, how he made me shatter.

Carefully, I rotate on the bed to face him, his arm tightening as I move despite his eyes remaining closed. Asleep, the usual taut line of his jaw is softer, and the sun's rays make his already golden skin look luminescent.

A white-hot, sharp *something* stings my chest, an inner cry at the unfairness of the situation. Though when is life ever fair? The upcoming battle, the odds of my survival, and even if I do beat them…what then? The Seven say mission complete and throw Draven back to sleep? And what if I don't survive? What if I fail?

No, I'll die before I let the Second use me. I'll do it myself if it comes to that and flip the Second off while I'm at it.

The weight of that truth settles inside me, and it's not such a scary thing. In order to protect Ray, to protect the people on this earth who I care about...my life does not seem such a high price.

I can only hope I'm strong enough to survive. To give Draven and me more time.

And Ray.

I tuck myself closer to his chest, inhaling his scent, allowing the crispness of it to calm my thoughts.

"Honey badger," Draven whispers, stretching against me.

A thrill of heat jolts down the center of me at the hardness of his body rolling against mine.

He slowly opens his eyes, a lazy sort of gaze as he looks me over. "Thank you," he whispers.

"For what?" I scrunch my brow.

His arms around me tighten. "For letting me hold you."

The words tangle in my throat—emotion weighing down my chest. How freeing does it feel for him? To be able to touch without killing, to experience contact without fear?

He rolls to the side, glancing at his phone on his nightstand before tucking around me again. "We slept for a few hours," he says. "But we still have time..."

Time to just live here in this moment.

Time before I have to tell Ray I love her and then face the biggest battle of my life—and after living with the man I thought was my father for eighteen years, I never thought I'd face anything more difficult than him.

Time because we want to play this right—to call out the Second when we're both rested and ready and on our own terms.

And if we're going to pretend like all is well and live in *this* moment for a little longer, there is something I want to know.

"Tell me something," I say, catching my breath, willing my body to work properly.

"What?"

"Another story," I say. "Tell me about your brother."

His eyes dart to mine.

"You told me so many stories earlier," I say. "Taking me on a journey through your past. And you never once mentioned him."

An old pain colors his features, and he leans his head against the wall. "My brother—my twin—was Called the same day as I was. We went to train with The Seven before being passed on to one of the respective Judge mentors. He accelerated faster than I did, earning his mentorship and actual fieldwork in a matter of weeks."

"How?"

A slow grin. "The ability to control lightning and storms is not so finicky a power as mine. They rarely put him in the divine sleep, and he was nowhere near as much of a threat to The Seven as a siphon."

"But there must've been others like you—"

"Not any of record. I'm the first to show the power. The Seven has never known what to do with me. They are all terrified of me, and many think the Creator has endowed me with such a power to punish them." He rolls his eyes. "I was passed down through each of The Seven, always treated as a problem. Who could possibly be *good* when they absorb the powers of every demon they come into contact with? What else could possibly be absorbed? The evil intent?"

I gape at him, shaking my head, but he merely shrugs.

"The last of The Seven, Esther, is the only one who was kind to me." He smiles softly. "She's the reason I excelled at all. Her patience and compassion allowed me to train with a seasoned Judge before finally being afforded missions of my own. But even she can't save me from the sleep they put me in when I'm not needed."

I instantly like whoever this Esther being is.

"My brother," he continues, "loved the Judge gig. Thrived on it. Practically the golden boy of The Seven." There is no bitterness in his tone, only longing, regret. "When we were kids, we were inseparable. We thought the same, could read each other without speaking, and we always had each other's back."

My stomach tightens like the floor is about to be ripped from underneath me.

"But once we were Called...everything changed. Something fractured between us—he couldn't see the hate I held toward the Calling, and I couldn't see the love he had for it. And once we were given missions of our own, we'd be separated, never put on the same task. Then, whenever we did get to see each other again, there was such...contempt between us." He shook his head. "I lost track of time, thanks to the divine sleep, and on one of my brief awakenings, Esther came to me. I couldn't remember the last time I'd seen her."

I swallow hard, the tension coiling Draven's muscles tightening around me.

"She came to talk to me. To tell me...a greater demon—one with a vendetta against me because I'd vanquished his mate the mission prior, the same female greater demon I told you about earlier. Her mate *took* my brother."

"Where?" I ask when he doesn't continue.

"To Hell."

Hell.

My blood runs cold.

"The demon thought he was *me*," he says, his voice breaking. "He thought he'd taken *me* to Hell. To torture for an eternity for what I'd done." A tear rolls down his cheek. "That was more than a hundred years ago." Ice runs through my veins, thinking there is no telling how much suffering his brother has endured in there. "And I'd sell my soul to get him back. To take his place."

And I can't fault him that logic, even when the mere idea of him being tortured in Hell makes the power roil in my blood. Because I would do the same for Ray without question. There's something about the love of a sibling that can't be severed or matched regardless of the way they left things.

"Draven," I say. "I'm so sorry."

He doesn't respond, instead absently fiddling with the colorful bracelet Ray gave me.

"What can I do?" A pointless question, really. What could I possibly do to help soothe the hurt of this loss? If anything like that happened to Ray…

I shudder at the thought.

"Stay alive," he says, his fingers moving over the stone in the bracelet my mother gave me for a moment before he jerks them back. "You never take this off." Not a statement, a question.

I lift my wrist, twisting it back and forth. "It's supposed to fall off on its own," I say. "It's one of those wishing bracelets. I've had it for years."

Draven's eyes flicker up to mine. "Who gave it to you?"

"My mother," I say. "It's the only memory I have of her. Why?"

He sits back, leaning against the wall again, his eyes churning with *something*.

"Draven?"

"It's… I thought…" He blinks a few times, shaking his head and forcing a smile to his lips. "It's nothing. Is there anything you want to do today? Before…"

Whiplash. The boy is the king of it. But after the truth he just laid bare? I'd want to change the subject, too. I'd want to run as far away from that darkness as possible. Because the idea of Ray taking our father's abuse in my place would be enough to turn me into the monster the world wants me to be.

And yet, Draven is *good*.

Despite the tragedy.

Despite the horrible treatment from those who should be his confidants.

He has not become what he could've easily justified.

"Yes," I admit. There are two things I know I have to do before night falls. Before I dive headfirst into the battle.

I don't have a clue how I'll manage it all in a way that will leave Draven unscathed, Ray protected, and the world safe.

And I hate the voice in the back of my head, whispering that such hope is useless. That in the end, I'm going to burn.

CHAPTER FORTY-THREE

ME: I need to talk to you. Can we meet up?

I chew on my lip as we walk toward the El, Draven silent and understanding at my side. He didn't hesitate when I told him what I needed to do before tonight. Before the spell wears off, and with the sun just now setting? I need to swallow my fear and do what I need to.

KAI: I'm busy

ME: Later? Please, it's important. Where are you? I'll meet you anywhere.

I have to talk to him. Have to make things right between us before...

KAI: I'm near Jackson Park. I'll meet you in front of the museum in half an hour.

ME: Perfect

Elation storms through the center of my chest at his willingness to see me. To give me the chance to mend what is broken between us before it's too late.

"I have to go," I say, changing directions on the street we walk down.

"I thought we were going to the hospital to see Ray?"

"We will. Right after. Kai's agreed to meet me, to let me explain things."

Draven furrows his brow.

"I'll meet you at your place after I talk to him, then Ray," I say when he matches my steps. "Then we can go to the library."

"We're on the last hours of the protection spell," he says. "You think I'm letting you out of my sight?"

I part my lips to argue. "I don't need a bodyguard."

"Don't you?" he challenges, arching a brow at me.

I stop, stepping into his path. A few pedestrians hustle around us, grumbling at the block in foot traffic. "Not sure Kai will be too eager to hear me out if you're hovering around me."

"I don't have the faintest care what Kai thinks," he says.

"I could stop you from following me."

"You could *try*." That damn connection we share shakes awake at his words. The sensation is palpable—a white-hot tension between us.

"You think you could take me?" I ask, tipping my chin up at him.

"In *all* sorts of ways," he croons, and heat trembles along the edges of my skin. "This morning was just a taste, honey badger."

My head spins from the power in my position—at holding his rapt attention, someone as strong and dangerous as he is. I can feel it, his endless well of power rolling off him like a signature sound that resonates inside me. A *craving* instead of the terror any normal person would cower at.

"Say the word, Harley," he dares.

"You—" I clamp my lips shut. "Ugh, you're distracting me," I groan and wave him off as I turn on my heels. "I don't have time to argue with you." No matter how delightful it may be. We're close to Jackson Park, and I'm content to wait for Kai the half hour he's asked for.

"It was working so well," he says, a light teasing to his voice as he follows me.

"One of your more endearing qualities," I say, trying to mimic his stoic tone when he said the same thing about me. Draven huffs a laugh but remains silent the rest of our walk.

The moon is rising, full and bright tonight, illuminating the limestone pillars of the building in a soft, silver glow, and we make it to the entrance of the museum with fifteen minutes to spare. The water feeding off Lake Michigan into the Columbia Basin laps at the pathway just beyond the wide expanse of stairs leading up to the museum, the gentle waves casting a peaceful veil over the night's scene.

"He's not here," Draven says, hands tucked in the pockets of his jeans.

"We're early." I shrug, scanning the area as I settle on one of the bottom steps. "When he shows up, can you—"

"Make myself disappear?" There is an annoyance to Draven's tone.

"Yes, thank you," I say. "I let you tag along, but I need to talk to Kai alone." He'd looked so hurt and betrayed when he caught Draven and me mid–make-out session. And despite that being totally my choice and my right to do so, I hate that I hurt him. The last thing I need is Draven lurking around when I try to make amends.

"Let me?" Draven raises his brows.

I give him an equally challenging look, daring him to argue.

He merely shakes his head, eyes scanning the area.

We're essentially alone this evening—I don't spot a single person around the park surrounding the buildings. I wonder what Kai can possibly be doing on this side of town that he suggested meeting here.

"You don't happen to have the power to speed up time, do you?" I ask, the waiting pushing me to my breaking point.

"No," he says. "Not one of my endless talents—"

A menacing growl cuts him off. We both leap to our feet, scanning for the source.

"What the—" The air whooshes out of my lungs as a massive creature hurtles itself at me.

"Harley!" Draven screams, launching atop the thing's back and hauling it off me.

I roll to the right, closer to the water as I gasp. Draven wrestles with the beast—it looks like a giant alligator with six legs instead of four. Scales of white armor plate the creature's back, spiking up near its skull and all the way down to its forked tail. The maw on it is ridiculously wide, with rows of razor-sharp teeth dripping with thick black saliva.

It goes for Draven's arm, but he lashes out with a whip of pure silver, ensnaring the beast's neck. A quick jerk is followed by a bone-snapping crack, and the thing goes limp at his boots. Its body dissolves into that black glittering powder, the bulk of it carried away on the wind.

Fire itches my fingertips, the ground a pulsing, living thing beneath my feet. "Goddamn it, not now!" Kai will be here any minute, and if he gets hurt, I will *absolutely* lose my shit. I glance at the tattoo on my wrist, noting the color in the vines hasn't faded entirely. "What the hell?" I look at Draven. "The tattoo still has time; how did that thing smell me?"

"I'm not sure," Draven calls from where he remains by the stairs.

"Are there more?" I ask, taking a step toward him, my eyes darting around the vast area near him.

"Harley!"

Something sharp hooks around my ankle and yanks me backward, slamming my stomach against the ground, rattling my teeth. I tear at the pavement as it drags me back and back until the cold water of the Columbia Basin swallows me entirely.

I jerk my leg against that heavy force, panic clawing at my mind. My lungs ache, desperate for air as I'm pulled deeper and deeper under the water. The same white demon glows beneath the murky liquid like some terrifying mythical sea creature.

Air.

I need air.

Darkness slides along my eyes, the water growing pitch-black the deeper we sink.

And *screw this*. I have zero time to die right now.

I mentally shout that truth at the flames in my blood, focusing on letting them out from behind that door that keeps them trapped.

The water lights up with a brilliant black and silver, the demon's slitted eyes flying wide at the sight of the dark flames swirling around my body like a tornado. Fire licks at the three-clawed limb it sinks into my ankle, the release instant as it roars underwater.

The minute I'm free, I kick my legs, reach for the surface. My heartbeat slows, dulling that fiery glow around me until only a wisp of fire remains. I call on that second power, the earth thrumming next to my fire, begging it to yield to me. A cold, ropey root encircles my wrist, yanking me upward until my mouth breaks the surface of the water.

I gulp the air, my lungs searing as that muddy root pulls me until I can haul myself onto the ground. Instantly, the root unleashes me, and I feel the release of control in my blood.

Snarls jerk my attention forward, my mind clearing enough to take in the scene before me.

There are nine of them—the giant albino alligator monsters—and their razor-sharp teeth glow in the moonlight.

Blood drips from a gash above Draven's right brow as each one of the creatures encircles him, and I scramble to my feet, a scream lodged in my throat as they all attack at once.

CHAPTER FORTY-FOUR

Like some perfectly initiated plan, they converge on Draven, their claws digging into the grass, churning up the earth as they rush him.

My entire focus narrows on the sight of those monsters covering him in a massive pile of claws and teeth.

I dig my heels in, rushing for the center of that pile, the blood in my veins *screaming*.

But a wave of power blows me off my feet, launching me through the air until my butt hits the pavement near the water. Thuds and wails pepper the air as the demons writhe under that power as well.

I roll, leaping to my feet.

Draven rises from his knees, his arms raised, hands flexed in either direction. Blood covers his face, his eyes a molten gold as he holds the demons in the air with his telekinesis power. Necks crunch, four of the demons' bodies twisting at awkward angles until their limbs hang limp, their thick black tongues dangling from their mouths.

Water gurgles behind me. I whirl, raising my fists because I'll be damned if I'm dragged to that murky bottom again.

From the water come six more, the white armored bodies glowing sickly under the moonlight as they stalk toward me.

Draven hollers, but I don't dare take my eyes off the demons whose claws now *click-clack* against solid ground. Their black eyes glisten as they go for my ankles.

Power, searing and saturated in earth, pounds against that iron door inside me as I scramble backward, closer to where Draven battles the remaining five.

One demon bares its teeth, the black spittle spraying over my pants. The world slows—Draven's heaved breaths behind me, the scraping of claws, and the sick cracks of bones fill my ears.

The demon closest to me leaps through the air, giant mouth open and ready to claim my head for its dinner, and I throw my hands up, dodging the serrated teeth, but its massive body lands on top of me. I choke for air, the weight of the snarling creature suffocating as I do everything to push it off. But my muscles are weak, no match for the ancient strength the monster possesses. And this is only *one*. Three more encircle us, waiting…for what? I don't know and don't care.

My body can't match theirs.

But my power can, if I can hold it long enough.

The dark flames snake from my fingertips, sliding over the monster's scaled flesh. It rears off me, dodging my dark fire. And as it regroups with its three buddies, creating a half circle around me, I know I need more power to stop them.

I drop my hands, digging my fingers into the soft grass beneath me. My tongue crackles with mud and rain. And I feel the interconnectedness of nature, of the earth pulsing in my blood and the power of it. I beg it to work, to not short-circuit when I need it most.

Like insects skittering over my skin, it answers my call. And one by one, the agonized screams of the monsters split the air.

Roots older than I am and thicker than the demons encircle each of their necks, jerking and yanking against their attempts at escape. I get my feet under me, holding that focus, drowning in the taste of vegetation, the scent of wet earth filling my nose as I control the ends of the roots.

I curl my hand and the roots tightening until their black eyes bulge.

And their necks crack.

The rush of them disintegrating into ash is both a relief and a weight that threatens to pull down the earth in my blood.

My knees bark against the ground as the power—both earth and fire—slips from my grasp, yanked back behind that iron door with a scream of outrage.

Draven groans behind me, and I spin around on all fours, my muscles trembling.

Two demons have his shoulders pinned to the ground, their acidic saliva sizzling against his cheeks as the third and final demon hovers over him from behind. Draven struggles beneath their weight, his eyes blazing.

That third demon lowers its mouth, a monster playing with its food.

"No!" I scream, and Draven's eyes jerk to mine.

"Harley, don't—"

But his order comes too late. One second, I can't move. The next I'm *there*, digging fingers covered in black fire into the third demon's back as I launch atop it.

The thing flails back and forth, screeching as it tries to shake my grasp. My body whips from left to right, but still I hang on. The fire coating my fingers flickers and wanes, like a candle dying in the middle of the night.

Until I'm just a girl on top of a monster, desperate to stop its attack.

The moon-white armor on its back pricks my skin, the pain stinging every nerve. I will each muscle in my body to lock, to stay on the thing's back as I glance up.

Draven is on his feet again.

No longer pinned, he dodges claws and teeth.

I scream, the tips of those plated scales ripping through my clothes and piercing my flesh.

Draven whirls, concern furrowing his brow before his eyes shift to a lethal fury that slicks my skin with an icy terror. He tilts his head back, raising his arms palm-up toward the sky, and shadows snuff out all the light.

Submerged in a blanket of darkness, the demons wail. The one beneath me lifts off the ground, the motion jarring enough to throw me from its back. Darker than midnight, I choke on the lack of sight. Overwhelmed by the sound of splitting flesh and gnashing teeth. A primal roar swallows the screams of the demons, the rage within it enough to make me tuck into a ball. A metallic smell laced with sulfur swirls in the rushing air around me, the cold touch of shadows tickling the edges of my skin as I cover my head.

A loud *pop*, and the shadows draw back enough for me to see. I uncurl myself, eyes wide as I find the source of the roar.

Draven.

His knees hit the ground, and he rages at the sky like a cornered beast from an ancient time. Wisps of shadow jerk back and forth at his shoulders. A slew of dead demons floats in the darkness, disintegrating into that fine black powder until it becomes one with his shadows. A mixture of his blood and theirs cakes his skin, his golden eyes churning with a blazing glow.

He doubles over, his jaw flexing and cracking until his lips snarl around rows of serrated, razor-sharp teeth.

My blood runs cold, all fire and earth trickling into a watery stream.

He's siphoned their power.

One more drop in the endless well he already possesses.

One more element that can consume him if he isn't careful.

And something in my heart breaks at the sight. At the way the monster merges with the boy I can't stay away from.

I crawl toward him, but he growls, scrambling away from me as the transformation keeps its hooks in him.

"Draven," I say, my voice calm if not breathless. *"Draven,"* I say again, catching up to him as he stills at the sound of his name on my lips.

He flinches as our knees touch.

I swallow hard while scanning his face. A magnificent beast, that's what he is. Muscled body, golden eyes, and a now-reptilian mouth capable of ending someone in one bite. But there is such devastation in those eyes, and shame. So much shame.

My fingers tremble as I reach up to cup his face, and he goes deadly still under my touch.

"I'm not afraid of you." I've said the words tons of times before, but in his current state, he needs to hear them more than ever. He needs to *feel* them. "I don't care what The Seven say," I continue. "You are good." He shudders beneath my touch. "You are not what you absorb. You are *good*, Draven."

His eyes close as he leans his forehead against mine.

The air between us hums, and I feel his deep sigh against my skin.

"Harley," he says, drawing back enough for me to see his face.

Wholly his again, cleared of the blood that covered it before the transformation. The shift disappearing somewhere deep inside him to be called upon later if needed. How many times has this happened to him over his hundreds of years of service in a war he had no choice in fighting?

"Draven," I echo, smoothing my hands over his face.

He snakes his arms around my back, hauling me closer. "When they came out of the water," he says, his voice raspy, raw. "When they took you...I thought..."

"It'll take more than some creepy alligator monster to take me down."

Draven's grip tightens on my body, a thrill of heat jolting down my spine at the primal touch. "Lagartis." He says the name, identifying the demon.

"One of the baser creatures from the inner levels?"

He nods. "You are good, too, you know," he says, smoothing back some of my wild hair.

I furrow my brow, shaking my head. I've never been the good one—the good daughter, the good friend, the good worker. I've been the worthless one, the pitied one.

"I don't deserve your kindness," he continues, closing his eyes. "If you knew the truth about me—"

My phone buzzes from my pocket, cutting off Draven's words. I frantically fish it out, reality catching up with my mind.

KAI: Can't make it. Something more important came up.

My stomach sinks as I read the words over and over again. Was showing up to hear me out *ever* a possibility? Or did he merely say he would just so he could blow me off? In truth, I should be grateful he didn't show up, with what just happened—

But his words…they hurt like hell.

My thumbs hover over the keys, but I don't have a thing I can say. I shake my head, pocket my phone, and return my attention to Draven where we still kneel, knee to knee.

"Why are you still here, Draven?" I whisper. "Clearly, even I get the magic tattoo wrong if those things found me. There is no telling what else I'm going to screw up."

"Isn't it obvious?" Draven asks, his free hand gently grasping the back of my neck, tilting my head ever so slightly.

My body shivers in his embrace, as if I can feel his powers flickering in and out after all he used.

His lips crush mine as he kisses me with deep strokes and teasing flicks. I sigh between his lips, and just as quickly, he tears his mouth away, a near-wicked smirk shaping his mouth. His chest heaves, both our breaths ragged and unkempt.

"You're *mine*," he growls, the words so final, so lethally claiming, that I feel them like a brand across my soul.

And I love the way it burns.

M y body aches in places I didn't know were possible as I walk into Ray's hospital room. Nathan gives me a hug before he abandons the chair at her bedside, telling me he's going to grab coffee. Unknowingly giving me the time I need with her.

I managed to talk Draven into going home for an hour, his use of power exhausting him to the point that he was barely coherent by the time I helped him fall in a heap in his bed, but after we agreed to meet at the library in two hours—him setting his alarm to be certain—he instantly passed out to recharge.

His scent still clings to every inch of my skin, and the thought sends a warm chill over my skin at the memory of his claiming kiss.

"You're mine."

The words he spoke after I faced the beast in him and didn't cower in fear. The way he kissed me. The way he seemed determined we could win the battle ahead, it all fills me with a sense of hope.

"Hey!" Ray says, her eyelids fluttering open as I sink into the chair at her bedside. She shifts on the mattress, her little forehead puckering a bit.

"How are you feeling?" I ask. I expected her to be asleep, since it's so late, the hour so close to my protection wearing off, if it's even fully working anyway. How the hell did those things find me? Could it be a coincidence?

"I slept half the day," she says, a strain in her voice drawing me out of my thoughts.

"Are you in a lot of pain?" I ask, wanting to murder my father all over again.

"Just a little. I'm okay," she says, leaning against her pillow. "You okay?"

I tilt my head. "Why wouldn't I be?"

She fiddles with the hospital blanket over her legs, chewing on her bottom lip. "I had another nightmare earlier," she says. "It was worse than the others. Maybe it's just that, but Marid…he keeps…" Her voice trails off.

Cold combats the fire in my blood. "What?" I urge. "What about Marid?"

Ray stares up at me, a cringe creasing her forehead. "You'll think I'm crazy—"

"Never," I say. "I'll *never* think you're crazy."

"He's been asking about you. A lot. And he gets angry when I don't know the answers." She pinches her lips together. "Sometimes it's like I can *feel* him. And he says he's going to hurt you, steal you. That he'll never leave me alone if I don't tell you…" She shakes her head. "They're just nightmares, though. My imagination running wild, right? Like we've always said."

I swallow hard. I have no idea if these are just nightmares—after what I've seen, what I know about the world, my gut says they aren't. No matter how much I wish they were.

"I have to tell you something," I say, my voice tight. A weight presses down on my chest, a silent plea to protect her from the darkness of the world. As I tried to shield her from our father our entire lives. I sigh, rubbing my palms over my face. She *deserves* to know the truth. People have kept secrets from me forever, and I can't do that to her. I don't want to disappear and her be left with the constant pain and grief of not knowing *why*.

"But it'll be *your* choice how much you want to be told." I can give her that, at least. Her own right to choose if she wants to remain blissfully ignorant of some things.

"I want to know everything," she says, her blue gaze too mature. A product of my failure to protect her from the lifestyle our father put us in. Also my fault, since he was hired to torture me.

At least I didn't let him kill all the good in me. And I know that has everything to do with the little girl staring at me with expectant eyes.

And these nightmares of hers that are about me? Those—I can feel it in my bones—those are somehow my fault, too. So after I leave here? I'm going to make sure the Second feels every ounce of my anger over it.

"You don't even know what I'm about to say—"

"I don't care," she argues. "It doesn't matter what it is. You tell me. We're sisters," she says. "We don't keep secrets, remember?"

Tears bite the backs of my eyes as I nod.

"Okay," I say. "You absolutely can't tell Nathan. Or anyone." I eye her.

"Does Draven know?"

I nod.

"Kai?"

Guilt hits my chest, his harsh words from earlier gripping my chest like a vise.

"No," I say.

"What is it, Harley?"

So I tell her.

Everything.

Even about the connection to Draven I can't deny.

And I finish the story with the battle from earlier.

Ray sits silent the entire time, her eyes widening in some parts, her nose crinkling in others.

"Well?" I ask after I finish and she's been silent too long.

"Show me," she says, her voice soft. Accepting.

"It doesn't always work," I admit but raise my hand. I cast a look at the closed hospital door, making sure a nurse isn't hovering near the small window there to see. Then I ask my leashed power for a little slack and snap my fingers.

Ray gasps, her eyes focusing on the lone black flame dancing on my fingertip.

It sputters and extinguishes, that chain at its throat yanking it back. Maybe I exhausted it earlier.

Her little brow crinkles.

"I'd love to know what you're thinking," I say, crossing my arms over my chest. I wish I had Draven's ability to read minds at will. Maybe I should've had him tag along just so I could know the truth of her feelings.

No. That'd be a violation of her trust, something I'd never risk.

"In mangas," she says, "sometimes a character's powers are accelerated with a special talisman or something."

A soft smile breaks my lips. Leave it to Ray to relate my supernatural abilities to anime.

"Maybe all you need to do to get your powers to work right is to find your talisman." She has such hope in her voice, such love. I told her everything, and she wants to *help* me.

"You're not afraid of me?" I dare ask, needing the verbal confirmation.

"No." She snorts like it's the silliest question of all time. "I'll never be afraid of you." Her little shoulders drop. "Even if we aren't really sisters—"

"Hey." I scoot to the edge of my chair and take her hand. "We're sisters," I say. "We'll always be sisters—I don't care what he said. You're my family. You're my *heart*, Ray."

"Always," she says. "Promise?"

"Promise."

She nods. "Draven is special."

I didn't tell her about the full extent of his powers, seeing as that isn't my story to tell, but I agree with her.

"I knew that," she says. "When he put my drawing back together."

I grin at the memory, knowing that now that she's going to live with Nathan, she'll have so many art pieces never in jeopardy of being destroyed. "How do you feel about staying with Nathan when you get out of here?"

"I'm excited," she says. "I love him. Love it there."

"Good." A knot forms in my throat. She deserves that happiness; she deserves everything. "You can cover the walls with your drawings—"

"I don't want them up."

I furrow my brow. "Because of the nightmares?"

"Marid is the only character I've been able to draw for a long time," she whispers. "Except for that one of you." She glances up at me. "And my fingers have been itching to draw, but I won't."

"Why?"

"Because I don't like what I see."

"What do you see, Ray?"

"He hurts you." She shivers. "Chains you up. Uses one of those blood bag things you see when you donate."

The image chills my blood.

"And Draven is there, too. Watching."

My eyes widen. Draven will never stand by and let me be hurt. Maybe she overheard us talking, and her mind has conjured this story and played it in her dreams and that's all this boils down to.

"Am I like you, you think? Is what I'm seeing…real? I drew you with fire before you showed me."

I hate that I don't have an answer for her.

"I'm not sure," I answer honestly. "But maybe my world has just somehow subconsciously rubbed off on you. Creating these dreams, these drawings." I lean forward to squeeze her hand. "And Draven would certainly never stand by and watch if I'm in trouble." He's proven that with the numerous times we've been attacked.

Ray nods, sighing. "Good." She chews on her lip. "I wonder what kind of talisman you need," she says, jumping back to our earlier conversation.

I laugh softly. "I don't think the real world will work like your anime."

"Writers take inspiration from real-life events all the time," she chides me. "Maybe some of these storytellers have the sight or whatever you're talking about."

I purse my lips, not able to argue that. "Well, with my luck," I say, "it's probably just my dirty blood that's making my powers short-circuit."

"You know that isn't true. You are what you decide to be. *You* taught me that."

"What do you mean?"

She rolls her eyes. "Every time I got scared. Every time I cried in your arms and worried that we'd turn out like Dad. That we'd be mean and bad." She raises her brows. "You're the one who would hold me and say, *'It doesn't matter whose blood runs in our veins. We are who we decide to be.'*"

She listened.

All those years, she listened. I figured the moments would be blotted out in her memory thanks to the strenuous circumstances surrounding them.

But here she is, seven years old, taking me to school with my own words.

"Who are you going to decide to be, Harley?" she asks when I remain silent too long.

"Someone you're proud of," I say.

"You already are." She smiles, and I feel it in my soul.

"I love you, Ray," I say. "No matter what happens. No matter if I disappear. I need you to know that. You're the bright spot in my world. I don't know how I got so lucky to have you as my sister."

"I love you, too." She tightens her grip on my hand. "But do me a favor?"

"Anything."

"*Don't* disappear. Don't do what you've always done."

I tilt my head.

"Don't play hide-and-seek with the world."

I freeze in my chair but force a smile to my face, not wanting to cause her any more pain. "I've never liked the world much anyway."

She laughs, sinking back on her pillow.

A soft hum sounds from my phone.

KAI: You still around Jackson Park?

KAI: I finished up my work. I'm ready to talk to you now.

My heart clenches, his last text still hurting. But I don't have much time left—if this is my shot, then I have to take it. Even if it means risking another battle with whatever demons may still be out there. Kai is worth that.

I scoot out of the chair, leaning down to kiss her forehead. "Get some rest, Ray."

"Where are you going? It's close to midnight."

"I have to meet Kai."

"You're not going to tell him, are you?"

"The more people who know, the higher they're at risk. I told you because if anything happens to me, I don't want you to spend your life thinking I left you on purpose."

"You won't," Ray says. "You're stronger than you know." She blinks, not closing her eyes for a few seconds. "You just need to find that talisman."

I look down at her, a soft smile shaping my lips. I don't know much about my new supernatural world, but I doubt there are objects that grant power like that. Still, the hope in her eyes threatens to crush what remains of my heart.

"Talisman, huh?" I say, an idea taking shape in my mind. I fiddle with the bracelet my mother gave me. "Like a wishing bracelet?"

Ray raises her brows. "You've never taken that off," she says.

"Maybe it's time I *do*. Maybe it's time I broke it myself to make the wish come true." I'm *way* past needing to take control of my fate. Plus, now that I know the truth—that my mother willingly gave me to a monster who wasn't my real father—I don't need this reminder anymore.

"Besides," I say, grinning down at the braided rope of color she gave me. "I have a better bracelet. One that means more to me than all the wishes in the world."

Water glistens over her blue eyes, but she swallows hard. "What are you going to wish for? To make your powers stronger? Easier to use?" she asks, her eyes wide as I slip my fingers under the thin black cord.

"I can't tell you or it won't come true." I smile as I kneel next to the bed, motioning for her to take the cord, too. She hooks her fingers beneath it.

I wish for Ray to be safe and happy and free of nightmares for the rest of her life.

"Together?" I ask, and she nods. I yank on the cord, and she pulls from the opposite direction. The material is stronger than I ever thought possible, so much that we both groan as we yank and tug and pull—

The bracelet flies against the wall so hard, it leaves a small indent—how cheap are these hospital walls? The black cord breaks in half, and the paper-thin stone in its center fissures in the middle—

My knees smack against the tiled floor, and I throw my head back, arching as I groan.

A searing hot force works its way through my body, and I know exactly what it wants to do, what it's racing toward... It melts the iron door, the steel collar choking my power. Melts it down into a liquid ore that snakes through my blood with a surge.

I double over, fingers splaying against the tile as my power floods my body, my soul, my *mind*. Ash and dirt burst along my tongue as I gather myself enough to stand. My muscles meeting my demands without strain or effort.

For the first time in my life, I feel *strong*.

Capable.

In control.

Ray's eyes are wide as saucers as she gapes at me. At the dark flames encircling my hands, my forearms.

Half a thought from me extinguishes them—my powers delighting in the freedom as they course through my blood.

"Harley?" Ray asks as I scoop up the broken bracelet and examine it. "What was that?"

I shake my head, staring at the crack in the thin black stone I've worn for as long as I can remember. The one my mother fastened around my wrist before she disappeared. Did she know what I am? Did she use whatever the hell this damn stone is against me? Was it her way of trying to subdue my powers my entire life?

Anger pulses in my chest.

"I'm not sure," I finally answer Ray, laying the pieces of the bracelet on the little table by the hospital bed. "But it doesn't matter, see?" I show her the beautiful rainbow braid around my wrist. "This one is safe."

"Are *you* okay?"

I smile down at her. "Better than okay," I say, my head swimming with the fire beneath my skin. For the first time since all this started, I feel...

Powerful.

"Does that mean your wish came true?" she asks.

"Yes," I say, half lost in my mind at the possibilities. She told me I needed to find a talisman to enhance my powers. Turns out I needed to shed myself of one that held them down. "Yes, I think so," I say, smiling at her. "I have to go." I hate that I need to leave her. But Kai is waiting, and my time is up.

"Be careful," Ray says.

"I'll do my best," I promise. "I love you."

"I love you."

I linger in the doorway, my hand on the knob, praying to whatever higher power exists that this won't be the last time I see my baby sister.

CHAPTER
FORTY-SIX

I spare some cash and hail a cab to Jackson Park, knowing I have absolutely no time to waste. And I hop out of the taxi with a new sense of purpose smoothing the jagged edges of my soul with this *unleashing*.

I confidently walk over the grassy area near the water, the moonlight still shimmering off its calm ripples. I almost dare something to come and get me. Dare the world to test me right fucking now.

I take a steadying breath, calming that itch to fight. I certainly don't need to be a living flame when meeting up with my very human best friend. I'm on shaky ground with him enough as it is.

First, I'll make amends. Make things right between us.

Then I'll meet up with Draven at the library as planned and let him know what's happened. That I've taken control of every inch of my power. Now that I rid myself of the bracelet that has, unknowingly to me, been holding it back, I can feel the depths of it—and it is extensive.

That has to count for something when we call out the Second, right?

"Kai!" I yell his name once he comes into view.

He leans casually against one of the trees near the water, arms folded over his chest. He shifts when he sees me, dropping those arms to his sides as I hurry toward him. Seeing him there, having him *actually* show up makes all the worries about our fight slip away. He's here. He's willing to work out our issues and save our friendship.

And I don't realize how much I *need* that reconciliation until

I wrap my arms around his neck and nearly cry in relief when he holds me back. He doesn't push me away, doesn't immediately lash out.

"I'm so glad you're here," I say, sighing. "Look, I know things have been off between us, but you have to understand that the last thing I ever want is to hurt you—"

Some metallic groaning happens from just beyond the trees, and I crane my head over Kai's shoulder to scan the area. It's so dark I can barely see, but panic claws my chest at the thought of more demons coming for me now of all times.

Kai squeezes me harder against him, shifting our embrace slightly, drawing my attention back to him. "I know," he says as he runs his fingers through my hair.

"I am really sorry, Kai. You know how much you mean to me. I told you before, I don't want to lose you. I don't want what happened to drive you away."

"You won't," he says. "I'm never letting you go." He sighs into the crook of my neck, and I swallow hard. "What time is it, Harley?" he asks, his tone so soft, so low that I almost miss the words.

I narrow my gaze, shifting out of his hold enough to grab my phone. "It's fifteen past midnight," I say, pocketing it as I look up at him. Shit, past midnight. I didn't realize how long it had taken me to get here, too caught up with my powers storming me. Draven is probably wondering where I am.

Kai grins down at me, a smile I've never seen before—one that looks more like a predator toying with its prey. I drop my arms from around his neck, taking a timid step back. He smooths his knuckles over my cheek.

"What's wrong?" he asks, scanning my face.

My instincts are tugging me in the opposite direction, begging me to run. Is that because I know Draven is waiting for me? Because I don't want him to go after the Second alone?

"You're shaking," he says, his hands curling around my trembling fingers. His thumbs smooth over the skin of my wrist.

"You're not wearing your bracelet," he notes as he tilts his head at me. "Did you lose it that night at the library?"

"No, I just—" The words die on my tongue, my throat tensing. I swallow around the mass, taking another step back. Kai keeps his gentle yet firm grip on my hands. "I never told you I went to the library."

Those green eyes widen, the unfamiliar grin stretching. "Whoopsie." He drags out the word.

I jerk my hands from his, and he gives me an incredulous look. "Oh, come on, Harley," he says. "You've faced Aspis and Hypnos, Cannis and Lagartis demons, but you're suspicious of *me*?"

I'm not sure I'm breathing.

"I wondered," he continues, eyes on the tattoo on my wrist, now wholly black as he matches every step I take away with a step forward. "I *wondered* why I couldn't touch you after your birthday. Drove me nearly up the wall when I couldn't get my hands on you enough. Though Kazuki has always liked to meddle in places he shouldn't."

"How?" The word is a choked plea.

He clasps his hands behind his back, bowing toward me. "Haven't you figured it out? I'm a *Judge*. Just like your precious Draven."

I furrow my brow. "You're lying," I say, shaking my head.

"I have no reason to lie to you anymore."

"We *grew up* together." He can't possibly be as old as Draven.

"We didn't," he says, shrugging as he steps closer to me.

The ground tilts beneath my feet, my mind whirling.

"Those memories were planted," he says.

"By who?" I snarl, finally holding my ground.

"By the one I work for—"

"The Seven."

A manic, dark laugh. "Clever, but no." He shakes his head. "They are content to sit on their white thrones and do *nothing* to save the world. To cleanse it of all its wretched evil." He curls up his nose as if the air around him stinks. "They won't listen to my pleas to demand an audience with the Creator. To convince them that the world needs razing." Another shrug.

"I'm taking matters into my own hands now," he says, narrowing his gaze on me. "Funny thing about having the unique ability to control demons—I can make them do whatever I want. The Seven always delighted in the power because until recently, all I made them do was die."

Ash clogs my throat, and everything around me slows.

"I always told you I wanted a better world. And when he came to me with a proposition...well, you know how these things go. Two birds, one stone." He smirks again. "All I had to do was get my hands on the Key." He points to me. "And unleash enough demons from Hell to get the Creator's attention."

A cold sweat breaks out across my skin, chilling me to the very marrow of my bones.

"Who..." I say, my voice cracking. "Who came to you—"

"I suppose you should know," he says, his face turning serious, grave. "Since you're about to meet him."

My eyes widen, the powers in my blood thumping.

"Aren't you curious why I asked you to meet me *here*? In this spot?"

"Oh, I'm curious about a few fucking things right now."

A small uptick of the corners of his mouth. "There are specific spots where the veil between our worlds is the thinnest. All over the earth. That's why we travel so much, because demons can slip through the cracks—"

"Here," I say, glancing at the ground as if a gaping hole to Hell will open up beneath me.

"Yep." His lips pop on the end of the word, his eyes scanning me from head to toe. "And you're the Key to fully opening it. Your blood."

"I'll never let you—"

"Never"—he cuts me off—"say never." He flicks his wrist, and as if on an invisible string, Draven flies from behind the trees, halting a few feet off the ground, his head pointing down. His body is wrapped in chains of black stones that look eerily similar to the smaller version that was on my bracelet.

And blood…that's *blood* dripping to the ground from a wound I can't see.

"Found this one sniffing around my library," he says. "And Marid might've given me a few extra powers to fulfill his wishes, like concentrating the power to a new demon every other day so Draven couldn't sense me," Kai says as my mouth hangs open at the display of power—maneuvering Draven as easily as Draven did the demons with his telekinesis. "It was quite funny watching him think he was getting close at the Belluk den and then the library."

My eyes lock on Draven's, and I mentally shout toward him. *"You couldn't warn me my best friend was a Judge?"*

He told me that he couldn't stay out of my head when my emotions were high, and they're pretty fucking high right now.

"I knew he was a prick," Draven says into my mind, but even his mental voice sounds strained. *"I didn't know he was an evil prick. He told me he'd been sent by The Seven to help protect you. He's the source who told me about the Belluk den. But I begged him to tell you the truth as soon as you showed your powers—he wouldn't listen. Now I know why."*

"You could've!"

"Couldn't. We're bound by magic to not reveal other Judges' identities."

"You told me about your brother—"

"He hasn't been considered a Judge for more than a hundred years."

Kai is still bragging about the powers Marid gave him when I spare him a glance. I return focus to Draven. *"How hurt are you?"*

"I'm weak," he admits. *"I need out of these chains."*

"On it," I say, swallowing hard. *"Don't die, okay? This conversation is so far from over."*

I turn back to Kai, flames dancing on my fingertips. "Let him go."

Kai laughs, but there's no humor in his eyes. "*Him?* The

sight of *him* is what draws your power forth?" he screams. "How *truly* naive you are, Harley. Don't you know why he's *here*? Why he's stuck to you like glue since arriving?" He wags his finger at Draven. "I must admit, a clever plan, making you fall for him. I had thought I had the upper hand there. Was certain our years of friendship—"

"Fake."

He glares at me. "Our *history* would lead you to trusting and loving me. Adoring me so much that you'd do anything for me. Freely, willingly give me your blood when the time came." He purses his lips, shaking his head.

I shift my feet for better balance, my instincts roaring.

"Draven came here to *kill* you," he continues. "Use your blood to free his precious brother." He spits the words over his shoulder, and Draven's eyes clench shut as he tries to groan through the binding between his teeth. "Marid told me all about it," he adds, shaking his head. "He's had this one's brother for more than a century now, torturing him for what Draven did to his mate." Kai glances over his shoulder. "What do you think he'll do to you when he arrives?"

My lips part, a gasp shaking me. Draven's story—about how he lost his brother—it matches Kai's words. My stomach bottoms out.

Draven struggles in his chains, anger flaring in his eyes as he shakes his head.

"Oh, don't try to deny it!" Kai snaps his fingers, the gag in Draven's mouth evaporating. "Go on, tell her the truth for once, you lying waste of power."

"Harley," Draven groans, the sound of his voice so raw, so broken.

"Is it true?" I ask, grateful to actually voice the question. "Is he telling the truth?"

Kai raises his brows, a delighted, manic smile on his lips.

"You know me," he says. "I won't...I can't—"

"Boring." Kai flicks his wrist and the gag returns to Draven's mouth. "I give you this *one* chance to confess, and you waste it. Useless. Garbage. I have no idea how you've survived this long, but Marid will most certainly amend that fault in the Creator's choices."

Draven's chains tighten around his body, a muffled cry escaping from behind the gag.

"Stop!" I yell. "Release him now!"

Kai tilts his head at me, a shocked look on his face. "Even after what I just told you? He's a liar, Harley—"

"And you aren't? My whole life...our friendship was a lie."

"Not entirely true," he says, tapping a finger on his lips. "I came into your life a year ago. Marid's memory magic worked on anyone already in your life—Nathan, Ray, even your father. Suspicions were abounding about you even then—"

"And here you are trying to use me to open the gates of Hell and unleash a greater demon."

Kai shrugs. "If that's what it takes to draw the Creator down from their pedestal and burn this world anew, then that's what it *takes*. And what a year it was," he says, those eyes grazing my body again. "Until he showed up." He jerks his head in Draven's direction. "I had such big plans for us. For you to stand by my side. I was going to beg Marid to spare you. To use his endless power to restore you after we used all your blood. But you had to go and betray me. Fall for him instead of me. You were meant to help me reshape this world." He glares at me. "Oh, well. I suppose, in a way, you still will." He reaches out to me, his palm upturned like I'll easily drop my hand in his. "Your wrist, Harley," he demands.

"Go to hell," I spit, my chest fracturing as my world tilts. At the loss of the one friend I ever had. The boy I trusted.

A lie.

Another. Fucking. Lie.

Draven's groan mounts, those stone chains around him cinching tighter and tighter.

"Your wrist," Kai demands, and I fasten him with a glare. The fire in my blood roars, and the earth rolls right alongside it. "Don't be silly," he says, reading something in my eyes. "You're a baby in your power. I've seen it. Tested it. I had to be sure you were the right one. And your blood may be the Key, but *you* are no match for me. Especially not with the extra bits of power Marid has endowed me with." He motions to himself like he is mightier than the Creator.

"Tested it?"

"You didn't think all those attacks were random, did you? Harley, I thought you were smarter than that." He rolls his eyes. "I had to," he says, his voice light like we're still the best of friends. "I had to see the extent of your power. I couldn't simply snatch you up and risk your blood opening the *wrong* gate, now, could I?"

Wrong gate? If I open the gates of Hell, is there someone who opens the gates of Heaven?

"And then Kazuki had to go and place that protection spell on you. I couldn't touch you, no matter how hard I tried. Not with harmful intent."

I tilt my head, racking my mind for when he tried—

"I came to you while you slept, and that invisible spell of protection prolonged this moment every time." Kai shrugs again, eyeing me with a mild curiosity. "So I sent the lower levels after you and still, your powers proved erratic at best every single time. Quite the disappointment," he says. "After the rumors across both the divine circuit and the Darkness, I had thought you'd be more of a challenge." He shrugs. "Though people love to exaggerate legends, demon and human alike."

The attacks race through my mind—all those times, Kai knew where I was. The apartment, Myopic, *here*—

Draven struggles against those chains, his scream muted by the gag.

"Let him go."

"Give me your blood." He extends his hand.

I don't move an inch.

"He'll die. He doesn't have much time left. The fight with the Lagartis earlier helped me with that," he says. "And I'm afraid I may have caught him by surprise on his way to the library. Blades can be so tricky."

My heart races as it wars with my mind. I can tell how weak he is from our silent conversation seconds ago. And I can't let Draven die...I can't believe what Kai said about him. He could've slit my throat any of the times we were together to use my blood to get his brother back. But he didn't. At the very least, he's going to live long enough to explain himself.

"Kill him, and you'll never get one drop," I challenge, adding a sneer for good measure.

"I assure you, I will."

"Everything about you is *fake*." I shake my head at his threats. "Nothing between us was ever real. You had to have a greater demon implant memories into my mind to *force* me to care for you." I scrunch my face at him in disgust. "You're nothing. And I'm not afraid of you."

"Is that so?" His eyes narrow with amusement as he raises his palms toward the sky.

The water lapping at the edges of the grassy area where we stand gurgles and...

More than twenty albino-alligator demons—Lagartis—slither and waddle onto the land. Ruthless jaws, sinewy, armored bodies. Tails swishing this way and that as they gather in one massive circle around Draven, ready and willing to make a meal out of him. Maws open and dripping that black saliva all over the ground.

Kai presses his middle finger to his thumb, poised to snap. To unleash those beasts on Draven. "Your blood?"

My body trembles with hate and rage. Shakes as I slide my gaze to Draven's, hanging there, defenseless. He gives me the most subtle shake of his head.

Not worth it.

He doesn't even have to speak into my mind for me to know that he doesn't think he's worth it.

As I have thought so many times my entire life. Not worth

the love of a father who can't stand me, who beat me down. Not worth the affection and kindness of my too-perfect friend. Not worth the trouble I bring to Nathan's world.

Alone and weak.

But not anymore.

Not since he walked into my life.

And Kai? He doesn't have a clue who I am—not like Draven does.

Which is why Draven's golden eyes flare, silently shouting at me to stop as I step to Kai and drop my wrist in his outstretched hand.

Because Draven is worth it.

And Kai?

He doesn't have a *clue* who he's dealing with.

CHAPTER FORTY-SEVEN

"Struggle, and he dies," Kai says, curling his fingers around my wrist with one hand. He reaches into his pocket with the other, withdrawing a silver blade that winks in the moonlight.

Draven thrashes against his bonds. One chain moves on its own like a snake slithering up to encircle his neck. His eyes bulge as that chain grips and constricts.

Draven's skin turns a sickening shade of blue—

"Do it!" I scream, jerking my wrist toward the knife. Draven groans, shaking his head. "Do it and let him go!"

Kai smirks, and the chain around Draven's neck loosens, some color returning to his face as he breathes. Some inner piece of me cries in relief—

A sharp sting slices across my skin. Kai's eyes widen as he holds the blade to my wrist and *cuts*. I groan as his grip tightens. As he turns my wrist over and splashes my blood upon the ground.

"Not long now," he practically coos, and I jerk back my wrist, flames engulfing my fingers.

"You got what you wanted. Let. Him. Go."

"Not until the gate opens." His eyes train on the ground where my blood sinks into the earth.

I glare at him, my heart shattering, battling the image of the boy I thought I knew, the friend I thought I had.

My only friend.

A lie. All a lie.

He's as twisted and cruel as my father. Worse even, since he wants to unleash Hell on earth. All under the guise of drawing out the Creator to fix the world.

I shake my head, two tears slowly gliding down my cheeks. Kai tracks those tears, his eyes softening.

"I'm sorry," I say, the words clipped.

"For what?" He tears his gaze off the ground and back to mine.

"That hate festered in you," I say. "When you were given gifts and abilities others would die for."

He clucks his tongue. The ground trembles beneath our feet—a tremor that has nothing to do with my power. The grass curls backward, turning black and swirling as if Draven's shadows have created a hole there.

"Most of all," I hurry to add, panic clawing at my insides. "I'm sorry that *you* were so naive."

He stares from me to the spinning black on the ground and back again, his eyes alight with anticipation. "Naive to what?"

"That my whole life I've been beaten down. Everyone treating me like I'm a weed. An ugly thing that didn't belong, but you know what weeds do?" I dart out my free hand, clutching the forearm that holds the knife with a viselike grip. "We thrive in the cracks, until we're strong enough to shatter the whole foundation."

His eyes flash wide at the flames igniting my hands, wrists, arms. A midnight inferno of brilliant dark fire that scorches his skin so fast, he leaps back. The earth shakes, sucking at his feet, encasing his ankles in mud and roots, right near that swirling hole. He wails an agonized scream as my earth stops him from running.

"Release him."

Kai's eyes are wide, just the hint of terror shining through the madness. "As you wish," he says and snaps his fingers.

All twenty demons break free of their invisible bonds, teeth chomping for Draven.

A scream rips through me, instincts roaring. Flames burst from my hands, cutting through the armored circle and hitting those stone chains encircling Draven, melting them to ore. He falls to the ground, righting himself in just enough time to shift into a swirling whirl of smoke that flickers from corporeal to smoke and back again.

Oh God, he's exhausted.

A sharp pain slices into my side, and my eyes drop. The knife is sunk into my belly, Kai holds the hilt, his ankles still encased in the earth, eyes filled with hate as he glares up at me.

"You're too late," he seethes. "The gate is opening! He's coming—"

I blast him with dirt, using the earth to send him soaring toward the water. My knees hit the ground as I curl my fingers around the blade, yanking it free from my gut. I gag, the pressure in my lungs compacting as I heave with the release of the blade. My fingers are wet with my blood as I hold the wound, as I coax the power inside me to knit and seal and bind. To not let one more drop of my blood spill upon the already cracking and swirling ground.

Demons are snarling at the shadows, at the erratic pattern, as Draven does what he can to defend himself.

And Kai is clawing at the ground as he heaves himself from the water. Soaking wet and livid, his eyes only for me.

And they promise death.

I'm dizzy from the blood loss, but I clamber to stand on unsteady feet, the world all at once tilting as that black hole grows and grows. The power radiating from it dark and just this side of familiar.

But I unleash that power inside me, yank on it and send it hurtling toward the beasts that snarl and fight for Draven's blood.

The wall of fire lights up the night in a brilliant glittering black and silver.

And the agonized wails of the demons in its path fill me with hope, because if they're screaming, that means I'm buying Draven time.

One after the other falls, piles of ash turn to dust and join the smoke. Shadow and flame curl and dance around the other. Draven and I push our powers to the very dregs as the beasts keep coming. The rigid tail of one hits the smoke, and a pained cry sounds from it as Draven's form takes shape. He rolls to the ground, the momentum from the hit propelling him closer to the water. He rights himself but stumbles.

The beast snaps its teeth near his throat, and Draven's hands barely stop it before it can rip his flesh to shreds. I throw my fire spiraling after it, the final demon igniting into a black ash—

Something strong and heavy hurtles into my wounded side, and the air rushes out of my lungs as we hit the ground. Kai straddles me, pinning me down, and then he pulls a fist back and slams it into my face, his fist crunching the bone beneath my cheek.

My vision sputters between light and dark as he hits me.

Again.

And again.

Until the hold on my powers slips, and I go limp beneath him.

CHAPTER FORTY-EIGHT

"You've nearly cost me everything!" he screams in my face, and I groan. *"Look!"* He jerks my head to the left, and the breath in my lungs freezes.

Snakes.

Hundreds of black snakes slither out of that swirling black hole, sliding over one another, climbing higher and higher until the shape of a man forms. A man made entirely of serpents, his hands clawing at the earth as he tugs his form from the hole.

Too late.

I'm too late.

Marid is here, and behind him? Hooves and horns and claws and talons, just the tips of terrible things as they each claw at the edges of the black hole.

I can't breathe, can't think.

Kai laughs, a dark, manic sound.

And I tear my eyes away from the horrific sight, searching for help.

Draven lays still on the ground, piles of black ash scattered all around him.

His powers...how much did he use? How *much*?

Panic claws up my spine, ice filling my bones as Kai moves atop me, leaning to the right as he scrambles to pick something up. My vision clears enough, my mind screaming at me to snap the fuck out of it. Marid is here, and his buddies aren't far behind. He'll *ruin* the world. Drench it in blood and terror and panic. The world my sister lives in. The one she'll grow up in—

"Harley." Draven's voice is weak as he enters my mind.

My eyes tear away from the hole, the snakes, from Kai. Narrowing to his body on the ground, to where his eyes are almost drained of color and barely able to meet mine as he slowly crawls toward me.

"I'm coming," he says. *"The power… I need your help to ground it. We can shut the gate."*

"No, it'll kill you," I silently argue. *"I'll get the knife. I'll stop my blood. No life, no power, right? The gate will shut like you said—"*

"So it's okay for you to die for the world but not me?"

"You wouldn't be dying for the world," I say, my heart shattering. *"You'd be dying for me."*

"Same difference." He's almost to us now, Kai's back to him where he remains atop me, that knife raised, his eyes enraptured with the gaping hole and the snakes coming out of it.

"Draven." I'm so tired, the blood I've lost, the power I've used—

"You're not alone, honey badger," he says, a breath away now. *"Even after I'm gone, you won't be alone. Never again."*

I want to cry.

I want to fight and scream and turn everything around me to ash.

I want to tell him I can handle it alone, that he doesn't have to do this…

But we're out of time. And we both know—we've always known—we can't let the world go down like this.

The pulsing in my blood prickles and aches and *hurts* as my head clears of the cobwebs from Kai's hits. My power returns to me, churning like a maelstrom.

"To ensure you can't seal it," Kai whispers in my ear. "I'll stop your heart, and the gate will forever be open. Only the Creator themself can seal it. Finally, they'll come. They'll come," he repeats, his eyes wholly glazed with power.

Time slows—moving at a snail's pace—as Kai hauls his arms upward, the blade back in his hands, poised over my chest.

This is it.

The dark fate I've run toward. Dying by my best friend's hand.

Rage and betrayal and guilt and shame curl inside my aching body.

Tired.

I'm so tired.

I reach up with my hand, and Kai's movements stop, his eyes going wide. Some battle raging there as he eyes my hand, raising his free one like he might interlace his fingers with mine.

I jerk past him, my hand locking with Draven's—

Power like I've never felt hurdles through me, through that chain that connects us. It's vast—like the sea of stars above us, dark and endless and consuming. It vibrates every cell in my body, the tremors causing me to shake, but Draven holds strong to my hand.

"No," Kai gasps, that blade swiping down, his face a terrifying thing as he slashes it.

It bounces off a wall of hardened fire, the knife flying across the air, snicking into the ground next to Draven's and my joined hands.

That wave shifts with the swirling earth I call upon, twisting into something new, something strong.

With Draven's power and mine combined, all intertwining and pulsing between us, it's all at once brilliant and terrifying.

And it propels Kai off me and back toward Marid, whose form is still gathering at the lip of that swirling hole.

I draw up to my knees, staying connected to Draven as I shift closer to him.

"What are you doing?" Kai whispers, terror clinging to his voice from where he scrambles to his feet near the hole.

"Closing it," I bite out, then send a wave of earth rolling for him.

"No—"

Flames, black and brilliant and a million times more magnified because of the endless power slashing through me thanks to Draven—turning my fire as big as a tidal wave—encompass the entirety of Kai's body and his power—

He screams as they slide over him, around him, inside him—slipping through his nostrils, his ears, his mouth. Shoving him back and back until his spine hits Marid, now fully formed and glaring at me with those black eyes.

"You dare—" Marid's grainy voice is cut off by a wet, choked gasp from Kai.

Betrayal flashes over those green eyes. The ones I thought I knew so well.

I push the power harder, Draven's grip on my hand weakening. Kai's body falls back and back, his shoes raking through the mud and swirling earth.

Knocking Marid into that black hole, the power streaming from me crashing over it.

Marid roars as Kai's body propels him farther back, as he fights and pushes—

Kai combusts in a pile of ash.

The power flowing through me exploding in a painful burst of endless, glittering black.

The force hurtles Marid and his army over the edge of that hole.

And down.

And down.

Until the wave of power shrinks it...

And it *seals*.

Swallowing the vengeful cries of Marid with it.

Draven's hand goes limp in mine, the sudden silence suffocating.

I roll him over to his back, my ear on his chest.

He's not breathing.

"No." The word wrenches out of me. "No, goddamn it!" I punch the ground by his face before I scramble to lay my hands over his chest. I go through the steps of CPR, tears streaming down my cheeks. "We did not just close that fucking gate for you to be dead, Draven," I bark at him. "Come back. Come *back*."

I work him—chest to mouth and back again—trying and failing to get his heart to start back up. To get him to open those damn eyes, to flash me a smirk, to say something infuriating.

"Draven," I whisper, my arms giving out when I realize he's not coming back. Devastation hits me harder than the knife to the gut earlier, and I fall over his lifeless chest.

I sob, angry, terrified cries that rake my throat raw. He gave everything to stop this. To save the world.

To save me.

I lift up, glaring down at him. "Didn't I tell you I wasn't a girl who needed saving?"

I clench my eyes shut, silently begging anyone who will listen to fix this. To make the world right again—one where he exists.

And that's when I feel it...

The chain.

The one that I've always felt whenever he's near me. It's still there. Still buried deep inside me, pulsing, breathing, aching.

I go deathly still, my palms on his chest, and I spiral down internally, swimming in my own soul for the source of that feeling...

There, sparkling black and with thousands of interconnected links glittering deep inside me. And somehow I *know* Draven's soul is on the other end. Just like I've sensed him through this chain before—an irritation, a worry, a brief moment of joy. I don't know what the fuck to call it, if it's normal for what I am, what he is, and I don't care.

I race across that chain, every fiber of my being hurtling over the seemingly never-ending length of it. I push and push until I feel like my mind might explode, my lungs might burst from the effort—

There. At the end of the chain, a mass of power, of shimmering golden smoke the same color as Draven's eyes. It hovers there, swirling around the end of the black chain in chaotic spirals. I mentally reach out, send my phantom fingers into that smoke.

It stills for a breath before curling around my hand, my wrist, up my arm, until it's entirely wrapped around my body. God, it smells like him.

I don't think; I just move.

Turn around and race back up the chain, the effort like lifting a car.

But I don't stop.

I can't stop.

And just when I think I'll never find the other side of the chain, just when I feel the cold dread of doubt sink into me—

I see the end.

And I crash over the edge, taking that smoke with me.

CHAPTER FIFTY

Movement lifts my head in a steady rise and fall, and I snap my eyes open.

We're still in Jackson Park.

I'm sprawled atop Draven's chest, falling over it at some point—

He's breathing! I haul myself up, my hands on his cheeks.

"Draven!" I say. "Draven—"

He shifts beside me, his hand covering mine on his cheek before his eyes flutter open.

A choked gasp tears through me, tears filling my eyes. He furrows his brow, raising his other hand to my face. "I always pictured you screaming my name in a different way," he says, his voice low and rough as he shifts to sit up.

"Omigod," I say, then throw my arms around his neck. "Don't you ever fucking do that to me again."

His arms slide around my back, hauling me to him. I situate my knees on either side of his hips, our bodies pressed together without an inch of space between us.

"You're in no position to give me orders, honey badger," he says, his fingers trailing up and down my spine.

I shift slightly, just enough to meet his gaze. Our noses nearly touch, we're so close. "Don't," I demand.

His eyes go distant for a moment, something churning there. "What happened?" He glances around, noting the no-longer-gaping hole leading to Hell beyond us.

"You died." I say it like an accusation.

Draven visibly swallows, clarity filling his eyes. He shudders beneath me, drawing up one hand to rub at the center of his chest. "Sorry?" he says after a few heartbeats.

"Not acceptable," I reply, shaking my head.

He grabs one of my hands, laying it flat over the spot he was just rubbing. Presses his hand over mine until I can feel his heart beating. A relieved cry rips through me at the stark difference from his lifeless body moments ago.

"What about now?" he asks, his voice a whisper between us. "Forgive me?"

I shake my head, unable to speak.

Slowly, he inches toward my lips, brushing the lightest of kisses there. "Now?" he asks, and I shake my head again.

A smirk shapes his lips, and he moves underneath me, his free hand on the small of my back urging me against him. I gasp at the contact, at the thrill of pure *life* that jolts right across that chain connecting us.

That beautiful, dark chain I can't explain.

The one that brought him back to me.

He captures my lips with his, stealing my thoughts. There is nothing gentle in this kiss—it's powerful and hard and…everything.

I moan at the taste of him, at his growl against my mouth as I fist his shirt, holding him to me like I'm terrified he'll disappear. His tongue slides over mine, his taste erasing every worry, every hurt, every doubt.

Until nothing is left but the pure, raw sensation of him and me and everything colliding between us.

"How about now?" he asks, drawing his lips from mine, his eyes molten gold.

"I'll think about it," I say, trembling atop him, my forehead resting against his.

"Beautiful, wicked honey badger," he says, and a rush of heat floods me at the roughness in his voice, at the way he darts his tongue out to tease my bottom lip.

And I fall into his kiss, his embrace, not once looking back.

EPILOGUE

"Are you sure you're feeling okay?" I ask, towel drying my hair as I come out of Draven's bathroom. He's sitting on his small couch, eyes blank as he stares at the carpet.

We came back here to clean up—both of us were covered in blood and ash—and I knew I couldn't go back to the hospital looking like that. Elation lifts my heart at the knowledge that I get to see Ray soon, that we shut the gate and I have the chance to be with her—free of our father.

Draven blinks a few times like he's just registered I asked him a question. His eyes widen at the sight of me before him, donning a pair of his black sweats and one of his T-shirts. While I would love the reason behind me needing his clothes to be that he got me naked—he didn't, not that I would've objected. But ridding myself of Kai's blood on my clothes became a number one priority once I'd convinced myself that Draven was real, he wasn't dead, and that we had time to figure everything else out.

"Feel better?" he asks instead of answering my question.

I scrunch my brow and head over to him, sinking into the open spot on his right. "Draven," I say, and he shifts to face me. "What's going on in there?" I ask, shucking the towel to the floor and leaving my hair hanging damp on my shoulders. I know we have a million and two things to talk about, but right this second isn't the time. "We won," I say, as if he could use the reminder. I don't need him to head straight to The Bridge and dance with me in celebration, but fuck. The distance he's set up since we got back to his place? It's totally messing with my *we survived the apocalypse* vibe.

"Harley," he starts, and the way he says my name has my stomach sinking.

"Why do you look like we lost?" I whisper. "Why do you look like—"

"I died," he says, and the words hit like a punch to the chest.

"I brought you back," I say, like that will explain away the shadows haunting his eyes.

"I died, Harley," he says again, eyes on mine. "I saw…" His voice trails off, and each heartbeat he doesn't speak is like a physical blow. "This isn't over," he says, that muscle in his jaw ticking. "It's so fucking far from over."

My eyes widen, fear skirting over me. "What did you see, Draven?" I manage to ask.

His grip on my hands tightens. "I know what you are now, without any shred of a doubt. When I died… He told me."

"Who told you what?" My skin goes tight.

"I was in Hell."

"What…" I can't make my tongue work. "What do you mean? What am I, Draven?"

That familiar devastation swirls in his eyes. "They're all going to want you now. They're not going to stop—"

"What the hell am I?" I ask, my voice cracking.

"I met the Devil," he says.

I huff. "Did he say *hi*?"

But there is no humor in his eyes. "You're not actually the Key after all. The reason you can open the gates, bring down the veil, have the Dark Flame…" His breath shakes. "You're something else. Something *more*."

I'm terrified to ask a third time, but I manage to force out the words. "What. Am. I?"

"You…you're the Antichrist, Harley."

A jagged laugh rips from my lips. "You've got to be fucking kidding me."

ACKNOWLEDGMENTS

My first thank-you always goes to you, the reader. You are seriously everything to me, and I'm so glad you picked up *Ember of Night* and took the journey with Harley and Draven!

Dare, my mate, without you this book wouldn't be possible. We had conversations about Harley and Draven years ago, and even after all this time, you've never once shied away from helping me talk out their story. Thank you for supporting me while I poured my freaking *soul* into this book. Through countless hours of shaping their journey, through the tears and the sheer rawness this book draws out. I love you more than words can ever express.

Thanks must be given to my family for supporting this dream of mine, even when I started dreaming about it in the second grade. The encouragement to chase my dreams no matter how hard it is stays with me every single day.

Liz Pelletier, you know how much I need to thank you. The work you put into this book is nothing short of awe-inspiring, and I'm beyond grateful. Thanks for loving these characters and seeing all the diamonds they had hidden inside as well as giving me the tools I needed to dig them out. And, I must say, working with you really sizzles and crackles and is a blazing, damn near searing kind of awesome. ;)

Stacy Abrams, I adore you and your willingness to answer a flood of texts filled with questions that likely have no coherent train of thought. And for the calls consisting of much the same. You're always an amazing, calm, brilliant presence, and I quite simply love working with you.

Elizabeth Turner Stokes, you are MAGIC. I remember when I first saw your stunning artwork for the cover and I legit gasped. Thank you for breathing life into Harley's character and her world! It's so beautifully on point and I'm forever your fangirl now.

To Jessica Turner, Alex Mathew, Curtis Svehlak, Toni Kerr,

Greta Gunselman, Megan Beatie, and all the wonderful people who are at my Entangled home, thank you for all the work behind the scenes! Each one of you has put so much into this book, and it wouldn't be the same without all your incredible talents! I'm so honored to be part of this awesome family.

To Beth Davey, my amazing agent, thank you for everything you do! I appreciate all the calls, ideas, and insight! You're absolutely amazing!

Molly McAdams, you will always be the coolest half of #MollySquared. Thank you for reading this in its rawest form and then every draft thereafter. I have no idea how I got so lucky to call you my friend. Take me to the moon-eye-eye!

Stoney, my woman, there aren't enough pages to express my thanks to you. I swear your ability to send us into unstoppable laughter at any given moment is your superpower. That and being genuinely awesome. You bring my life so much joy and I simply love you. Let's keep rolling down that freeway, 'kay?

Esther. I love you. Then, now, and always.

To the amazing bloggers who constantly work on behalf of authors and readers alike, you are EVERYTHING. I'm grateful and honored and appreciative of every single one of you who sacrifice time in the name of love for books!

Mayhem Members! Thanks for making our group so positive and fun and for being understanding when life has me hiding in the writing cave for months at a time!

Attention must be given to those of you who read this book and related to certain pieces of Harley's journey. I see you and I'm sending you strength. You are worth it. You will find joy. You're stronger than you know. I believe in you. And if I could hug you to siphon off your pain, I would. Thank you for choosing this book. You make all things possible.

Sink your teeth into the smash-hit series from
New York Times *bestselling author Tracy Wolff*

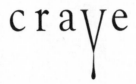

crave

My whole world changed when I stepped inside the academy. Nothing is right about this place or the other students in it. Here I am, a mere mortal among gods…or monsters. I still can't decide which of these warring factions I belong to, if I belong at all. I only know the one thing that unites them is their hatred of me.

Then there's Jaxon Vega. A vampire with deadly secrets who hasn't felt anything for a hundred years. But there's something about him that calls to me, something broken in him that somehow fits with what's broken in me.

Which could spell death for us all.

Because Jaxon walled himself off for a reason. And now someone wants to wake a sleeping monster, and I'm wondering if I was brought here intentionally—as the bait.